The bestselling novels of

# William E. Barrett

## THE SUDDEN STRANGERS

"Barrett brings his customary narrative skills and some of his deepest, subtlest character insights to one of the best of his novels."

Chicago *Tribune*

"A warm and human romance."

*The Kirkus Service*

## THE SHADOWS OF THE IMAGES

"Exciting, readable, deeply meaningful."

Boston *Herald*

"Powerful!"

Washington *Post*

## THE WINE AND THE MUSIC

"Remarkable understanding and compassion—very human and believable."

Denver *Post*

"An enchantingly beautiful love story."

Meriden, Connecticut *Journal*

Avon Books by WILLIAM E. BARRETT

*THE WINE AND THE MUSIC*

*THE SHADOWS OF THE IMAGES*

William E. Barrett

# The Sudden Strangers

AVON
PUBLISHERS OF
DISCUS • CAMELOT • BARD

AVON BOOKS
A division of
The Hearst Corporation
959 Eighth Avenue
New York, New York 10019

First Avon Printing, June, 1970

AVON TRADEMARK REG. U.S. PAT. OFF. AND
FOREIGN COUNTRIES, REGISTERED TRADEMARK—
MARCA REGISTRADA, HECHO EN CHICAGO, U.S.A.

Printed in the U.S.A.

To Dora Rollman
and Jessica Hemp

OVERTURE

Dorinda Daly was a personality. She had been starred in four fabulously successful musical comedies, had been pictured on the covers of *Time, Life, Newsweek,* and *Theatre Arts,* had been featured in *Collier's* and *Saturday Evening Post* articles, and had been profiled in *The New Yorker.* Her phonograph records sold by the ton and her early platters were collectors' items. The public knew everything about her that was unimportant, very little that mattered.

She had an apartment on Park Avenue with a long living room decorated in soft green and primrose which she called the spring room. The small adjoining room, off the entrance foyer, was a study in russet browns and gold. This, inevitably, was the autumn room. Mary Norbert had her desk there.

Mary was twenty-two and she was merely a voice on the telephone to the columnists, agents, actors, publicity people, and unclassifiable individuals who called Dorinda's number hopefully and seldom reached her. Mary wrote verses, some of them moodily obscure and some of them funny. She had sold two of the humorous ones to magazines. She played the piano moderately well and her voice was a small lyric soprano. She could do clever impersonations of people whom she had an opportunity to study. She had a dancer's body and a face with a projection range of from pretty to beautiful, depending upon the time of day, the lighting, and the eye of the beholder.

Dorinda's new show, *The Seventh Wife,* was opening in New Haven within two days and it was a time of tension: fittings and photographs, rehearsals, changes in dialogue, more rehearsals, two new songs, and a doubtful one that might come out. Dorinda was harried and hurried save for occasional intervals. She sat in the spring room during one of the intervals with Carter Brill, whose place in her life was undefined.

"I don't know what to do about him, Carter," she said. "I knew once upon a time. Now, all that I can do about him is stew and fret and walk around with a handkerchief in my hand, wadding the damned thing."

Carter Brill's laugh was softly modulated, polite. "You can throw the handkerchief away, darling," he said. "You don't have to do anything about him. He's old enough to do his own doing."

Mary Norbert could not look into the other room from her chair behind the desk, but the conversation in the spring room was as clearly audible to her as if she sat in the seventh row center. Dorinda's most casual conversation, if her foil proved responsive, was a little like a scene from a play. Given a situation of any emotional content whatever, the conversation *was* a scene from a play. The situation this afternoon involved Dorinda's most honest emotion. She was not reading lines; she was genuinely worried.

"At twenty-five, he's weaned," Carter Brill said, "or he should be."

"He is. He's a MAN. In caps. I'm proud of him." There was a passionate intensity now in Dorinda. "But he's a fool about women. He believes in them."

Mary Norbert raised her eyes to the portrait on the wall above the bookcase, facing her desk. Bart McBride, Dorinda's son, stared at her from the wall through all of her days, grinning at her. She had grown accustomed to him as she had grown accustomed to the toy leopard in her own apartment, or the French poodle paperweight on her desk. He was better-looking than the poodle and almost as handsome as the leopard. Moreover, he was the only male in her life for hours at a time, sometimes for days.

"Hello, fool," she said softly. "Are you really like that about women?"

In the other room, Dorinda's voice picked up a slow and hesitant line. "I made a mistake somewhere, Carter," she said. "I thought that he would meet the right kind of girl in college. Especially if it was the Ivy League. Was that too naïve?"

"The Ivy League part throws the galleries into hysterics," Carter said. "Otherwise, it's a reasonable notion. College life is rather notable for women. Sometimes they seem like the main idea."

"I thought so. Anyway, I can't blame the ivy. The only woman he ever saw, apparently, was a rich little stinker with no morals. He got all jammed up with her, somehow. After he was in the Army, away to hell over in Japan, he got the cute idea of marrying her by proxy. Imagine anyone being married that way! My God! An understudy going on for the bride."

Mary Norbert raised her eyes again to the smiling portrait across the room. This was a new angle. In all the months until today, she had been given no glimpse of Buster's feet of clay. She had been given only his mother's highly improbable word picture of a mental marvel with the body of Hercules, a right halfback who probably spoke Greek or Latin in the huddles. She felt slightly let down with him now. She had listened reluctantly to the conversation, yet reluctantly fascinated. When Dorinda wanted her excluded from a conversation, Dorinda knew how to exclude her. Her phone rang and she answered it.

In the spring room, Dorinda moved restlessly back and forth, a tiny figure in a deceptively simple black wool dress. Her fingers played nervously with a long green handkerchief. In her younger, more obvious days she had stolen scenes with a handkerchief. She used one now, as some people used cigarettes: nervously, an occupation for her fingers. Carter Brill sat in one of the striped overstuffed chairs, his legs straight out, his fingers meeting at the tips, the forefingers touching his chin.

"What I want to know," he said, "is did the boy marry her, proxy or no?"

"Certainly not."

"Too bad. It might have been the best thing for him. And for you!"

"No. That girl was wrong, Carter. Terribly wrong. I'm afraid of another one like her. I didn't raise him, and put so much of myself into him, for somebody like that."

"The moving finger writes——"

Dorinda ignored him. "I know what *I* want," she said. "I always knew. I never had anything but needs and wants when I was growing up. Bart shared a lot of that, too, but his life has been different. Very different."

Carter Brill smiled. "And now you don't want somebody with needs and wants to get him."

Dorinda threw her head back. "Somebody like me, you mean? No, I don't! He's coming to New York now that his season is over and there's nothing here that I want for him. There's nothing in my life that I want him to have."

The girl in the other room heard that statement between phone calls and considered it infinitely sad. Dorinda Daly's son was twenty-five and Dorinda played women of that age convincingly on the stage. It was fantastic that she should have such a problem, but she had it, and it was very real to her. The phone rang again. Carter Brill frowned at his shoe tops.

"I won't have it, Carter," Dorinda was saying. "He's too good for that."

"Maybe so. On the other hand, maybe he's got to prove that he's good. Let him alone."

"I can't. He means too much to me. You'd never know. If I was a pious soul like my mother, I'd want him to be a priest, I guess."

"A priest?"

"Certainly. It's the only club left where women can't get in."

"And that's good?"

"Not for you. This is a clean kid, clean-minded."

The audience of Dorinda Daly paid that line the tribute of momentary silence. Mary Norbert, between phone calls, glanced at the portrait of Bart McBride doubtfully. Carter Brill let his held breath out in a sigh.

"You don't know a damned thing about that," he said.

"I do. I've known all about boy children since I was five."

"But you don't want this one to be human."

"I don't want him to be a heel, like the men I know."

"That's all right. I don't bruise easily. How about the

men you don't know? Who should he be like, Abraham Lincoln?"

"No. I just can't imagine. That's the trouble."

Dorinda stood still in the middle of the big room, looking small and strangely helpless, as she so often did when she was dominating a scene, a cast, a theatre filled with people. Her forehead was faintly creased. Her lovely voice picked up words again.

"I wasn't making cracks at you, darling. Present company always and et cetera. But there aren't any heroes any more, Carter. You know that. Just a lot of rutty bums, some of them dressed better than others, but all just alike. I don't want Bart to be like them. Maybe I should have worked on him sooner instead of putting him out to grow."

"You'd have made a swish out of him. Mother's little image!"

"That's what I feared. I kept him out of show business. I put his feet down in soil and let him grow."

"So, he grew. Are you afraid now that you were wrong?"

"No. I was right. I just don't want some wise little slut cutting him down. I want him to keep on growing."

"Does he have to be sprinkled with holy water to grow? And have a Roman-collar wall around him?"

"No. That's just an idea. Priests scare me. I wouldn't go near one. That's the idea of a different kind of woman than I am. I can't use it. All I want is an idea as good. Maybe I have one." She paused. "I hope so. But I had to talk, darling. I think with my voice. I can't just sit in a corner alone and do it."

Mary Norbert had a respite from the telephone. It had not rung for nearly five minutes. The afternoon was fading. She listened for a few moments, curious about the idea that was as good as a Roman collar for the protection of the vulnerable Bart. Dorinda had moved on to the discussion of *The Seventh Wife*. Only one subject—her son— would have diverted her from it for so long at this stage of rehearsal; particularly now, when everyone behind the scenes knew that she was fighting against odds for her professional life. The girl felt strangely moved.

Her feeling for Dorinda was deep and warm and wordless. It was the sum of many things: admiration, gratitude, sympathy. No one in her life had given so generously of herself as Dorinda. No one had ever understood her so well. She might have had from her own mother, if she had ever known her mother, what Dorinda had given her, but that was mere speculation; Dorinda was a reality.

She could close her eyes now and go back to that dimly lit stage of a year ago. She could enter into the person and the personality of the girl she had been. The room around her became less real than the memory. There was a naked drop lamp, swinging slightly, causing the shadows to dance. She could look out at the empty seats, smell the dust.

She had come to that stage, to a reading for a small replacement part after long months of making the rounds; jobless, proud, hungry, hoping desperately, frightened. She had faced Clement Roler, one of the most patient of directors, and she had blown up completely in her reading. Memory and voice and poise deserted her, leaving her figuratively naked on the stage. The director, holding his own voice down, tried to pull her together—and, in her panic, she resented his very compassion. Her resentment was the only honest, real thing that she gave him. Clement Roler, of course, did not have to accept that.

She could see now his pinched, pale face, his dark, angry eyes. "This is not a high school class play," he said. "I believe that will be all."

The dreams and the hopes, the study, the hard work, the carefully bound clippings, the letters of introduction—all the assets that she had brought to her first real opportunity —were swept away in an instant, discounted, wiped out. She had met a professional opportunity with raw, ignorant, amateur incompetence. She reached toward the empty seats, trying to call the opportunity back, but the director was already turning away. Her hand dropped and she was alone with her failure for the ten seconds that it took her to turn her back on the chilly vastness of the theatre, to cross the shadowed stage. From the deeper shadow of the wings, a soft, crystal-clear voice spoke to her.

"I wonder if you will have lunch with me," it said.

She looked up, startled. It was improbable that Dorinda Daly should be in the theatre that morning, impossible that

Dorinda Daly should be inviting her to lunch; but there it was. Musical comedy's star of stars was standing within two feet of her, small, trim, assured, waiting on the reply of a would-be actress who had just blown a bit part. Mary Norbert drew a deep breath and the genius of disaster still ruled her tongue.

"I guess so," she said.

She sat across a table from Dorinda Daly in a small, quiet restaurant and she was never able to recall afterward what she ordered or what she ate. Seen close up, the face of Dorinda, which was often beautiful in photography and always glowing with the illusion of beauty behind the lights, was a plain face with a too obvious bone structure, a lack of feature balance, a certain coarseness in a skin that had known too much make-up. The eyes, however, were deep, dark blue, intent and alive, interested, warm with understanding. After a few minutes the eyes—and the marvelous deep-toned voice—were all of Dorinda Daly. It took time to become aware of her extraordinary mobility of feature, the sheer magic of her hands.

"You are not an actress at all, child," she said gently. "What made you believe that you were?"

Mary made a stand against further retreat. "I am one," she insisted. "I acted in Denver." She bit her lip, recalling the director's cold voice. "In school plays," she added defiantly. "I had a straw-hat season in New England. Not big parts. I am a good mimic. I do impersonations. Good ones."

Dorinda Daly smiled. "Performance," she said. "Not acting. Do you know the difference?"

Mary stared at her. "What did you start out to do?" the older woman asked.

"Sing."

"Ah! What did you sing?"

This was the first person in New York who was sufficiently interested to ask questions, the first person, even among those who had been her friends, who seemed genuinely to care what she hoped and planned. Mary Norbert forgot that the woman across the table was one of the great names of the theatre. This woman was her audience, voluntarily her audience. She came out of herself, out of her defeats and her discouragements, out of the humiliation of today's reading. She talked.

She told Dorinda Daly about the orphanage in which she grew up, about her native gift for mimicry that won her attention, the voice that earned her a preferred position in the choir.

"Mother Superior said that I had a rare gift, that I had been born with a perfect sense of pitch."

"A perfect sense of pitch is a nice thing to have."

The eyes across the table encouraged her and she plunged onward. She told about the monsignor who directed the Cathedral Choir and who was a great musician, of his interest in her voice; about the scholarships that took her beyond an orphan's reasonable hope: to high school, to business college in the summer months as a prudent hedge against the failure of talent, the two years of college. She spread her hands then, helplessly.

"My voice wasn't big enough. It was just a voice."

Dorinda Daly nodded. "By that time you had faced audiences. Nothing else would satisfy you? It is really a very familiar story, my dear. How old are you?"

"Twenty-one. But that doesn't matter. I really feel that . . ."

Dorinda shook her head. "No. You haven't got it. Believe me."

"You don't know. You can't tell. I'm better than I showed today. I'm not like that at all. I never really got started. I lost my head."

The deep blue eyes across the table continued to regard her gravely. They seemed to say that not getting started when one had an opportunity was part of not having the priceless ingredient; that losing one's head was another part; that such things would not happen to the professional that she aspired to be. The girl's desperate determination faltered before that level look.

"I could learn," she said humbly.

"You could!" Dorinda Daly inclined her head slightly. "You could learn many things, but they would cost more than the learning would be worth to you. Nobody goes far enough on the things that are merely learned, not in the theatre. It's the something extra inside of you that does it. It's there, or it isn't."

Mary's hands clenched on the table top. "What haven't I got?"

The answer came right back to her. "You are not obvious enough. You wouldn't project to an audience. You haven't got the kind of intensity that spends itself. You lack combative hardness. Because you lack those things, you have an unspoiled quality that is very rare. Believe me, it is very rare; in the theatre or out."

"I sound like an unhatched egg."

"Hardly so," Dorinda laughed. "At any rate, I like you. I need a personal secretary. You might enjoy the work. You will learn a lot about the theatre. You can take voice, ballet, whatever you want, on your own time. If, in a year, you decide that I am wrong in what I said today, you can step out and try to prove it."

Mary Norbert recalled practically every word of that conversation now, nearly a year later, staring across the room and seeing nothing.

On that afternoon Dorinda Daly had been, in her own person, all of a girl's dreams of eminence in the theatre: grace, charm, generosity, culture. Today, after nearly a year of intimate knowledge, Dorinda was only a little less; and that less was wrapped in the warmth of a very deep affection.

In the course of the months Mary had learned that Dorinda Daly was not always generous to other women, not always wise and seldom thoughtful, that her beautiful diction was part of her but no greater a part than her command of slang and even of profanity. The actress in Dorinda could guide her with certainty to any pedestal and sustain her in acting perfectly at ease there; but the woman who was the actress did not belong on a pedestal and could not live on one. Mary Norbert, who aspired to no pedestals herself, preferred Dorinda as she had found her.

The position of private secretary involved mainly the steady stream of fan mail, charity solicitations, requests for personal appearances, invitations to social affairs. Contracts and the purely professional matters were handled by

Dorinda Daly's agents or the producers of her shows. Mary
Norbert had only slight and casual contact with show business, where she had anticipated a virtual living of it.

There was a break in the rhythm of voices in the other
room, a sudden stirring. Mary moved some papers around
on her desk and looked up as Dorinda emerged with the
faithful Carter Brill in tow. Dorinda was wearing her
black wool with a blue fox across her shoulders, and a
black satin beret that rested jauntily against the soft gold
of her hair. She was drawing on her gloves.

"I'll be back after my fitting, Mary," she said. "If I
don't make it by six, call Hugh and tell him I'll be a
little late."

Carter Brill nodded his head, smiling as though the in-
structions needed his confirmation. His very white teeth
gleamed beneath the precise black mustache. He always
seemed like the tail of a kite when he entered or exited
with Dorinda. Actually he was a better than average playwright and Mary had once been in awe of him. The door
closed and she looked up at the portrait on the wall. After
all that she had heard, the smile seemed a bit brazen. She
rose abruptly and snapped her fingers.

"Get thee to a nunnery, McBride," she said. "I want to
think."

She walked into the spring room. In spite of her flip-
pancy, her objective was the young man whose pictures
adorned the room. She wanted to renew her impressions.
He sounded like such a miserable specimen of a man, even
in the words of a mother who idolized him, that it was
difficult to imagine him.

"Dorinda didn't know, of course, how she made him
sound. She'd have known if somebody else wrote the dialogue and if she had had time to study it."

The girl stopped before the portrait on the baby grand.
In this one, Bart was the stalwart football hero, posed a
bit self-consciously with his arm drawn back to throw a
pass.

"Conceited fool!" she said.

She knew that she was being unfair as soon as she
rendered the verdict, and she mentally amended it. Bart
McBride had not been responsible for that photograph and

he had no way of knowing that it would ever ornament a grand piano.

There was another photograph on top of the bookcase, a very intent, earnest picture of a young man on the threshold of the world, wearing robe and mortarboard. Mary Norbert had always liked this one best. It was so very human: proud, uncomfortable, determined; a little harried, not in a mood for the camera. She had studied that photograph before and it always seemed younger to her than the undergraduate photographs.

There was another photograph on the record cabinet. In this he wore the uniform of the infantry and he looked big, capable, sure of himself, a little amused at life. A certain battered quality in his face was more apparent in this photo than in any of the others; the heavy eyebrows seemed strangely flat, the nose looked as though it had been broken and set slightly awry.

"Gargoyle!" she said.

That wasn't right either, of course. The Army photo had always puzzled her because he was not in a glamour outfit like the Air Force. Dorinda had never volunteered any information on that score; probably because it never occurred to her. The mere fact that her Bart was in the infantry would automatically invest that branch with more glamour than any other branch of the service.

The fourth photograph, in a silver frame, hung on the north wall; a news service action photo of a catcher in chest protector and shin guards crouched on the base line waiting for the ball, with another ballplayer sliding into him. Bart McBride, of course, was the catcher and in this instance he was unaware of the camera: concentrated, almost desperate, stretching for a ball that was too slow in coming, about to be cut down by the high-riding spikes of the slider, but seemingly unaware of that too; his chin high, thrust forward, the muscles of thigh and biceps straining against taut flannels. The violence of the man's life was in that picture—a pointless violence like rough play, the violence of games.

The story of Bart McBride, the girl thought, was probably all there in four photographs—his story and his personality and everything there was to know about him, save one thing. There was no picture of Bart McBride with a woman.

"I wonder?"

The girl stood there and now that she was relaxed, with no phones harassing her, Dorinda's voice and phrasing took on a new meaning. There had been something about putting a Roman-collar wall around Bart and about an idea that was better than that as a protection against predatory women. Mary's eyes widened.

"She couldn't mean me," she said.

The room was very quiet with the strange emptiness noticeable in any room that Dorinda Daly left. Dorinda brought vitality with her and she took it away again. The room remembered her, holding her scent like a faint breath, preserving it against the more pervasive odor of Carter Brill's tobacco, the stale reek of the butts over-flowing two ash trays. Mary Norbert read again the compass of the room, her eyes moving slowly from one photograph to the other. She shook her head.

"No," she said; then, more emphatically, "Definitely not!"

# PART ONE

# Yesterday

## CHAPTER 1

Bart McBride stood on the Forty-fourth Street side-walk with the Algonquin Hotel at his back and drew New York into his lungs. It was enough for a few minutes merely to stand there, letting the memories flow into him, catching the rhythm again, watching the traffic jostling and banging eastward, the cars flowing in and out of the parking structure across the street. There had been a parking lot over there through the years that he remembered best, but a single level no longer held all of the cars that must be parked. Parking lots, like everything else in New York, were climbing skyward.

He had a decision to make in a few moments and he spun a quarter in the air, watching it spin and catching it as it came down. The doorman also watched the quarter. "Taxi?" he said. McBride shook his head. Taxis were for the people with time schedules or rational objectives, or flabby legs.

He could turn to his left and walk eastward; past the Iroquois and the Seymour, the City Club, the Bar Association, the Yacht Club, the Harvard Club, the Fifth Avenue Bank, and the Guaranty Trust, and ultimately into the Grand Central Station. He could turn right and cross the Avenue of the Americas, which was still Sixth Avenue as far as he was concerned. He would pass the Lambs Club and the Belasco, the Woolworth store and the drugstore which was on Times Square. He could keep going, cross Broadway, pass the Astor and the Shubert Theatre, with its famous alley and with Sardi's facing it; the Majestic, the St. James, and ultimately the Hudson piers where the great ocean liners lived when they visited New York.

Forty-fourth Street, which offered a man such a choice, was the greatest street in town. He put the quarter in his pocket without looking at it and turned to his right. He strode out confidently, eagerly. The direct route to his mother's apartment, the only objective that he had, was in the opposite direction, but he would be more relaxed with her if he walked in her world first, on the streets to which she had brought him from all the nameless streets of the half-forgotten towns they had known together.

The sun, which liked to visit New York but did not care to live there, was somewhere over beyond Jersey. The long lines of late afternoon light lay in shafts and streaks and geometrical figures in the street. Bart walked as far as the Majestic Theatre and stopped. Shirley Booth was playing there in something called *By the Beautiful Sea*. He could remember when Dorinda opened at the Majestic in *Buffalo Nickel*. She had her first starring role in that one. He was ten or eleven and it was very wonderful. He knew what the dressing rooms were like in the Majestic, and how it smelled, and how it looked in the morning when it was empty. He knew the St. James across the street, too, where Dorinda once played in a rowdy musical called *Lush-a-bye, Baby*. At the end of the street, long blocks to the west, were the piers. He had come down from Cornell to see Dorinda off when she sailed for the London opening of *All the Girls You Know*.

Memory was satisfied. He retraced his way and stood, momentarily, on the Broadway corner, looking at the two nudes in the Bond sign, with the waterfall between them. The male figure reputedly stood fifty-three feet tall and weighed six tons. "Reminds me of that big Dartmouth guard, that Polack," Stub Miller said one night. Somebody always said something like that—or something like "Let's sign that guy up!"—but the sign was still there and the men who played football a few years ago were gone. McBride shrugged and turned left, breasting into the sidewalk crowd. It would be easy to get sentimental about that, and sentimentality was silly stuff. Why wouldn't the football players be gone? A man didn't stay in college forever.

The faces of Broadway had not changed. In no other

part of New York did one see such a concentration of faces. If the faces were different elsewhere, then the slow, shuffling, jostling pace of Broadway did something to the people who jammed these blocks north of the Times Building. They crowded and elbowed one another; people on the make, people wanting something, under the illusion that they were getting it by taking it; abused, frustrated, resentful, when the cup remained unfilled. He stepped out of the current at Forty-sixth Street where a small boy, nine or ten perhaps, stood beside a shoeshine box, soliciting business with a shrill voice. The boy went to work on his shoes without conversation, but his alert eyes measured his customer, noting perhaps the breadth of shoulder, the deep tan.

"You a sailor?" he asked at length.

Bart nodded solemnly. "*Ja*. Dutch Navy."

"You don't speak Dutch."

"We never do. Not the Navy. Only the Army speaks Dutch."

The boy snapped his polishing rag in a final salute to the left shoe and started on the right. His face was expressionless. "Sailors tip good," he said.

Bart grinned. Economics towered above the Arts and Sciences, the Army, the Navy, and the Marines. He had several silver dollars in his pocket, legal tender in the West where he worked, but oddities in New York. He flipped one to the boy when he left. He was no longer aware of the faces of the crowd, nor of the crowd itself. He turned east on Fifty-second Street and this was a different rhythm, the rhythm of brownstone houses with colorful pasts, of French restaurants, of Twenty One, of Leon and Eddie's.

The apartment house on Park was tall and elegant, and it looked like scores of other tall, elegant apartment houses. There was a doorman in a wine-red uniform and a lobby filled with accumulated hush. Bart McBride paused for a moment, adjusting his eyes to the dim light. A girl who stepped from the elevator paused too. His eyes adjusted swiftly. This girl was slender and straight and medium tall, with softly curled brown hair that seemed almost a part of her tiny beret. She wore a simple straight-line suit with two parallel rows of absurdly large buttons above the belt line.

His eyes took her picture, his brain developed it, and something—his soul, perhaps—supplied the editorial comment. She was lovely; not spectacular-lovely, merely lovely.

"Are you Bart McBride?" she said.

"Yes."

He was vaguely disappointed that she knew who he was. For a moment she had been something brand-new in his life. He groped back into his memory, tossing around the trivia which filled his mother's letters. There was a girl, a secretary, whom she had mentioned a number of times with enthusiasm. Somebody named . . . ?

"I'm Mary Norbert," the girl said. "I'm sure that Dorinda—that your mother—did not expect you so soon." She retreated one step. "I'll tell her."

"I don't have to be announced."

"Oh yes. I'm certain." She faltered momentarily, then managed a smile. "It wouldn't be fair."

Bart forgot that the girl was lovely. It didn't matter. The reason for her hesitation was obvious. He had gone through all of this before with other people. He could disconcert her by asking, "Who is he?" but one didn't do that. For many years, well-meaning people had tried to shield him from the knowledge of men in his mother's life, as though something like that could, or should, be hidden away in some dark closet. It always infuriated him.

"Okay," he said curtly. "You phone her from the lobby, if you have to do so, while I'm on the way up."

He did not wait on protest or argument and he wanted no feminine fencing. He walked away from the girl and entered the elevator.

A man opened the door of Dorinda's apartment. He was a pale, flabby man with a small black mustache, medium-tall, unimpressive. There was a lazy good nature in his greeting.

"Hello," he said. "I've wanted to meet you. Didn't know if I'd have the chance. I'm Carter Brill."

Bart shook the extended hand. Why not? He had never heard of Carter Brill. The man had anticipated a certain awkwardness in the meeting and he talked right through it as he led Bart into the apartment.

"I'm doubling as butler, maid, and secretary," he said, "answering doors, bells, and telephones for a few minutes. You met Mary going out, didn't you?"

"Yes, I met her."

"Good girl. Like everyone else, she has to take time out to eat, though. Annoying necessity sometimes."

They had crossed the autumn room and entered the spring room. Bart had never been in this apartment before. He did not have anything to say to Carter Brill, and he could not think of anything to say to him. That inadequacy annoyed him, as had Mary Norbert's maneuvering in the lobby, because he recognized the identity of attitudes. He was being self-conscious about a man in his mother's life; the very thing that he resented in others. Carter Brill did not seem to notice.

"Now that you are here," he said, "I'll check along. Off duty when a replacement comes along." He smiled and his teeth were very white. He was, or seemed to be, secretly amused at something. "Your mother will be out presently, I'm sure. I called in to her."

It was all very casual, proper, and circumspect. Bart was still annoyed with himself because he could not shake off his awareness of the undercurrent, nor his resentment of a vague intimacy that seemed immediately established between this man and himself. He said something polite in parting, but the words spoke themselves. He did not think about them. Alone, he returned to the spring room. He liked the cheerful lift of color, the spaciousness. He looked with interest at his own pictures spaced around the room. A door opened and closed somewhere to the right and a light, breathless voice said, "Bart!"

She came into the room like something small and fragile and fragrant, wafted by the wind. She was in his arms before he actually saw her and there was a wordless sob in her voice as she kissed him.

"It's been so long," she said, "so very, very long."

He held her close and she was incredibly slender, dwarfed by the corduroy robe that enfolded her, a bit steamy still from her bath, scented like a florist shop with no single scent dominant.

"Dore," he said, "I've missed you."

It was true. He always missed her. She was true north in his life. His compass needle always swung back to her. Her fingers dug into his biceps and she threw her head back, looking up at him.

"You look marvelous," she said. "All that black tan!"

She was without make-up and she did not need it. She had her own special and peculiar light that glowed behind the oddly assorted features, the odd gamin face. "You look wonderful yourself," he said. "How's the new show?"

"Marvelous! I love it." She backed away from him, still looking at him. She snapped her fingers. "I'm lying, of course. I'm scared to death of it."

"Why scared?"

He knew instinctively how to establish a mood with Dorinda. It must never remain emotional for long, and he must enter her world before he shared his own. Her right hand lingered a moment on his arm, then she waved him to one of the big chairs and seated herself on the divan. It was a two-tone green and the robe was yellow.

"I can't talk," she said. "I just want to look at you. You're so damned big! You get bigger all the time."

The vital statistics did not support her statement. He was six-one and he weighed 180. That had been standard for several years, within five or six floating pounds. He let it go. "The show?" he said.

"They say I'm going to fall on my funny face."

"Who says so?"

"Everybody. I've got to sing against a broken-down tenor from the Met, Rico Moreno, for one thing."

"If he's broken-down, why worry?"

She moved her shoulders slightly, opened her clenched right hand. "This little job isn't Verdi or Rossini," she said. "He sounds bigger than God singing what we've got."

"You'll sound all right."

"Thank you, darling. I do. But this isn't a hayride. We also have the chubby and beautiful Emmet Dane, fresh out of TV, with all that build-up."

Bart shook his head. "I'm vague about him."

"He's Liberace with lungs. Nobody is going to convince him that all the people out front are not his personal fans."

Dorinda bit her lower lip. "Then there's the ingénue, Gilda Skara, a conniving little stinker from Hollywood. She's planted in the show. She'll sing my role in the movie version. Certain as sunset."

"Why do you stand for all that?"

"Pride, darling. A silly something. That's one thing. If I didn't do it, they would whisper about it. I'd rather lay a thing out where everybody can see it, then prove it, or maybe not."

Bart watched the play of expression in her face, the movement of her hands. He did not know whether she was actually afraid of this show or whether she was dramatizing the situation for him. It was difficult to tell. She was a little like a football coach who always loses on Friday the game that he expects to win on Saturday. This time she might be sincerely frightened. There was always a last show, always a point on the other side of the peak. He couldn't imagine it for Dore, wouldn't let himself imagine it, but he had read somewhere that *The Seventh Wife* was a mistake of hers, a show that she should not do.

"The backing comes from Hollywood," she said. "Most of it does. It costs an awful lot to bring a musical to Broadway these days. We had to make control compromises for money."

"How is the show itself?"

"Good. An amusing book. The music is wonderful." She smiled slowly, her right hand following an arc outward. "It should be. It's all adapted from Dvořák. Why steal from Tschaikowsky, Grieg, and Borodin? We're too original for that. A couple of songs aren't right yet, but——"

She shrugged and threw the show away. "That's enough. Positively! Tell me about you."

"It's practically a blank page. I played ball for a bush town in a bush league all summer. I batted .254. The big leagues will not be interested."

"Girls?" She leaned forward, hugging her knees.

"Waifs and strays. Nobody that added up. I don't meet

anyone but baseball fans. They wear jeans or beaten-up slacks and they have shrill voices. They live on hot dogs and hamburgers."

"Stay away from them!" Dorinda was emphatic. "A stage door is a stage door, even when it's in a ball park. Nothing good hangs around it."

He grinned at her. "Still and all, there are two sexes. A man can't change that."

"I never met one that wanted to."

Dorinda rose and moved restlessly around the room. Her slippers, like her robe, were oversized and they flopped; but she managed a strange grace of movement. She stopped abruptly with her distinctive dismissing movement that was partly a movement of shoulder, partly a sweep of arm. "How do you like my apartment?" she asked.

"Fine." He gestured to the four photographs. "Who's the guy, Noel Coward?"

"No, thank God! There's another one in the other room. Mary is fond of it. You met her downstairs, didn't you? How did you like her?"

"I didn't give her much thought." Bart felt again the irritation and resentment of the moment in the lobby that had carried over into the encounter upstairs. "I liked her better than that monkey, Brill, who was hanging around up here."

The words slid out before he could stop them. Dorinda stiffened and stood rigid.

"Carter Brill isn't a monkey," she said. "He's a loyal friend of mine."

"I didn't like him."

Dorinda's eyes were steady. "If you're building up to the closet scene in *Hamlet*," she said, "I won't have it. I've seen that one hammed by experts."

"I wasn't building up to anything. I——" He stopped and snapped his fingers. "I'm sorry, Dore. I apologize."

"Thank you, Bart."

She stood there looking at him and he thought that not another woman in the world would say "Thank you" under the circumstances; yet nothing that she could say would mean exactly what that meant. She had had to live her own life by the rules that she found in the odd world of illusion and make-believe. She had always been discreet in the years of his growing up. She had never embarrassed him nor disowned him. If she wanted now to keep that corner of her life inviolate, out of bounds to him, she was entitled to do so. He had no right in his maturity to hammer down the walls that she had built for the protection of the boy he had been.

"Have dinner with me, Dore," he said.

"I can't." The sleeves, which were too wide, slid around on her wrists as she gestured helplessly. "I didn't know you were coming today, Bart. I'd break anything, darling, but this is Hugh Hyland. He's fixing those two songs for me. He's so very sensitive. Temperamental. You understand, don't you?"

"Of course." He swallowed his disappointment. "It's all right, Dore. Another night. I'll be around. I'm at the Algonquin."

"I hate it. Your first night in! Let me show you my apartment."

She brightened and all the lights came on behind her eyes as she took his hand. She had always been like this. She had never refused him anything without giving him something in exchange. She gave him herself now, as he remembered her best; loving the things that were hers because they were hers.

He did not see much of the apartment because he was remembering more than he saw. There had been a little figurine long ago, a fairy dancer with a wand, that Dore had bought when they were bitterly poor. It was an extravagance and she knew it, but she defended it. "A person should always own one beautiful thing, just to look at," she said.

There was a night when she was very tired after two shows, when the room in which they lived was very small. She brushed against the dancer and knocked her from the dresser top. There had been an appalling moment then when the boy knew what she had done and when she knew, before she dared to look. She had dropped to one knee, sobbing before her fingers touched the fragments.

"My dancer!" she cried. "Oh no! Not my little dancer!"

She wept bitterly that night and Bart had been too

young, too ineffectual, to comfort her. He picked up every piece of the shattered figure from the floor, but it was beyond all mending. He had the fragments still, carefully wrapped, in his old trunk. As Dore led him through these bright rooms, touching her possessions lovingly with her fingers and her voice, that heartbroken cry came across the years to him.

"My dancer! Oh no! Not my little dancer!"

He was being sentimental; but so much of Dore was in that one simple memory. They came back to the spring room. He lifted her by the elbows, then, and kissed her, holding her aloft for a few moments; proud of his own strength, proud of this exquisite tininess which had produced him. He kissed her again.

"This is good, Dore," he said huskily. "It's wonderful to be home."

## CHAPTER 2

The bar was in the East Fifties. It was dimly lighted.

It had tables and booths and a red leather atmosphere. A bored young man ground gaiety out of a piano and sent the alluring sound out into the night through the open door. Few people were lured. There were couples scattered around in the shadows; not many couples. Bart McBride sat on one of the leather-covered stools at the bar proper. He drank scotch and let thought move in him. He had all of New York from which to choose his company and his entertainment, and he did not choose. Or maybe this was choice. He had entered through an open door in search of a drink. Once within the place, he stayed. It neither charmed him nor repelled him. He was merely here.

He had a habit of regretting and he had never been able to break that habit. He regretted his curt treatment of Dore's secretary. The girl had merely done what she felt

she must. Carter Brill, for that matter, had been courteous
and polite, a friend of his mother's, extending a friendly
welcome to a son. He had not matched courtesy with
Carter Brill. He could not, somehow, regret that.

"To hell with him!" he said.

It was irrational to feel that way. Dorinda was right. He
would look pretty silly playing Hamlet to her Gertrude, or
Telemachus to her Penelope.

"The Freudians would make quite a thing out of that,"
he thought. "An Oedipus thing. But they would be wrong."

There wasn't any of that in his relationship to Dore. She
wasn't possessive and she did not cling. She had not ruined
other women for him. There had never been a silver cord
holding him. Dore was his mother and she was also a
woman whom he knew very well, a very glamorous woman.
First and last, she was his mother. It was a special thing,
a precious thing, and nobody had ever written any rules
for it.

He ordered a fresh drink and listened to the music of
the carelessly played piano, letting the memories flow. He
could remember so much.

He remembered a night somewhere in the South, long
before Dore became famous. Dore was talking to a man.
He could not remember the man, nor anything about the
town except that it was in the South.

"I have a boy to raise," Dore said, "and I have a career,
I hope. I'm not going to be a tramp, Eddie."

It was very funny to Bart then. He knew about shows
and roles even if he did not know much of anything else.
He thought that somebody was offering Dore a tramp role
and he laughed, thinking of how she would look in a tramp
costume. Later, of course, he understood what it all meant,
remembering it, although he did not know when he was
hearing it. There were many memories like that which
took on meaning long after the event. Dore would not be
ashamed today of any memory that he had if she could
know what he remembered. She had her faults and her
weaknesses, and she had made mistakes, but she had kept
the pages clean on which his memories were written. That
was a big thing, considering the route they had come.

She had let him use his own name, Bart McBride, from

the beginning although it led to questions and confusions when she was billed as Dorinda Daly. She had name trouble at best. On contracts, programs, or billing, someone was always spelling her name "Daily," "Dailey" or "Daley." There was a day when she blew up and tore a program in half.

"The name is Daly," she said. "D-a-l-y. I'm a four-letter word."

Dore's parents were Roman Catholics and she had raised Bart scrupulously as a Catholic. She sent him to Catholic schools. When he was very small he had recited his prayers for her, and the answers in the Catechism, wherever they happened to be. She had taken him to Sunday morning Masses, even when she had late shows on Saturday night; but he had known very early that there was no religion in her, no personal belief; that it had meaning to her only in relation to himself.

In those early days, Dore sang and danced in choruses, in smoky places that smelled of liquor. He had slept in boxes, or on boxes, off stage in clubs and vaudeville houses. He walked home with Dore in dark and in dawn, when home was a room in some rickety boardinghouse, or a bench in the bus station of some one-night stand.

He had never asked himself then if Dore's way of life was necessary, and he did not ask it now. It had been necessary to her and he had shared it.

They had had fun together even when things were not very good for them. Dore used to tell him stories and she made jokes, many of them in one dialect or another. She liked going to zoos, too. He remembered zoos that most people did not know existed. She knew how to enter a child's world, probably because she always had, as she had still, a certain childlike quality, something within her that had never grown up and that was part of her stage magic.

There had been people who asked Dorinda why she did not leave him with someone while she did her act in night clubs or theatres. She had one answer to that: "If there's a fire I want to be where I can get him out," she said.

There hadn't ever been a fire. When he was old enough for school, she had to leave him with her parents in a small Missouri river town. He liked his grandparents and he liked school and he liked the town. He liked the novelty of play, of boys and girls his own age, the river and the caves and the Huckleberry Finn legends. He was glad, however, when vacation time came and he went out again with Dore.

His neighborhood, the neighborhood of his growing up, was not a place; it was an atmosphere. It was the all-night eating places, stage doors and alleyways, the call boards where actors looked for mail, the old men who were theatre doormen, the flashlight fire-flies blinking backstage when scenery was changed while the show was on. It was clubs with loud brassy music, and travel in busses, resorts and straw-hat theatres in summer. It was an odor compounded of paint and glue and canvas, grease paint, cosmetics, and spirit gum. It was the enchantment of seeing ordinary, familiar people transformed into figures of romance, and of being a part of the magic; of the breathless expectancy of curtains going up; the contrast of castles and drawing rooms and elegance on stage, of mice and cockroaches behind the scenery.

He had had all of that, wanting nothing else. Dore had never hidden him, disavowed him, or been embarrassed by him. He was hers and people had to accept the reality of that as they accepted the illusion that she created behind the lights. He had had a happy childhood.

When he was thirteen, she was studying Shakespeare to improve her diction, although she was already in the lights then. She never played a scene of Shakespeare on the stage, but she rehearsed many of them with all the intensity of a real performance. He was her foil, her stooge, the player in her fantasies. He learned "comment" from her then, which, in the theatre, is a form of mental paraphrasing to get inside the lines. She studied something called "conversational French," which was French by brute memory without grammar or rules. He had to study it with her and she was fiendishly good at it. She was good at anything that she studied and she was always studying something.

In their earliest, most poverty-stricken, hungry days, she squeezed out dollars for voice and music and dancing lessons. He had memories, that predated his first school, of Dore in narrow rooms they shared, doing exercises on the floor or practicing dance steps solemnly, all alone. He remembered early mornings in theatres, and dull gray clubs, where she played the piano and practiced songs. He learned to play the piano himself so long ago that he could not remember his first lessons. Later, he played accompaniments for her while she built up that frail voice that was today so fabulous, such a perfectly controlled instrument. He had been part of it all—the diction, the delivery, the timing, and the range, that added up to the inimitable Dorinda Daly style. It was inimitable because no one else ever worked so hard or carried so little so far.

Bart McBride drank scotch tonight in a strange bar and when his glass was empty he reordered. He was not, ordinarily, much of a drinker. His life had demanded physical fitness above all else. He had escaped from Dorinda's life there and yet, even in that, he was tangent to it.

She taught him ballroom dancing because she considered it necessary for him; but she was furious when she discovered a male dancer in the cast of *Buffalo Nickel* instructing him in stage dancing. He had not understood her fury then as he understood it now. The dancer, as he remembered him, had been all right; but perhaps not. At any rate, the incident had marked the beginning of the end as far as his participation in backstage life was concerned.

"It's not for you, kid," she said. "I won't have it."

He thought it strange that it should not be for him when it was the only life that he knew, but Dore was resolute and uncompromising once she made up her mind. The fact that an argument was reasonable did not sway her if she felt that she was right. She distrusted logic. She substituted boxing lessons for the dancing lessons because, she assured him, they were exactly what he needed. She sent him to a broken-down ex-champion with a sadistic streak who not only taught him to box but taught him to hate and, ultimately, to enjoy combat as a release from hating. That fall—again because Dore was certain that it was the best thing for him—he went away to boarding school, to the Christian Brothers, a very he-man, realistic group of dedicated teachers.

He still remembered vividly that day in Grand Central Station when he went away. Dore was trying hard not to cry and she succeeded. She fussed around, doing little things for him, like straightening his tie and picking lint off him. She made a lot of jokes. When the actual moment came, she took a deep breath.

"They'll make a man of you, boy," she said. "I can't do that. You've got your father's body and that's good for a boy, but I can't cope with it. You've got a brain, too, thank God, and you're going to have a good education if it kills both of us."

It nearly killed him. His brain had been conditioned by Dore. It wanted all of the things that she taught it to want: literature, drama, the understanding of poetry, music, languages; but he was a natural athlete with a tireless body. Whatever he was himself, inside, he served those two masters. He won honors, scholastically, in the subjects that interested him, and he made letters in football, baseball, and track. Twice he ran away from school and for an entire school year he imagined that he had a vocation to be a missionary in China. In his final year he neither rebelled nor dreamed of a vocation; he merely conformed.

The piano player rattled off a tune from Dore's second big show, a screwy number called "Pop Goes for Weasels." Bart ordered a fresh drink. Silly as it was, that song had disturbed him once. The word "Pop" had never meant anything to him personally as it did to other people, boys whom he knew and even adults. He had no memory of a father, no associations, no pictures, no anecdotes. He did not know if his father was dead or alive, but he took it for granted that he was alive somewhere. Dore said simply that "he went away" and there was nothing evasive or indirect about her. If she meant to say that he died, she would have said just that. "He went away" and Dore refused to talk about him, so he wasn't even a ghost. Like the year of running away from school and the year of wanting to be a missionary, there had been nearly a year of wondering, every once in a while, about his father. After that year Bart did not care any more. It didn't make any difference.

"A man could dive off a ferryboat," he said aloud, "and remember his whole life in a few seconds. It takes longer in a bar."

The bartender paused in the polishing of a glass. "How's that?" he said.

Bart rattled the small fragments of ice in his glass and looked at them with distaste.

"I've got a problem that's too big for whisky to solve," he said.

The man in the white jacket shrugged. "How big does that have to be?"

Bart continued to stare at the melting ice. He did not know why he had made that remark. He didn't have a problem, big or little, if one ruled out Aleta and the problem that had proved insoluble long ago. One did rule out Aleta. One had to do it. That was all over and there was no problem, nothing that a man could do anything about. Maybe the whole problem was that he had no problem.

"There's nothing the matter with my life," he said, "except that it doesn't add up. I like it. I like it just the way it is. The only trouble is that I know it can't stay the way it is. If I don't do something about it, I won't go on liking it."

The bartender grinned. "You can always move to Brooklyn, Jack," he said, "and never know the difference."

Bart McBride pushed the stool away and stood for a moment catching his balance. "Right," he said.

He walked away from the bar and he remembered that this was his first night in New York in a long time. He hadn't done a thing with it except get drunk. He shook his head, mildly astonished. One way or another, it didn't seem to be important.

There was a light wind moving from river to river down the street. He stood for a moment breathing it, amazed at the freshness of the air. It was a thing that people forgot, that no one ever said about New York, and that no one ever wrote. There were times when the air was clean and cool and moist, like a sparkling drink for a man's lungs. He started walking west.

## CHAPTER 3

Mary Norbert sat in the lobby of the Algonquin, waiting. The first hour had been difficult; the second was embarrassing; the third hour, which would start in ten minutes, would be impossible.

"I'll leave as soon as the after-theatre crowd starts coming in," she vowed grimly. "Not even for Dorinda!"

She let the thought float in the air. It was too light a thing to bear the definition of an ultimatum. She had never failed Dorinda yet; more important, Dorinda had never failed her. But this!

She felt that the waiters, the people behind the desk, the bellhops, and the lobby groups had all classified her and were either pitying her or despising her. Something reasonable inside of her debated the question. It was entirely possible that none of these people gave her a thought. Still, the situation was fantastic and she could no longer pretend to be interested in a magazine nor act convincingly the role of a guest who enjoyed lobby-sitting. For one thing, it was bad casting. She was not the type for a quiet sitter role.

The Algonquin lobby was a place of rendezvous, a place where people, of the stage and literary worlds mainly, met and visited. The battered, noble old chairs and divans were arranged cannily to provide easy seating for small parties or large ones, couples or groups. In a sense, the lobby was a cocktail lounge since drinks were served there on the small tables which were conveniently placed relative to the chairs; but it was also the living room, or parlor, of those who resided in the hotel. One was not disturbed by a waiter unless one tinkled a table bell for service. Mary sat in one of the single chairs, the stag or wallflower chairs, against the west wall. The chair was, in a sense, badly placed. Between it and the cigar stand, there was a door to the men's room. Nobody, of course, waited alone in a lobby for long except men. Nobody.

The minute hand of the clock marched on. They were setting up the buffet table at the north end of the lobby for the after-theatre parties and late snackers. In a few minutes people would be drifting in, animated and stimulated from an evening at the theatre. Seats in the lobby would be at a premium. There would be laughter, conversation, eating, drinking, companionship. What would people think of a lone female then? Even Reason could not argue convincingly that no one would notice her.

"I won't wait," she said.

She saw him, then. He loomed large behind the half-partition that separated the lobby from the desk. He was stopping for his key. The girl bit her lip. This was the most difficult moment in all of the preposterous business. She had to cross the lobby and accost him before he reached the elevator. "Accost" was the word and the only word. She rose and the couple on the divan near the screen looked up at her, curious. All the reasonable elements of her nature had been unreasonable. She *had been* noticed and speculated upon. She raised her chin and walked toward the elevator, the one elevator of the hotel. She met him there.

He had his key in his hand and a vague, dazed look in his eyes. He did not see her at all until she thrust the envelope at him.

"Mr. McBride," she said curtly, "I was instructed to deliver this to you personally."

His eyes came to focus immediately. His hands were slower than his eyes. He let her hold the envelope stiffly over space while he recognized her.

"Your name is Mary Something," he said. "I was thinking of you. I was rude to you today. I'm sorry."

"It is Mary Norbert. And I thought nothing of it. Please take this so that I can go home."

He stared down at the envelope, then took it gently from her fingers and put it in his pocket. "Let me buy you a drink while you tell me what this is all about," he said.

His hand touched her elbow and she resisted his touch. "No, thank you."

"All right. No drink."

His fingers pressed more firmly now and he turned her deftly, masterfully, away from the elevator. He towered over her and the alternative to accepting his lead was the making of a scene. She had had a sufficiently bad time in this lobby already.

"Let's sit down," the man said.

He seated her near the entrance to the main dining room. The small glass-topped table had a sign that read "Reserved." He looked surprised and before he took the chair facing her he removed the sign. He handed it to the waiter who swooped down on him.

"Put that on another table, please," he said.

"But——"

The waiter was prepared to be firm until Bart McBride looked at him. There was something formidable, despite his polite amiability, in Bart's shoulders, his dark tan, the set of his jaw. Mary Norbert, who had felt it and who had allowed herself to be intimidated, experienced a momentary satisfaction at seeing that force work on someone else. The waiter held the card in his hand and retreated one step. Mary's sympathy swung immediately to him. After all, it was outrageous and presumptuous to ride over the man, to usurp a reserved table.

"We have no right to this table," she said, "and, anyway, I'm leaving right away."

Bart looked at her thoughtfully. He had, she knew, been drinking, probably a lot. He did not show it save for a certain deliberation in his movements and his speech—almost a slow-motion photography effect—and in the redness of his eyes.

"You won't change your mind about a drink?" he asked.

"No." She felt that she was too vehement, that it wasn't necessary to slap a man in the face with a refusal; it was enough to refuse. She reached with slender finger for a softening phrase. The one she found was not the one that she wanted. "I would not be starting even with you," she said.

He watched her fingers. "That's right," he said. "You

certainly wouldn't. It has suddenly occurred to me that I have not eaten in weeks."

He looked up at the still hesitant waiter. "Cold plates. Two. Turkey, ham, tongue, whatever. And rye bread. And coffee."

"No, please."

Neither Bart nor the waiter paid any attention to her protest. The waiter's expression had cleared. He put the "Reserved" sign on another table. Bart's eyes followed him.

"At the risk of being cynical . . ." he began; then he shrugged. "What were you saying?"

"It doesn't do any good for me to say anything. You pay no attention to me."

"I do. I watched your hand. You're an actress."

"I tried to be."

"Same thing. Most of them that *are* merely try to be."

She smiled in spite of herself. "I aren't."

"That's nice. You look better now. Do that more often. What was your trouble when I came in?"

Mary stiffened. She had been carried along on a current of male dominance and it was a good feeling. The men she knew did a lot of pretending and more than a little conniving, but they did not dominate. Now, however, she came swiftly back to reality. She had waited for hours to deliver a message to this man, only to have him ignore it when she delivered it. It was a small thing in her that let itself be impressed by whisky-arrogance.

"My trouble is that I am heartily sick of this lobby," she said. "I've been here since seven forty-five because your mother considered that envelope in your pocket so important that it must be handed to you personally."

He stared at her, then glanced, startled, at the clock. "Good Lord!" he said. "We can't have that!"

"We've had it."

"It's ridiculous," he said. "Columbus stopped in this hotel on his first trip to America. People have been getting their mail at that desk ever since. You should have tossed it on the counter and gone to a show."

"That isn't what she asked me to do."

He looked at her gravely, so intently that her own eyes

conceded the victory to him. "How long have you worked for my mother?" he asked.

"Nearly a year."

"It isn't long enough. I've worked for her much longer. I could tell you about her. Did you ever hear of the White Queen?"

"In *Alice?*"

He made an impatient gesture. "Where else? She used to believe six impossible things before breakfast. Remember? Well, that's Dore. Only she doesn't get up early enough to believe them before breakfast. She believes them before dinner."

"I don't get the point," Mary said. "Aren't you going to read her letter?"

"No. Of course not. That is one of the impossible things. I never read mail at night. Another impossible thing is that you sat here playing post office. All by yourself."

"And the other four?"

He shrugged. "They are so impossible that even you would not believe them."

The waiter started to serve their cold plates and Mary was suddenly aware of the after-theatre crowd which had filled all of the available space around them. She had dreaded their coming and when they arrived she had not noticed them. She had not even noticed the voices, the chamber music of companionship from trios, quartets, quintets, and sextets. Aware now, her chin lifted and she surveyed the room. At least two of the women were watching Bart surreptitiously. He was not watching them.

"Do I impress you as being slightly drunk?" he said.

"Yes. Why?"

"Wouldn't you be?"

"Probably not. I never have been. Why should I be?"

"That's something I find impossible to explain to you. Another impossible thing is that after a bout of this delicatessen I will be incredibly sober."

"I'll wait and see."

"Do. But join me. After all, I had to drink alone."

She did not ask him why. She was becoming intuitive about him. It was incredible that a man of his compelling appearance could be lonely in New York, or anywhere else, but she knew a lot about loneliness and she recognized her own particular kind of loneliness when she found it in someone else. Some people could be lonely in crowds because companionship was more to them than the mere active presence of other people.

Bart McBride was not as she had imagined him. For one thing, she had not been prepared for his brush cut. In the photo that she knew best, he had dark hair that curled. She had not been prepared for his eyes, either. They were a deep warm shade of brown. She had taken it for granted that they would be blue, like Dorinda's. She had often wondered about the man who had been married to Dorinda. It was an intriguing thought that she had at least a partial answer before her. The man was big, no doubt, and dark-eyed. She stopped there. When you said something like that about a person, you said nothing at all. It wasn't even a clue to what the man was like. One could learn that much from actors: that the person was inside and only the illusion on the surface.

The man across the table was eating with silent concentration and he seemed unaware that she was studying him. She tried not to be obvious about it and she did not have to be. The food, when it was served, had appealed to her mainly as a prop, a piece of business to be moved around, an occupation for her hands. She discovered, to her surprise, that she was hungry, and said so.

"It's the bracing air of the Algonquin lobby," Bart said. "They pump taste-bud tantalizers into it every half hour."

He spoke absently, devoting all of his attention to the food on his plate. He looked a little like each of his pictures, not precisely like any of them. He was more mature than the young man who stared at her from the photo on the wall all day, more rugged than the football picture. He had not shaved since morning, obviously, and his beard was dark against the tan. He was not, the girl decided, so very much larger or huskier than other people. That was what, in the theatre, they would call his quality. It was an effect that he created. He drank his coffee black and he emptied his cup with one swallow. He leaned back.

"As you were saying, when I was taken suddenly drunk?" His eyes had inquiry in them and, amazingly, they were clear. She laid her napkin beside her plate. "I said something about going home."

"That doesn't seem right. I'm sure you were saying something much brighter. Something with wit and sparkle in it."

"No, I wasn't. I'm not. I have to go home."

"Who's waiting?"

"Nobody."

"Then why do you have to go?"

She paused, studied him. "Because there isn't anyone waiting," she said slowly. "Does that make sense to you?"

His eyes held hers. "Unfortunately, yes," he said. "Let's go."

He would have hailed a taxi, but she shook her head. "If you can walk a mile, I can," she said. "All that food!"

"A mile?"

"I haven't measured it. East Fifty-sixth, near Lex."

He nodded. "Want to run it?"

"Positively not."

"Thanks."

He was amiable, good-natured, and he did not miss any of the conversational balls that she threw to him, but she knew after a few minutes that the idea of complete sobriety was another of the illusions that he created. Without knowing what he was like normally, she sensed a discord in his personality, an offbeat something. The man, himself, whatever he might be, was not completely present. They strolled Fifth Avenue and they exchanged comments on windows and window displays. He stopped abruptly before one window which featured smart woolen street dresses. His eyes weighed and measured a forest-green creation that had red piping on the cuffs and the shoulder tabs.

It was something that Mary Norbert could wear and would be more apt to wear than would Dorinda Daly at this stage of Dorinda's career; but the girl knew that he was seeing Dorinda in it and not thinking of her at all.

"He has window-shopped with her," she thought, "and he knows what's good on her. It must have been a very, very close relationship. It makes it easier to understand——"

The man was staring at the window display and he

seemed to have forgotten her. When he spoke, his voice startled her.

"You're close to her," he said. "How is she? Is she all right?"

It was, the surprised girl thought, a little like telepathy, or mind reading, at least a synchronization of thought. He took it for granted that she, too, would think of Dorinda when she looked at that dress. He was right, of course. She had; but only because she was with him.

"How do you mean?" she said.

"This show of hers. Is she in trouble with it?"

"I don't know. I wasn't with her when she had other shows. I don't know what's normal. She's nervous about it."

"Frightened?"

"A little. Yes, I'm sure she is."

He frowned as he turned away from the window. They walked again. The wind was cold and the girl huddled into her coat. Bart McBride was not wearing a topcoat. He did not seem to notice the wind.

"Even before she could actually do it," he said, "she always believed that she could sing or act anyone else right off the stage."

There wasn't any comment that Mary could make. The comment belonged to a memory that was his own. She did not know his Dorinda Daly. It wasn't vital that she should. She shared the more important thing with the man who walked in the wind with her. They were both concerned about Dorinda, affectionately concerned.

"She's always had that strange stuff that they build miracles out of," Bart said. "Something called faith. Not many people have it."

The girl looked up swiftly. "That was an odd thing to say."

"More obvious than odd, when you know her."

"No. I don't feel it as obvious. I wouldn't think of faith at all in connection with her. Maybe I should." Mary reached out with her fingers, instinctively, seeking a word, a way of saying something that she felt. "Would it be right to say that she doesn't have faith—real faith—in anybody but herself; that if she cares for people, she hopes for them, but——"

Bart nodded his head slowly. "That is nearly right," he said. "Not quite."

They turned the corner into Fifty-sixth and the wind was stronger. It was difficult to talk against it. Mary Norbert was aware of a dull wonder that they had talked so much of Dorinda, so little of themselves.

"He knows nothing about me at all," she thought. "I'm not even certain that he remembers my name. I'm not certain, either, that what I know about him is right. He isn't the way I expected him to be."

She wondered about the girl that Dorinda said he would have married, the girl who was all wrong and associated with him in some kind of an unsavory thing. It was not the kind of wondering that she wanted to do about him, but it was in her mind and she couldn't get it out.

He stood with his hat in his hand when they reached the three steps and the narrow doorway that led to her walk-up apartment.

"I'm sorry that you had the long wait," he said earnestly. "Dore never expected you to do that. She must have thought that I'd be there."

"It doesn't matter at all. I had a good time."

"Did you?" His eyes searched her face, then he smiled. "I hope that you are ever a truthful child, Bianca. The entertainment was not first rate. I was, unfortunately, two other people."

"They were nice people, both of them."

"I'm glad for them. There will be another time."

He took her hand, held it in his palm, and looked at it. She let him look, then withdrew it. "Good night," she said.

"Good night."

She knew that he was still standing there when she opened the door but she did not look back. She ran up the stairs, and it was like running away from something vague and undefined. In her own apartment, she threw herself down, breathless, on a chair.

"I liked him," she said. "Damn it all to hell! I didn't want to. I won't!"

Her hands tightened into fists. Out of loyalty to Dorinda she had put aside resolutely the thought that there could possibly be purpose or design in Dorinda's kindness to her. She was not prepared to accept that thought yet; but there was not and could not be, once she let herself think about it, any sane reason why that letter to Bart had to be delivered personally.

"She wanted this to happen," she said, "and just the way it did happen. She wrapped me up and threw me at him."

She stared across the room and she resented bitterly the stupidity of cleverness. Why couldn't Dorinda see that it spoiled every lovely, gracious, thoughtful, and generous thing that she had ever done to use her this way?

She rose and removed her hat, resisting the temptation to look in her mirror and see herself as he had seen her. "It doesn't matter," she said. "He's the one man in the world with whom I could never be myself; the one man who is completely ruined for me."

There couldn't be any mystery, or magic, or beauty in anything that two puppets did; only the illusion of the real, never the real. It wasn't enough.

"He called me 'Bianca,' " she said. " 'Fair and virtuous.' He didn't know that he was a puppet. He thought that he was discovering me. That makes it harder. I wish that I didn't know."

There was a photograph of Dorinda on her dressing table and she stared at it. The face that the camera had translated into beauty smiled at her. Tonight she did not smile back.

CHAPTER 4

Bart McBride had been willing to accept the fact, without any mental arithmetic, that it was a mile from West Forty-fourth to East Fifty-sixth, but the return trip, over the same route, was two miles, or perhaps three. His muscles took the blocks easily, but the will that drove them was weary. He looked with approval upon the turned-down bed in his room, then he remembered Dorinda's letter. He drew it from his pocket and weighed it in his hand.

"She was all right physically," he said. "Not sick or anything. The girl would have told me. If there was an emergency, or anything that had to be done tonight, she would have phoned or had me call her back. It doesn't make sense."

He laid the letter on the dresser top and went to bed. Sleep came down on him like a collapsing wall, with no preliminaries of thought or sensation. There was a moment in which he was, and the succeeding moment in which he was not. He opened his eyes to the morning.

It was a luxury merely to lie there, with no voice calling him, no obligation waiting, no duty to be served. He had neither hangover nor headache, he was merely awake. He thought back to the night before and his first thought was of the girl who waited in the lobby and with whom he walked across town. Her name was Mary but the last name eluded him again. He found that annoying.

"From here she looks wonderful," he said, "but she's an actress. She was probably whatever she felt like being at the moment."

He had many things about which he should be thinking, but thinking imposed the condition of arriving at conclusions. He lay with his hands clasped behind his head and stared at the ceiling. How in hell did anyone ever reach any conclusion about anything? He concluded that he was hungry, rose, showered, and remembered Dorinda's letter. He took it with him when he went downstairs to breakfast. She had written his name on the envelope, although she was sending it by her own trusted messenger. Her handwriting was distinctive, large childishly formed letters driven by a hurried, impatient hand that spilled them across the paper at an absurd slant. He opened the envelope and shook out the single page that it contained.

*Bart darling* [he read],
*I felt so helpless with you today. I don't know if I have*

*anything I can give to the man you are, and until a man*
*marries, anyway, he needs parents. I think so anyway.*
*Who else has he got? Maybe you should know your father.*
*I've worried and worried about that many times. Anyway,*
*if you want to know him he is in a monastery upstate. A*
*kind of Monk or Brother or something. It's St. Urban's*
*and his name is Brother Anselm. I hope you do whatever*
*you decide to do without asking me to talk about him.*
*And I'm shattered about tonight and not having dinner*
*with you. This damn show. You understand, darling. Please*
*let's do things together.*

> *All my love,*
> *Dore*

He sat at the table, staring at the letter, with his eggs
getting cold. In all that he had thought and imagined about
his father before he stopped thinking about him, a monastery had never occurred to him.

"Why?" he said.

The question seemed to echo from the four walls of
the room, and down all the corridors of his life. He could
not imagine the man or the motivation. Two people met
and married and had a child, but the child knew only one
of them. The man went into a monastery. It was incredible.
What could a man take into a house of souls, a fortress of
God, if he left his obligations and responsibilities behind
him? How would the man, by his own standards and
before his own Judge, measure up in comparison to Dore
—who wasn't a saint, but who did the job that she had
to do and did it with all that was in her?

He made an impatient gesture that brushed out of his
life again the father who had entered it so briefly and so
late.

He should, he thought, feel some emotion, but he felt
nothing at all. Perhaps everything that he should be feeling
now was felt long ago to the point of depletion. He folded
the letter carefully and put it in his pocket, then he ate his
breakfast.

He smiled when he thought of the urgency behind the
letter, of the girl who had to wait for him in the lobby
until he came in. He was twenty-five years old and he had

lived the years without this message, but when Dore reached a decision, the news moved to her front page and he had to have it immediately.

The ghost of the man who had sired him moved for another moment in his mind as he stood in the sunlight on Forty-fourth Street, spinning a coin. He was, he thought, fearfully and wonderfully made, indeed; the son of a cloistered monk and of Dorinda Daly. The doorman watched the coin and said, "Taxi?" Bart McBride shook his head. He walked east.

It seemed to him when he reached the apartment house that he should have made a phone call, but he had not thought of it in time. "If she's busy, Dore can have me thrown out," he said. "Maybe Mary Something will do it."

He had not given the girl more than a passing thought or two all morning. When he saw her again, he wondered why he had not. Even in the morning, behind a desk, she was enchantingly lovely. There was no single feature that impressed. He had forgotten that her eyes were so wide and so softly gray. He would not have been certain that her hair was brown. Her quality was total effect. She was politely aloof to him, not unfriendly, but definitely impersonal. She reached to a button on her left.

"Your mother expects you," she said.

"I don't know why. Feminine intuition, perhaps."

"Perhaps," she said. She did not smile.

"It could be, too," he said, "that I'm a predictable type."

He walked through the spring room. Dorinda was in the breakfast room with Carter Brill. She was wearing a peach-colored negligee and her morning make-up. Bart bent across the nook table and kissed her.

"You look twenty-eight this morning," he said.

"Twenty-seven," she said.

She was pleased with him and amused. He had not, he thought, exaggerated very much. Dorinda did look like a woman in her thirties. Carter Brill, who rose when Bart came in, remained standing.

"I'm moving along," he said. "It's been nice, Dorinda." His smile included Bart. "I haven't earned my leisure in New York, as you have," he said. "I work here."

He was very friendly, very courteous, and he played his

role of the casual visitor well. Bart tried not to be annoyed with him, not to think of him at all. It took effort.
He looked at Dorinda and her eyes were intent upon his
face. There was momentary anxiety in those eyes, which
cleared immediately. She did not encourage expressions
that betrayed her.

"Sit down, Bart," she said. "Breakfast?"

A maid appeared like a djinnee out of a bottle. "No," he
said. "Just coffee. I should have waited. This is free."

"How are you doing at the Algonquin?" Dorinda asked.
"Are they treating you right?"

"As always."

They exchanged memories in a glance. They had both
been frightened when they first stayed at the Algonquin. It
had been pretty impressive then after boardinghouses and
fleabag hotels in places like Memphis, Nashville, Atlanta,
and Richmond, not to mention the smaller flag stops on
the way.

"I can't get over how wonderful you look," Dore said.
"What are you going to do to keep looking that way, now
that your season is over?"

He shrugged, embarrassed. It was the question without
an answer. "You might say that I am between engage-
ments."

"I might, but I won't. You're not an actor, thank God."

"Baseball is show business, Dore," he said softly. "We
play every day, a matinee on a double-header day. We
take the show on the road."

He saw the astonished look in Dore's eyes and he knew
that she had never thought of it in that way, obvious
though it was.

"It's acting without art, Dore," he said. "We substitute
agility for art. And we don't get better with experience
because experience is not a good substitute for agility."

Dore widened her eyes, studying him. She had never
understood baseball. There had been no time in her life
for it. If she had ever been in a show that was written
around baseball, she would have known everything about
it. She had seen him play once in New Haven against Yale.
She had seen him play football several times. She did not
understand football, either.

"You have to get out of it," she said at length. "It's not for you. What do you want to do, Bart?"

"I'm open to suggestions."

He made the tone light, but he hated the futility of a statement like that. It had the single virtue of honesty. He had a gentleman's education in a practical world. He had taken Dore's dream, made it his own, and partially fulfilled it. He had opened doors to the riches of mind and spirit, doors that had always been bafflingly closed to her. The mind and spirit, however, lived in the flesh. The world, thus far, had offered employment only to his flesh; none for his intellect and none for his imagination, which was the stepchild of his soul.

"I'm not good at sensible things," Dore said. "I always have to ask somebody. There must be something."

"There is, Dore," he said gently. "Don't worry about it. I'll turn some corner and there it will be."

"I'm sure you will."

She smiled at him, genuinely happy for him about the corner that he would inevitably turn, the pot of gold that he would find at the foot of some rainbow. He forgot when he was away from her that she was like this. In the world of his childhood she had known what to do in all of his emergencies. Her instincts and her intuitions had been grounded in his realities. He had gone, as a youth and as a man, where she had been unable to follow. She had only her fairy wand with which to cope with men: her command of illusion, her invocation of make-believe, her naïve faith that wishes were horses and that carriages would be provided.

Freed from the necessity now of confronting a problem, she chatted happily with him about life as she lived life. She told him about the people he had known backstage with her, and what they were doing. When she mentioned an actress, she became that actress. She was fascinated that Mary Martin had elected to do a show in which she did not sing. She had seen *Kind Sir* and for a few moments she *was* Mary Martin in a scene with Charles Boyer. She was a half dozen women in swift succession; instinctively, naturally, without any consciousness of mimicry. Her own voice was music, but it changed in color and tone and emphasis, became husky or shrill, offbeat, syrupy. Her eyes widened, narrowed, flashed, or became round and cowlike. Her hands were still or they fluttered, the fingers took on individual life. Her slender body moved into new attitudes, and in some of the characterizations she seemed heavy.

Bart played straight to her, saying just enough to feed her, to evince interest, to keep her talking. He was fascinated, as he had always been fascinated. Once upon a time, he had been puzzled that with her great ability she did not seek the big dramatic roles. She had laughed at him.

"No emotional strip teases for me, darling," she told him. "I like my soul decently clothed on the stage."

He understood that now and he was not certain but that her genius for comedy, her satiric gift, constituted the greater art. He had met great tragediennes who were humorless and dull. The mercury did not seem to flow in their veins as it did in Dore's. He remembered Dore in a dozen or more roles which no audience ever saw, the roles of the diction-training years when he himself was, of necessity, an actor. He had no way of knowing if she had been as good in those roles as he remembered her. Probably not.

Her mind darted suddenly to the subject that he had considered neatly wrapped with blue ribbon and put away. "Bart dear," she said. "You could go back to college and take a postgraduate course in something."

"I could."

He smiled at her earnestness, the intent way she leaned toward him. "If I could imagine the something," he thought. "Or maybe I should just go somewhere and earn letters in basketball and track. I missed them the first time around." He laid his rough, scarred hand over her small one.

"I'll think about it," he said.

She had not mentioned his father, nor her urgent note of the night before, and he knew now that she would not. She had given him opportunities to introduce the subject and she had knocked twice on the door of his immediate plans The note might have been sheer impulse or she might have given him the alternative of seeking his father to test his devotion to herself, some feminine thing within her needing reassurance. He didn't know and couldn't know. When Dore played a situation by ear, she was far from obvious.

She looked, with sudden panic, at her watch. "Oh, darling," she said. "So late! And I have so much to do. With a rehearsal at one!"

He rose swiftly. There were always startling reminders that Dore's relaxed moments were stolen ones, that she was a woman who worked, and worked hard. She had a ticket envelope on the table beside her plate. She held it out to him.

"The World Series opens today," she said. "I have tickets for you."

He took the tickets, strangely moved. "Thanks, Dore."

He kissed her and held her close to him for a moment. "There are two," she said. "You can take someone."

"I will." He remembered suddenly that he was a stranger in town. Doubtless there were many people he knew if he cared to look around or make phone calls. Nobody stood up in his mind waving for recognition; and it did not seem worth while to dig.

"The girl outside! Mary Something?" he said. "Does she rate an afternoon off?"

Dore looked at him, interest in her eyes. "If she wants it, and if you want her to go."

"I'm not certain. I want to make a test. If she asks you, then you'll know that I asked her."

"I'll be curious."

Dore laughed, then laid her hand on his arm as he turned to go. "Are you all right, darling? I mean—money and all that?"

He made a mock punching motion at her small chin. "Just fine," he said. "Rolling in it. Thanks."

That wasn't true, of course. He wondered for a moment about Dore herself. She would be sound enough right now, but she had come up in the era of high taxes. Her expenses were enormous, she was generous, and she was exploited. If she missed with this new show? She had missed once before with *Lush-a-bye, Baby,* a raucous show that was wrong for her. She had gone out on the road with a war horse and it took her two years to get back on Broadway. She was younger then. He shook his head. He didn't like to think of her missing with this one.

The girl behind the desk raised her eyes when he came out. "If a batter strikes out," he said, "and the catcher drops the ball on the third strike, what happens?"

The girl did not change expression. She remained aloof and impersonal. "The batter runs to first," she said.

"Perfect."

"What do I win?"

"Nothing. I didn't want to be stuck with someone who doesn't know what's happening. Will you go to the World Series with me this afternoon?"

Mary Norbert's feature control failed her. She looked startled, then excited. "I never saw a World Series game. I'd love to. But?"

"But what?"

"I don't know if I can get away."

"You could ask."

"Yes."

She rose swiftly and he stepped back to let her pass him. She moved swiftly and she was a very graceful girl. He took a half dollar from his pocket and spun it. It came down in his palm heads up, which didn't prove anything. He put it away and the girl came back. Her eyes were shining.

"I can go," she said.

## CHAPTER 5

Mary Norbert watched her first World Series game from a box at the Polo Grounds. There was a catch-in-the-throat expectancy and excitement about it all: the nervous agility and grim seriousness of pregame practice, the crisp new uniforms and the sparkling infield grass, the singing of "The Star-Spangled Banner" and the throwing

out of the first ball. The man beside her was cheerful,
very good company, lazily relaxed; but he was a professional watching professionals. Once the game began, he
was like an actor at a play, following it not only with his
mind and with his attention, but with his hands, his body,
his whole being. He did not overwhelm her with techni-
calities but he often anticipated events on the diamond
before they occurred. In fan-to-fan conversation, she held
her own.

Midway in the game, as the Giants came trotting in
from the field to take their turn at bat, Bart McBride
bought her a hot dog. "Where did you learn so much
about baseball?" he asked. "Brothers?"

She shook her head. "No. I just learned. And football.
I was a big girl before I knew that boys did anything
else but play games. I never talked to any of them."

"How's that?"

She bit into the hot dog. "It's a dull, drab story," she
said, "and this is a good game."

He looked toward the field. Jim Hegan, the Cleveland
catcher, had his shin guards and chest protector on. He
was adjusting his mask. "Do you wish you were down
there?" she said.

"I'd like to be. Yes."

He nodded his head, watching the catcher. He had a
very strong, bold profile, nothing actorish about it. She
remembered that terrific action picture in the spring room
where he strained toward the ball while the runner, with
spikes high, slid into him. He had done what these men
on the field were doing, but in a smaller arena. From what
she knew of him, from his attitude, from the expression on
his face, she sensed that he would never play in a World
Series, nor, for that matter, in the big league. It gave her a
feeling of kinship with him. She had aspired once to such
roles as Dorinda played.

She doubted now that the aspiration had ever been
more than a dream. She would not have let a reality go
so easily, so completely, in so short a time. The dream had
been one of the stations at which she'd stopped briefly on
her journey to something, somewhere, a destination that
she could not see.

The Giant batter walked to the plate and knocked mud off his spikes with his bat. Bob Lemon, the Cleveland pitcher, leaned forward to read the sign of his crouching catcher. The game held her again. The score was tied.

"A quarter that the Giants score this inning," Bart McBride said.

"It's a bet."

They had been making freak bets throughout the game and the luck evened out fairly well. They had a blind bet on the outcome of the game. If Cleveland won, Mary could dictate the program for the evening; if New York did, Bart would decide what they would do.

Her eyes intent upon the field, the girl marveled that she had allowed herself to be maneuvered into such a bet. The making of it was a commitment. Spending an afternoon with the man, she would spend the evening also. Faint misgivings stirred in her. She had not meant to have anything to do with him, but here she was. She finished the hot dog. She was having a good time. The Giants failed to score and she held out her hand. The man dropped a quarter in it.

In the eighth inning she came to her feet with everyone else in the park when Vic Wertz, the Cleveland first baseman, hit the ball as hard as she had ever seen a baseball hit. It traveled incredibly far and the New York Giant center fielder, Willie Mays, was a tiny, ineffectual figure chasing it. Then, no longer ineffectual, the outfielder reached up and caught the ball over his shoulder, almost against the fence. Mary pounded her clenched fist hard on the shoulder of the man beside her, and did not know that she was pounding or that she was screaming until the ball was back in the infield. Bart McBride laughed at her. His eyes were shining.

"You won't see many like that," he said.

She felt slightly foolish, but she experienced, too, a sense of physical release. Something had happened to her that let all of the accumulated tension in her body escape. Her nerves were tingling but they were no longer tense. She had a vague consciousness of meaning in the experience, an understanding of the reason for sports and games, the spectator need for this mysterious release that they provided; but she did not probe her own consciousness for meaning, nor care if there was one. This was another stage of her journey to somewhere and the train was beginning to move.

The Giants won the game in the tenth inning and that, too, was wildly exciting, but not in quite the same sense as the other, the unexpected play. Bart McBride smiled down at her as they moved in the press of the crowd from the ball park.

"Do you have an old tweed topcoat or a trench coat? Something warm, not too good?" he asked.

She looked up, puzzled. "I have a jersey trench coat," she said, "but it is a bit beat up."

"That's fine. You're going on an ocean voyage."

"Probably not."

"Yes. You lost a bet."

"Stakes within limits."

"I know. Did you ever ride the Staten Island ferry?"

"No."

"I thought not. It's difficult to find people who have. It's a must for me when I come to New York. It's not as much fun alone."

"Is it fun anyway? A ferryboat?"

"You'll see." He looked at the sky. "I'm sorry it isn't going to be a better night, but sometimes the foul nights are best."

Mary shook her head. "All right. I lost a bet. Have fun. But I'm not dressed for dining out, and if I dress for a ferryboat, I won't be, either. What is this? Shouldn't I have a portable dressing room with this date?"

"No. We won't dine. We'll merely eat dinner someplace where they serve food."

"That's settled," she thought. "A little masculine dominance is nice for a change. Any of the little juveniles I know would talk about it and make it seem like a charming thing to do; then we'd go Dutch on it."

Aloud, she quoted: " 'Sir, to your pleasure humbly I subscribe.' "

"Sister, content you in your discontent," he said immediately. "Nice of you to remember that you are Bianca."

They laughed together in that peculiar intimacy that

grows out of quotation and response, the memory of plays and lines, the mingling of memories that were not shared and yet are matched. There was, for the girl, a sense of curtain at the rise and all the play to come. The man made a path for her through the crowd and she walked it.

They shared a table in a restaurant that was not French nor Belgian, Italian, German, or Armenian; that merely served good food quietly. There was no music, no floor show, nothing to distract two people who were interested in each other.

They talked about the game they had seen and Mary asked the question that she had to ask. "All those players out there! After the Series, they won't play ball again till spring. What do they do all winter?"

"They find hollow logs," he said, "and hibernate."

"Seriously?"

"Seriously the question becomes foolish. They're people; not just ballplayers. What do people do all winter?"

"Work at various jobs, mostly."

"So do ballplayers."

"What are you going to do?"

He moved a salt cellar around on the table top. He had huge, ugly hands. "I'm a special case," he said. "There's some question as to whether I'm really a ballplayer. You can't make a career out of playing in the Western League. It's a training ground. You move up or you get out."

"And you don't even know if you'll play baseball next summer?"

"That's the view from here. Visibility zero."

"And if you don't?"

"I know a man who wants to sell a pretty good organ, a monkey in the prime of life, and a collection basket. Package deal. The price is very attractive."

"I shouldn't have asked, of course. It really isn't any of my business."

"I didn't mean to act cute, either. I go to great lengths to avoid admitting that I don't know."

"You don't have to know right now."

He shrugged. "I could go to a small college. I have had an offer. I could teach English lit. A few other subjects, I guess. I could work for degrees. I could coach the football team and the baseball team. That would be the main job, of course, the reason they would take me on."

"What's the matter with that?"

"Practically everything. I'd be perpetuating myself. Teaching youngsters the subjects I studied and the games I played. Taking them on a conducted tour into my own personal blind alley."

"It could be more than that."

"I don't think so."

"Then it's out for you, of course."

Mary frowned at her plate. The conversation was swinging very close to an old dilemma of her own. "It is possible to be in slavery to freedom," she said.

"I'd have to think about that." Bart was silent for a few minutes and the girl waited. They concentrated on the dinner before them.

"Maybe you've got something," he said at length. "If someone has no ties, no obligations, no responsibilities, no job, he is theoretically free. Actually, I suppose, he would be drawn into the orbit of other people who did have direction, and he'd do what they did, or what they wanted him to do."

"Or the idea of freedom would enslave him and prevent him from assuming jobs, ties, responsibilities, obligations."

The girl was remembering other long solemn discussions about life and meaning; discussions held under incredible circumstances in improbable places. There had been late soul-exploratory conversations to the accompaniment of juke boxes in all-night cafés after long, wearisome days of rehearsing. There had been forums on a sandy beach between performances at a summer theatre. Young actors and actresses, however, were more prone to the striking of attitudes than they were to probing thought. The best of their lines were usually quotes or paraphrases from Chekhov, Pinero, Ibsen, or someone else who wrote plays.

Bart smiled suddenly and he looked very much like the picture that faced her each day from the wall. Something in her expression, she thought, must have amused him. Perhaps she had become too serious, too dedicated, too portentous.

"The ideal life," he said, "was that of the galley slave. A man couldn't go wrong while he was chained to an oar. And speaking of boats——"

CHAPTER **6**

They rode the subway to South Ferry and they walked through the turnstiles to the ferry slip. The boat was a double-decker with a barn-red superstructure, ungainly, without grace of line. Mary viewed it with misgiving. She had ridden the ferry to and from New Jersey when she traveled B. and O. It had been interesting, but brief, lacking in glamour. She shrank from a possible anticlimax to a day that had been memorable.

They had talked, she and Bart, about so many things. They knew surface things about each other and she had had intriguing glimpses of a man for whom she had not been prepared. The idler picture of a youth living on a mother's bounty was not true. He had told her of a summer when he worked his way to Spain on a boatload of mules from Missouri. He had worked with a construction crew in Oregon another summer, and on a dam in her own state, Colorado. He had liked books that she had liked and had seen plays that she had seen. He had humor.

There was a large, enclosed cabin on the boat, but Bart led her to the upper deck. There were life preservers, as on an ocean liner, and directions for using them. Fog was settling over the harbor and a misty spray wet the wind. Bart was silent and something in his air of expectancy was contagious. The deep-throated whistle emitted two hoarse and husky notes. The girl turned. There was a grinding sound, a sudden lurch, a rattle of chains, then movement. She looked up at the man's face.

Bart McBride was happy: a man experiencing again an old, remembered pleasure. The girl walked beside him toward the stern and she was totally unprepared for the scene upon which the curtain rose.

New York came up out of the water as the ferryboat pulled away. The lights in all the towers glowed through the mist, buildings piled against buildings like castles in some old fairy-story illustration. Bart took her hand in his and she returned the pressure of his fingers.

"It is marvelous," she said.

"It's incredible on clear nights."

"It doesn't have to be more incredible than this."

The slender shafts that were merely tall buildings to the groundlings seemed to float, detached, on a cloud of luminous mist. This was New York without streets or people to walk them, without greed or struggle, lust or pain. This was beauty. This was the dream, the spiritual concept, the sum of man's striving without man himself to mar it. This was the ideal city in which poets lived without ever touching earth.

The girl sighed softly. The day had been too much. She was an emotional fool, blown up like a balloon and floating in unreality: the excitement of the ball game, the talk across the table, and now this fantastic Arabian Nights across water. "I'll have to stop it," she thought; but she did not want to stop it. The man's hand felt rough and gnarled in hers and he turned her away from the receding buildings. They walked the deck and on the Brooklyn side they glimpsed momentarily the delicately spun and distant bridges. The fog was thickening as they walked forward and the fog horns of unseen ships spoke to one another in deep, mournful voices.

"Those long minors! Bart, I love it."

It was the first time that she had called him Bart. She felt very close to him, not only physically, but spiritually, in understanding, in yearning. After all, he knew what was here and he had brought her with him to share it. The long, gray tentacles of mist curled and writhed around them.

"Ellis Island is over to the right," he said.

His voice was unsteady and its unsteadiness steadied her. He, too, was feeling something down deep.

"Starboard," she said.

"Okay. Be nautical. But you don't seem the type."

"I am. I played in *Pinafore* once when I was in school. That's very nautical."

He nodded solemnly. "Very. But I don't remember any mention of port or starboard in *Pinafore*. What were you—dear little Buttercup?"

"I was Josephine."

He shook hands with her gravely. "I'm glad to meet a girl who was not dear little Buttercup," he said.

It was nonsense that moved like the wet mist around the reality of themselves. They were all alone in the night on this mystic barge that carried them into the immensity of sea. The Statue of Liberty was a sudden apparition starboard, wet green in the half-smothered floodlights. They stared at it.

> *Give me your tired, your poor,*
> *Your huddled masses yearning to breathe free . . .*

The words had more meaning out here in space. There was salt in the air, an odor like the smell of seaweed. A long black tramp steamer crossed their bow, heading for the Jersey shore. It could be from anywhere; anywhere, that is, that had a wondrous name. "The velvet-footed camels on the road to Samarkand," she thought. "But that is silly, of course. It would be a caravan to Samarkand and not a boat. Still, 'caravan' is a wonderful word, too, and this is a place where words are not good enough if they are less than wonderful."

"Mary!"

She turned to him and he kissed her. His lips pressed down on hers and he was big, rough, as strong as the sea or the ships that sailed it. Her fingers rested against the solid, tense muscles of his shoulders. She yielded to him, returning the kiss, floating as the buildings had floated above all the realities. She drew herself away from him, looking into his eyes. They were wide eyes, dark, but there was nothing frightening in them.

"I had to——" he said.

"So did I."

One had to be honest about it, but when he tried to

kiss her again, she twisted away. "That was then," she said. "It's as you said last night—we were two other people. Let's be ourselves now."

"I wasn't anyone else. Not tonight."

She put her head down but she remained within the curve of his arm. There was a throbbing in her veins that was like the steady, powerful beat of the boat's engines. She had been stirred before, but not like this, not at all like this. She had to tell herself that it was not the man, that it was something within herself, her response to the night. She tried to hold fast to thought, but it blew away from her like the spiraling streamers of fog. The man did not speak but he held her close and there was warmth in him.

The song of the boat engines changed, dropped to a lower register, rose again. They were turning and now, dead ahead, were lights, haloed lights that were rainbow-tinted.

"We're there," she said.

There was regret in her voice, though she tried to keep it out. The end of the journey was inopportune. It left something unresolved. It was the *deus ex machina,* the outside force that meddled in human affairs when humans should be permitted their own solutions. Bart McBride drew a deep breath.

"Yes," he said, "we're practically in. Le Havre, or Liverpool, or Naples. Take your choice."

He released the pressure of his arm, picked her up as though she were a doll, and kissed her again swiftly. He let her down and stood then, holding her hand as the lights came closer.

"You are going to get yourself hated," she said.

"Not if I can help it."

She did not know that the Staten Island terminus was St. George until she walked off the boat to the gleaming arcade and the shops.

"We could go back on this or wait for another," Bart said.

"Let's wait for another."

She wanted time and she was not quite certain why: to postpone a possible issue, to prolong an interval of pleasurable suspense, to experience the unreality of the real after the enchantment of fog. It was difficult to accept the bright lights and the bustling movement of people. They seemed exaggerated, preposterous, lacking in dimension. She tried to think, but thought eluded her. Her tongue rummaged around in all the words that she knew, finding none that would fit.

It was good to walk with Bart and look at displays and sit with him, drinking coffee. He talked and she made answers, not knowing what she said nor caring. The knowledge that they would shortly board another boat was like sitting in the theatre as the lights dimmed, waiting for the curtain to rise.

She had not been able to see Dorinda in Bart, but she was more sensitively aware of him now. Dorinda in Bart was elusive, something in swift motion, the passage of a ghost through a room; a gesture, a fleeting expression, the emphasis upon a certain word, the shape of his mouth in repose. She was most certainly present in his diction. He had no noticeable accent that one could classify as Boston or Harvard, Oxford or Southern, and neither did Dorinda. He pronounced words clearly, without slurring them, and there was a sure rhythm in his speech, without discord or dissonance. It would be pleasant merely to listen if his words had no meaning whatever. Of few people in her lifetime could she say that.

"Do you know how long that voyage took us?" he said.

"Years."

"Or seconds. Actually, twenty-five minutes."

She pondered that. It seemed incredible. It would, she was certain, take more than an hour to remember all that had happened.

"Did you ever see Philip Barry's *Second Threshold?*" she said.

"No."

"It was hoke. But there was a line in it—'Even a stopped clock is right twice a day.' "

He watched her expectantly but she had no more to say. She did not know why she had said what she did. She spread her hands helplessly.

"A ferryboat stops the clock," she said. "Does that make sense?"

"No."

"I was afraid not."

It was time to go again. There had been few passengers coming over, but there were many more for the return trip. She climbed to the upper deck with Bart but by common consent they chose seats forward on the port side instead of walking the deck or standing by the rail. The girl still felt bemused, outside of herself. The actual presence of the man beside her was merged with past impressions, misconceptions, speculations. She could not talk to him as she talked sometimes to the smiling photograph that faced her desk. She could understand now, however, that terrific action photo where he awaited the ball and the spikes. She had thrilled to baseball this afternoon and she had heard the cheers of the crowd.

There had been times when the crowd cheered him, but she wasn't there. She wondered how it had been, what he felt. "You have always been an athlete, haven't you?" she said.

"A long time."

"I've seen your football pictures. It must have been thrilling to know that you were very, very good at something, to know that people were talking about you and writing about you, to hear them cheering you."

He nodded slowly, "It *was* good, Bianca. I won't pretend with you. But it's over. There is nothing very interesting about it now."

She was about to protest, but the protest died before she voiced it. He was right, of course. He was a man. She wouldn't like him if he was one of those beings who never grow up; if he never got over his past glory. Still, she wished that the past would roll back for a little while. She would like to see him do the things that she imagined him doing: the electrifying runs, the daring passes, the fierce tackles, which were the wild thrill of football. He had played for Cornell. Her love of words trapped her again. "Cornell" was one of the wonderful words, and there was a certain awe in the phrase, "the big red team."

"Tell me about you," he said.

"That's all past, too."

He laughed. "I won't ask you about any of the roles you played in Horseshoe-by-the-Sea, or wherever it was."

"I didn't play any real roles."

"I'd like to know why you never talked to boys, and why you only knew them through the games they played."

"Would you?"

The boat was moving. She stared out into the fog and, suddenly, she wanted him to know about her, to know the things that were important only to her, and not the concern of anyone else on earth.

"I was an orphan," she said. "Technically, at least. I don't know what I am, really. I was left at the orphanage when I was a few days old, by a person or persons unknown."

She felt the man's body tense, but she did not look at him. "I was left there on June 6, 1932," she said. "It was the Feast of St. Norbert. That is where my last name comes from, the name you can never remember. The Mary is, of course, from Mary Immaculate, the only mother I had. We were all girls at the orphanage and we wore gray uniforms. We slept in a dormitory and we marched into meals at the refectory, and we said grace. We had hours for study and hours for recreation and hours for prayers. It sounds very dull now, of course, but it wasn't, really. The nuns were very good to us and they understood, before we knew it ourselves, that, because we were girl children, we would be curious about boys. They used to take us to baseball games and football games where we rooted for the teams of boy orphans. It was very good for us."

The man's arm tightened around her and she was content within the circle of his arm. "Did you ever learn anything about your parents?" he said.

"No. There wasn't any way of learning. I liked that better. Some of the girls were half orphans, or real orphans whose parents died. They knew who they were. The rest of us, some of us, wondered and made up dramatic stories about our parents. I know that I felt very mysterious about it all for a time." She found it difficult to explain and she groped with her fingers for the words she wanted.

"We all looked alike," she said, "but we didn't feel that way. We, each of us, knew that we were different, not like anyone else at all."

"What could you do about it, about being different?" The man's voice was hoarse.

"I had a talent, a gift. I could sing. I had an instinct for music. The nuns interested people in me. I had scholarships. I had to work, but I got through high school and two years of college. My voice wasn't as good as it promised to be, and I was a show-off, stage-struck. I liked the stage better than working seriously at music."

"But the others? Those without talent? What happened to them?"

There was an urgency, something desperate, in the man's voice. She looked up into his face and the intensity of his eyes frightened her. "Why?" she said.

She knew, then, that there was nothing in her personal story that could stir him like that. She had come very close to him, intuitively, tonight. She had a flash of memory, of Dorinda talking to Carter Brill. She turned in Bart McBride's arms. Her own voice sharpened, took on urgency. "Why do you want to know?"

He stared at her without answering and her fingers tightened on his forearm. "Did you do that to someone?" she said tensely. "Did you give a child away?"

"I don't know, Mary," he said.

"Why don't you know? You must."

"I don't." He took a deep breath. "Look out at the fog, the way you were. I'll tell you."

Reluctantly, she turned her head away. Her body was rigid, no longer accepting the comfort of his arm. His voice came to her muffled, like the horns in the harbor.

"There was a girl when I was at Cornell," he said. "Her name was Aleta. I have no excuses to offer. Let's leave it like that. There was a girl. I was ROTC in college and I went right into the Army. I was in Japan when she wrote to me and told me that she was going to have a baby—mine."

Mary could feel her nails digging into her palms. The Statue of Liberty floated like a ghost in the mist. *"Send*

*these, the homeless, tempest-tossed, to me.*" The man's
voice pushed on, doggedly.

"That letter did something to me. Maybe because I'd
never known my own father. I couldn't get back. I wanted
to marry her by proxy. She wouldn't have it that way."

"Why not?"

"Say that I didn't mean enough, that I never did, that
she was a girl of wealth and family. At any rate, she didn't
want me."

"Or the baby?"

"She said yes. Knowing her, I couldn't believe it. She
went somewhere to have the baby. She wrote to me later
and said that it died. I didn't believe that either."

"Couldn't you find out?"

"I was in Japan. I wrote a lot of letters. She told me
to stop writing. Unless she told me what she did, I could
never know—and she won't tell. Never."

"Didn't you try to find out when you came back?"

"I didn't go near her. No. I knew her. It wouldn't do
any good. She would stick to the story that the baby died.
Maybe it did. I hope so. But I'll never be sure."

Mary shrank away from him. She was seeing the precise lines of gray-clad figures, all alike, the stiff little
braids. She was remembering things she didn't talk about:
the sudden, wild, unpredictable fits of rebellion, the lonely
weeping after lights out for no reason at all. The eternal
"Who am I?" that never had an answer.

The night was suddenly wet and cold. There had been
a man just minutes ago who stood across her path as no
man had ever stood, and now there was only shock—such
a shock as she would experience if she were to meet her
parents after they had ceased to have meaning. Sitting
where she sat, listening as she had listened, *was* like meeting her parents. They were destroyed, as the man was destroyed. She could no longer believe in them as the child
she had been believed in them: star-crossed lovers, romantic, dashing, unfortunate.

The reality was not like that. It was two young animals
lusting for each other, not even loving each other, sacrific-
ing nothing, giving no thought to the child who might
be, not wanting that child, deserting it, nameless, in the

night. The story of Bart McBride's child was her own story, in all of its ugliness, and she could not reject it.

"I'm sorry," Bart said. "I should not have told you."

"I asked for it."

"I couldn't have told anyone else. I've paid for it, Bianca."

"Have you?"

She was thinking again of the dormitory, the bed she made so many times, the nuns who came and went and the children who stayed. She had been one of the fortunate ones.

"No, I guess not," the man said. "What can I do?"

She was silent. She had no answer and it was not her responsibility to find an answer; it was his. "I would not know where to start, where to look," he said. "I've been over that a thousand times in my mind."

"My father never found me either. As far as I know, he never tried."

"Don't! It isn't fair."

"You could make her tell you."

"She's married. Do you think that I could?"

Mary bit her lip. She did not want to think. Bart was probably right. The girl would stick to her story now, would have to stick to it if she were married. "If he's haunted, it's his own ghost," she said.

The song of the engines changed, deepened. The boat was swinging on an arc. The buildings of lower New York huddled together in the fog. Some of them were partially blotted out and many of the windows were dark. The fairy castles had been bombarded and shattered by the guns of reality. In a few moments the passengers of the boat would be landing, ferryboat passengers. The landing was not Le Havre or Liverpool or Naples or any place with a magic name; it was merely South Ferry. The girl rose and the man walked beside her, not touching her.

"It was very lovely for a while," he said, "and I'll remember that."

She knew that she would remember too. She stretched out her fingers but words eluded her. Her hand dropped.

"It's too bad for you," she said. "I was the wrong girl."

They rode uptown in silence and there was a moment

at her door when he stood with his hat in his hand, when she knew that she was being childish and immature, and that he needed something that she had to give: a word, a gesture, anything. She knew it, but she was drawn too far into herself. It was the man who brought understanding to that moment and to her own need.

"Your parents were different, Bianca," he said. "They had talent to give a girl, and beauty, and grace, and imagination. They would be worth knowing."

He smiled at her and then he was gone, swinging down the street with long strides.

## CHAPTER 7

There were fourteen bars and after that a man stopped counting them. When a man counted fourteen bars without entering any of them, the rest didn't matter. He no longer wanted to enter one.

Bart McBride sat in his own room and stared at the two-suiter on the rack. He had unpacked it yesterday. That was a long time ago. He couldn't unpack it now because it was already unpacked. A man should be able to remember a simple thing like that. He had made a mistake tonight because he didn't remember. Yesterday was back there where a man could no longer reach it, do it or undo it.

"I had something for a minute that didn't take brute strength to hold," he said. "So I dropped it. It's broken and that's that."

The orphan asylum was something else again. It was the confusing element because, unlike the rest of it, it wasn't just yesterday. That, if there was a little girl sleeping tonight in a dormitory and getting up in the morning to put on a gray uniform, was today—and it was also tomorrow.

She would be nearly two years old. Unless, by some

miracle, she had some of Dore in her, she would be a little girl without a talent.

Aleta, of course, had never said that it was a girl. She refused all details. It was a baby and it died, she said. Aleta, who was wealthy and spoiled and a liar, said that. If it was a boy he might be a husky little brute and play football while little girl orphans watched and cheered.

Paternity was something that a man didn't think about very much. If he had never known a father himself, a man didn't have much to go on. Still, a part of himself that was living and lost couldn't be forgotten—if it was living and if it was lost.

Bart rose and walked around the room. It was a small room, too small for floor-pacing. There were men, he knew, who were singularly undisturbed about such problems. He did not know how their minds worked. How did they reason it out, or did they?

What did his own father think or feel about paternity? He was safe now in his monastery with his immortal soul wrapped up in burlap or whatever it was that they used to make a monk's robe—but was that all that there was to it—every man for himself and the devil take the rest?

He picked up Dore's note, which he had left on the dresser top when he emptied his pockets. He studied it a minute, then crossed the room to the phone and asked for the porter's desk.

"Brownie," he said, "there's a small town upstate. It's got a monastery in it called St. Urban's. I've got a hunch that the town will be called that too. When can I get a train?" He waited a minute. "Five-fifteen A.M. Thanks."

He thought of Dore then, but there was nothing that he could say to her which would make sense. She wouldn't have time to miss him, anyway. Her show was opening in New Haven. The rehearsals would be killing and there were two new songs. There would be fittings and the costumes wouldn't be right because they never were, and there would be more fittings. Dore had problems enough.

On the edge of sleep, Mary Norbert came through all of the barricades that he had erected. He remembered the candor of that "So did I," when he kissed her, the warmth of her hand in his when they walked the deck. She was very nautical because she had played in *Pinafore*.

"It was nice knowing you, Bianca," he said.

At 5:15 A.M. on Thursday, September 30, 1954, he boarded the train in Grand Central Station and went to meet his father.

PART TWO

**Today**

CHAPTER 1

The first permanent building of St. Urban's Monastery
was erected in 1878 as the home of contemplative
monks who worked the fields for their food, made their
own clothing and shoes, sang the sacred office at the
canonical hours, and offered up the austerity of their lives
for their less fortunate brethren in the world. It was isolated, remote, undisturbed, until a frivolous incident
changed it.

The publisher of a powerful magazine and a wealthy industrialist lost their way one night after some enthusiastic
drinking at one of the country estates. They drove aimlessly on back roads, not knowing where they were, until
they came to St. Urban's. It was very late and the monastery was dark. Neither man was a Catholic, but the publisher recalled that ancient custom required of a monastery that it provide sanctuary to the weary traveler.

"They have a bellpull," he said. "Let's ring and see what
happens."

"Nothing. Probably a prop. This isn't the Middle Ages."

"Let's try."

The idea of waking up the monks and demanding hospitality as weary travelers appealed to the two men in the
mood of the moment. They parked their car and the publisher pulled the bell rope beside the monastery gate. The
lay brother who opened the gate for them did not betray
any surprise or even interest. He admitted them. After
some hesitation, he went in search of the coffee that they
demanded and returned with hot tea. They were provided
with cots and no questions were asked of them.

The following morning a monk served them with breakfast and refused to accept payment. They drove thought-

fully, soberly, to the city and they discussed the joke that had not been a joke. They had actually spent a night in the atmosphere of the Middle Ages. They had discovered something which supposedly did not exist.

The publisher publicized St. Urban's to the world and the industrialist gave the monastery money for a guest-house.

The money, earmarked for that special purpose, might have been refused, but the gift that was bracketed with it made acceptance mandatory. Publicity changed the external life of St. Urban's forever. The solitude of the monks was invaded. People sought the monastery out of curiosity, out of piety, out of world-weariness, and out of despair. No one was ever turned away save women, who were referred to a convent eight miles away, and who seldom went where they were directed.

"Since it is manifestly the will of God that people seek us, and that we minister to them, and since He has gener-ously provided us with the means to meet this new re-sponsibility, it is not our right to question," Father Bernard, the Prior, said. "We must build the guesthouse."

St. Urban's became, almost overnight, a place of retreat, a place of refuge. The more people sought it, the more it was discussed, written about, and esteemed, by men of all faiths. It was an Abbey in 1954, still with an inner, hidden, monastic life of its own, but reconciled to the presence of the perpetual stranger at its gates.

Brother Anselm had come with the second wave of those who learned about the monastery through its pub-licity. He had come while the guesthouse was being built. He had stayed to become an oblate of the order, with the simple vows which were permitted to a man of his past. He, with several other oblates, shared the life of the professed brothers and the priests. He worked in the fields and he worked as a carpenter, and he had a certain skill with pipe. He learned to eat less in a day, every day, than he had once considered necessary for a single meal, and he averaged less than seven hours of sleep out of the twenty-four. He was in the fiftieth year of his life, healthy, happy, needed where he was, needing nothing personally that he did not have.

On the Feast of St. Jerome, Brother Anselm came down from his ladder when the bell rang, fifteen minutes before Vespers. He was pleased with the bell. It had rung at the precise second that saw the completion of his task, the installation of a new railing on the guesthouse balcony. Such precision of timing was like a benediction on his work.

He took the sectional ladder down and put it in the storage shed. It was starting to rain again, after a lull, and he saw the guest-retreatants hurrying in from the garden to the shelter of the building. He had seen many retreatants and visitors and guests. He was no longer curious about them. He was rounding out a decade in the order, and the life outside, whence these people came, no longer had reality for him. In ten years a man put much of himself and much of his work into a physical place, entirely apart from the experiences of his soul. He could not walk far in any direction, from any starting point, in the Abbey without touching upon some piece of his own work; not that he remembered it in foolish pride, but a man was aware of his own imprint upon the house in which he lived. Because of his work, more than by reason of his simple vows, he was forever a part of St. Urban's.

Brother Anselm drew the cowl over his head and strode up the gravel path: a tall, long-limbed man, lean but broad of shoulder. His work for the day was over and he looked forward eagerly to Vespers in the chapel. That hour of prayer, that visit with the Blessed Sacrament, was his home-coming, the laying aside of the day's weariness and its vexations, the interval of great peace and beauty before supper.

His course crossed or paralleled that of other monks coming in from their various tasks. Monks did not waste words, or disturb God's silence, by senseless greetings or salutations, but he recognized them in his mind, giving them names that their work suggested: Brother Rumpus, who awakened the others in the morning, and Brother Nostrum from the dispensary, Brother Mumble, who read this week in the refectory, and Brother Scalpus, the barber. Sometimes he thought of new names for them, but if he did not, the old names served for months at a time, providing him with quiet amusement. By the occasional gleam in a passing monk's eye, he knew himself as similarly recognized; as Brother Sawhorse, perhaps, or Brother Awl. It was a form of soundless laughter in the silence and a happy thing.

In the corridor that led to the chapel, Father Prior bore down upon him. He had no name for Father Prior. He drew himself erect when he sensed that the Prior was about to speak to him.

"Father Abbot will receive you immediately after supper, Anselm," Father Prior said.

Brother Anselm proceeded to the chapel, shocked out of his quiet mood, as startled as if a bomb had exploded within the cloister. Nothing like this had happened in his ten years. He had entered no request for an audience with the Abbot and he knew of no reason why the Abbot should think of him or be aware of him. His mind was distracted as it seldom was at Vespers. The chanting of the choir monks, instead of lifting his prayers and buoying them up like sea water, was a monotone background to his own thought.

He examined his conscience for a grievous fault that might have come to the attention of the Abbot, but, in all humility, he could find none. There were faults and imperfections, of course, but the humblest confessor could reprove them such as they were. The Abbot did not have to bend to the weaknesses and the inadequacies of a mere oblate who prayed best with his hammer and his saw.

It could not be that he was about to be expelled from the Abbey. Such things did not happen without cause, and he had merited expulsion only before he was first admitted. The order knew all that he had been. It was in his enrollment and they had accepted him when his term of probation was up. The past was buried in the mercy of God and the charity of the order. It could not rise against him. What then?

Father Abbot might have it in his mind to transfer him to another monastery. He did not know of any oblate who had ever been transferred, and there was the vow of

stability which bound a man to the monastery of his pro-
fession, but all things concerning a monk's life came under
the authority of the Abbot. If the Abbot decreed that he
should to go another monastery, he would have to obey.

The thought terrified him. He did not want to leave
St. Urban's. It was his home, the fullness of happiness
that he had found in a troubled life. He loved its gray
stone and its silence, the chill in which he rose and the
drowsy mood of Matins, the fields and the barns, the clean
wood that knew the bite of his saw. He loved the shrine
of the Blessed Mother at the end of the garden, and the
orderly cemetery beyond it where the monks slept after
the last Compline. He loved the Masses and the chapel,
the feel of its rough flooring under his knees, the voices
that chanted there. No other monastery would provide such
brethren, men he would love so well, Brother Rumpus,
Brother Nostrum, and the rest. Anselm, and a few others,
had come here marred, with little to offer but damaged
lives; the many had come here fresh and clean, offering
everything, with the world untasted. He had learned from
the many and he loved them for what he had learned,
for the happy poverty that he had shared with them.

The mists of distraction parted as the moment of Benediction approached. The priest held the monstrance, with
the white Host, aloft. Brother Anselm raised his eyes
for a moment to the face of his God. His body bent
then as the priest carved the sign of the Cross in the in-
cense-clouded air. "Lord, let me stay here," he prayed.
"Let it be something else, some cross to carry, but permit
me, please, to stay."

Brother Anselm was still worried and anxious, as he had
not been in years, when he took his place in the refectory
for the evening meal. This, he saw clearly, was a fault in
him since nothing could happen to a monk that was not
the will of God and for his own good. Even his prayer
before the Blessed Sacrament had been a presumption since
he could not know, as God knew, whether it was best
that he stay or go. It was a poor prayer that instructed
God in what should be done.

The reader had been changed tonight. It was not Brother
Mumble in the pulpit. This was the one whom he thought

of as Brother Tremendous, the one who made even dull homilies sound like great drama. The meal was nearly over before he discovered the substitution. Normally, he was a good listener. He had had very little education before he came to the monastery and he had learned much from the reading at meals. When the reading was very dull, as it often was, he derived amusement from its dullness, making comments on it in his mind. This night it had no meaning.

The time came at last and he made his way to the Abbot's suite. Father Abbot worked at an ancient rolltop desk with a long, bookstacked refectory table between his chair and any visitor. He turned when Brother Anselm entered. He was a man of large frame, deep in his sixties with the hawk nose and bold features of a fighting man, the soft gray eyes of a contemplative.

"Sit down, Anselm," he said gently.

He had a single sheet of paper under his hand in a space on the table cleared of books. Anselm had seen such sheets before. All of Anselm's life that mattered, his full biography, was written on the one page.

"You have a son?"

"Yes, Father."

"A young man came to the Abbey this morning. He registered with the retreatants. During his conference with Father Stephen in the afternoon, he asked if he might talk to you. Father Stephen was impressed with his resemblance to you. He told him that such permission rested in me. The young man's name is Bart McBride."

The Abbot paused, glanced down at the paper, then raised his eyes. "Is there any reason, Anselm, why you should not see your son, or talk with him?"

Anselm had difficulty in finding his voice. He had come into the room insulated against shock. The worst had happened to him within his own mind. His only emotion, when the Abbot started to speak, was that of relief, of gratitude that his presumptuous prayer had been answered. He did not have to leave. Now, with tremendous force, this new reality struck him. Was there any reason why he should not see his son? His *son*. He had never seen his son. He had seen a baby, but a baby is not a son. There was a dryness in his throat.

"No reason, Father," he said.

"That is good."

Panic welled up in Brother Anselm. He was not ready. "I would like time to pray," he said. "I do not know how to talk to him."

"He, doubtless, needs time, too, though he may not know it." The Abbot nodded his head. "I will send word to him. You will be in the cloister garden tomorrow at three-thirty and he will come to you."

"Thank you, Father."

The Abbot rose. "If a problem arises, if you need assistance, call upon Father Stephen."

He raised his hand in blessing and Brother Anselm knelt for it.

## CHAPTER 2

Bart McBride had not reached the Abbey in a leap, nor on the swift wings of impulse. The train to St. Urban was the slowest local on the line. It stopped every few minutes, and at every stop people left it or boarded it. Many of the passengers rode from one town to another five miles away, to a town that looked exactly like the one they had left. Bart felt detached, remote, like a man from Mars. He could not imagine the motives and the impulses which moved these people from one place to another. They were strangers and he had no deep interest in them; but, because he had nothing else to do, he thought about them.

These were the living symbols of the freedom that he so often pondered. They were free to move around, to step onto this train or to step off; but behind that simple fact there was something driving them and they were not free of that something. He was riding the train, too, and as the result of his own decision, his own free choice; but it was not an experience that he wanted, neither a profit nor a pleasure. He was going to St. Urban's because he had decided to go there, but he had no interest in St. Urban's. He was going to meet his father, but his father as a person meant nothing to him. He did not have to go, of course. Nobody commanded it.

He shook his head impatiently. Thought habitually took him into such blind alleys. Dore used to say: "I can't think unless I have someone to talk to."

That might be slightly exaggerated, but, for Dore, only slightly so. Dore talked things out, or acted them out. She ran no mental rat races. He had never been like her in that respect and it was strange that he was not. Anyone would say, from the pattern of his life, that he was an extrovert.

Two men in the seat behind him were talking about Willie Mays's amazing catch yesterday and the surprising victory of the New York Giants. "It will be different today," one man said. "That Wynn is terrific in the clutch."

Bart looked at his watch. It was incredible that, less than twenty-four hours ago, he was asking Mary Norbert to go to the game with him. So much had happened after that.

"Did you ever read your letter?" Mary had said. "The one I carried into darkest Africa."

"Yes," he told her. "My mother knew that I was a Catholic, so she sent me a bingo ticket and two chances on a Chevrolet."

"That is almost blasphemy."

"No. It is merely sacrilege."

Dore had the right system. Talking to someone was much more fun than thinking. If nothing profound developed in conversation, nothing was lost. The world had quite enough of profundity.

There was no point in telling Mary Norbert about Dore's letter, even though she had delivered it. He could not tell her about his father because he did not know his father. So he talked nonsense and she replied in nonsense and they crossed that bridge to something else. In con-

versation there was always something else; one did not
have to run in circles around a single pivot.

The trip seemed endless and the train was as aimless as
life. It welcomed new passengers out of nowhere and it
dropped old ones into nowhere, all with a vast, impersonal calm. It moved, however, when it moved, into startling beauty.

Upper New York State was framed in the train window
in a series of living vignettes: hills and lakes, splashes
of fabulous color, farms, orchards, trim houses, roads that
curved into the trees and curved out of them. Bart Mc-
Bride looked upon it with the pride of a returning prod-
igal. It was not the state of his boyhood but, of all
the states in the Union, it was the loveliest. New York,
city and state, took itself for granted. The people who
knew it best and loved it best were either inarticulate
or disinclined to enlarge upon the obvious. It was New
York, and the other states could have the adjectives.

As the familiar landmarks became more numerous, Bart
regretted that he had not picked up some literature on
St. Urban's Abbey. Past a certain external point, he would
be going it blind, uncertain what to expect. He knew only
the obvious legends. As an undergraduate at Cornell, he
had driven past it a number of times, and there was a night
when he parked at the foot of Monastery Hill with Aleta.

It was the night of the Darmouth game in November,
after a big and noisy celebration. The sturdy sons of
Dartmouth had been less sturdy than usual and the big
red team had annihilated them. Bart McBride had scored
two touchdowns and had been in most of the action. He
was exhilarated beyond the point of weariness, glory-
drunk, half in love, reckless.

The snow lay heavy on the ground and weary clouds
spilled a fresh supply lazily, letting it drift down and float
and blow around. He drove the roads aimlessly with Aleta
for a time because they liked to do that, running out the
momentum of one excitement, building to the next. They
stopped on a climbing curve below the monastery because it was a picture for some artist who hadn't been
born yet.

The gray mass of stone towered above them and the

snow was like a screen of gauze that softened its grimness.
The steeple outlines were blurred and the cross was suspended in space. Aleta huddled close to him. Her beaver
coat was new then, a birthday present, and there was
something sensual in the feel of it. Her oddly narrow eyes
with their uptilted corners lifted to Bart's. He had never
seen another face like hers, with the sharply defined cheekbones, small mouth and chin; dark eyes that forever promised impossible things, or dared one to impossible things.

"I want to ring the bell," she said.

"Don't be silly."

"They'd have to let us in out of the storm. It's in their
vows. Do you suppose they'd put us in the same cell?"

"They wouldn't let you in the place."

"Why not? Can't a woman be a pilgrim, or a weary
traveler?"

"They're not supposed to be. You're supposed to be home
in bed, or traveling with two chaperons who are too smart
to get lost or weary."

"I'm not. I'm lost and weary with a big lunk who isn't
smart. I want to ring the bell."

Bart McBride did not think now that it was funny. He
didn't think that Aleta was funny, or ever had been funny.
She was in his life, however. She walked arrogantly in
and out of his memories as though she owned them. As
far as women were concerned, she did own a dispropor-
tionate share of them. Because she had been in his life,
many other things were missing from that life.

He stared out of the window. There was a light rain.
The clouds in the west were black. He had liked the rain
on the upper deck of the ferryboat with Mary Norbert.
He had liked everything about her and about the time
that he had spent with her. There was an eagerness in her,
a freshness, a candor, that he had met in few people, and
she apparently had no fear of being thought naïve. They
had ridden the subway to South Ferry and she had la-
mented the passing of double-decker busses from Fifth
Avenue.

"The first time I ever rode one," she said, "it was
crowded downstairs and I wanted to ride on top. So I
asked the driver if there were any seats upstairs, and he

told me, 'Lady, I haven't the slightest idea. I haven't been up there in years.' "

Bart had discovered New York all over again in sharing with her the experiences of her initiation. If there had been shocks and frights and disillusionments—as there must have been—she did not dwell upon them. It had been an adventure and, taking the bad with the good, she had obviously enjoyed it.

The rain was beating against the windowpane and blotting out the landscape. It had been raining on the return from Staten Island when he pressed the question that, probably, he should have left unasked.

"I was left at the orphanage when I was a few days old, by a person or persons unknown," Mary had said. "I was left there on June 6, 1932. It was the Feast of St. Norbert. That is where my last name comes from, the name you can never remember."

He did not like to remember it now. That last name opened the door of memory again to Aleta. It was a barrier between himself and the girl he had called "Bianca." It reminded him that there were people born into the world so poor that they did not have names. It made him wonder helplessly what saints there were in January. Some saint of January, perhaps, had been called upon to provide a name that he should have provided.

The train was slowing for another station. It was twelve-five. This one was St. Urban.

He thought that he would be alone, but eight other men from the train went up the hill with him. The Abbey was a group of stone buildings, with a tall spire that supported a gold cross. The partly encompassing wall was covered with ivy and the red tile roof of the guesthouse topped the wall near the iron door of the entrance. The stone arch above that door bore the inscription "Pax." One of the other men pulled the bell rope and Bart was amused at his original idea that he would approach this door alone and ask for his father.

He could not imagine it now: standing at this gate like a house-to-house salesman and talking to a cowled figure; "Pardon me, but I happen to be your son."

He entered with the others and took the curve in the

graveled path that led away from the cloister to the guest-house. He waited on a stone bench before a massive crucifix until it was his turn to be interviewed by a cheerful young monk named Father Michael. The monk did not write with a quill pen; he had a modern ball point.

"They call me Father Statistic," he said amiably, and he asked his questions of name and date. He raised his eyes when he asked the question "Purpose?"

Bart hesitated. It did not seem the proper time, nor Father Michael the proper monk. He could not ask for his father yet. The monk misread his hesitation.

"By purpose I mean only, did you come to make a re-treat, or do you have a spiritual problem?"

"No spiritual problem especially. I'll take the retreat."

"You make me want to ask what flavor," Father Michael said dryly. He passed a leaflet across the desk. "Here are the rules for retreatants."

Bart was a retreatant then and he moved in silence with the rest because idle talk belonged to the world they had left outside, and because the voice of God can only be heard in the silence. In midafternoon Father Stephen, the retreat master, talked with him, and there was no longer any logic in masked purposes.

"I would like to see a brother here," he said. "His name is Brother Anselm."


Bart lay on his bunk when the day was over and stared at the ceiling. Word had come from the Abbot just be-fore Compline, the chanted good night of this cloistered family to God and to the Blessed Mother. The sweet simplicity of Compline had enfolded him and his mind had not cleared for thought until he was alone.

Tomorrow he would meet his father. It had ceased to be a mere idea or an intention; it was a time and a place. He would meet him in the cloister garden at three-thirty. There was no eagerness in him, no great anticipation; his resentment was too deeply rooted for that. He felt, how-ever, the stirring of an old curiosity. He was as he was partly because of this man whom he did not know.

Earlier in the day he had been impatient because the Abbey seemed indifferent to his request, and because the

Abbot took his time; now he was glad that the meeting was to be tomorrow rather than today. He had stood before the Algonquin, a lunatic playing with a coin, spinning it for a decision and making a decision without looking at it. That day he had known that he would walk on Dore's streets before he talked to her. Here in the dark and the silence, he faced a like necessity.

Some phrases from the retreat talk of the afternoon were suddenly alive in his consciousness. "Whatever your apparent purpose for coming here, whatever the surface reason," Father Stephen, the retreat master, said, "you were moved by the grace of Almighty God. Make no mistake about that! Because you were so moved, your life will never be the same again. However little you may change, however little you may recognize the change, you will be changed."

Bart McBride listened to the silence as it repeated the words of the afternoon. He was not positive that he wanted his life to be changed; certainly not blindly, without his own participation in the change. It was easy to believe in this atmosphere that miracles happened, that God spoke to man, that people were transformed and lives directed into new channels; not so easy to submit as to believe.

These were the streets of his father's life. They were strange streets. A man could lose his way in them and never find the route back.

"Back to where?" asked the silence.

## CHAPTER 3

In the Abbey of St. Urban, October 1, 1954, was the First Friday and the Feast of St. Remigius, Bishop-Confessor; if it was anything else, the else did not matter and one was not aware of it. The monks' day began at dawn with the chanting of Matins and Lauds. The stream of prayer, once flowing, picked up the sleepy and reluctant retreatants, carrying them along to Prime at five-thirty and Mass at six, followed by breakfast. Somewhere in late morning, during the silent recreation walk, Bart McBride suddenly remembered the World Series.

"I wonder who won it?" he said.

He was mildly surprised that it made so little difference to him. He looked beyond the wall at the cumulus clouds grouped in the west. If he were out there, this would not be the Feast of St. Remigius because he wouldn't know about that. What would it be? "Hell," he said, "the Series isn't over yet. It's only the third game today."

It didn't seem right. Yesterday was too long ago, and the day before yesterday was beyond belief. He and Mary had watched two teams from a box at the Polo Grounds in New York. That was on Wednesday. Today, the two teams were in Cleveland and he was here. He wondered about Mary Norbert. It was easier to think about people than about events, because people were timeless and events had only the importance that one assigned to them. He wasn't very interested in the World Series because he couldn't place it in the reality of time. In the Abbey of St. Urban, the World Series was not happening at all.

Mary Norbert would be in the spring room of Dore's apartment. He wondered, irrelevantly, what she had had for breakfast, and whom she saw. "She will hate my picture now," he thought, "but Dore won't let her take it down."

He thought of Dore and the thought enfolded her gently. She would be working hard, on the top of her nerves, pointing to her opening in New Haven. Her lovely voice, her pliant body, her exquisite timing, all that she was would go across the footlights to another triumph—or not. He knew how it was. He had hit a home run with the bases full in Denver in a game that didn't matter, that was already won—and he had struck out with the bases full in Wichita in a game that was crucial. He had felt as well one time as the other, with the same skills; but he had, and then he hadn't.

"She can't win or lose in New Haven or Boston," he thought. "In show business, you haven't done anything until you've done it in New York."

He worried about her. She had no place to go but up, and with each year it was more difficult. He had prayed for her at the morning Mass, and for Mary Norbert, and for the answers to the questions in his mind. It had seemed like the natural and the logical thing to do.

The bell rang and he was startled. It was time for lunch. An hour had blown away from him, over the Abbey wall. "And one hell of a meditation I made!" He shook his head. The day was not as long as it had looked during Matins.

The beautiful rhythm of rule and order picked him up again and moved him through the hours. At three twenty-five, Brother Porter came for him. He remembered Brother Porter well from his initiation to the monastery yesterday: a short, round-faced man with broken veins under his skin. Somebody said at the table, where discussion was permitted, that some of the brothers were oblates and had explained what oblates were. Brother Porter was obviously an oblate. He had insisted upon carrying Bart's bag, which Bart was far more capable of carrying than he was.

"It is my duty," he said.

There was no debating with that. In the room assigned to him, out of the habit born of many hotels, Bart had reached into his pocket. When he remembered where he was, his hand dropped away. The scars of life were deep in Brother Porter's face, and the shadows that bottles cast. He watched the pantomime of the hand that dipped and dropped away. There was amusement in his eyes when he lifted them to Bart's. The knowledge of what he had been, and of what he now was, lay like a gentle joke between them.

That was yesterday. Today Brother Porter moved swiftly up the path before the man he guided, held two doors and a gate for him, and bowed when he left him in the cloister garden. The monastery buildings rose on four sides of this rectangle with its four elms, its skeleton rose-bushes, its flower gardens marked in autumn's shadow on the ground. A tall monk in a smoky robe, his cowl thrown back upon his shoulders, stood before the shrine of the Blessed Virgin, his rosary in his hands. The monastery bell rang the half hour. Bart walked up the path to the shrine. His lips felt unaccountably stiff.

"Brother Anselm?" he said.

The monk turned. He had the lean features of the Southwest: long jaw line, prominent cheekbones, straight, thin nose, wide mouth. His eyes were dark brown, shadowed by his heavy eyebrows. He was nearly as tall as Bart.

"I'd know you as my son," he said huskily.

The moment rested heavily on both of them. Bart felt an intolerable tension inside of him. "I didn't know where you were until this week," he said.

"There was no need. I wasn't a father to you."

"That's something I never understood."

"Didn't she tell you?"

"Nothing at all."

"Then it's best forgotten."

They were walking, by unspoken accord, on the curving path. His father's sandals made an indefinable sound on the gravel. They seemed to press the surface where Bart's shoes crushed it.

"It's your story to tell," he said. "I think she felt it that way."

"It's past. No purpose would be served."

Bart drew a deep breath. "Look," he said. "This won't do. I'm not a child. I'm a man. I have a problem of my own. I've never had a father. Maybe I don't have one now. Give me a chance to find out!"

Brother Anselm walked quietly and Bart had the uncomfortable feeling that he was praying. "That is no longer my life," he said, "and I know little of anything that would be a help to you."

"I haven't been able to convince myself that you have any right to this life of yours."

Brother Anselm raised his eyes to the gray buildings of the monastery. A question was weighed in his mind, answered, and laid aside. "I will tell you what I can," he said.

They had turned in their stroll on a looping path around the exhausted flower bed. There was a stone bench that faced the shrine of the Virgin. Brother Anselm gestured to it and seated himself beside his son.

"I know nothing," he said. "What do you do?"

Bart spread his hands before him. They were gnarled, scarred hands, a catcher's hands. Two fingers on his right hand had been broken in Japan when he was catching for an Army wonder who had blazing speed and no control.

"Can you guess?" he said.

The monk looked gravely at the hands. He essayed a smile, the smile of a workman rendering judgment in a field that he understood. "Whatever it is," he said, "you're not good at it."

"I'm afraid you're right."

This was easier. Bart understood suddenly his father's need, the need that was so often his own: that of walking on another person's streets before entering that person's life.

"I've got a body like yours," he said. "No matter what I've tried to do with my mind, the body takes over. Even in the Army! I wasn't a soldier; I was a professional athlete in uniform."

He felt his father's eyes on his face, but he did not look at him. He told him swiftly about Cornell, the football and baseball letters, the opportunity to play professional baseball, the Army interruption, and then the Western League in which he was just an ordinary catcher.

"I played baseball once," Brother Anselm said. "In Missouri."

"What position?"

"Pitcher when I wasn't in the outfield. Oil company teams."

Bart looked at the statue of the Virgin. "Would you be scandalized," he thought, "if we stood up and started throwing a baseball around?" He had a warm feeling that he had not expected to have for this man who had played on small teams long ago. Another hero, poor devil! Dreaming of the big leagues, probably, and liking it when he struck somebody out because the crowd cheered him.

"Were you playing ball when you met Dore?" he said.

His father sat motionless, staring straight ahead. "It was a long time ago," he said.

"She came to see him play," Bart thought. "This is the chapter before I was born." He could not imagine it.

"You are Bartholomew McBride, Jr.," his father said. "But they tell me you don't sign that way."

"I never knew."

It was an unhappy remark. It called into being the missing years, the blank pages on which much might have been written.

"I want to know about it," Bart said quietly. "I have the right."

Brother Anselm was quiet for a long minute. He had his eyes raised to the Virgin in her shrine and there was no question now that he was praying. It seemed right that he should be praying. It was his life. The very stones of this place commanded it.

"I am not an educated man," he said at length. "I do not know how to lay it straight as it was. It would be wrong to make a judgment on my poor speech. It would be better if she told you. I'd rest content in her telling."

There was an odd flavor in his father's speech. It puzzled Bart until he remembered the silence here. A man like his father would pick up the rhythm of refectory reading, odd turns of expression, the language of the epistles, the gospels, and the psalms. He heard little else.

"I'll make no judgments," he said. "I know Dore."

"Yes. You'd know her. And for more years than I did. She was sixteen when I knew her first. I was twenty-one and I'd been working since I was fifteen."

Brother Anselm frowned at the pebbles on the ground as though it was difficult to remember, difficult perhaps to believe what he remembered. "I was big and strong," he said. "I worked as a swamper on pipe trucks. I'd worked on a wildcat well. I didn't know much. Dora was going to high school. She was a good dancer. She sang pretty good."

He paused and the shadow of a smile crossed his face. "She wasn't Dorinda then. She was Dora. And she didn't sing any better than anyone else though she thought she did."

Bart could believe that. His father held his rosary in his hand now. "We were married," he said, "in St. Peter's. You've been there?"

"Yes. My grandparents took me when I stayed with them."

"Good people. Always. Are they well?"

"Dead."

"May they rest in peace and may perpetual light shine upon them."

Brother Anselm made the sign of the Cross. He was a monk again. His eyes stared into distance and his fingers moved over three beads before he found his voice. It was curious to Bart that he seemed to pick up the vernacular of his past when he remembered that past.

"You were baptized there," he said. "But by then there wasn't much marriage."

"Why?"

"We were young. I waited till Dora was eighteen and graduated from the high school before we married. I had no high school myself, so there was that. It was a bad time because of the depression. I had a good job as tower man with a drilling outfit in Oklahoma, but where it's best for oil workers, it's bad for women."

Bart nodded. He'd worked in construction camps. It was difficult to imagine the exquisite Dore in one of them, washing and ironing and cooking with primitive equipment; still, there had been the back rooms and the cheap boardinghouses in the backwaters of show business which were little better. She had accepted them without a whimper.

"I'd have taken work someplace else if there was work I could get," his father said. "Dora lived in Oklahoma City for some of it and I'd come in once a week from the fields. She got a job there, singing. It wasn't something I liked, but it was something she could do and, as it turned out, it was better than anything I could do."

Bart was frowning now. The logic of that was more apparent than real. Dore had developed a great talent by years of hard, patient, incredible work; but it didn't follow that her talent, at that time, was bigger than her marriage. He looked at the image in the shrine. His father had warned him not to make judgments. There was no fear of that, of course, where Dore was concerned, but he wanted to get things straight. His father's voice was without emotion.

"I couldn't give Dora anything she wanted," he said, "and I couldn't make a living where she could sing. There were two sides to it, then, but not later. When she wasn't with me, I couldn't think of anything better to do than drink."

Bart could see Dore better than his father could describe her. She had been certain that she had to go, and she believed in her own star. A husband wouldn't fit in a box backstage as a child would. Dore would see it clear in her own mind as it had to be, and she would face whatever she had to face with her chin up. Still?

"You didn't pay much attention to me," he said.

He was feeling disloyal to Dore because of the question that hung in his mind. His voice was sharper than he intended it to be.

"You couldn't go where I had to work," his father said mildly. "Not without a mother you couldn't. I couldn't take you, either. You were better off with her. She got too far away for visiting in the time off that I had."

He nodded as though confirming that memory as right. "I sent money for you and her out of my pay every week. I never heard anything. She wasn't one for writing. When I was drinking, it didn't seem necessary to send money, and I was drinking all the time, so that stopped and I wasn't anything to either of you."

Brother Anselm's head was bowed. "When your mother made a success and had money," he said, "she hired detectives to find me. I was a bum. She had some people in Dallas take care of me. They put me in a sanatorium. When I came out I joined the A.A.s and I went to a priest who got me back in the Church."

It was very quiet in the cloister garden. A man in a smoky robe talked and a young man in tweeds listened. The image of the Virgin looked down on them.

"I came to New York to thank her when I got on my feet. It was hard to find her. I went to a theatre where she was."

Brother Anselm's voice came to a dead stop. Bart

sensed the fact that he had not seen Dore nor thanked her; he had merely seen her in a show.

"How long ago?" he said.

"Ten years."

Bart groaned inwardly. That would be *Lush-a-bye, Baby*, the worst thing she ever appeared in. If only he had seen her in *Buffalo Nickel*, or even *All the Girls You Know*, or *The Barber's Rich*, that Figaro thing she did; anything but *Lush-a-bye, Baby!*

"She's different off stage than on," he said lamely.

"She wasn't anybody I knew. It had been a long time. I came up here because I heard about it. I didn't come to stay, but I stayed. I was nothing outside and I had nothing. I am nothing here but God has given me everything."

"Everything?"

"All that I need. More is gluttony." Brother Anselm raised his head. He looked at the buildings as though reassuring himself that they were still there.

"I had a son," he said. "I lost him in the world. God brought him to me that I might see him. My son, who has no debt to me in affection, has treated me with respect. Who but God could give me this day, or know my need?"

He turned his face to Bart and there was a shining film over his eyes. "I have talked too much," he said.

"No." Bart was surprised at the huskiness in his own voice. He had not been talking. "I wanted to know. You've done better with your life than I've done with mine. I have a problem."

"I have no wisdom. Father Stephen . . ."

"No. I've talked to priests. You are my father. I want to ask you."

Brother Anselm seemed to be fighting a silent battle within himself. He looked up at the image of the Virgin, then looked away. He rose and stood tall. "We will walk and you can tell me," he said.

Bart kept step with him around the silent paths. They passed two monks who did not look at them. Bart told him about Aleta. It was a story so very like his father's. Aleta was not the girl he should have married, but he would have married her and she was in his life. She wrote him about the baby when he was in Japan. There was distance and necessity to keep him where he was. The problem about which he could do nothing was the problem about which he did nothing. It did not vanish, however, because he ignored it. The problem survived his neglect of it. It lay like a shadow across his life.

"I met a girl who had been in an orphanage," he concluded, "and she told me about it. I keep seeing those little kids, all different because their parents were different, but all treated alike because that is the way it has to be done. I'm haunted by it. What can I do?"

Brother Anselm straightened his shoulders. He threw aside, figuratively, the robes of a monk and became a man, speaking, as a man must, out of his own human experience. His words betrayed the fact that he, too, saw the similarity of pattern between his son's problem and his own.

"You must see this girl," he said. "You must give her a chance to tell you the truth. It is her right to have that chance now that she is older. It is your right to demand the truth."

They had rounded the shrine and the ground sloped upward beyond an arched gate. The cemetery of the monks was here, a simple geometrical pattern of wooden crosses. To come upon it at this moment seemed particularly apt. All of his father's story was told, even to this, the inevitable ending of it. He had heard somewhere that a monk was buried without a coffin, wrapped in his habit with his cowl drawn over his face. There was beauty in that, and poetry. The body knew no glory; it went back directly to the earth. He raised his head.

"Thank you," he said. "I always knew that, I guess. I knew that I should see her. I didn't. Now, I will."

"It is the only way," his father said.

They walked back and the bell rang for the ending of work, the work from which Brother Anselm had been relieved so that he might talk with his son.

"I must go now," he said. "I thank God for this." He stood for a moment, facing Bart. "I ask you to consider," he said, "that your mother is fine in herself and that God must have loved her to make her His instrument. Through her, His grace reached me. Because of her, I was able to come here."

"I will remember that."

"Do. I have prayed for her every night and for you."

Their hands met for the first time and everything had been said. Bart walked again across the garden and through the gate. When he reached the guesthouse, the bells were chiming the call to Vespers and to Benediction.

## CHAPTER 4

The telephone rang steadily all Saturday morning and Mary Norbert answered it, patiently, impersonally, almost cheerfully. Most of the calls were from people who wanted tickets to the New York opening of *The Seventh Wife*. It was amazing that so many people, strangers and casual acquaintances, knew the unlisted telephone number of Dorinda Daly, even though a columnist had published it once, with some other unlisted numbers, to prove how smart he was. It was more amazing that these people did not know that she was in New Haven, and that they could expect to talk to her personally if she were not. As though Dorinda Daly, before the opening of a new show, could concern herself with someone's desire for tickets! Each person who called, however, was filled with self-importance. Something must be done! Yes, indeed.

At eleven-fifty Carter Brill came in. He wore a beautifully cut charcoal-gray suit and carried his topcoat over his arm. He was a welcome break in the day, someone she liked and who liked her. In her year with Dorinda, he was the one person whom she had come to know well. She had never known a man who wore clothes better. He had a nice taste in accessories and a well-barbered look, but there was nothing effeminate about him. He had a surface softness, but there was strength in him and character despite the supporting role that he accepted in his relationship to Dorinda. There was nothing mean in him. He had a tolerant attitude toward other people and it was a tolerance that did not patronize. He was seldom astonished at anything that anyone did, but he was always interested. He liked people and he was amused by them. More of the amusement than the liking went into his plays.

"Hello, Mary," he said. "Did you see the New Haven notices?"

"Yes."

"Like them?"

"No."

He nodded. "We are on the same team. Neither did I. They treated our girl with respect because the gods had permitted her a place in the same show with Bigvoice of the Met."

"That is the way it read to me too. You were there. Was it really like that?"

Carter Brill lighted a cigarette and took his time, making a ritual of it. "Well," he said, "I've seen her better. She never really loosened up. I've got to admit that she seems in awe of this guy."

"How was he?"

"Having the time of his life. He hams all over the place in good old Met fashion and there's nothing in the score to run him out of wind. He projects."

"And Miss Hollywood?"

"Better than she figured. She's giving it all she's got."

Carter Brill sat in the straight chair to the right of the bookcase that faced Mary's desk. Mary answered the phone again, then took the receiver off the hook. She did not like people who did things like that, but she had to talk to Carter while he was willing to visit. He picked up the conversation where the phone call had interrupted it.

"So it's a good show and a fine cast," he said. "The rough spots will iron out in Boston. But a long run for it could be as bad as it's good."

Mary understood him perfectly. A long run for *The Seventh Wife* would be very, very hard on Dorinda if she were overshadowed, if it fixed her in the public mind as a bright talent supporting a star. It was unthinkable. The top spot was hers. She could afford to share it graciously, but not yield it.

"She won't let anyone take the New York notices away from her," she said.

"No, of course not."

They both spoke bravely because to do less would be to acknowledge a lack of faith in Dorinda; but Mary knew that Carter was worried and that he was too astute not to know that she was worried too. It was a bond between them.

"Why hasn't she ever married, Mary?" Carter Brill asked suddenly. "It hasn't been the fault of men."

Mary did not look at him. The question was revealing, and because it was revealing, it was embarrassing. Carter Brill had known Dorinda longer than she had. He couldn't hope to receive an answer that meant anything. "He's in love with her," she thought. "He's asked her to marry him and she won't. Curious!" She fastened two paper clips together, frowning at them. If Carter thought that Dorinda was going to be hurt in this show, and if he was in love with her, he'd want to take care of her.

"She *is* married," she said. "Isn't she?"

"That's a Catholic answer."

She looked up swiftly. "What do you mean, a Catholic answer?"

"You are a Catholic, aren't you?"

"Yes. But I don't see where that has anything to do with what I said."

"It does have. Catholicism inflicts wounds on the mind, and the wounds leave scars."

"That sounds like a line from one of your unwritten plays."

"Some of my best lines occur in my unwritten plays. But that doesn't get us anywhere. The point is that an ignorant country kid went through a marriage ceremony with some stupid clod when she was eighteen. She is now Dorinda Daly and the clod is still a clod, if he's anything. She hasn't seen him since she was twenty. Do you call that a marriage?"

"There's a son to show for it."

"A biological accident."

This touched a sensitive nerve in Mary Norbert's awareness of the world. "Do you consider children biological accidents?" she asked.

"Aren't they?"

"No."

"What else? You wouldn't try to tell me that Dorinda selected this big farmer to be the father of her children, or that she ever thought of such a thing?"

"She selected him. Or she let herself be selected. At eighteen, she was a big girl. It must have occurred to her that there might be children. As a matter of fact——"

"I know. There was one. Which doesn't prove your point at all."

"What does it prove?"

It seemed strange to be talking to Carter Brill in this vein. He had stopped to talk to her many times when Dorinda was out, or busy, and she had usually found him stimulating. His mind was as restless as his body, as the fingers which played with interminable strings of cigarettes. Only when Dorinda was trying to talk something out, and he was trying to help her, did he relax into relative inaction. He was prowling around the room now, frowning, not answering her question. She wondered what urge had driven him to discussing Dorinda with her.

"It happens to two people who aren't married at all," he said abruptly. "It happens all the time. It's the same damned thing inside a marriage as it is outside it. It's just what I said: a biological accident."

"Can you name another *accident* that operates by rules?"

"What do you mean, rules?"

"Nine months' gestation for one."

"That's an irrelevancy. I refuse to be drawn into it. A broken leg is an accident, but not the length of time that it takes to heal it."

Mary laughed. "That's not the same thing, and you know it."

"To hell with it! The point is that you take the attitude that Dorinda has to be married all her life to someone who isn't her husband, and who hasn't been for so long that it's ridiculous. She lost him and she hasn't even got a widow's right."

"Probably because she isn't a widow. But why blame me? I wouldn't dream of telling Dorinda what to do, and she wouldn't ask me."

Carter Brill crushed his cigarette out savagely and lighted another. He flipped the dead match at the wastebasket with his thumbnail and seemed to take a melancholy satisfaction in his own skill. The match dropped in neatly.

"It isn't you," he said. "I like you. If I didn't, I wouldn't be playing Maypole with you. It's the damned Catholic mind that drives me crazy, so that I want to smash things. Dorinda has it too, though I'll swear I don't know how or why."

"Has she?"

"You know it. She never goes near a Catholic church. She doesn't believe any part of it and probably doesn't even know much about it. But she was married in the Church, and the Church says she has to stay married and can't marry again, so that part registers. She's superstitious about it. Does it make sense? In any manner, shape, or form does it make a bit of sense?"

"If it makes sense to her, then it makes sense."

Carter Brill sat down heavily. "Let's quit," he said. "Let's quit right here while there's a speck of sanity left in this screaming world. The Catholic mind is bad enough, but when you gild it and bedeck it, and bedizen it, with feminism, Reason dies at the stake in agony."

"I'm sorry," Mary said mildly. "I *am* feminine gender, you know. So is Dorinda."

Carter Brill smiled suddenly. He had a fine smile that not only revealed his white, even teeth but lighted behind his eyes. "Your apology is accepted," he said. "You are a fine specimen of the gender. I'm certain that the gender must be very proud of you. And I'm sorry that I popped off."

"You didn't pop off. We seem to have had a debate."

"Let's call it something else. Let's call it a sonata for two pianos in G minor, Opus 88. Don't let's call it a debate."

"Right. It's a sonata for two pianos in G minor, Opus 88."

"With flutes."

They smiled at each other, content that one thing at

least was settled. In this mood, or in argument, Mary decided that she liked Carter Brill even better than she had realized. He was as sincere in his convictions as she was in hers. That was the baffling thing with people like Carter. You could not throw out their sincerity and you could only throw out their logic on the basis of your own definitions. People like Carter Brill did not reject; they merely denied that there was anything to reject.

"Where is Dorinda spending the weekend?" she asked.

"With the Bertfields. They'll keep it quiet."

"Good."

That was always the problem with the out-of-town openings. Dore considered it unlucky to return to New York until she returned with the show, and there were few places she could go where she would not be exploited, or annoyed by bores.

"What is the lad doing with himself?" Carter said.

"I wouldn't know. He's dropped out of sight."

Carter Brill crushed out a cigarette and forgot to light another. He raised his eyebrows. "Incredible development," he said. "I'd have laid odds."

"Dorinda asked me to call him at the Algonquin," Mary said stiffly. "She wanted to offer him tickets for New Haven. He had checked out."

Carter Brill was studying her, his eyes speculative. She felt herself flushing and resented it. "You heard Dorinda talking to me about him the other day?" he said.

"Some of it."

"Some was probably too much. I have an idea that he's a much better man than Dorinda gives him credit for being. The fond-mother role is Dorinda's worst."

"She's sincere in it."

"That's why she's so very bad. She'd be wonderful if she played it. Not a dry eye in the house."

"He is very keen about her. And in a very special way. He wouldn't be if she made a role out of being his mother."

Carter Brill took a fresh cigarette and tapped it against his hand without lighting it. "I stand in awe," he said. "Motherhood as a rule does not endow females with either wisdom or with intelligence, Mary. Perhaps you've noticed! My mother considered me a personal possession, like a toothbrush. Any evidence that I had human impulses, outside of her plans for me, was a personal affront to her; as shocking as if her toothbrush were to waver in its singleminded devotion to her teeth. Any interest I showed in young women was practically infidelity to *her*. If I had married while she lived, my wife would have had a hell of a time. I never hated any girl enough to make her my mother's daughter-in-law."

Mary Norbert stared at him, too startled to speak. This was a Carter Brill whom she had never known or imagined. He continued to tap the cigarette against the back of his hand. Despite his words, there was no expression of bitterness in his face.

"I am doing this bit of indecent exposure," he said, "with intention and design, and with the mental reservation that I should be minding my own business."

He finally lighted the cigarette. "Dorinda is the opposite pole," he said. "She's crazy about that kid of hers, but she never used her son as a replacement for her husband—which is a common practice among women! I leave that thought with you. She has no cords on him, silver or otherwise."

He had been holding the dead match in his hand. He flipped it at the wastebasket and missed. Mary rose as he picked up his topcoat.

"What are you trying to tell me?" she said.

His eyes met hers. "You are a bright girl, and I draw diagrams badly."

"You drew the diagram and I don't like it."

"Dark glasses do not become you."

"It isn't a case of dark glasses, or rose-colored ones either. If you're trying to tell me that Dorinda considers me a safe companion for her son, I've already figured that out. It isn't flattering."

"It is very flattering."

"It is not! Would you like it? After your little speech about toothbrushes, can you contradict yourself and tell me that I should consider myself a very lucky girl because——"

Carter Brill raised his hand. " 'My child is yet a stranger

in the world,'" he quoted solemnly. "Juliet, you distress me. Imagining you in the listener role when Dorinda was expounding to me, I foresaw this."

"And yet?"

"And yet Dorinda can do nothing but hope. Can a hope hurt you? Have you ever introduced two friends you liked and hoped they would like each other? Why blame Dorinda, who introduced two people she loved, if she hoped that they would love each other? Be a good Catholic, Mary. There is no such thing as predestination. Sail your own bright ship. If you find a port you love, don't love it less, or sail on past it, because Dorinda loves it too. You are not compelled!"

He blew a kiss at her and went out. She stood staring at the door and she could feel the flush in her face. Her legs trembled and she sat down.

"I hate them," she said, "all of them!"

There was a feeble smoke wraith wavering above the corpse of Carter Brill's final cigarette. It was the only sign of life or movement in the room, and it belonged to someone who was gone. The quiet enveloped her, a strange, unnatural stillness that was unnerving. She remembered suddenly that she had taken the receiver off the hook. She replaced it and immediately the phone rang. She braced herself for the inevitable, obvious nuisance call, but a deep voice said, "Bianca, you certainly talk a lot."

"I wasn't talking."

"Then you are the world's best listener. I've been trying you for a half hour. Will you have dinner with me?"

"No."

"That's so definite that it must be a mistake."

"I'm afraid not. I have an engagement."

Mary steeled herself against his voice, against her own curiosity, against any possible argument. She wasn't going to be a straight for Dorinda, or a character in one of Carter Brill's plots, or Bart McBride's idle hour.

"It's important, Bianca," the voice said.

She breathed deep. "It can't be," she said. "It can't be important to both of us, and if it isn't, then it isn't important."

The words tumbled out and she was appalled at them.

She had been keeping everything on a high, cool plane and some nervous, undisciplined thing within her was suddenly speaking gibberish. In her panic, she hung up. The hush flowed back into the room and she sat there alone with it. "I don't care," she said.

## CHAPTER 5

Bart McBride waited patiently in the apartment house lobby. "I owe it to her," he thought, "after her long sentry go in the Algonquin." He watched the people who entered or left, couples usually or groups of women. Whether paired with a man or grouped with other women, women were noisy, their voices high and shrill, their laughter unconvincing. He was particularly sensitive to their discordant qualities after the tranquillity of the monastery. When Mary Norbert stepped out of the elevator, he was almost as surprised as the first time that he saw her, in this same lobby.

She was so straight that she gave the impression of marching. She had a dancer's grace, but not the ballerina duck walk; her feet tracked. She was wearing a very small hat with a rhinestone knickknack on it and her head was high. She looked unhappy.

She was not aware of him until he intercepted her at the door. " 'Supper is done,' " he quoted solemnly, " 'and we shall come too late.' "

She looked up startled and her eyes were wide, but when he held the door for her, she looked straight ahead, her forehead furrowed in concentration.

" 'I fear, too early: for my mind misgives,' " she said.

"Good girl."

"Don't you know anybody but Shakespeare?"

"But certainly. Chekhov, but only in the original Russian. Ibsen, but only in the original Scandinavian."

"Aeschylus, but only in the original Greek," she said, "and Plautus in Latin."

"O'Neill in Sanskrit."

"And Eliot in High Church." She broke off abruptly. "I told you that I couldn't see you."

"I mistrusted the emphasis. I don't believe in noon, or midnight, or any extreme. If you'd been less emphatic?"

They were walking south on Park Avenue and the lights were on. The street was thronged with taxicabs, but nobody who waved succeeded in flagging one. It was the familiar New York evening scene. Everyone who was not riding a taxi seemed to be seeking one.

"I have a date," Mary Norbert said firmly.

"Name him—and the place. Instantly!"

She faltered and Bart shook his head. "Good quoters are poor liars, always."

"It doesn't follow. There is no connection."

"It's Freudian. Very profound. One quotes because it is easier on his id than inventing."

"I don't know how we get into these idiotic conversations. And I'm not a liar. And I meant it when I said that I'm busy."

"You meant it, too, when you said that importance is as importance does, or something. It was very interesting. I'll make a bet with you."

"I don't bet."

"You lost the last bet. It's your turn to win."

"What's the bet?" she said warily.

"If I get us a taxi within one block, you come to dinner with me. If I don't, I'll believe you have a date and no more questions asked."

She looked at the fast-flowing traffic, the frantically waving people at the curb. "Within *one* block," she said. "It's a bet."

Bart did not break stride. He had a fatalistic feeling about bets. One won them if one deserved to win and if there was some point in winning. He did not stand and signal. He merely walked closer to the curb. Ten feet ahead of them, a taxi pulled to the curb to discharge two passengers beneath an apartment house awning. He helped Mary in.

"Lüchow's," he said.

"It wasn't fair," Mary said.

"Why not?"

"You sold your soul to the devil, or something, to get this cab."

"Not exactly. I kept strings on it."

"There isn't any point in our seeing each other. We settled that the other night."

"We didn't settle anything the other night. We merely fell apart."

"I didn't. We talked about something that involves issues, convictions, basic realities. When we got through there wasn't anything left."

"Since then I've been in a monastery. I discovered that there are many things left."

She looked at him quickly, wary of humor where humor did not belong. "What things?" she said.

"Silence, solitude, faith, decision, patience, humility, refraining from judgments, prayer—and love."

"You are trying to confuse me."

"Quite the contrary. I don't want you to be confused."

"I don't trust you. You are too masterful about everything. There is no reason why you should feel that you can walk up to me and start making my decisions for me, or that you should——"

"I did not make any decisions for you, did I? You merely lost a bet."

The cab drew up before Lüchow's on Fourteenth Street. It was a very old restaurant and it looked very old, with high ceilings and vast cavernous rooms, and crystal chandeliers. "I'm in a mood for hearty German food in large quantities," he said, "and schmaltzy music and a lot of people."

"You didn't ask me what my mood was—or is."

"Your mood was canceled when you lost the bet."

"All right." She smiled suddenly. "And I like this. It's fun. Not good for a girl's figure, but fun. Satisfied?"

He looked across the table at her. He thought, as he had thought before, that one would call her face "heart-shaped" if that were not such a horrible cliché. When you threw the cliché away because it was horrible, she was still a girl with a heart-shaped face, broad and high of forehead, smooth of cheek, rounded chin, a controlled but vulnerable mouth, gray eyes of compelling candor.

"I am not only satisfied, Bianca," he said. "I am deeply grateful."

They walked to Washington Square when they left the restaurant and he told her about his father as they walked. He had debated that decision in his own mind coming down on the train. His father was Dorinda Daly's hidden chapter and this girl worked for Dore. There was that, but there was also the fact that Dore had used this girl as the messenger to bring him word of his father. Starting from that point, Mary Norbert had become more to him than to Dore. He could not unlock the gate that was closed between them without telling her about his father. So he told her.

"I learned from him what I should have known," he said, "that two people can stand for different values and move in opposite directions, with neither of them wholly right or wholly wrong. I liked him. I'm glad that I know him. He's a better man than I am."

"How better?"

"His life is better. He bought something for what seems a terrific price. It's worth what he paid for it. I can see that, and I have the price, but I'm not capable of paying it."

"I don't understand."

They came into the square. Bart's memories moved on its paths and benches like ghosts. Dore had a night club spot the first time they came to New York, and Broadway had never heard of her. They had stayed in the Village, in a small furnished apartment, and he had played in the square. Dore told him that Constance and Joan Bennett played there, too, when they were children. She showed him where John Barrymore used to have an apartment. Now he was walking down one of the paths with Mary Norbert and two old men were playing checkers under one of the park lights, possibly the same old men he used to watch, with the same checkers. Two people rose from a bench and strolled away. He took over the bench with Mary.

"It's the same thing that you do about taxis," she said.

"It frightens a person. But I still don't understand all this about your father being a better man than you are, and about the price of things."

Bart remembered the retreat talk which had made such a tremendous impression on him, the one that had closed his visit to the monastery. It had seemed then, and seemed now, to sum up all of his bewilderments, to offer an answer to all of his problems.

"The world is God's showcase," Father Stephen had said, "and we all come to it with spiritual wealth to spend. There are rare and beautiful things in God's showcase, which the most humbly born of men can afford. God has given to each man the true riches which will buy the rarest and the richest gifts, and He has given to man the very great gift of decision. Yet so many spend their wealth for the world's penny candy, sicken with it, and return to sicken again. Others stand before the showcase, irresolute, choosing nothing, spending nothing, tempting the patience of God."

Remembering, Bart tried to tell Mary Norbert. The words did not fall so eloquently from his lips as they had from Father Stephen's, but he held the thought intact.

"I am one of the irresolute ones," he said. "I've drifted into what was convenient, or what seemed necessary. I've never made a bold choice of what I wanted; probably because I hesitated to commit myself to the price. When we want something, anything at all, we have to give up something to get it."

Mary frowned in concentration. "Do you really have a choice?" she said.

"That is what I asked him. Father Stephen says that everyone asks that, and that most people deny that they have any choice, even in the act of choosing; that every decision of every day is a choice."

"I can see that. But in the big things? The really important things?"

"I think so. It's the thrift principle applied to the spiritual and the intangible. You can't have the big things if you waste yourself on the petty things."

"I'd have to think about it. What did it do to you?"

"I'm not certain—yet. I came out of it with a decision. That's why I had to see you."

"Why me?"

They were two people sitting on a park bench in Washington Square which had seen generations of young people sitting on the benches; where great poets and painters had rested or despaired, and poets and painters who were not great; where idlers had idled and drunks had slept and prostitutes had walked. Bart looked into the shadows at a group of children who played an intricate game of their own devising.

"An honest answer might be long, Mary," he said, "and at this stage it might be complicated. Let's say we started a discussion on a ferryboat that, for some odd reason, turned into a snowball rolling downhill. It grew into something pretty big. I find I can't live with your picture of little girls in gray uniforms wondering who they are."

"I'm quite positive that I do not want to discuss that subject any more. That's why I didn't want to go out with you tonight."

"I was certain of that. You are the only person I know with whom I can discuss it, because you are the only one who understands it."

He watched her, waiting. She pressed her lower lip with her teeth, looking at something far away from him. "You take me too seriously. I overdramatized it."

"I don't believe that you did."

"It's a fact of life. There are thousands and thousands of us." She clenched her hand, then opened it, spreading the fingers wide. "A man quoted something to me today. Everybody who has anything to do with the theatre quotes things. He did: 'My child is yet a stranger in the world.' He meant me, for another reason than the one that is right. Say that all those little girls are strangers in the world. That's why they wonder who they are."

"It's still sad."

"Many unchangeable, inescapable things are sad."

"Yes. And we are all strangers in the world, asking who we are, wondering where to go. But that's a digression, Mary, and you know it. I'm going to see Aleta and demand an answer. That's my decision."

The girl raised her head. She looked into his face. "Demand?"

"How else?"

"If she laughs at you, then what?"

His jaw tightened. "She won't laugh."

"Maybe not. I don't know her. But I know that women laugh at men to cover up the fact that they don't have answers, or are afraid of the answers that they know. If she laughs, it's her perfect answer, because it leaves you without another question."

Bart looked beyond the square into a monastery cloister where a tall man in a robe and cowl walked with him. "She's older now," he said, paraphrasing his father. "I have to give her an opportunity to tell me the truth. She has that right."

Mary Norbert said, "Oh!"

"Don't you agree?"

"I don't see where it makes a bit of difference whether I agree or not. What is she like?"

What was Aleta like? Bart looked into the past as he had looked into the monastery garden. He could see her on the screen of his mind. "She is dark," he said. "Olive-skinned. Her eyes are oddly shaped, narrow, almost black."

"You'd certainly know her again. You aren't vague about her." Mary Norbert laughed. "You must have thought about her a lot."

"No. Not particularly. I knew her pretty well."

"Unquestionably. Are you still in love with her?"

He turned, startled. "Are you crazy?"

"I asked a logical question. I'm not crazy and I won't be shouted at."

"I didn't shout at you. But that was a fantastic question."

"Was it? She isn't a subject on which you are indifferent or objective, certainly. If you can't think of her without raising your voice and getting violently emotional!"

She was tense, her hands clenched. There was a flush in her face and her eyes were angry. Bart drew a deep breath. "For God's sake, Mary!"

"Leave God out of it. I asked you what the woman was like. I meant as a person. I was trying to help because you asked me to help. I had to know first what she was like as a person. All that you could think about were the nauseating physical details. Her olive skin! Her black eyes! As if I wanted to know that!"

"It's part of what she is like. I didn't know."

"I don't want to hear any more."

She made an attempt to rise and he gripped her wrist. "Wait!" he said. "I do want your help. Aleta is past, long past. We broke up before I left Cornell, before I went in the Army. I didn't see her before I left for Japan. We were all through before I got that letter."

She was fighting his hold on her wrist. "Let me go!" she said.

There was no point in trying to talk to her or reason with her. He released her suddenly and she rose swiftly without looking at him. She marched down the path, her heels clicking. He had to take long strides to keep pace with her. "Look," he said. "Maybe I word things clumsily, but I'm not in love with Aleta—if that's the issue. It was——"

"Her olive skin and her black eyes! Let me alone! You make it worse. It's all so sordid and disgusting that I feel unclean just listening to you. It was bad enough the other night."

"Look!"

"Stop."

"Will you listen a moment?"

"No."

She walked toward the bus stop, her body straight, her heels tapping angrily. Bart kept pace with her, searching desperately in his mind for something to say, some word key that would turn the tumblers of this preposterous lock. Adults, he told himself, didn't act this way. There wasn't any misunderstanding that couldn't be cleared up with just a little patience, a reasonable attitude. If she'd just listen, he could convince her of how wrong she was. He hated Aleta and all that she had done to him. He hated his younger self for being Aleta's fool. My God! Hadn't he proved that? He'd been back from Japan for more than a year. He hadn't gone near Aleta.

"Let me get you a taxi," he said.

She didn't answer him. There was a bus waiting and she

boarded it. She had her money out before he could pay her fare and he had to change a dollar in order to pay his own. He had to walk down the aisle, then, of a bus that had only a few people in it, and sit beside a girl who looked out of the window, refusing to speak to him.

"Bianca!"

He gave up. He could not think of anything to say either. They rode in silence up Fifth Avenue. He walked beside her across Fifty-sixth Street and as they neared Park he tried again.

"Mary," he said, "I'm sorry. I was clumsy. I looked forward to tonight. I wanted to ask your opinion before I went out there. Doesn't it mean anything to you that——"

The unresponsive silence chilled him. "Okay," he said. "Have it your way."

He left her at the doorway to her apartment house and he did not say good night.

In her own apartment, with the light on, Mary Norbert was suddenly cold, which was an absurdity on such a warm and humid night. Her hands trembled so violently that she spilled dry coffee all over her two-burner stove before she succeeded in putting two tablespoonfuls into her two-cup percolator. She sat down, then, staring at the stove.

"Why did I?" she whispered. "How could I? Only a fool does the same stupid thing twice."

She was no longer angry or jealous, merely a little sick. She saw herself in grotesquely exaggerated terms as she imagined that Bart McBride saw her: shrill, unreasonable, quarreling in an open park, walking ridiculously away from him while all those people stared. She remembered the attempt that he had made to placate her after they left the bus. She could have wiped all the rest out then with a single word and she had not uttered it.

"He did come to me," she said miserably. "He meant it when he said that I was the only one who could understand. He said that even after the other night when I didn't give him understanding. He'll never say it again. Never. How could he?"

She wept, silently, with more tears inside than out. The coffee started to perk and she turned down the gas, grateful for the something outside of herself that demanded attention. Images piled upon images in her mind, and words upon words. He was probably the most decent, most sensitive, most desperately in earnest man she had known in her entire lifetime. He was going into something where he was going to be hurt and defeated. He asked her about it first, and instead of advising him or helping him, she had turned into a virago. He was making a big mistake, and because she had had a chance to do something about it, it would be her mistake when he made it.

"He's idealistic about it," she said.

She remembered then the phrase of Dorinda's that she should have remembered earlier. "He's a fool about women," Dorinda said. "He believes in them." The men whom Mary Norbert had met, most of them, who were "fools about women" were fools for reasons other than belief.

"He believed in me," she said.

The fragrance of coffee permeated her kitchenette. She turned off the gas and while the coffee settled she walked into the other room and took a book from the bookcase beside her bed. It was Rilke's *Letters to a Young Poet*. She turned the pages to the passage that she had read, marked, and many times reread.

*We have no reason to mistrust our world* [she read], *for it is not against us. Has it terrors, they are our terrors; has it abysses, those abysses belong to us; are dangers at hand, we must try to love them. And if we always hold to what is difficult, then that which now still seems to us the most hostile, will become what we most trust and find most faithful. How should we be able to forget those ancient myths that are at the beginning of all peoples, the myths about dragons that, at the last moment, turn into princesses? Perhaps all the dragons of our lives are princesses who are only waiting to see us once beautiful and brave. Perhaps everything terrible is, in its deepest being, something helpless that wants help from us.*

Tears were flowing down her cheeks when she closed the book. "I was not beautiful and brave," she said. "I had an opportunity to be." She thought of that other opportunity, of the empty theatre and the shadow-filled stage, the patient director who did not have to tolerate her temper. "All the dragons!" she said. "All the dragons! And never once have I been beautiful and brave. Never once!"

## CHAPTER 6

Bart McBride awakened in the middle of the night. He had been running around in a walled place that was like the inside of a cylinder. The wall was a closed curve with the smooth surface of steel and there was no way out. He lay blinking at the ceiling, awake yet not quite awake, half convinced yet of the dream's reality. Slowly, very slowly, the true dimensions of the hotel room asserted their reality and he sat up.

"Hell!" he said. "What brought that on?"

The dream of walls, and of the place without a door, belonged to his childhood, particularly to the first year at school with the Christian Brothers. He had outgrown that and forgotten it; now it was back. He got out of bed and walked around the room. There was nothing to keep him in the room. It was an ordinary room with a door. He could walk out of the door and do anything that he wanted to do. He looked at his watch. It was two forty-five.

This was New York. There were shows that stayed open all night, and eating places. It would still be bright over on Broadway, with people milling around. There was an all-night shooting gallery on Sixth Avenue where a man could go in the middle of the night and improve his aim. In a few minutes, in several Catholic churches scattered around town, Mass would be starting for printers and other workers of the night. It was Sunday morning. He could get dressed and go to Mass before dawn.

He crossed the room and stood at the window looking out, across Forty-fourth Street and the parking garage roof to the bulk of the Stern store on Forty-second Street. He remembered Father Stephen at the Abbey, telling him that his life would be changed, changed forever, because he went there. He could feel it changing, feel the slow relentless pull of a powerful tide, and he had a sense of helplessness. That, perhaps, was what the dream was all about, and why it had come back.

He thought about Mary Norbert in Washington Square. Mary Norbert might be the dream. He had been as helpless with her as he had been in the bottom of the metal cylinder. She did not have to be as she had been with him. He could talk to her, or he could listen. All that she had to do was tell him where he was off base, or what he said that was wrong. It should not ever be necessary for a woman to flare up, or slash or cut—or for a man to do it either—if the other party was even halfway reasonable, or trying to be reasonable.

"I was honest with her," he thought. "I didn't hold anything back."

It might be that a man couldn't be honest with a woman, that no woman wanted honesty from a man, or wanted him as he actually was. They enacted roles, all of them, and so many of the roles were so charming that a man liked them and applauded them, even when he knew they were roles. That was all right. A man could be the audience of a woman any time, but he couldn't always play the role she wanted him to play, the role that wasn't written in his book, that existed only in her mind.

He walked away from the window. You couldn't replay scenes any more than you could replay games. You couldn't get up before dawn on Sunday and make the touchdown that you missed on Saturday afternoon. The slow tide of thought took him back to Father Stephen.

There was God's showcase to consider and what did he want from it? Until he answered that question and offered what he had for what he wanted, his life would have neither point nor aim, shape nor dimension. He could not answer the question until he saw Aleta and paid his debt to the past. He did not know what he had a right to ask, nor what he had to offer, until that debt was paid.

He went back to bed. "Tomorrow," he said.

He awakened to bright sunlight and the sense of a hot day in the making. It was another thing so often remarked of other places in the country, so easily forgotten about New York: the Indian summer that could carry August into October and splash the autumn with summer heat. He rose slowly, still oppressed with the feeling of ill-being that had come to him in the night, the feeling of weight to be carried and problems to be borne.

He went to Mass at St. Malachy's on Forty-ninth Street. He had gone there first when Dore was playing in *Buffalo Nickel* and he had served Mass there one morning as a volunteer when neither of the regular altar boys showed up. It made him a part of St. Malachy's, somehow, and he had gone there many times since. It was the actors' church, with Masses, Confessions, and devotions at all kinds of odd hours to meet the necessities of people in show business. He had seen men and women there in make-up and even in costume, snatching a few minutes for God during a break in a show role or a night club act or a revue. It was his parish church, the church of the neighborhood in which he had grown up, the neighborhood of backstage.

He came back to the street again after Mass with the feeling that he had been an indifferent and distracted worshiper, that he had not yet escaped from the cylinder of personal bewilderment which had imprisoned him in his dream. He glanced across the street at the shabby, run-down apartment houses that looked just as he had first seen them, no better or worse. Just east of the church he stopped before the windows of a phonograph record supermarket, the largest cut-price record store in the world. He had bought two of Dore's shows there on L.P. records a year ago. The store was closed today, but Dore's voice was in there, waiting to be released for any casual buyer. It was a weird sensation, thinking of that.

He ate breakfast at a counter and he watched a man enter a phone booth. He wanted to enter the phone booth himself, to call Mary Norbert. In the light of day, with something as prosaic as eggs on a plate before him, and coffee in a cup, the scene in the park seemed fantastic and unreal, of no significance. It would be different if he talked to her now, and he felt the need of talking to her. He enjoyed talking to her. He finished his breakfast and walked toward the phone booth with the change in his hand. The man was still in there and he stood for a moment, jingling the change, then he turned away.

"She wouldn't want to talk to me," he said. "I'd probably wake her up."

He went back to his room at the hotel and he had a phone there that required no change, and for which he did not have to wait. His mood, however, had changed. He was confronted now with the call that he had to make.

There was no direct line from his room to the girl who had once been Aleta Waringly. She was married and Bart McBride had sent her a wedding present, but he could not recall the name of the man she had married. It had never been important to him. He did not know what the man was like, nor what he did, nor where he originated. Aleta might have gone anywhere with him: Chicago, Omaha, Walla Walla. Somehow, he could not imagine that, or accept it.

There were five huge phone books that carried the phone numbers of Greater New York. She might be listed in one of them if he knew her husband's name. On the other hand, she might be living in one of the Westchester towns, or in Connecticut, or out on Long Island and still be, for all practical purposes, a New Yorker.

"Let's quit stalling!" he said.

There was a sensation of actual physical relief in picking up the phone, feeling it in his hand, committing himself to something that he had sought to evade. Her parents would be where they had always been, and he remembered that number. He called it, and when he was connected a maid answered and he asked for Mrs. Waringly.

It was one of the long waits of his life. He could hardly expect friendliness. He had been in Japan when Aleta wrote and told him that she was pregnant. He did not know how she had handled that problem at home, but she certainly could not have kept it a secret. All of his letters, after that, by her request, had been mailed to a postal box number in another Connecticut town. Her parents would believe that he had betrayed their confidence, as probably he had, and that he had run out on Aleta when trouble came, which wasn't true.

"Hello," a light breathless voice said. "This is Mrs. Waringly."

"Mrs. Waringly," he said, "this is Bart McBride."

His hand held the receiver tightly. There was a pause, the briefest of hesitations, then she said, "Why, Bart! It has been ages and ages. Where are you?"

"In town. At the Algonquin."

"Oh dear! On Sunday in New York! And it is so unseasonably hot! You can't even get anything to eat on Sunday in New York. You must come right out here."

The warmth in her voice, the invitation, everything so far from his imagining, threw Bart off balance. He shook his shoulders. "That is very nice of you," he said. "But I couldn't think of it. You must have plans of your own. Actually, I called you to obtain Aleta's address."

"Aleta." Again there was a pause. "You knew that she was married, didn't you, Bart?"

"Yes. I knew that. Of course."

"A lovely boy. You must meet him. He and Aleta are coming over in a little while. You must come out. We won't take no for an answer. It has been so very long and you must tell us all about yourself."

"It would be an intrusion."

"Not at all. How very silly of you. You come right away. We will be having a drink. You are driving, of course."

"No. I'll take the train."

"Oh dear! That's so uncomfortable. But it can't be helped, I guess. You get the very soonest train, Bart. Somebody will meet all the trains till you get here. It will be so nice to see you."

Bart hung up the receiver and stared at the instrument. This wasn't the way that it figured to be. This wasn't it at all. Florence Waringly had always bewildered him. She commanded a fast flow of words, and she overwhelmed one with her friendliness. Strangely enough, the friendliness had always been genuine. But today?

"What in hell did Aleta tell them?" he said. "How?"

Aleta was mercury. She was evasive and elusive, impossible to pin down when she did not want to be pinned. She lied boldly when she lied, and she defended any lie that she had told with horse, foot, and guns; but he could not imagine what she had done with the situation as he knew it.

Did she blame someone else, someone out of reach and out of reason? Did she play fair and tell them that he had done all that he could, and that it wasn't anything that she wanted?

He had been prepared for hostility, but he did not know how he could face masked knowledge in these people, or feel his way carefully where he had planned boldly. How was he going to talk to Aleta if this was to be a jolly family group, with a "lovely boy" husband in the background?

On the way to the station, his sense of humor came to his rescue. After all, it was too much to expect that he could call up late Sunday morning and find another man's wife all alone, all set up for his big scene.

Life wasn't so simple. He would have to do with Aleta as he had done with Dore, with his father, and to a certain extent with Mary Norbert; he would have to walk awhile on the streets of her life, catching the rhythm of them, before he could talk to her.

It was hot, blasting hot. Florence Waringly had been right about the discomfort of the train, too; but the ride was not long. He saw Aleta on the platform as he swung down from the step.

She was wearing plaid shorts and a white blouse. She had gained a little weight, not too much. Her hair was short, much shorter than he remembered, and the red of her lipstick was very red as it had always been. She moved swiftly to meet him, but not with the impetuous charge of another year that was over the hill. She held her pace today to the stride of the tall young man who walked beside her. She gave Bart both of her hands.

"How very nice, Bart," she said. "Let me look at you!"

She took a slow backward step, her head on one side. "Tut, tut," she said. "I kept remembering you as bigger than anybody." She flashed her eyes at her husband. "You aren't as big as Roger." Her hand waved through a circle. "Roger, my husband, Bart McBride."

Aleta's husband was at least an inch taller than Bart and probably twenty-five pounds heavier. Quite a few of those pounds were lard, Bart decided. This Roger hadn't been running around in ball parks all summer; as why should anybody? He was a handsome man, dark, with good features, but he looked surly. It wasn't something that anyone could hold against him under the circumstances. "In his spot I wouldn't like any former candidates who came around, either," Bart thought. "I wonder how much he knows."

He felt uncomfortable because that knowledge—or non-knowledge—was suspended between them as he shook hands with Aleta's husband.

"We have orders to bring you right out to the old homestead," Aleta said. "Mother and Dad are eager to see you."

"You are very fair-haired with the family," Roger said. "You and God and George Washington."

"Hush," Aleta said. "How did George Washington get in there?"

She slid under the wheel of a long two-tone convertible. Roger stood aside and let Bart sit in the middle. Aleta swung the car deftly out of the parking space and turned it around. "We were wild to go to New Haven for the opening of your mother's show, Bart," she said, "but we'd rather see it in New York. Didn't want to take the edge off. How is it?"

"She doesn't appear in many flops, Al."

"She posilutely doesn't."

"I saw her in *The Barber's Rich*," Roger said stiffly. "She was very good."

"That was one of her best."

Bart wondered who had seen it with Roger. Aleta and he had seen it together when the flame was burning brightest. It didn't seem right to sit between a man and his wife on the seat of this car, to feel the movement and thrust of Aleta's body as she drove, and to remember as he could not help remembering. It wasn't right, or fair, or even decent, perhaps; but it was, it simply was, existent in time as the car existed, as Aleta did, and Roger.

"It's really a thing for her to be singing in something with Rico Moreno," Aleta said.

Bart watched the town rolling by: the Spinning Wheel Antique Shop, Gibson's Gifts, Stanley's Barber Shop, Emerson Barlow Real Estate, Caslon's Pharmacy.

"It would be something for her if she appeared with him at the Met," he said slowly, "but it's something for him to appear with her in a Broadway show."

Aleta drew a deep breath and exhaled slowly. "Bravo, Bart!" she said.

The car followed the curving road, through aisles of trees, past the old stone houses at the edge of town, and those beyond which Alex Waringly called "1939 Colonial." Aleta swung to the left between two granite pillars. The white road led them to the house, one of the first of the ranch type in this area when it was built, a sprawling affair with wings stretching from the hub in a half wheel. Alex and Florence Waringly were seated at small tables in the patio under gaily striped awnings. There were a half dozen other people.

Florence was as he remembered her: a soft, short, round woman with bracelets on her arms and rings on her fingers. She seemed blonder than he remembered, but that was probably an illusion. Aleta once said, "My mother is blonder than anybody." She still was. Florence had her daughter's trick of extending both hands in welcome, or maybe the trick was hers and Aleta the borrower.

"Bart darling. How very brown you are!" He took her hands in his and she held up her face. He kissed her cheek. "Stalwart," she said, "you were always so very stalwart."

Alex, Aleta's father, thrust out his own hand. He was a square-built, round-faced, genial man, who had always stories to tell that he had heard at one of his luncheon clubs. His face was a two-tone red that evidenced an adequate amount of whisky, a reasonable amount of golf.

"It's good to see you, boy," he said. "Come here and meet the public."

There were introductions and the names meant nothing, although two of them sounded vaguely familiar. The guests whom one met at the Waringlys' were apt to have names that one had heard before. Bart bowed, shook hands, made the bewildering round, and heard himself eulogized as the "best damned all-round football player that ever came out of Cornell." Alex had always been a fan of his, a great Sunday morning quarterback and replayer of games. "Me, a Harvard man, rooting for Cornell," he used to say. "Tie that!" He was still a fan. His heartiness was disconcerting and his effusive praise left Bart without anything to say. After all, the significant thing about past glory was that single word, "past."

There was a young Puerto Rican boy with a tray of drinks. Bart accepted a tall Tom Collins and settled into a big, comfortable chair which offered relaxation to a man's whole body. An atmosphere of friendliness and good-fellowship enfolded him.

"This is wonderful," he said.

He had again the sense of a great tide that was carrying him forward to changes in his life that he could not foresee; but for the moment he floated on it. This was what his life had been like once. There had been nothing in his life to prepare him for the Waringly home when Aleta first invited him down. It awed him then, and it still did. All of this had been a part of Aleta herself, and of the glamour with which he invested her. There had never been any snobbery about the Waringlys. They knew that he had nothing at all, that he was just an athlete, but if Aleta had wanted to marry him, he was certain that her parents would have had no reservations about him. There had been a time, too, when he had wanted to marry Aleta. He looked across two tables to the man whom Aleta had married. He still didn't remember his last name.

Roger seemed at home in this setting, but he added no sparkle to it. He seemed to be brooding about something. It was possible that he and Aleta had quarreled about Bart's coming. Looking at it from Roger's point of view, it was something to quarrel about. After all, what was the object in this McBride's coming down?

Florence was talking about Dore and the people under the awning awoke to a new interest in Bart. As Dorinda Daly's son, he was more interesting to them than he had been as an ex-collegian, a onetime football player. It was one of the pleasant things about the Waringlys that they had given him his own personal rating first, something for which he stood personally.

"I've seen her in all of her shows," one of the women said. "I'm mad about her. It's incredible that you should be her son. She looks so young."

It was the inevitable comment and the one that he avoided. Dore was not exploited in his publicity. In the Western League, he had been a catcher named McBride, as at Cornell he had been a halfback named McBride, and in the Army a lieutenant named McBride. Dore had never covered him up, but, except for people close to him as the Waringlys had been, he had kept her out of his public life. He was not a secret, of course. Columnists referred to him from time to time and he had been mentioned in articles about Dorinda Daly; but he stayed out of her limelight.

"She *is* young," he said now. "Dore will always be young."

"But physically? How does she do it?"

"She is young physically too. It's the way she is."

Aleta came into the conversation. "Bart said something priceless as we drove up from the station. He said that it would be something for his mother if she appeared at the Met with Rico Moreno, but that it is something for Rico Moreno to appear in a Broadway show with Dorinda Daly."

The feminine voices murmured appreciation. Alex Waringly laughed aloud. "Good! Damned good!" he said. Bart was ill at ease. He had not tried to be clever; he had merely expressed a conviction. Aleta clapped her hands. It was another trick that she always had. She did it as a man might snap his fingers.

"Darn!" she said. "Talking about her makes me want to hear her."

"I was thinking the same thing, my dear," one of the women said.

Aleta turned swiftly. "Roger, pet," she said, "be an Eagle Scout! Run over and get my Dorinda Daly albums. They are all together, and the singles are in the D album."

Roger rose reluctantly. "I would not look for them under

Q, darling," he said. He looked at Bart. "Maybe you'd like
to come along. See the country."

"Certainly."

Bart had seen the swift protest building in the faces of
Aleta and her mother. He forestalled that. For one thing,
Roger obviously did not want to go and leave him behind.
It made no difference. There was no immediate possibility
of speaking to Aleta alone. This guy was the Main Street
of Aleta's life. It was better to walk him now and get
him over with. Aleta spoke sharply as he rose and pushed
his chair back.

"Bring the Rico Moreno records too, Roger," she said.

There wasn't any "pet" in her voice this time, either
spoken or implied.


## CHAPTER 7


Roger walked around the convertible and kicked the
white-walled tires, frowning at them. There was no
point to it, but it was the kind of thing that a man was
apt to do when he was angry and pent up. Bart had done
such senseless things himself, so he could understand the
impulse. He wondered about the other man. They had both
been drawn to Aleta. They might be alike in many other
ways.

This Roger had a body that could have made him an
athlete. Bart doubted that he ever had been. On sight,
there was something missing. He lacked the look of combative hardness, of endurance, and the second-wind lines
that mark a man's mouth. Bart knew his own kind and
Roger was not one of them. In that sense, at least, they
differed.

The man kicked his last tire and slid in under the wheel.
"I saw you look surprised down at the station when she
took over the driving," he said. "Well, it's her car. I've
got one of my own. She lets me drive it."

Bart got in beside him without comment. There wasn't any reasonable comment that he could make. The man had been watching him more closely than he thought. The distinction of "his" and "hers" in automobiles was interesting but not earth-shaking.

"Do you live near here?" he asked.

"Over the hill." Roger circled the flower-garden island in the driveway and drove down the private road to the pillars. "You used to be Number One Boy," he said. "Are you still carrying a torch for her?"

Bart shrugged. "I shouldn't have to remind you that she is married."

"No. You shouldn't. But you can't tell me that you came out here because you love listening to Alex and Florence. I can't buy that."

"It's a friendly family. They were good to me. I like them."

"I still can't buy it."

Bart frowned at the road. This was his cue to get angry and cut loose, as he very easily could. He had the uncomfortable feeling, however, that the other man was more honest than he was. Roger was laying it on the line. He believed in matching honesty with honesty, and he hated evasion; but he had to accept the evasive role. He couldn't tell Roger why he was down here. There just wasn't any way of being honest.

"Let's put it this way," he said. "I was invited to your wedding. I couldn't come. I called Aleta's mother to get your address. I would have called you, then, and maybe I'd have been invited out, maybe not."

"Why would you care?"

"I probably wouldn't. Not too much. I knew Aleta. She was a friend of mine. I hadn't met you."

Roger was driving fast, viciously fast, angry. The car topped a hill and Long Island Sound was below them, incredibly blue. "A girl like Aleta doesn't know any men who are friends," he said. "All she ever knows are men who make passes."

"I won't make any passes."

"Damned nice of you."

"Look," Bart said, "up till now this has been a quiet,

peaceful Sunday afternoon. I'd like to keep it that way; but if you start looking for trouble, I'm not going to climb any trees to get away from you."

"The big red team," Roger said.

"Not lately."

"Okay."

Roger was looking straight ahead, anger still dark in his face. "I've got to put it the way it looks to me," he said. "I didn't like the idea of your coming around. Maybe I was wrong about it. There are a lot of things I don't know. I don't know what happened or how you lost out with Aleta. Saying that you lost out and I won is only one way of putting it. If you think it's the garden of Eden, you're crazy."

Bart shrugged. He wasn't liking the conversation. There was something wrong with a man who talked of personal matters with a stranger. Even if he was torn up with the suspicion that there was something in his wife's past, he was still wrong. None of the Waringlys would do it. Bart McBride would not do it. There was a code about such things. The car swept away from sight of the Sound and topped another low hill.

"There it is," Roger said, "Vannin Acres."

So his name was Vannin, Roger Vannin. Bart remembered the name now as it had looked on the wedding invitations. It was good to have that settled. The house loomed up ahead of them, a ranch house like the Waringlys'; smaller but still impressively large.

*"Her little* place," Roger said bitterly. "The house that suds built!"

"It's your home," Bart said quietly. "Why deal me in on the personal resentments?"

"Because you happen to be here, and because that's how I feel." Roger braked to a stop in the driveway and turned in the seat. He had his chin thrust forward belligerently. His lower lip was thrust forward, too, and that spoiled the effect; it diluted the anger and reduced it to petulance. "You can spend the rest of the evening saying, 'There, but for the grace of God, go I.'"

"Probably not."

"You should. I'm twenty-eight years old. Look at that place! Could I buy it?"

"I wouldn't know. You might have inherited slabs of pure gold, or a bunch of oil wells."

"I didn't inherit a damned thing. I didn't inherit eating money. I came from a jerk town in Ohio. I was drafted out of high school into the Army. I went to Columbia on G.I. money. That's how much backing I had. I'm a poet. I wanted to write plays."

Bart looked at the house. All of the young poets were probably trying to be T. S. Eliot this season. He didn't know. There had been poets at Cornell, probably Columbia attracted more of them. "Roar, Lion, Roar!" He had heard that cheer rolled out across the fields on which he had played against Columbia. There wasn't much roar, and not an awful lot of lion, in Roger Vannin. Maybe the young intellectuals of Columbia refrained from roaring. Or maybe all of this was unfair. That house, that he couldn't buy himself, might be Roger's steel cylinder in which he ran around helplessly.

"Do you know what I'm doing?" Roger said. "I'm writing ad copy for detergents. Detergents are suds. Dear old sparkling, scintillating suds!"

Bart was still looking at the house. If he had married Aleta, it would be his house. How could he avoid it? And would he want it?

"Even a poet has to make a living," he said.

"Money!" Roger sneered at the word. "Does everything have to be measured by what it brings in the market place? Can you measure art that way? Or beauty?"

"People do."

"People! There are only a few people in the world who know what art is. People weep about peasants in places they couldn't find on a map, and about crumbs in slums; but the greatest tragedy leaves them unmoved."

"Does it?"

"You're damned right it does! The waste of the artist is our greatest tragedy, and nobody gives a damn. Let him write about suds! Take your own mother. Suppose she had to waste herself, singing commercials about suds!"

Bart thought about Dore. She had gone hungry. She

had saved dimes and quarters to pay for dancing lessons, diction lessons, courses in sight reading and in harmony. She had done three, sometimes four shows a day in smoky night clubs. She had done one-night stands and learned to sleep on busses. She would have been delighted, along the way she had come, to sing about suds or any other thing. She was an artist. In her own field, she was at the very top. She had not always been. If she had insisted upon being an artist before other people were willing to acknowledge that she was an artist, she probably never would have become an artist. You lived knowledge like that; you couldn't put it in words for people like Roger Vannin. He wouldn't put anything about Dore in words for the likes of Roger Vannin.

"We better get those records," he said. "They'll be sending out the St. Bernards."

Roger laughed shortly. "I can see why she rated you away up there," he said. "When you're sent, you come right back."

He opened the door on his side and stepped out. Bart followed him up the path to the house because it would be a self-conscious thing not to do so. His temper was still under control, but the electricity was running through his nerves. He had had all the combat that he would ever need, but if he had to hit just one more man in his career, he would not mind if that man turned out to be Roger Vannin.

It was growing dark. Roger opened the front door and snapped on the light. The living room looked startlingly like the Waringly house. It was in the same pattern: fireplace, stark walls, modern blond furniture. The furniture was good, expensive, artistically arranged, but it did not have the solid, settled, enduring look of mahogany or walnut in traditional designs. This furniture cried aloud that it belonged to people who could afford to wheel it out tomorrow and replace it with something still more modern, something brighter, or something merely more amusing. The Waringly place had always impressed Bart that way, too, even when he was most in awe of it.

Roger crossed the room to the built-in cabinet beside a

recessed loudspeaker and drew out four L.P. envelopes. He took six records from two cases and straightened.

"Here," he said, "you'd better carry them."

They went back to the car and Roger drove faster on the return trip. He was withdrawn into silence and Bart left him there. Aleta was waiting for them in the patio. She was wearing a wide skirt now, presumably over the plaid shorts. The others had gone inside. "What in hell took you so long?" she said.

"Your damned records. If you filed them in any kind of order, it wouldn't take so long."

Roger still sounded angry, but genuine anger did not lie. Weighing one thing with another, they had not been gone for a sensationally long time; not long enough, certainly, for a woman to make an issue of it. A man could stand on that if he wanted to be belligerent.

Something of what he felt must have showed in Bart's face. Aleta glanced at him and clapped her hands. "Think nothing of all this, Halfback," she said. "It's merely our manner of waltzing."

"Halfback" was her favorite name for him long ago. Bart shrugged. "I didn't think anything of it," he said.

That, too, was a lie, of course. It was difficult for a man to keep his own sense of values on the line when the values around him were scrambled and confused.

"Okay," Aleta said. "We've got time for a quick one before we eat. It's only delicatessen, a buffet thing, but we have to get to it."

She led the way inside. The others were grouped around the living room with the drinks. Florence looked concerned in a fluttery, aimless way. "What in the world, Roger?"

"He's already been interrogated." Aleta's voice was light, but there was an edge on it. "He had two flat tires, lost his way, and couldn't find the records. Now, let's give the boys a drink."

Bart had nursed one Tom Collins outside. He took another one now from the little Puerto Rican in the white coat. It seemed indicated. When a man didn't keep to a schedule around here, the result could be quite a production. That was Roger's problem and he could have it.

Bart chatted idly with two women and a man, faces without names, and he thought again of how like this room was to the other. Aleta was a girl, obviously, who did not leave home; she took home with her. There was a moment when they rose to go into the dining room; she moved close to him. Roger had gone ahead with Florence.

"What did he tell you?" she demanded.

He looked down into that strange face, the oddly shaped eyes that he had once found so disturbing. Her eyebrows were thin, black lines and there was shadow on her lids.

"The history of Connecticut," he said.

"Stop it! What were you talking about?"

"Houses, neighbors, colleges. He went to Columbia."

"Cute. He still goes to Columbia. I'll buy that part, not the rest. Roger never talks about anything but himself."

"All right. That's settled. He talked about himself. Now, when can I talk to *you?*"

There was quick fright in her eyes. She looked over her shoulder. "Not here. And not tonight."

"When?"

"I don't know. Let's work on it."

Her voice was a husky whisper. She met his eyes, held them, then abruptly turned away. He remembered more than he wanted to remember in that moment, and he swore under his breath.

It was with a feeling of relief that he joined the others who moved in a line around the long table, taking cold ham and turkey, potato salad, tomatoes, celery, and an assortment of other things onto his plate, conscious suddenly of hunger, weary of problems, discords, and disturbances. "I'm not an ulcer type, thank God," he thought. "Anything that I can eat, I can digest—and if it's eatable, I can eat it."

He sat with Florence and two of the guests at a bridge table. They talked and nothing that they discussed was important, but he enjoyed himself. These were pleasant people, friendly people, doing exactly what millions of other Americans did on Sunday evening. Later, in the living room, he settled back in a chair and Aleta lifted the top of the record player. She held a record in her hand, careful that her fingers touched only the edges.

"This is a recording of the songs from *Buffalo Nickel*," she said. "I'll play only one band, the one I like best."

The player was a superb instrument. Bart knew that when the first few bars of music poured out of the speaker. He leaned forward and suddenly she was there in the room with them; Dore in her first big Broadway triumph, Dore with all the yearning and longing in her voice. She held eleven people silent, unmoving, with only her voice, a voice on a record.

> *"This day, this hour, this moment,*
> *This mad delight,*
> *This dizzy height,*
> *This—loving—you."*

When her voice floated into the quiet that it had commanded, there was a collective sigh that was, itself, applause. The song was old, they had heard it often, but they were regretful when it ended. "Marvelous!" one of the men said. "She has something that no one else has, no one at all."

Bart lifted his eyes. Aleta was staring fixedly at him. She held his eyes for a split second, then turned to select another record. He felt uncomfortable, indefinably uncomfortable. She selected the Dorinda Daly hits deftly. She could have forgotten *Lush-a-bye, Baby,* but she didn't. She gave them a Dore who was doing her best with subhuman material.

> *"When the first fiddle looks like the second fiddle,*
> *When a man looks just like any other man,*
> *And the other man is a chump,*
> *When life's all a-clutter,*
> *When no one's a-flutter,*
> *Then a girl's in her summer slump."*

Aleta changed the program after that. "I think it should be interesting," she said, "to hear Rico Moreno since he is singing with Dorinda Daly in her new show."

Bart watched her at the machine. Aleta had not liked Dore and Dore had not liked Aleta. They had met twice and it had been too often. No one would know that now. Aleta had Dore's records, and she had been generous in every comment. He wished, however, that she hadn't concluded Dore's program with the fiddle number, immediately preceding Rico Moreno.

The orchestra was playing the introduction to *"Che gelida manina."* The full, rich voice of the younger Moreno, one of the Met's finest then, poured from the speaker. Bart closed his eyes. He was not seeing Rico Moreno; he was seeing Dore. She had a *La Bohème* party number that she did strictly for show people, the toughest audience in the world. It was a Dorinda Daly that the public never saw.

She seated herself at the piano, looking very solemn, as primly dedicated and precious as a high school genius about to give a Chopin recital. She ran through the opening bars of *"Che gelida manina,"* and uttered an explosive "WAH!" She rang scales with it, and wah-wahed it, sounding just a little like Ethel Merman: AH, WAH-WAH-DA, WAH-WEE-NAH, WAH, WAH, WAH. "It was really too bad," she said sorrowfully. She ran it over again then in her own voice, exaggerating the sweetness—and dropped to a chest tone, grimly dramatic, for the opening of the recitative which called upon all the versatility of her voice before she was through.

> *"Mimi was arty, Montmarty* [she sang],
> *His kind of a party;*
> *Tender and tough, little bit rough*
> *With a heart—a heart—*
> *A heart of gold—go-old . . .*
> *She was* FLAME, *she was game,*
> *Her eager hands—Mimi's tiny hands—*
> *They sought him . . .*
> *They caught him . . .*
> *Chilled him—half killed him . . .*
> *Her little hand . . . che gelida manina . . .*
> *Che gelida . . . Mimi . . .*
> *Her little hand—Mimi's little hand—*
> *Was* CO-LD."

There was more of it, much more, and only Dore could do it, mixing the aria music in with husky, half-whispered narration and an occasional deep stomach note, her eyes wide and innocent and guileless. He smiled, remembering her, and then the big voice swelled out full and round on the high C and Rico Moreno was singing it all straight, taking Mimi's cold hand seriously and finding pathos in it.

"Beautiful," one of the women said. Bart looked around the room and for a few seconds one could read a verdict there. They had liked Dorinda Daly, loved her, but they did not believe—not any of them—that she could sing on the same stage with the tenor from the Met.

Aleta removed the record carefully, reverently. "I can hardly wait," she said.

It was the end of the party. The guests were standing. "I'll have to impose on somebody for a ride to the station," Bart said.

Alex Waringly waved the suggestion away. "Nonsense," he said. "You are spending the night here whether you know it or not. We haven't seen you in years."

"I didn't bring a bag."

"We have pajamas and all manner of things," Florence said. "Even toothbrushes."

"New ones," Aleta added.

Bart looked at her and her eyes were asking him to stay. She was, after all, the reason why he was here. "Dinner at our place tomorrow night," she said.

He glanced at Roger, but for once Roger was not looking at him. He had been conscious of the other man's eyes measuring him while the music was being played. Roger was the only one who had given him what he had expected from all of them: hostility.

There was the usual flurry of good nights, the milling around of people. Roger and Aleta left with the rest. Alex Waringly rested one big hand on Bart's shoulder.

"How about a nightcap, boy?"

"I'm not much of a drinker."

"You don't have to be when you're within crawling distance of a bed. I'd like to have a talk with you."

"Fine," Bart said.

He was not certain that it was fine, but it seemed to be inevitable. Florence gave him her two hands to hold and her cheek to kiss as she said good night. Alex walked over to the sideboard and the whisky decanters. "This," Bart thought, "is it. Now that the guests are gone!"

## CHAPTER *8*

Alex Waringly mixed two highballs and passed one of them to Bart. He led the way down the hall to the library. Unlike the rest of the house, it was dark-paneled. The walls were lined from floor to ceiling with book-shelves, and the shelves were crowded with books. Two heavy chairs were angled companionably to the fireplace, which was dark now on this July night in October.

"I don't know why I call this a library," Alex said. "I talk in it, but I never read in it. Look at all those books! Would you believe it that when I bought them I intended to read them, all of them? I don't know what happens to a man's personal time."

Bart glanced at the shelves. There were expensive sets in fine bindings and brightly jacketed books from book clubs, a lifetime of reading for anybody. The shelves overwhelmed him and he could sympathize with Alex Waringly.

"There's too much of everything in the world," he said. "Too many books to read, too much fine music on records that you want to hear, too many shows to see."

"Do young people feel that too? I thought that it hit me only because I can feel the sand running out sometimes."

"Everybody feels it, I guess."

Alex Waringly took a swallow from his glass. "You've got a lot of sense, Bart," he said, "and you're balanced. Tell me something. What in hell is the matter with your generation?"

Bart grinned. "We're young."

"Everybody was young once. It's a good excuse for some things. It doesn't excuse everything."

Bart waited. Suspense built up inside of him. He liked

Alex Waringly. There were questions that the man might ask, questions for which Bart could offer only inadequate answers. Aleta was his daughter. What answer was good enough to the question Alex Waringly might ask?

"My friends are pretty decent citizens," Alex said. "A man shares a lot with his friends. He finds out that most people try to do the right thing, no matter how dumbheaded they may be. Hell! We all guess our way through when problems come up. Sometimes we guess wrong. It's got to turn out that way."

"I guess so."

"My friends are people with money. That's the way it has to be. It's a case of doing the same things, living the same way, being interested in the same things, and having the same kind of problems. Hell, it's how everybody makes friends! Anyway, most of us raised families. Some of my friends have sons who are pretty much damned fools. I don't know much about that problem. Unfortunately, I don't have a son. But I've got a daughter."

He took a swallow of his drink, raised his eyes over the rim of the glass. "You've met Roger. What do you think of him?"

"I've met him. I don't know him."

"Yes. Of course. Unfair question, I guess." Aleta's father brooded over his drink. "Three of my friends have daughters about Aleta's age," he said. "They all have the same problem. It seems damned strange to me. I'd like your opinion."

Bart took his first swallow of the drink in his glass. The suspended ax had fallen and fallen harmlessly. Either— incomprehensible though it seemed—Alex Waringly did not link him to Aleta's pregnancy, or, equally incomprehensible, Alex was letting the past bury the dead past.

"You don't raise a daughter the way you'd raise a son," Alex said. "You don't put it up to her at some point to prove that she can support herself, or make something of her life. Perhaps you should. Most of us just rock along, figuring she'll be married anyway and why argue with her? We spoil daughters, I guess, but what in hell else can we do? We live a certain way because we've got a certain amount of money, and certain standards. We've earned what we have, and she hasn't, but she's one of the family. What can we do? Move her out in the garage?"

"No. I guess not."

"No. So we spoil them, hoping all the time that they'll want to do what we can't seem to make them do. Maybe that's stupid of us. All they want is what comes easy. They go for the ride. Then they get married. That doesn't solve a damned thing. The problem gets worse."

Alex Waringly looked at the bottom of his glass, then rattled the ice around in it. "Have another one of these?" he said.

"I'm still doing fine."

"I'm not. Must have shorted myself."

Alex rose and stalked heavily out of the room. He was wearing a brown sport shirt, a well-worn pair of gray flannel slacks, and the sports jacket that he had donned for the buffet supper. He looked like his own gardener or like a country squire at his ease, but he wasn't at ease. Bart did not know where the conversation was leading, nor where he fitted into it, but the problem, as it was unfolding, interested him. He had always taken the parents of people for granted; if they had problems, he never knew about them.

Inevitably, he thought about Mary Norbert. Nobody had provided her with background or money. If there had been at any time a garage into which she could have been moved, it would probably have been a break for her. The blunt facts of her life were that she earned money if she wanted to eat today, and saved it if she wanted to eat next week. She clothed herself and she kept fit and she stayed out of trouble, because if she got into trouble there was no one to help her. She stood firmly on her own two feet with a lot less arrogance than Aleta, who had never proved that she could last a week away from home base.

Alex came back into the room. His glass was filled and he carried the decanter. He sat down with a grunt. "I should have done this in the first place," he said. "God knows I'm no camel."

He stared somberly at the cold fireplace. "It's always been considered a pretty snobbish thing," he said, "for a family with money to stand pat on their daughters marrying young men with money. Parents got themselves made into villains in books and plays doing that. Since the war, we've been pretty proud that we weren't that way. I don't know. A man can be so stupid in some ways that he is proud of being a damned fool."

He drank and his shoulders shook. "The daughters of three of my friends married young men with college backgrounds, service in the Army or Navy, no money. What the hell? We've got money. The idea was to be patient. The young men had had their lives disrupted by military service. Set them up. Help them over the hump. Let them get their feet on the ground."

He raised brooding, disillusioned eyes to Bart's. "None of them is worth a damn. All they want to do is stay in colleges taking courses. It isn't education, just college. They like it. They don't like anything else. They don't want to work. They just move in with the spoiled daughters and become spoiled sons-in-law, going for the ride behind the patient horses."

He paused. "All that your generation seems to want is security. That's why I asked you what in hell is the matter with it?"

Bart met his eyes. "I don't think young people really want security," he said slowly. "It isn't natural. Everybody tries to give them security: the government, prosperous parents, colleges, schools, everybody. What we want, all of us, whether we know it or not, is insecurity. That's where the thrill is."

"Nobody wants that kind of thrill any more."

"They do. Juvenile delinquents are kids looking for insecurity, risk. School is cut-and-dried. No competition. Passing is automatic. Everybody is trying to take care of them. I don't know. I'm just thinking out loud. I don't know anything except football, baseball, and a few subjects that most people find boring."

"I'm interested in your ideas."

"Thank you. I played football. The thrill of the game was the uncertainty. That's what made us work hard. Even when we opened against Niagara or Syracuse, we knew that we could miss. If somebody had set it up for us so that we knew we were going to win every game, we'd have quit. There wouldn't have been any point in going through the grind any more."

"I can see that. Bring your argument back to my problem."

"I'll try. You asked my opinion of Roger. I don't know him. But I saw his home. I've had a look at how he lives. That's his ball game. Somebody won it for him. What does he have to win? Where's his thrill?"

Alex Waringly held his glass suspended. "They have to live somewhere," he said. "Aleta's had a lot. She's always had it. We couldn't take it away from her because she wanted to marry somebody."

"Sometimes you take a lot away from a person by giving him something."

"I don't quite follow that."

Bart emptied his glass. The liquor was warm and it bit. He had something clear in his mind that he had never expected to make clear to someone else; it had to do with giving and taking away.

"I've just come from a place, a monastery," he said, "where they rise by descending."

Alex looked alarmed. "Come now!" he said.

"That's true. They descend into humility and poverty, and incredible self-deprivation, and they rise by it to a very great dignity and holiness and power. You can feel the power and the rightness when you're with them."

Alex Waringly shook his shoulders impatiently. When he spoke, he ignored everything that Bart had said. "Industry provides all the thrills and excitement that anybody needs or can handle," he said. "That could be Roger's game, as you put it; not the house, or how he lives in it. The house, and the rest of it, is the bench where he rests when he isn't playing."

Bart waited. Alex, too, had his vision of what was true. It was worth hearing. "I like games too," Alex said. "Nobody likes them better. My life has been a game, an exciting game. I've built something where there wasn't anything. I like to think that I put something into the world that wasn't there when I came to it. I've offered Roger what I would have offered my own son if I had one."

He laid his glass aside. His broad hands became suddenly eloquent as he gestured to emphasize his point. "Our newest division is detergents," he said. "It needs chemists and engineers and lab workers, but it also needs men to write about what we're doing. Roger wanted to write. I put him there."

He leaned forward, laying his right forefinger on his left palm. "Men have been making soap since the time of the Romans," he said. "It's a necessity of life. In the past five years the production of synthetic detergents has been gaining steadily on the production of soap. Now they have surpassed soap. In five years! And we're just beginning. We have a new process for making petroleum sulphonates, the base for new commercial detergents. I find that exciting at my age. We're creating new plants, new careers, new jobs, changing old habit patterns. I thought Roger would find it exciting. He doesn't. He wants to write poetry and plays."

Bart felt the weight of the room pressing down on him, the weight of all those unread books. There were people who put their lives into the writing of poetry and plays and novels, people as sincere as Alex Waringly, but not any more in earnest, probably, nor more dedicated to the task that called them. He could see the excitement of production in Alex Waringly's eyes. It would be heady stuff for a participant, a good player. "If detergents beat soap," he said slowly, "they aren't Roger's detergents. His team can't lose, the team that produces that house of his, and makes him a two-car family. A play that he writes can lose, or a poem. That's his insecurity. He wants it."

"No sane man could want it." Alex Waringly's voice was gruff. He poured himself another drink and downed it neat. "How about you?" he said. "You're not writing a play, are you?"

"No. I couldn't. I've been playing ball in the Western League."

"That's no good."

"It's peaceful."

"What do you mean, peaceful?"

"No problems. No worries. We were too many games out of first place to have a chance at the pennant, and too many games out of last place to finish last."

"It's no good. You've outgrown it. I'll give you a job."

Bart straightened. "Yours is a technical outfit. I haven't any technical training."

"We're knee-deep in engineers now. The colleges are rolling them off the production lines for us. We ought to have a few men around who can think without the help of a slide rule."

Alex Waringly rose. "I won't give you a house or two automobiles, although I don't think those things make a damned bit of difference. I'll give you a job. If you're not worth ten thousand a year within twelve months, I'll fire you. Let's go to bed."

They went upstairs. Bart's room was at the end of the hall. His covers were turned down and there were pajamas laid out for him; shaving equipment and a toothbrush on his dresser. He felt slightly dazed. He was regretting that last drink.

"I made a dope out of myself," he said, "all that stuff about rising by descending. He thought that I was crazy. Not to mention the brilliant little essay about peace and contentment in the Western League."

He walked around the room. He remembered Mary Norbert's plaintive "How do we get into these ridiculous conversations?" Wherever he went, he seemed to have a genius for that. He thought about Mary Norbert. He wished that he could talk to her and tell her how it was, how he felt about all this. He probably wouldn't say anything that made sense. He didn't even have it clear in his own mind.

He had the offer of a job. Alex might forget it in the morning, but he did not believe that Alex would. The Waringly interests were big business. It might solve a lot of his problems if he found a place with Alex and settled into it. His life would begin to assume some kind of recognizable shape.

He still could not understand the fact that he was treated as he had always been treated. He did not see how Aleta could have handled her problem and left him out of it. He stiffened as a sudden thought hit him.

Suppose that the family had met the problem by sending Aleta someplace to have the baby quietly, secretly, with-

out any of their friends knowing about it? Suppose the
baby had lived and they had surrendered it to an orphanage, or for adoption, so that the secret would never
be revealed? They would want to forget it all now, pretend that it never happened; especially since Aleta was
married.

"Hell, they couldn't!" he said.

He wasn't sure. Aleta was their only child. They had
spoiled her, and still did. They'd do anything for her. He
lay in bed for a long time, sleepless, thinking about that.
The task of forcing the truth from Aleta loomed up before
him like a labor of Hercules.

"Suppose she laughs at you?" Mary Norbert said.

Well, suppose she did? He had waved that away as
preposterous, but it no longer seemed preposterous. Aleta
was on her own home grounds. Everything favored her
if she wanted to avoid a discussion.

He thought about his father, walking into a theatre and
seeing Dore on the stage in *Lush-a-bye, Baby*. "She wasn't
anybody I knew," his father said. Aleta wasn't anybody
that Bart knew, either, but his mind moved in confusion,
insisting that it knew her because it had known the girl
she used to be. Memory was a tricky sorcerer. It blended
the real with the unreal to achieve its effects. He had to
fight the physical visions out of his mind. Some of them
belonged to him, and to his life, and to the passion for
Aleta that was over; some of them were mere fantasies
of what might have been, or might yet be. Those were
dangerous.

Thought ran in circles, descended in spirals, ascended in
spirals, turned to vapor. The phrase about rising by descending no longer seemed absurd. The Abbey had given
him a vision of peace and beauty such as he had not
known existed; less a vision, perhaps, than the glimpse of
a vision. He had been only a pilgrim at the gates, but he
had touched the edge of life as it was lived within the
cloister. There was an invisible line just beyond the guest
house, a line that divided those who offered a little to
God and those who gave all. No armed sentry barred the
way, no locked gate; but a casual visitor, a niggardly giver

such as himself, could never cross it or know what the inner cloister held for those who crossed.

When those men stood before the showcase of God, they chose nothing for themselves; they had sought only a gift that would be, in some small measure, worthy to be offered back to their Creator. They had beggared themselves, given all that they had or ever hoped to have, in order to obtain that gift.

Because he knew that he was incapable of such faith and of such generosity Bart McBride felt humble. Within the cloak of humility, his clamoring flesh stilled. This bed was soft and luxurious, and the cot in St. Urban's guest-house had been hard. There were bright pictures on these gay walls, and only a crucifix on those other walls which were without color. He looked into the semidarkness at the crucifix that was not there. The day was over. Hours ago the monks had chanted Compline.

He slept.

## CHAPTER 9

Aleta awakened before Roger did. She lay quietly, floating gently into the consciousness of a new day. In a few minutes the alarm clock would ring. She had trained some silent bell ringer of her subconscious to awaken her before the noisy clamor of Roger's alarm started. There was nothing civilized about coming into a new day out of a sense of shock.

She thought about Bart McBride, as she had thought about him on the edge of sleep. It had been interesting to see him again, but not thrilling. She had been disappointed in that. It should have been thrilling. He was as big and as hard and as fit as ever, but there was something missing. She was not certain what it was that she missed. She would find out if she had a chance to probe a little. She had been wary of Roger and his edginess, unwilling to challenge it with so many people around.

She drifted lazily back in time to her first meeting with Bart. She had never cared too much about football players or other athletic cattle. She had never rated Cornell too highly, either. To her, Cornell was Mob Institute, a veterinary school. Her roommate at Vassar, Julia Reed, had a brother named Randall who went there, and that was pretty quaint. He belonged to something called "Book and Bowl" and his portrait made him look like a character out of a French farce—not at all like anything Cornellish.

After Mountain Day in her junior year she went to a Cornell dance with Julia because Randall Reed looked interesting. Randall turned out to be merely another type, but a big animal in a dinner jacket that seemed ready to explode cut in on her, and he was the only reason she remembered that one dance out of the many.

He didn't say anything at all to her the first time he danced with her; he merely danced. And he didn't have to bow low when he met Fred Astaire. He was somebody who knew what the music was saying. The second time he cut in, she was interested. "What are you trying to do," she said, "stake a claim?"

"No," he said. "I don't even know who you are. You can dance. I like to dance with you."

"Do you want to know who I am?

"No," he said. "After tonight, I'll probably never see you again."

Later, many months later, he told her that on their second dance together the music was "Erie Water" from *Buffalo Nickel*. She didn't know then, nor care. All she knew was that if there was any arrogance to be exhibited it would be her arrogance, not that of some lunk from Cornell. On a no-break with Randall, she said: "There's somebody here that I want you to run out of my life. If he cuts in on me again tonight, drop whatever you're doing and take me away from him."

Randall Reed looked noble. "Name him!" he said.

That was Randall's last gesture, the last thing she remembered about him. When he found out who annoyed her, he wilted. "Now look!" he said. "If it was some drunk, or somebody crude, or somebody that made passes —but that's Bart McBride."

It was the first time she had ever heard of Bart McBride. She discovered then that he was a campus celebrity and very big news in the Ivy League on Saturday afternoons; moreover that he was not a run-of-the-mill big shot but a highly respected individual.

He kept on cutting in and dancing with her, and in the waning minutes of the dance he walked her out into the magic of the Cayugan night. She would say that for Cornell, it had a setting: luminous landscape and sparkling water, towering trees, and, on that night, a big moon. There were waterfalls all over the place and one could hear them.

"Who are you?" he said.

"You didn't want to know."

"I do now."

The simplicity of it got her. It was different and she was one move behind him. Before she got back in step, she told him who she was and that she was from Vassar.

"I'll come over," he said. "When are you doing something interesting over there, something for the males?"

She told him about the skating carnival and it was a date. He didn't make a pass at her and that was unnerving. She had a technique for repelling passes, none at all for people who absent-mindedly overlooked the fact that she was desirable.

"Let's go someplace and have a drink or something," she said.

He looked at her gravely. "Who invited you down to this?"

"Nobody. That is, he's just my roommate's brother."

"The dance is nearly over," he said. "You're his date. I'll be down for the skating."

He took her in then, unkissed, unrumpled, and unmanned. His brand was on her from that moment, and he did not seem to know it. That was Bart McBride.

The alarm beside the bed shrilled noisily, urgently. Roger awakened with a curse, rolled over, and fought with it. It growled and muttered beneath his muffling hand before he found the shut-off switch. Aleta swore softly under her breath. It was almost as great a shock to be jerked abruptly out of the past as it was to be awakened. Roger blew his breath out in a snort.

"Brrr!" he said. "What day is it?"

"Monday, darling. The gateway to the shining week."

"The cellar door. To hell with the week."

He rolled over, reaching for her, and she rested content for a moment, drowsily relaxed, disinclined to surrender the mood of night to the urgencies of morning. She remembered then what day it was. It was not merely Monday. Bart McBride would be at her mother's. The day might not be as dull as most. She twisted away from Roger swiftly, kicking the covers aside and coming to rest with her feet on the floor, sitting on the edge of the bed.

"Come back here," he said.

"We can't. Betsy is moving around out there. She disapproves of us as it is."

"Forget Betsy. She works here. Let's have breakfast in bed."

"She wouldn't like it."

"It's her job."

"Maybe not. Anyway I have enough trouble with her. I don't want her to quit."

Aleta sat where she was, waking up with conversation, but savoring the sensual joy of the moment: Roger's hands seeking her, calling her back, knowing that she wouldn't go but warm with the knowledge that she could. That was the nice thing about Roger. She knew how to trigger him when she wanted, but she could stop him when she wanted not. So many of her friends were twin-bed people and they were scandalized at the double bed. She liked it. "I'm saving the twin beds for my second marriage," she said. "After all, I don't know my second husband as well as I know Roger."

"Come here!" he said again.

It was time to go. She jumped to her feet. She was wearing a sheer blue nightgown. She stood a few feet away from the bed. "You better rise and shine, Buster," she said. "Work and classes wait."

"To hell with work and classes," he said sulkily.

She laughed and turned away from him, moving swiftly

across the room to her own bathroom. Her bathroom was blue and yellow. It was bright and cheerful even on days that were not. She would have liked a leisurely tub, luxuriantly soaking in the warm water and letting her thoughts stray; but with Roger in a mood, it was better not. She settled for a shower. Her mental motion pictures during a shower and toweling were always old silent pictures, jerky, episodic, with a lot of fading and cutouts.

She couldn't recapture her earlier mood. She had brief flash scenes in her mind of skating with Bart, who skated as gracefully as he danced, of the way he lifted her off her feet the first time that he kissed her. She remembered seeing him play football against Yale, and of going primitive with all the rest of them when he scored the touchdown that he had dedicated to her before the game began. She had been as weak as jelly that night, all gone for him inside, and he didn't know. Practically nothing happened.

She put on a robe and came out. Roger was still lying in the bed, on his back, staring up at the ceiling. "Say hey!" she said. "This won't do."

"It's going to do."

"You'll have to hurry."

"Not me. The dauntless detergents will continue to make their phenomenal gains today without my help. The mills of Columbia will still grind."

"Roger, you can't!" She was suddenly concerned. "Dad won't like it."

"He doesn't like it one way or another."

"There's no sense in needling him. After all, you draw a salary."

He flung the covers aside angrily. "You have to throw that lousy salary at me every time you need it in an argument," he said. "It's bad enough to have to take the damned salary."

"I didn't."

"And if you think I'm leaving you here all day with that muscle-wonder of yours, I'm not that crazy."

He stalked off to his bathroom and Aleta stood in the middle of the room, frowning, after he had slammed the door. "So!" she said.

She went down the hall to the breakfast room and nodded brightly to the prim, middle-aged woman who brought her coffee. "Good morning, Elizabeth," she said.

Only in the semiprivacy that a ranch-house room affords was Elizabeth referred to as Betsy. She was an angular woman whose light hair was streaked with gray. She rarely smiled. To her, life was a serious matter.

"Good morning, Mrs. Vannin," she said. "Shall I prepare Mr. Vannin's eggs?"

"Better hold them a few minutes."

It was an unnecessary question and answer. Elizabeth, Aleta reflected, probably knew to the second when Roger's feet hit the floor and when he entered the bathroom. It was outrageously embarrassing to think even briefly about all that Elizabeth probably knew about them. "We should have a room like a broadcasting studio, all soundproofed," she said. "I wonder what one would cost."

She tried to interest herself in the morning paper, but the affairs of a world full of strangers did not hold her attention. Her day was going to be extensively revised now that Roger had decided to hang around. It not only would not be as she had planned it; it might easily be an all-time low among dull days.

Roger came into the breakfast room briskly. He was wearing an atrocious sports shirt that he had bought for himself, a sickly green-blue thing with enormous red spiders splashed all over it.

"Good morning, darling," she said. "I still think that shirt stinks."

"I'm not trying to charm anybody. What are you going to wear?"

"I haven't decided. And I'm laying aside all of the things I resent until I have my breakfast."

"Are you in a resenting mood?"

"Keep on the way you are going and you are going to find out."

"I can hardly wait."

Elizabeth brought the orange juice and it was like a flag of truce. Aleta divided the paper. She was accustomed to Roger's blustering gestures. She could always take the bluster out of him fast when she felt like it. They didn't have any problems that way.

"Do you suppose this guy McBride would ask his mother to read my play?"

The question came with the eggs and it caught Aleta off balance. "If you don't like him," she said, "why ask favors from him?"

"Where does the favor come in? Actors and actresses need plays to act in, don't they?"

"They haven't needed yours so far."

"Never mind the cracks. You know as well as I do that the big thing is getting a play read by the right people."

Aleta shrugged. "Dorinda Daly doesn't act in plays. She sings in musicals."

"She might want a change. Like Mary Martin."

"I doubt it. And this new one of hers will probably run forever."

"I'll ask him anyway."

"Suit yourself."

Aleta tried to see an advantage to herself in having Roger obligated to Bart. It annoyed her that she couldn't see it because she felt certain that there must be something that she was overlooking. "It will come to me," she thought.

She went back to the room and the resentments raised their heads, small resentments and large. If nothing else, she thought, resentments gave one a good reason for doing something that might be difficult to do without them.

She took a pair of shorts from a drawer. They were pretty brief, white with a blue stripe. Roger had raised hell when she bought them and even her father, who should have been used to anything, had said, "Get a skirt on. That's too much."

She put them on now, and a pair of pale blue ankle socks with white saddle shoes. She had a blue bra and she tried the effect—bare midriff—before the full-length door mirror. She whistled and for a moment her eyes gleamed. She shook her head.

"I couldn't get away with it," she said regretfully. "Roger won't give that far."

She put on a sleeveless cotton blouse, but she did not do anything about her legs. They were very good legs. She had worn a pair of shorts like these when she went canoeing on Lake Cayuga with Bart that June at the end of her junior year. It was the end of his junior year, too, and he was staying over a couple of weeks to get some ROTC work done before he went to Spain with a boatload of mules. He was an obsession of hers, then, because she had never been able to take the mastery out of him. She would date him, armed to the teeth with all the weapons in her arsenal, and he would take over. She always ended up doing what he wanted to do, as he wanted to do it—and he didn't even let himself imagine what she wanted to do. No other man she had ever known had been like that.

He looked wonderful in uniform and he was somebody to notice in swimming trunks and a T-shirt, too. She had been something for the boys on the fence, herself, in the white shorts and a red blouse. He was aware of her, very much aware of her. He was disturbed, too. "And if he hadn't been, I'd have drowned myself," she thought.

They had sprawled beside the fantastically blue lake when they were burned with sun and soaked with sweat. The red blouse was clinging to her like a wet bathing suit and they were all alone in a silent world, with white sails far out on the lake, the noise of motorboats muffled and far away. His mastery broke then. She had watched the animal in him growing stronger by the minute and she had waited with a feeling that was excitingly close to stark fear, teasing it a little. He was the bull, she was the toreador and she had never faced this moment with him before.

He pulled her to him and kissed her roughly, savagely. The mastery in that was his as it had to be. She floated on her own emotions and made only a token struggle. He found some enormous bull-stopping brake, then, somewhere in the strange being that he was. He held her shoulders with hands that were brutal in their unconscious strength, holding her away from him.

He asked her to marry him.

If Cayuga had ever known a comedy like that, the stones were silent. He took his honest lust and wrapped it in romantic ribbon, made a valentine out of it, and handed it to her. She hadn't laughed because she ached too deep for laughter, and because he made an apologetic speech, humble in his poverty. She was the girl in the golden coach and he was the mule-herd on his way to Spain, with another year of college when he came back.

"I'll have my Army commission when I graduate," he said. "It isn't much, but it's something."

There was no arrogance in him, only hunger. A hungry man has no mastery; but even in defeat he defeated her. She didn't want to marry him, and she didn't want the only kind of victory that she could take out of a comedy like that.

She didn't break him, her way, till that October. It was the night after the Princeton game when the Tiger tore the Big Red Team to tatters, and half killed a halfback named McBride. He lost his chance at All-American in that debacle and she was gentle to his wounds.

She smiled, remembering, her lips parted, looking into her own eyes in the mirror. She heard Roger whistling as he came down the hall and she took refuge in the bathroom. She wasn't ready for him to see the shorts yet. She'd gone soft. She had to take her resentments out and polish them before she faced Roger. She stood for a moment, biting her lips, looking at nothing at all; then she opened the door and walked out.

Roger took one look at her and his jaw jutted. "You're not going to wear that," he said.

"I certainly am."

"No."

"It's a damned hot day and I'll wear what I like."

His eyes were angry. "What are you trying to do?" he said.

"Do you want to know?"

"I asked you, didn't I?"

"All right. I was just as cheerful and pleasant this morning as a TV housewife. I didn't even make an issue of it when you decided to ignore your job and the courses you insisted that you had to take." She took a step toward him, her hands clenched. "Then you made that trusting, innocent remark about staying home because you weren't crazy enough to trust me with another man around."

"That isn't what I said."

"It is exactly what you said. So, as long as you stayed home to protect your honor and your home, I'm giving you something to protect. Stay close and protect it, big boy!"

She pirouetted slowly, then walked deliberately to the door. "We'll take my car," she said.

## CHAPTER  10

The morning was bright and hot, with no breeze stirring. October had come in like a lamb, and a lazy lamb at that. There was color on the hillsides, but it was pale color. The trees waited patiently through the mock spring for the frost that would set them aflame.

Aleta drove with a feeling of expectancy, of eagerness, ignoring the silent man beside her. Her victory over Roger had given the morning a certain flavor. She felt ready for anything.

Bart was sitting in the patio with Florence when she parked the car in the driveway. He was wearing his gray flannels, but he had discarded his white shirt for a blue sports shirt that belonged to Alex. He rose when she walked into the patio. The blue was good on him and it intensified the magnificent bronze of his skin. Florence seemed to be suspended in mid-sentence.

"Hello, Al," Bart said. "Your mother has been telling me about your trip abroad."

"That's ancient history."

"It isn't," Florence protested. "It's only a little over a year ago. It was your wedding present. And your letters were priceless, especially the one from Genoa."

Florence, Aleta thought, had an amazing talent for the trivial and the obvious. "This is terribly amusing," Flor-

ence said. "When I told Bart that it was your honeymoon,
he said that he made his only trip to Europe with a boatload of mules, and that it wasn't a honeymoon."

She laughed and Aleta ignored her. "I remember those
mules," she said.

Her eyes were on Bart's face. If he remembered that he
had once brought his damned mules into a passionate moment beside Cayuga, he did not betray himself. His eyes
entered into no conspiracies with her. He showed no awareness, either, of the shorts. He had to be aware of them,
but there wasn't a flicker of a lingering glance. "It's the
masterful streak again," she thought. "The stinking hypo-
crite! Maybe I overdid it. Damn!"

Roger moved quietly up beside her. "Did I hear Florence say that you went to Spain?" he said.

He was cheerful, cordial, friendly, and that, Aleta knew,
was neither natural nor honest. It was a planned, cal-
culated, and connived assault upon her own intentions.

"Yes, I did." Bart brightened at the cordiality. "I traveled
sixth class, or whatever the bottom is, but I saw a lot of
Spain."

"We missed it," Roger said, "and Spanish is the language
I speak best. We spent all of our time in England, France,
and Italy. Tell me——"

"Aleta darling, I have something to show you," Florence said. "If the boys will excuse us?"

"They'll excuse us. It's practically a stag party already."

Aleta followed her in. She was seething a little, but only
a little. She permitted herself a feeling of grudging respect
for Roger. He had figured out a way to top her and
he had caught her off guard. The challenge promised to
be more interesting than an easy victory would have been,
especially since Bart was being so excessively the gentleman. Florence turned to her when they were inside the
house.

"Really, Aleta," she said. "Whatever possessed you to
wear those shorts?"

"What's the matter with them?"

"Didn't Roger tell you?"

"He didn't get very far with that line. Neither will you."

Florence raised her eyebrows. "With Bart here," she said, "it is too, too obvious of you."

"What do you mean? You didn't notice him having St. Vitus' dance, did you?"

"No. He's a gentleman."

"A gentleman? My God, what does that have to do with it? Gentlemen, if that's what he's turned out to be, go to bathing beaches and break their necks buying tickets to shows where women wear flowers—little flowers, like dandelions. Women with less excuse than I have wear shorts when they go to the supermarkets and——"

"Calm down, dear. I know all that. I knew about men before you were born, too. Those are not mere shorts and you know it. They're vulgar. They're—pornographic." Florence shook her head. "It's your intent that distresses me, not your body. Why, Aleta?"

"I just felt like it. Particularly when Roger stayed home to chaperon me."

"Oh!" Florence sank into a chair suddenly. "I forgot about that. It was on my mind. Aleta, he shouldn't do that. Alex has been very patient, but if one of them retires and leads a life of leisure, it should be Alex, not Roger."

Aleta's body tensed. Experience had taught her never to compromise on this subject. Her personal security was involved. "Dad likes what he's doing," she said. "Roger doesn't. When he can spend his time writing plays . . ."

"But he doesn't! Alex let him take time for those courses. Roger is missing his classes today too. And he isn't writing."

"He wants to talk to Bart about that play he wrote. Bart knows people in the theatre."

Florence looked distressed. "But he wrote that play in college," she said, "before you were married. Surely, Aleta!"

Aleta drew a deep breath. "All right," she said. "We're no good. I'm just a vulgar, naked woman and Roger is a bum."

"Now, darling. Don't exaggerate! I didn't say that."

"You're too damned genteel to say it. You have to dress it up, with a fancy skirt over its bare legs."

Aleta whirled on her heel and walked swiftly out. Her

anger had come to an easy boil and she could feel the bubbling in her nerve ends. She was in a mood to pass along a little trouble to Roger and Bart if they wanted it; holding the boiling just beneath the surface, permitting only a little gentle steam to escape.

There was no one in the patio and she walked out to the edge of the grass. She saw the two figures small in the distance. Her lips tightened. "Damned Boy Scouts," she said. "Okay, hike!"

She walked back and there were cigarettes on one of the tables. She lighted one and walked around with it. When she had given Florence sufficient time to become involved in phone calls, or some other innocuous activity, she went inside. She rested on the couch until nearly noon. She gauged the time of Roger's and Bart's return nicely. She was seated at the piano, playing, when they arrived. She played badly because she never practiced, and had never accepted discipline, but she remembered enough of Chopin to summon sadly sweet sound out of the instrument. The two men came in noisily and she affected a mood of rapt unawareness for a moment before she opened her eyes. She let her fingers drift along the keys, barely touching them.

"How was the bird-watching?" she said.

"Damned good." Roger was a trifle too emphatic, too hearty. He watched her warily. Bart was not watching her at all. Esther, Florence's cook, was frying chicken. Bart inhaled audibly.

" 'A goodly house,' " he quoted. " 'the feast smells well.' "

Aleta laughed. "I knew that luncheon would bring the Eagle Scouts in from the fields," she said.

Bart's eyes were remote. He seemed far way. "Wrong line," he said. "You should have said: 'What would you have, friend? Whence are you?' "

"Why should I have said anything like that?"

Bart looked at her gravely. "That's the way it was written."

Aleta rose from the piano stool. She turned her eyes to Roger. "What happened to him?" she said. "Was the sun very hot?"

Roger looked puzzled but he laughed. "He was all right until he smelled the chicken."

Aleta picked up his laugh and echoed it, but she was frowning when she turned away from them. "I missed a cue," she thought. "It's a game. He never played it with me. He's been playing it with some girl. He either forgot, or he tried it on me deliberately. And isn't it cute that he and Roger are buddy-buddy. I'll fix that."

She was bright and cheerful during the luncheon. Several times she was aware of Florence watching her speculatively, but she was not concerned about Florence. Bart was being the simple son of nature, enthused about the day and the country and the hike that he had had with Roger. Roger was complacent, pleased with himself, holding something back. He held firm until the coffee.

"Bart is going to have my play read," he said.

"Not by your mother?" Aleta looked swiftly across the table.

"No." Bart shook his head. "I don't believe she would read a play." He looked embarrassed. "As a matter of fact, I don't know many people who have anything to do with plays. I thought of one man who might read it."

"Who?"

Roger leaned forward. "Merely Carter Brill, that's all," he said.

"Carter Brill?" Florence joined the conversation with an air of excitement. "Oh, that's wonderful! He's famous. I've heard of him. Let me remember. What did he do?"

"*Sailor's Moon,*" Aleta said. "*Last Man Over.*" She was impressed in spite of herself. "And that one about turtles— not the voice of them."

"*The Bright Swift Turtles,* darling," Roger said, "and the one that nobody forgets—*Dancers' Dawn.*"

"Of course. That brittle sophisticated style! Why, Roger, it's the same kind of thing you do."

"I'm not that good," Roger laughed self-consciously, "but there's nobody I'd rather have read *The Bells of Abandon* than Carter Brill."

Aleta rested her back against her chair. "Build high, you rat!" she thought savagely. "You'll have so far to fall."

She had no faith in Roger's play and she was seething again when she reflected that he had stayed home today because he didn't trust her with Bart; and he had used the time to make a little personal hay. Aloud, she said, "I'm glad that you boys have so much in common. I wouldn't have thought—well, it rather astonishes me."

She looked innocently from Bart to Roger and she saw the doubt implant itself. It hit them differently, for different reasons, but it hit. She saw her statement translated into a question in their eyes before they guarded themselves. The question hung there between them. If either, or both of them, came up with the inevitable answer that they had her in common, that answer was so crudely correct; but it was a hell of an answer for two big bounding Boy Scouts to face on the threshold of a happy, healthy, fresh air friendship.

"What's so astonishing about it?" Roger said sharply.

"I don't know." She tapped her fingernail against her teeth, looking off into space. "You are such different types," she said softly.

She stood up then. They could meditate awhile—and they would—on how distinctively different they were. She stretched her body slightly, then turned and moved away from them. Florence was busy creating a diversion.

"Perhaps we should all go outside," she said. "It is such a nice day. And I'm sure that I don't know what Aleta is thinking of. It seems to me that you boys have a great deal in common."

"That's right," Aleta thought. "Kick it around and then step in it. You're going to help a lot."

The Waringly patio not only had big comfortable chairs with chrome arms and reclining backs, it had big plastic-covered dice that converted a chair into a chaise longue. Aleta stretched comfortably and closed her eyes. She made no attempt to participate in the conversation that Florence was gallantly forcing upon two reluctant males. After a while the discord of uninspired and unwilling small talk got on her nerves.

"I never heard anything so dull," she said. "Let them sleep, Mother. They're growing boys."

Florence was indignant. "I'm sorry if I'm keeping you

awake," she said. "But I must say that you're not a very polite hostess, lying there without saying a word."

"I'm not a hostess at all. This is your house, remember. I'll take over tonight and I'll be awake."

She thought ahead to how awake she would be. Resentments moved in her. She permitted herself, for the first time, to consider Bart's motive for coming out. She had pushed it from her mind every time that it intruded because she had not been ready for it. She was ready now and she could face it without blinking. He did not come to Waringly because he could no longer stay away from her; he had stayed away easily enough, and long enough. She knew what was on his mind, and, knowing, she had an advantage over him. She would let him bounce around on a hot griddle for a while.

She no longer found Bart McBride exciting. That, of course, was not a new development. He had turned dull when he lost his mastery. When he became a pleader, he became a bore. Her mind traveled back in time, three years ago this month.

He had been pretty low that night of the Princeton game when the Tigers mopped up the earth with him. He was bruised and cut and battered and lame. It was Cornell's first defeat of the season and the first time that Bart had been stopped in his tracks, unable to score. She saw him beaten that game and she went out with him that night. He still had a lot of arrogance in him, at least outwardly, and she was very gentle to him.

They drove around in her car and Cornell was a place that abounded in waterfalls and secluded spots. They were not interested in waterfalls. They parked and they talked and it was a cold, dark night. She dug in under the shelter of his arm and pulled the car robe up around them. She held his kisses a long time, being very sweet and consoling about him. The bull-brake that always stopped him was slipping a little.

"Let's drive to hellangone," he said huskily, "and stop somewhere where there's a justice of the peace. We can get married, Al. Let's——"

She turned her face up to his. "Let's stay here," she said, "and pretend we're married."

She lay in the warmth of the patio now, remembering. Bart was over there, somewhere, on one of the other chairs, and he didn't mean a thing to her, not a pulse beat. He had started his slow dying in her life on that night when she discovered that she could command him. There had been a physical something after that which lasted for six months or more, but it probably would not have lasted nearly so long if they had not been separated by a wide area of New York State, seeing each other only at long intervals.

It was a maddening period. When he was with her, he wanted her and there was such a direct obviousness about his wanting that it bored her, leaving her no triumph of her own to savor. There was a certain thrill in it, of course, because he was a terrifically exciting animal; but he never got over the idea that they should be married, and that was the deadly, tiresome thing about him. He wouldn't accept the fact that a girl was entitled to at least one barbarian in her life, since she would probably marry somebody civilized eventually if she had any sense. He was a natural barbarian, a powerful physical something, but he wouldn't let himself go completely and be what he could be.

"I'm sorry that I ever started you," she told him one night. "You're like the dope habit. Nobody wants the dope habit, all anybody wants is the effect. Damn it, to get the effect, you have to have the dope habit!"

He thought that was funny. He never seemed to get the idea that she meant the things that he considered funny. As far as she was concerned, there was no humor in the idea that he did seem to regard her, deep down inside of him, as a bad habit that he had to break. He was putty when he was near her, but he could stay away from her, and he did. She was in Ithaca more often than he was in Poughkeepsie, and she found the neutral ground, not he, by going to the places where he played games.

This was a drowsy afternoon and nobody wanted to talk. They were just lying around like sluggish pythons digesting food. She wondered if Roger and Bart were thinking and remembering things, as she was—and if so, what?

When she was very young, before she knew much beyond what her imagination told her, she remembered telling Lina Curtis, a girl she knew, "I don't ever want to be a wife. I want to be a flame in the lives of a lot of men, a flame they will remember."

Lina must have been a wise little brat, because she laughed at that. "You read silly novels," she said. "I want to be a wife, and I'll snuff your flame out like a candle whenever I want to, and then you won't be anything."

She wondered where Lina was now, and what she was doing. She wondered if she was a flame in Bart's life and memory, and if she always would be, and what other girls he had known, and how well, and if any of them had been Japanese.

She looked through the slits of her eyelids when there was a sudden movement on the patio. Roger was standing. He held an empty beer can in his hand.

"Another?" he said.

"No, thanks."

Bart did not sound sleepy. Aleta had a moment of resentment at the fact that they did not include her, at least by invitation, in their beer drinking; but she could not remember their having the beer. Maybe they had invited her. She didn't believe she had been asleep, but how could one know; memory and sleep got mixed and mingled sometimes. It made one wonder if memories had any more significance than dreams. She parted her lids again momentarily when she heard Roger come back. He was carrying two cans, even though Bart was not taking any. Ordinarily, she would have put a stop to his afternoon beer drinking when there was serious evening drinking ahead, but not today. "Let him fall on his silly face!" she thought. "Maybe it will teach him not to play Horatius to my bridge!"

She did not turn her head in Bart's direction. She had reached a point of remembering in which she was hating him again. He came galloping over to Poughkeepsie in May just before commencement. There was no play in him, no ardor. She had seen him two weeks before that in Boston when he played baseball against Harvard and he had been fairly exciting, but he was as stiff as a character in a Victorian novel that evening under the oaks and maples of old Vassar. He was a knight asking for a lady's hand, no less.

"I'll receive my commission with my diploma, Al," he said. "I don't know where I'll be sent, but I won't have much time. Will you marry me?"

It sounded so damned silly after all they had done, and after the arguments they had had on the subject. It was difficult to be patient with him.

"Why?" she said.

"I've asked you before."

"I know you have. Do you love me?"

He didn't answer her, or look at her, and she had known the answer to that question before she asked him. He no more loved her than she loved him; they had merely shared a sort of slavery to each other.

"Do you love me?" she repeated.

He turned to her then. "No, Al," he said. "I don't."

She slapped him. She hit him as hard as she could with the flat of her hand, and the pain of the blow ran up her arm. He stood there looking at her, with the red mark on his face and the words tumbled out of her. She called him everything that she could think to call him. She had walked away from him and she had not seen him again until he came out to Waringly yesterday.

She hated him all over again, remembering. No man had the right to ask a woman to marry him because he felt guilty about her. A woman didn't have to take that from him, and she hadn't.

A dropped beer can tinkled when it struck the flagging and bounced. Aleta opened her eyes. Roger was starting out for more beer. He had a stupid, surly look on his face.

"Let's go over to our place and have a real drink," she said.

He looked at her, blinked twice, and threw the other can down for someone else to pick up. "I'm doing all right," he said.

He lurched past her and she followed him into the house. "See here," she said. "You can't do this. How many cans of beer have you had, for Pete's sake?"

"My business," he said. "Want to smell my breath?"

"I don't have to smell your breath. You're going to stop right now. We have a guest for dinner and I won't have you passing out on the table."

"Guest!" he said thickly. "Fellow named McBride. Old flame! What in hell am I? What did you mean, we were so different? How'd you know?"

"Don't be dirty-minded. Anybody could look at you and see how different you are."

"Florence couldn't. Just the same, she said. You could. How did you know? How well did you know this fellow?"

"You're drunk."

"Only a little bit. Just a little. Beer. Sweat it right out. What about this fellow?"

"He's somebody you buttered up to get a play read. Remember?"

"To hell with the play. I think you used to know him awfully well. I don't like it. Why is he down here? Sniffing after you again. Know what I'll do?"

"You'll fall flat into a big hangover headache."

"To hell with that. You're trying to change the subject. I'll shoot him, that's what I'll do. I know guns. One thing I know. I'll shoot him. Shoot you too, maybe. Depends on how guilty you are. Shoot myself. Triangle. Eternal triangle. How do you like that?"

Aleta gripped his arm and shook him. She was furious at herself. She had slept out there. She had not known that he was drinking so much. He must have had one can after another to achieve a result like this on beer. She was frightened, too. He had a collection of guns and he had waved one around when that silly ass, Gilbert, lost his head over her and became obvious about it. She had dropped Gilbert immediately on his stupid fat head, and nothing had happened; so she never knew whether anything would have happened.

In quiet moments afterward, she laughed about it all and was certain that the gun was merely a big gesture on Roger's part; but the incident gave Roger a new value in her emotional life. She wouldn't live with him if he was uncontrollable, or if he was entirely meek; but the idea that he was vaguely dangerous fascinated her. She did not regret Gilbert and the gun that did not go off, but she did not want to go through it again.

"Roger honey," she said. "We won't have any fun tonight if you get too drunk too early. Too much beer isn't good for you. Put your finger down your throat and get rid of it. Then if you'll lie down for a while, you'll be okay."

"Sure!" He swayed unsteadily. "I'll lie down and you'll go out and play with old Stalwart. That's what your mother calls him. Dear Florence calls him 'Stalwart.'"

"That's not so wonderful. It's just a word like 'sweat.' Let's go in and get fixed up. I'll stay with you till you're feeling good again."

"You will? Right there!"

"Of course."

"All right," he said.

He went into the guest bathroom and Aleta flinched when he thrust his finger down his throat. It was a remedy that she recommended but that she could never take. Florence came in as she was stripping the coverlet from the bed. She was wearing her most anxious expression.

"What happened, Aleta?" she said. "Is anything wrong?"

"Nothing. My boy just got too much fresh air. Go out and stay with old Stalwart, will you?"

"Who?"

"Whom, I think. Anyhow, stay with him. Whoever he is, stay with him. Leave us alone."

Florence sighed. She glanced toward the bathroom and shook her head. "Well, I must say——"

She didn't say it. She turned and walked out. Roger emerged from the bathroom. He looked pale. "Thanks," he said. "I couldn't have taken it."

He dived into the bed that Aleta had prepared for him and she brought a wet towel from the bathroom for his head. She sat beside him and in a few minutes he reached out and took her hand. She felt close to him then and a little tender. She glanced at her wrist watch. She'd give him a half hour.

CHAPTER **11**

There had not been much of memory in Bart Mc-
Bride's afternoon. It was a day for reverie rather than
memory; for resting with his body and wandering with
his mind, for seeking the truth about people and the definitions of things; not too much concerned that the truth
about people is at best relative truth and that most definitions are debatable. On a warm day, with insects buzz-
ing and other people out of the mood for conversation,
a man could listen to the voices within him that he seldom
heard.

This was a lovely segment of the earth's surface. He
loafed comfortably in furniture designed for comfort, in
surroundings of material luxury, where no expense had
been begrudged that would contribute to the well-being
and the happiness of the people who shared it; but there
was no harmony in it all. The people sang off key. They
were all at cross-purposes.

He had enjoyed hiking over the countryside with Roger,
but Roger was not a good hiker nor a comfortable companion. He did not have the knack of outdoor relaxation.
His geniality was a bit hollow and his friendliness seemed
forced; ultimately he wanted something that was not in
the earth or sky or in the experience they were sharing.

Of himself, for himself, Bart would never have considered asking a favor from Carter Brill; but when Roger
confronted him with the problem of the play, he had
not hesitated. His reluctance to ask a favor from one
man was overbalanced by the other man's need. Looking
at Roger's life from the viewpoint of what he, himself,
wanted from life, Roger lived in a trap. If Roger had
written a play as his sole hope of escaping that trap,
Bart was in full sympathy with him. What he was asked
to do seemed little enough, requiring of him only a small

sacrifice of pride and the momentary embarrassment of asking Carter Brill to read a play.

It might even be that he owed Carter Brill that sacrifice of pride. He had not met the man's cordiality halfway. It was more difficult to ask a favor than to grant one. In a sense he would be making amends, but there was irony in the thought that he was in such a position between two men to whom he had felt antagonism, and in that position by his own free choice. His sole link to either man was a woman; Dore in the one case and Aleta in the other, two women who did not like each other. Human relationships were intricate and complicated webs.

As far as Aleta was concerned, he had a better understanding now of the distinction that Mary had made so bitterly. The eyes, the skin, and the hair were not the girl. Aleta was inside of all that, and the Aleta inside was a self-centered and disagreeable person. He was not stirred or attracted or even interested in her. Only the remembrance of past intimacy was disturbing. He had to put that firmly aside. They were two ghosts, those shadowy figures of another year, not at all like the older selves who remembered them.

Aleta was sleeping now. Roger drank beer steadily, bringing it out from the house, two cans at a time. Florence had gone in some time ago, angry about something.

The one great noticeable lack in this establishment, and in the lives of these people, was "nonsense." They did not have any and they did not understand it in others. Nonsense, as he had known it, was a sort of high magic with its own values, beyond all analyses, beyond definition, beyond the dull mathematics of what humorless worldlings called common sense.

Nonsense was Dore pretending that they were rich and wonderful when they had barely enough to eat, believing it and making him believe it through a sort of contagion, holding fast to the pretense until, suddenly, astonishingly, it was so. It was Dore paying money that she could not afford for the little dancer, so that they would have one beautiful object in any shabby room they occupied. It was Dore insisting that all earrings were twins, and naming them. If she dropped one, she knew whether it was Clara or Camille, and if Bart found it for her, he did not find an earring, he found Camille. It was Dore keeping them both awake in a bus station, so that they would catch the right bus, by discovering characters from *Alice in Wonderland* all over the bus station. It was Alice itself and the capacity for believing in white rabbits and mad hatters when one was no longer a child.

Nonsense was the matching of tag lines from familiar plays that were studied in drama courses, quote, counter-quote, with Mary Norbert. It was believing that you could command a taxicab within a block when no one else could do so. It was taking a girl for a nickel date in glamorous New York and standing in the rain to see tall buildings in the mist. It was spinning words together without regard to meaning, knowing that the one other person will understand them and require no meaning from them.

He became very interested in the definitions of non-sense, lying there in the sun. It was woven into all the strands of his life.

Football was nonsense; twenty-two husky young men hammering each other for possession of a ball and for the privilege of carrying it across a line drawn upon the earth. Watching football and cheering the essentially mean-ingless violence on the field was nonsense. So was pro-fessional baseball; playing the same game day after day for months against a rotating series of opponents, travel-ing from city to city on solemn schedules that obliged the playing of the game; forcing oneself to play with sprains, strains, wounds, fevers, and broken bones. The magic which made it nonsense and not mere folly lay in the intangibles of loyalty, courage, team spirit, the in-dividual submerging himself in something bigger than him-self; and in the spectator need for the dramatization of struggle, the catalyst of conflict. Or perhaps not! If it could be explained, it was no longer nonsense; if any-thing about it could be proved or disproved, it was not magic.

He thought suddenly of the Abbey. There was nonsense there too, wonderful nonsense. From dawn till Compline, healthy, happy men lived and worked under a stern, ac-cepted discipline, voluntarily denying themselves what other men considered necessities. They followed rituals that were centuries old, and chanted chants that were centuries old, indifferent to either the praise or the ridicule of the world outside their walls. For what? For the Something that they had never seen, heard, or touched. For the faith in Something that they could not make believable to the unbeliever. That was Nonsense, the great Nonsense with the capital N. It was Nonsense so magnificent that it had to be Truth. Men denied their flesh for it, and laid down their lives for it, and rested at length in the earth under their simple wooden crosses, with their cowls drawn over their faces.

Here at Waringly there was brittle comedy or hearty laughter, but no humor; folly, but no nonsense. The Waringlys were pleasant people, friendly people, generous as lords of the manor are generous; but there was a missing element. The fine qualities were like a highly polished surface; underneath, Waringly was grim. There was nothing grimmer in the world, he thought, than the single-minded, uncompromising service of self.

Florence came out from the house. She did not look fluttery, or pleasantly vague, as she usually did; she looked angry. "Bart," she said, "what *is* the matter with Roger?"

"I don't know," he said. "Is something the matter? He and Aleta went inside a while ago."

Florence tightened her lips. She had a small mouth, as Aleta had. The startling thought came to him that she might, once, have been very much like Aleta; softer and less direct, perhaps, but still like Aleta. He had never seen that before; but then, he knew the Waringlys only on the lighter side of their lives, the guest side.

"He is probably drunk again," Florence said. "I don't know why people ever become parents."

None of the logical replies seemed appropriate. Bart merely waited. Florence was tapping the arm of her chair with her fingernails. "I nearly died giving birth to Aleta," she said, "and I was tied down with her during the best years of my life. I thought when she went away to college that Alex and I would have a little freedom to do the things that we wanted to do, but she was so demanding! We had to make so many sacrifices."

Instinctively, Bart looked beyond the house and the patio in which they sat to the broad acres beyond. Florence read the thought. "I know that it seems to you that we have a lot," she said, "but we made sacrifices, many, many sacrifices."

Florence reached to the box beside her for a cigarette and Bart held a match. "I wanted Aleta to be married," she said. "I thought it would be good for her. We gave her a beautiful wedding and a trip abroad. While she and Roger were in Europe, we built a house for them as a surprise. All that I ever get from them is worry and insolence. Where have I failed, Bart?"

Her anger had melted into the soft mood that he knew best. Her lips were quivering and there were tears in her eyes.

"I don't believe you have failed," he said gently.

He could say that honestly. It wasn't failure, it was something far over and beyond failure, something bigger than failure. He had no definition for it. He remembered what he had said to Alex: that it was possible to take away by giving. Alex hadn't understood him. Florence would not understand that either, because it was nonsense. Nor about rising by descending.

Florence was dabbing at her eyes with a small handkerchief. She held her cigarette in the other hand. "I wish you could tell me what to do," she said.

"I'm afraid that I can't."

He thought that he had been wrong in one verdict, when he rode with Roger yesterday. He had been uncomfortable because Roger insisted upon discussing his personal affairs. Bart had been certain then that it was a lack in Roger and that none of the Waringlys would talk, as he did, of intimate family matters to a guest, a comparative stranger. He had been wrong about that. They all would, and did.

Aleta came out on the patio. "Ready, Bart?" she said. "We're going over to Casa Vannin."

Roger followed her out. He looked all right. Florence rose. "Don't you think that you should wait until your father comes home?" she said.

Aleta looked at her. "No. I don't. Do you?"

"No. I guess not."

Bart said good-by to Florence, thanked her for her hospitality, and declined her invitation to spend another night. He had set a goal for himself. There was a late train and he was going to ride back on it to New York.

Aleta slid under the wheel. "Florence told me that your mother's show is opening in Boston tonight," she said.

Bart nodded. "I walked down to the town and sent her a wire this morning."

"Thoughtful youth! Do you realize what the opening date is in New York?"

"Yes. October twelfth. Her birthday."

"And mine," Aleta said softly.

"And Christopher Columbus'," Roger said.

Roger was trying to be cheerful again. He and Aleta were engaged in a mock argument about her birthday and why she was not named Columbine or Christine. Bart was thinking back. At the height of his obsession with Aleta, it had seemed a very significant thing that her birthday and Dore's coincided. It was an omen, a sign from the stars that she was the girl for him. How wrong that was! The stars were never half that stupid.

"Do you suppose that you could get me opening-night tickets, as a birthday present, Bart?" Aleta said.

Roger cut in swiftly. "Hey! You can't go around asking men for birthday presents."

"I can if there is no other way of getting them."

Bart shook his head. "I doubt if there will be a loose ticket anywhere," he said. "I'll try."

"Even one ticket," Aleta said lightly. "I'll leave Roger in some bar till after the show."

She swung into the driveway and parked the car. "Roger honey," she said, "do you think you could mix us a drink?"

"Best thing that I do."

Aleta vanished into one of the other rooms. When she came back, she was wearing a black jersey blouse with long sleeves, a wide, flaring skirt of pepper-and-salt tweed, stockings and black slippers. She had renewed her makeup and the shadow was deep in her eyes, her lips vivid. She wore earrings of extraordinary length with crystal pendants.

Bart thought about Mary Norbert. He could describe Aleta to her as Aleta looked now, and it would not mean a thing; but she would attach meaning to it. The axioms of feminine geometry were so cockeyed that women came up with preposterous lines of reasoning. All of their circles were squares and all their triangles straight lines.

He talked generalities with Roger and Aleta, their generalities, while they sat around with highballs. Nothing that was said involved him greatly. He felt detached, far away. All of this was the overture, an interval before the rising of the curtain. Somehow, before the evening was over, he would talk alone with Aleta. That was all that mattered.

Aleta rose suddenly and went over to the piano. This house, like the other, had a baby grand. Knowing Aleta's limitations as far as the piano was concerned, he wondered why. She ran her fingers idly over the keys as though searching for something, then settled on what she wanted.

> *Far above Cayuga's water*
> *With its waves of blue*
> *Stands our noble Alma Mater*
> *Glorious to view*

She did not sing, but she gave him Cornell. He saw Roger frown at his glass. Aleta's fingers quickened on the keys.

> *Cheer till the sound wakes the blue hills around,*
> *Makes the scream of the north wind yield*
> *To the strength of the yell from the men of Cornell*
> *When the Big Red Team takes the field.*

The beat of it shattered his detached calm. How often had he sung it, heard it sung? He had a sweeping panorama of memory that included many fields, many stands, many cheering crowds. Aleta had been in some of those rooting sections. She had heard his name rolled out across the field with thousands of voices powering it. They had met later when the bonfires were burning and the snake dancers writhing. Her fingers raced now and it was as though she was typing him a letter that said: "Remember?"

Roger rose and took his glass. "Time for another," he said curtly.

Bart looked up at him as he turned away. He knew then that Aleta's fingers had not been beating out anything so personal as a letter; hers had been an open thing, like a postcard that anyone could read. She swung to "Stand up and Cheer," then:

> *Roar, Lion, roar,*
> *And wake the echoes of the Hudson Valley.*
> *Fight on to victory ever more*
> *While the sons of Knickerbocker rally,*
> *Roar, Lion, roar.*

It was flat and anticlimactic. Roger did not seem to be paying any attention to it. It had come in as a postscript, and he had not been a football player. Once away from the music that stirred his own emotions through association, Bart felt detached again. College songs were never really good except when one was in college, or back for a reunion, or with a group who generated a mood. Aleta let the last roar die and jumped up.

"I won't miss a drink just to be a one-man band," she said. "Roger, you sing something!"

Bart looked up with interest. Roger was standing irresolute, with his glass in his hand. Obviously he liked to be asked to sing. He glanced toward Bart.

"How about you?" he said.

Aleta cut in quickly. "Bart will play the accompaniment," she said. "He's better than I am."

Roger looked sharply at her. Bart thought it tactless of her to remind Roger of yet another thing that she had shared with him. He rose and walked over to the piano. He was rusty but he could play accompaniments in this league.

"What will we do?" he said.

Roger downed his fresh drink in two swallows. He brushed the back of his hand across his mouth. " 'Water Boy,' " he said.

As soon as he opened his mouth, Bart knew that, no matter how much he might like to do this, Roger did not have what it took. He had no rhythm, no music, no style. His voice was strong but he did not know what to do with it; he merely powered the words into the room. Aleta had to know that he was bad, Bart thought. She had to know. But she applauded "Water Boy."

Roger was having fun. He sang: "Hear de Lambs A-Crying" and "Sweet Chariot" and "Old Man River" and "John Henry." When he decided to do "Glory Road," it was difficult to keep him in the room. He seemed to realize that in that one he had been a little less than Tibbett or Robeson.

"I'm out of practice," he said. "After that, I need a drink."

His face was flushed and there was a glow in his eyes. Aleta patted him on the arm. "I always wished that I could sing," she said.

She walked over to the piano, humming. "Bart," she said. "I've got a thing running through my head. How does it go? That one of your mother's about yesterday—something—and mist on the hill?"

Bart played the chorus softly, giving her the melody. "That one was in *All the Girls*," he said. "Believe it or not, I heard it first on a phonograph record that Dore sent me. I was at the Christian Brothers' school and they wouldn't let me go in for the opening."

"How did the lyrics go?" Aleta said. "I've been trying to remember."

The piano had taken possession of him. Bart felt the pull of it, the call to make music. He had always liked, "Did You Know." He played it again now and sang it, half voice. Aleta leaned across the piano, singing with him in pantomime, keeping time with one finger.

> "*Yesterday's rain is mist on the hill* [he sang],
>     *Yesterday's pain is with me still.*
>     *Why did you go when I told you, "Go!"*
>     *My lips were liars, my heart said, "No!"*
>
> *You should have known, my blinded lover,*
>     *Or did you know?"*

Aleta's strangely shaped, dark eyes were looking into his. There was something hypnotic about them. He held the note, swelled it a little. There was a splintering crash from the direction of the fireplace. Aleta whirled. Roger had smashed his glass against the tiles.

"What in hell is this?" he said.

Aleta walked slowly toward him. There was menace in every deliberate movement. "Just what do you mean?"

"You know damned well what I mean."

"I'll accept your apology if I have it in a hurry."

They stood motionless, facing each other. For six or seven ticks of the clock, Roger held his pose, his chin thrust forward; then he closed his eyes and his shoulders lost their rigidity. He brushed the back of his hand across his forehead. "I'm sorry," he said. "I must be drunk."

A precise, angular woman with gray hair appeared in the doorway. "Dinner is served, Mrs. Vannin," she said.

There was not very much that anyone could make of dinner after the scene that preceded it. Aleta was the only one who tried very hard. She seemed determined to act as though nothing had happened, and she talked. She received little co-operation.

Bart's sympathies rested with Roger. He could look back and see the scene through the eyes of Aleta's husband. It became, then, the singing of an intimate song; with Aleta leaning over the piano and accepting the song as sung to her. Bart did not believe now that Aleta had forgotten the lyrics. It was too pat. She staged it too well. He had played right into her hands, but once he embarked on the singing of "Did You Know," there had been no place to go, nowhere to look save into Aleta's eyes, no way of singing save to her.

He did not realize fully what he had done to Roger Vannin until after dinner when Roger, having eaten very little, insisted upon drinking brandy over Aleta's protest. Roger lifted his brandy to Bart. "My singing must have amused you," he said bitterly. "I'm strictly amateur. Nobody warned me that you were a professional."

"I'm not. It was one of my mother's hits. I followed her styling."

"If I'd heard you sing first, I wouldn't have made a fool of myself by letting you play accompaniment."

Bart felt the other man's humiliation and there was not much that he could do about it. He had sung Dore's number half voice and he had not attempted to give it much, but he had a pretty fair baritone. Dore had taught him many things. He had had rhythm beaten into his dreams when he was a baby, music into his mind when he was old enough to read notes, style into his consciousness as he grew. Dore had never permitted him to make serious use of what she gave him, but he had it. He could do naturally, effortlessly, what Roger would never be able to do. Roger knew enough about singing to sense what he probably could not define. Bart made a deprecatory gesture.

"Your voice is bigger than mine," he said. "If I tried to sing, I'd be singing for the fun of it, just as you did."

"Thanks. It's just a noise I learned to make."

Aleta laughed. "This is just too silly," she said. "I like the way you sing, Roger. Bart is just a crooner."

That did it. Roger looked at her, then turned away. He crossed the room and poured himself a stiff drink of whisky from a decanter. At the end of an uncomfortable half hour, he passed out and lay face down on the couch upon which he had been seated. Aleta watched him for a few minutes, silent, then she shrugged and rose quietly. She strolled toward the door and looked back at Bart.

Bart followed her. It was the moment toward which he had planned, but he did not like the way it had come about. It was a cloudy night, turning chill. Aleta walked a few yards away from the house, beyond the range of light from the windows, then turned.

"I'm sorry, Bart," she said. "He isn't always like this."

"You didn't cover yourself with glory," he said.

"What do you mean?"

"You'll have a hard time squaring this with him."

"I?"

She widened her eyes. Bart looked away from her. He didn't like the innocent look. It meant that she would put Roger on the defensive while he was still in the throes of hangover, berating him for the way he acted. The man just couldn't win; but that was Roger's problem. Aleta was standing close to him. He turned back to her.

"Look," he said. "It's your marriage. None of my business. There's something that is my business. I want to know about the baby, Al."

She reached up swiftly and laid the palm of her hand against his mouth. Her hand was soft, warm. "Hush!" she whispered. "You damned fool! He may be pretending. And Betsy is in the house. She can hear the grass grow."

"All right. Let's walk a mile if we have to. I want to know."

"That's over. All over."

"Not for me. It's never been over."

She drew herself straight. "You were always that kind of a dog, always returning to the vomit."

"I don't think of it that way."

"I wouldn't either if you didn't make it that."

"I want to know."

The clouds were rolling fast and the moon seemed to be racing in and out of the valleys. There was deep shadow beyond the house. Aleta walked only a few steps, then stopped.

"I have to go back," she said.

Bart gripped her wrist. "Al," he said, "where did you have the baby?"

She looked up into his face. Her skin was white, her eyes deep and dark. "I won't tell you."

"Yes. You will. I'll keep asking that question till you do —if I have to ask it in crowds, in front of Roger——"

"You wouldn't dare."

"I would. Doesn't he suspect?"

"He knows that I wasn't a nun."

"Is that all?"

"It's enough. He hates every man I ever knew."

"That's hard on him. I wouldn't want him to know any more. Tell me, Al, and I'll go."

"Is that all that brought you back?"

He was still holding her wrist. Her body touched his. She still looked up at him. He met her eyes. "That's all, Al. You're married."

"You were always a boy about marriage. And if I wasn't married?"

"We settled that the last time we talked."

"When you paid me the high compliment of offering me marriage, admitting that you weren't in love with me."

"You have the knack of making a man look bad. It wasn't quite that way. I've got to know where you had the baby, Al."

"Why?"

"I have the right to know. It was mine."

She drew her breath in and he could feel the tension in her. He was conscious of the scent she wore, her oddly shaped face with the prominent cheekbones emphasizing the short line of her jaw, the smallness of her mouth. He had stood like this with her on other nights, combative. There had always been a combative element in their relationship.

"You weren't there," she said. "I was alone."

"That wasn't my fault."

"It wasn't mine either."

"Where did you go? Who helped you?"

She turned a frightened look toward the house and pulled her hand free from his relaxed grip. "He's up, moving around——" she said.

She started back. Bart looked toward the light. He saw no movement and heard none. In two strides he caught her, whirled her around, and held both of her arms. "It's no good, Al," he said. "I've got to know."

She writhed in his grasp. "It's over," she said. "Dead. Let me go!"

"Was it a boy or a girl, Al?" he said huskily.

"It's dead."

"What was it?"

"A boy."

The word hit him like a hammer. He had a picture firmly in his mind, a picture of little girls in gray uniforms. He had no picture of the boys at all, save as ball players whom the girls were permitted to watch. Not all of them would play ball, and the very small ones couldn't. He shook Aleta like a rag doll and he saw the fright in her face.

"Barbarian!" she whispered.

"I can't believe you," he said. "I can't believe the baby died. I've got to find out for myself. I want to know when it was born."

"You're hurting me terribly."

He had forgotten the strength of his hands. He released her. The moment that he did, she ran away from him. She was at the door of the house when he overtook her. There was terror in her voice.

"Please, Bart! I'll write the name of the place, everything, and mail it to you."

"It's easier to tell me."

Her fingers dug into his biceps. "It isn't. It's complicated. I have to look up a couple of things. Oh!"

She looked toward the living room. "He is stirring. I know it. Bart, he's got guns all over the place. I'm scared. I'll truly write it for you. I'll prove it. Cross my heart! But not here. Not now."

Her panic seemed genuine. "I'm at the Algonquin," he said. "If you don't write it, I'll come back, and I won't care——"

She broke away and he made no attempt to hold her. When he followed her in, Roger lay where they had left him. She ran across the room and went down on her knees beside the couch. She put her hand under Roger's cheek.

"Roger darling," she said. "You can't stay here. You've got to get to bed." She lifted her face. There were tears in her eyes. "Bart, help me!"

Bart moved Roger around on the couch until he could get the grip that he wanted. The man was heavy and he was out cold. It was stevedore work, getting him into the bedroom and undressing him. Aleta stood with her fingers interlocked.

"I'm so afraid that he'll die sometime when he gets like this," she said.

Aleta, the frightened woman, was unconvincing, but Bart McBride was weary of the Vannins, weary of scenes. He had to accept the whole sorry business for what it was. He had done all that he could for Roger. He looked across the bed at Aleta.

"I won't compromise with you, Al," he said.

"I know."

"All right. I'm sorry it had to be this way."

He turned and walked out. It was a long walk to the station and a long wait for his train. He had time to be dissatisfied with himself. He hadn't given Aleta a kind word, or a word of sympathy for those months that she said she had spent alone. Still! Letters long ago had covered all of that. Aleta did not command sympathy.

He walked up and down on the empty platform. He thought about its being a boy. It became more real, knowing that much. A boy! He had, or had had, a son. He thought back to his own years of wondering and of wanting, to that one year at school, in which the need of his father had been a desperate, unreasoning thing. No child for which he was responsible would ever have to go through that.

"She'll write," he said grimly. "She has to. I didn't leave her an out. She knows that I'll do what I said I'd do."

The train was a humming in the rail and then a distant white light, the train that would take him back to New York. He wondered how Dore's opening had gone in Boston. He was glad that he had remembered to send her a wire.

CHAPTER 12

It was 8:55 P.M. in the Abbey of St. Urban. The monks' day was over. They left the chapel and walked quietly in the corridors, seeking their cells. Brother Anselm was still hearing the Salve Regina. The good night hymn to the Blessed Virgin echoed in his mind and memory normally until sleep came; but for three nights his sleep had been troubled and uneasy. The phantom chanters in his mind were dispersed by his own discordant thoughts. This was the fourth night.

He stood in his cell beside his cot and raised his eyes to the crucifix on the wall. He had with him, as he always had, the comforting sense of the presence of God in the place of his sleep. It was not a stern Presence, nor wrathful, nor demanding. There was an enfolding love where one felt God, a security, an exaltation that was not merely of the spirit but of the physical senses, a freedom from all fear and want forever. He had been alone with the awareness of God through all the nights of many years, but now there was another self standing beside him and he was no longer solitary.

The other self was the man who had stood straight in his pride before the image of the Virgin in the garden and who had presumed to advise his son in a grave matter out of his own faulty knowledge and experience. He should have prayed and been silent before he spoke, and he knew that, but he had grown foolish-tall with pride.

"I advised him wrongly," he said. "It was not the thing that he should do."

The self that had not listened was there beside him, intruding upon the joy of his solitude, disturbing him as the grave faults of his younger years no longer disturbed him. He could not call back the words that he had spoken, nor the opportunity that he had had for speech.

The chimes of the Abbey announced the hour of nine, the summons to slumber. Brother Anselm lay upon his cot. He was a simple man, born for simple thought, and he could not cope with complexity.

"It is not a matter that I can deal with alone," he thought. "I will ask for the counsel of Father Abbot in the morning."

At 11:45 P.M., Dorinda Daly returned to her hotel suite after the opening night performance of *The Seventh Wife*. She was staying at the big, old-fashioned hotel on Beacon Street. She liked the high ceilings, the feeling of spaciousness, and the privacy. Few people expected to find her there, and in Boston she preferred the few to the many; tryout week was a week of strain.

Carter Brill walked around the parlor, nervously puffing on his cigarette. It was not always pleasant to tell the truth. It was particularly difficult to tell an actress the truth, because actresses did not live realities, merely the shadows of realities. Dorinda came back, wearing a peach-colored negligee. She stretched in the chaise longue and closed her eyes.

"God, I'm tired all of a sudden. How was it, Carter?"

He took his time, crushing out a cigarette in an ash tray. "I'm no good to you unless I'm an honest pair of eyes out front," he said, "a pair of eyes that you can trust."

"In other words, I missed."

"You're not the star of the show. You should be."

"Is it my fault?"

"I believe that you know it is. If you stood up to that big ham, you could slap him right back into the boxes."

"That wouldn't be good for the show, would it?"

He looked at her. Her eyes were no longer closed. "Perhaps I missed," he said. "No, it wouldn't be good for the show. He is slightly terrific."

Dorinda nodded. "If he's good and if I'm good, the show will run forever; if he was lousy, I couldn't do anything with it."

"You can't afford to let him steal it."

"I know. Not to mention Gilda."

"She's better than I expected. But even at half throttle, you're still tops. Over anybody in the business. If you would only open up . . ."

"Maybe I have a psychological charley horse, or something. But I'm glad that you're honest, Carter. It's a lovely thing."

"It costs me. Queens once had the bearers of ill tidings beheaded."

"I'm not a queen, darling. And beheading has gone out of fashion. I wish you'd do something for me."

"Name it!"

"It's a big do. I want you to fix some of my lines. They don't speak right."

He stood staring at her. "You know that I can't do that. Kinzing wouldn't let me touch a line of his show."

"He doesn't have to know about it. I want you to write me some lines that I can sort of ad-lib, that I can use myself, just as if I'd forgotten the others."

Carter Brill smiled. For a few minutes he had been worried about her. It wasn't normal for an actress to be too "big" about other people in a cast. As soon as she started to connive a little, he relaxed. If she did a little more of it, he would feel better about the whole show. After all, this was only Boston. He shook his head.

"It's dangerous," he said. "If you monkey with lines on your own, you are apt to foul cues. Rico Moreno is out of opera, where he didn't dare scratch his ear except on cue."

"I know about cues, darling. I've been in shows. These are little things. I am going to do one myself. Maybe it's a good example. When I make my first entrance, I say: 'I saw your ad in the paper,' and Rico says, 'I didn't put an ad in the paper.' I am going to say 'want ad' instead of 'ad.' That doesn't bother anything, does it?"

"No. And Kinzing would change that officially if you asked him."

Dorinda shook her head. "I don't want that. He'd change it all, and Rico would say 'want ad' too."

Carter went back to pacing. "Let me think," he said.

This, he knew, was not a simple vagary of the feminine mind, this was the maneuvering of an actress. If he permitted himself to be drawn into it, his part would not be simple. He knew the show backward and forward. He could see it whole. He stood off from it for a few minutes, looking at it.

Briefly, the plot centered around Rico as the idealistic Doctor of Music who has many devoted pupils. He has finally done something for himself. He has written an opera. One of his former students has interested a nitwit, playboy millionaire in backing the opera for production. The playboy, played by George Kelsey, a veteran comedian, has just married his seventh wife, played by Gilda Skara. The students convince Rico that the playboy will never back a staid, respectable music professor. He has to have a Bohemian streak. They hire an out-of-work model, Dorinda Daly, to act as his mistress when Kelsey calls, so Rico will have some gay-dog color. Dorinda's first solo, "Mistress by the Day," was one of the best in the show.

The seventh wife, however, is determined to reform her husband and her solo—"You Can't Trust Your Husband with a Rake"—expresses her feeling about permitting Kelsey to associate with musicians and their mistresses. In the end, Rico loses his big chance at backing for his opera by refusing, on principle, to give up the mistress who isn't his mistress.

Carter Brill walked around the room with it, then sat down facing Dorinda, who watched him anxiously. "Okay," he said. "I see what you're doing. Rico gets all the attention now with his dumb bewilderment about the damned ad. You'll get it first, and perhaps a laugh, if you get that word 'want' in there and give it the emphasis you can give it."

Dorinda smiled and gestured lightly with her right hand. "It is just a little thing, but——"

"I believe I know where there are a few other little bodies like that one buried; or where they could be buried."

"Do you, Carter? I'm so glad. If you'll bring me the book, I'll show you what I think can be done."

She was very sweet, very deferent. He crossed the room for the book of *The Seventh Wife* and brought it back.

"I should be able to think of a good line to describe this predicament I find myself in," he said, "but maybe I'm not half the playwright that I think I am."

Dorinda turned the pages of the book. "I would not love thee half so well if thou wert Bernard Shaw," she said. Her finger found a line on a page. "Here, Carter," she said. "In this scene, when Gilda comes in and——"

Carter Brill bent above the book. It was an hour later when he made his last note. He stretched wearily. "I hope you know," he said, "that those few simple words will be tougher to write than five thousand."

"I know." Dorinda's eyes were eloquent. "I'm grateful, Carter."

"I'll fly back to New York and work on it."

"New York? Why?"

"It's the only place I can work."

"That's temperament. And superstition. You can be quiet here."

He shook his head. "The air of Boston is full of old,

used thoughts, everything that's been thought for centuries."

"New York isn't any different."

"That's where you're wrong. A thought doesn't last long in New York." He picked up the book of typescript. "When I finish, if I can't come up, I'll send Mary Norbert," he said. "Okay?"

"Ye-es." Dorinda hesitated. "I can use her. A thousand things! I've wondered. I had a wire from Bart. He wasn't in New York. He was out in Connecticut. Where that girl used to live."

"The lady snake?"

"That one. I hoped——" Dorinda bit her lip. "Mary is so damned right for him. They're so right for each other. Decent, high-minded kind of people, both of them. Damn it, Carter, I hoped that if I brought them together Mary would hold him, that he'd see——"

Carter Brill shook his head. "If the little Norbert had the holding knack, she'd be a she-serpent, too, and you wouldn't like her. Let be!"

Dorinda's shoulders slumped. "I will. I have. I won't try to play God, Carter. If they can't find each other now, then maybe I'm wrong and maybe it wouldn't work out. I gave Bart all I had left to give him: a girl I've learned to love like a daughter, and the address of his father."

"His father? That may have complicated matters."

"I don't think so. Anyway, there's nothing hidden any more. It's his show. He's got to put it together. I put mine together, don't I, Carter?"

Her voice was breaking. She had taken all that she could take in one day; too much, Carter Brill thought. He went down on one knee beside the couch and held her gently while he kissed her.

"You're pretty wonderful, Dorinda," he said. "Remind me someday to tell you so."

In a music studio on the fringe of Greenwich Village, Mary Norbert finished a rehearsal of her own. Doc Epstein, the old man at the piano, grunted and reached in his vest pocket for a cigar.

"It will do," he said. "Not wonderful. No big talent. No big names. But what the hell? Is this for posterity?"

"It might be, Doc. It might be. Maybe you are making history."

The short, dark-haired young man in the slacks and sports shirt laughed and winked at Mary Norbert. "Turillo and Norbert," he said. "It goes nice."

"Too much like Gorilla and Filbert," Doc Epstein said. "Go home."

"He's hinting at us," Mary said. "But I like his suggestion. It has box office. Gorilla and Filbert!"

"No class," the young man said. "No quality. Okay, Doc, we'll go quietly."

"See you tomorrow," Mary said. "I hope."

The old man chuckled. "Hope tight," he said. "Without me, would you be lousy!"

Mary ran lightly down the dark, angled staircase, with Frank Turillo following her. It was a good feeling to be using her voice again, to be at least playing at performance. The young man caught up with her on the steps outside. It was a cloudy night, cool, with a fresh feeling in the air. The air-conditioning system of night between the rivers was going into action as it had not for a week. Somewhere, blocks away or miles away, a clock struck midnight.

"A short beer?"

"Coffee."

"It will keep you awake."

"Never does. Beer will ruin your figure."

"On a tenor, a ruined figure looks good."

They walked across Eighth Street to MacDougal and there was no midnight curfew. Shops were open and people milled around on sidewalks. They sat at scarred wooden tables and watched an artist at an adjoining table do a pen-and-ink portrait of the man who had just bought him a dinner.

"That's a gift, like a voice," Frank Turillo said. "You can starve with it."

"There was a man who received a gift of two wishes from a great magician," Mary said. "He wished for what he thought he wanted, got it, then used the other wish to get rid of it."

"What does that prove?"

"You can starve even if your wishes are granted."

"I wouldn't." The young man stared gloomily at his glass. "The way I always heard that wish story, there were three wishes."

"The extra wish only confuses things and makes them worse."

"I'd like to try." He looked at her across the table. "With your talent and with that Daly connection, why aren't you in a show?"

"She doesn't think I have it."

"Did she ever hear you when you were really putting out?"

"No."

"Then she doesn't know."

"I'm afraid she does."

"Nuts! All those squawking squaws are alike. Afraid somebody can squawk better. Jealous. If you're out, nobody that's in wants to make room for you."

Mary shook her head. "Dorinda isn't like that. But never mind. How about you? Where are you going?"

Frank Turillo nodded toward the other table. "If I could draw people, that, what he's doing, would be a future."

"That bad? Why? You've got a remarkable voice and you've worked with it."

"I've killed myself with it. The money I've spent! Two years in Italy, even. But who wants it? Can I be Peerce? Never. Am I Lanza?"

"You're better than Lanza."

"Thanks. I think so too. But is anybody around screaming for somebody better than Lanza, not so good as Peerce? With half my throat cut, maybe I could be Eddie Fisher or Frankie Laine and make a million." He gripped the edge of the table, leaning forward over his tense hands. "The last good job I had didn't have a note in it. No singing at all."

"What was it?"

"*Mister Roberts.* Road company. I was Insigna." He

relaxed suddenly and there was a calculating look in his eyes. "I had one swell line——"

"I know." She cut in on him swiftly. "The binoculars scene."

"That's right. It's where I say——"

"I know what you said. I have a knack of remembering lines."

He sat rocking in his chair, a grin on his face, calculation in his eyes still. "How about you, baby?" he said. "Any birthmarks?"

Mary looked at him quietly. "Up till now, we've been getting along," she said.

"Like that, huh?"

"Exactly like that."

"Okay. You aren't my type anyway." He let the chair legs come down with a bang. He was still grinning. "I like the big dairies, and birthmarks, lots of birthmarks."

Mary nodded. "If I hear of any, I'll let you know."

The grin faded. There was a desperate earnestness in Frank Turillo's eyes. "Never mind," he said. "I can always find that for myself. But if you hear of a job?"

"I'll remember."

Mary Norbert paid her half of the check and they went out. She thought of all the stories about wishes. If she met a magician, or a fairy godmother, on the way home, would she wish for the stage again, for a career like Dorinda Daly's? If she had that, with one wish left, what then?

Bart McBride came into the Algonquin at one forty-five by the clock. There were people sitting around in the lobby talking. The clerk rose from his own small desk to give him his key. There was no mail. At his own desk again, the clerk noticed the date on the daily calendar and tore off the top page.

It was another day: October 5, 1954.

# Tomorrow

## CHAPTER 1

October fifth was the Feast of St. Placidus, martyr,
who died in the sixth century. To Brother Anselm, the
centuries were without meaning. St. Urban's had freed
him from the tyranny of time. St. Placidus, patron saint of
novices, had been his own particular intercessor during
his first year in the monastery. The saint lived in his mind
as vividly as the priests and brothers who had died during
his ten years. The saints unseen and the monks he had
known were members of a single company to which he, a
humble figure, was attached. It was easy to forget that
Father Bruno and Brother Damon were dead, although he
had carved the crosses for their graves; as easy to forget
that St. Placidus had died long ago. Time did not matter,
nor mere physical presence. It did not make very much
difference if a good man lived in time or in eternity.

Brother Anselm prayed to St. Placidus during the Mass
of the many martyrs, asking him to guide his speech in his
conversation with the Abbot. "I speak my thoughts badly,"
he said, "and it is important that I make myself understood. I will need help with Father Abbot because I am
not easy with him."

He did not know why this was so, and he put his bewilderment into his prayer. It was not the fault of the
Abbot, who was kind and wise, it was the fault of his own
education. He had always worked under other men when
he worked in the world and he had never been a boss.
Some of the bosses had no more education than he had,
and he had known how he stood with them, giving them a
day's work, which was all that he owed them. The engineers under whom he had worked were different. They
were men of education and he was less sure of what he

knew when he dealt with them. It was like that with the
Abbot. If he was clumsy in his speech and did not make
clear what was in his mind, he would not know if his thinking was wrong in the face of the Abbot's superior wisdom,
or if it was only the words of his thinking that were at
fault. It was a confusion that he could entrust to St. Placidus in prayer and it gave him confidence to do so.

His prayer to the saints always took the form of conversation. They were friends of his with whom he felt at
ease and, in so far as he pictured them at all, they were
older, wiser monks, but not too unlike himself or too remote from him. He never expected miracles from them or
direct intervention in his affairs, any more than he would
expect the extraordinary from Father Michael or Father
Stephen, or any other monk of St. Urban's. The saints
could guide him in his thinking and in his conduct and,
perhaps, help him to avoid mistakes; but above all they
were his friends.

The Blessed Mother was closer to him than any saint,
but his prayers to her were different. He sent up prayers of
devotion to her at odd moments of his day, and offered
her his work when he had a difficult task or one that called
for special patience and skill. He sought her aid only with
great problems, and in the dark hours of temptation. In
his early years at St. Urban's, when the longings of the
flesh were sometimes strong and the thoughts in his mind
were sensual thoughts, he called upon her for help. Nothing unclean could stand in her presence, or in the thought
of her—and nothing had. He had asked her every day and
night to watch over and protect his wife and his son; but
he laid no petty cares before her and he tried to offer
prayers of gratitude, and prayers of love, to her rather
than to be forever seeking favors. He felt very sure, very
safe, in his prayers to the Blessed Mother and she never
seemed far away. She was a gentleness in his life, which
was often a hard thing, even here in the peace of the
Abbey.

Before the great mystery of God he was inarticulate.
At the consecration in the Mass, his heart seemed to stop
beating. He could kneel before the altar with his eyes
raised to the sanctuary and lose all track of time, saying

no prayer, thinking no thoughts of his own, lost in the great wonder that he existed, and that the beauty of the world existed, and that he could kneel thus in the presence of his Creator and not be driven away.

God was the great Reality. All that he had, or ever would have, came from God. He thought of God best when he thought of the person of Jesus Christ, and Christ was God in most of his thinking. He was aware of the Father and the Holy Ghost although they were dimly realized in his mind. He did not trouble himself with attempts to unravel mysteries. If he were as wise as the Abbot, there would still be much in the ordinary world that he would never understand. The Creator of that world was beyond the most distant boundary of all that he did not know.

Prayer, then, was the bridge over which one crossed to Reality. Since a monk's personal needs were few, and his temptations light compared to those of his brothers in the world, the great prayers of the community were offered for the world and its struggling people. Somewhere in that world, at any moment, a human being in need of help, deserving none of himself, was fed on the energy and the devotion of men who existed beyond his knowing; and strength came to him. Something entered the world as a living force for good because there were men content to take nothing out of that world. A monk prayed his days, from the hour of Matins in the dawn to the hour of Compline, asking no question of the Infinite, secure in his faith that nothing offered to God is wasted.

Brother Anselm laid his personal problem before St. Placidus and, as he left the chapel, Father Sub-Prior spoke to him. "Father Abbot will see you in the first hour of the afternoon, Anselm," he said.

The work of the morning lay ahead. The screens were to be removed from all the windows of the guesthouse, repaired if they needed it, and stored for the winter. The gutters of the guesthouse roof were to be cleared of the summer debris so that the winter moisture would flow off freely. From the height of the roof, Brother Anselm could see monks on ladders in the orchard, picking apples, other monks husking corn, "Brother Bumble," the beekeeper, working on his hives. The sun was bright and the maples blazed scarlet and gold on the slopes. The oaks were waiting for cold weather before donning their autumn finery. There was smoke floating in the sky southward where the railroad ran, and birds wheeling in the western sky beyond the Abbey gate. It was a good day and he worked.

The Abbot received him in his study. There were letters stacked on the refectory table. The administrative detail of the Abbey was not light. "Sit down, Anselm," he said.

Brother Anselm sat on the edge of the visitor's chair. It did not seem right, even under command, to sit in the presence of the Abbot. The older man's soft gray eyes asked a question. Anselm felt his muscles tightening.

"My son had a problem," he said. "I presumed in my ignorance to advise him."

The Abbot smiled. "Be at ease, Anselm," he said. "Relax. This is your home. Did your son ask your advice?"

"Yes, Father."

"Then it was hardly presumption to give it."

"We were in the garden. I did not ask in prayer what I should tell him. I turned away from Our Lady when she would have put the right thought in my mind. I walked in pride. My advice to him was wrong."

"Pride?" The Abbot nodded slowly. "You walked with the many, Anselm. Pride is the sin of angels, the first sin of humans. The cure for it is to name it and acknowledge it, as you have done, because that calls for humility. In what way was your advice wrong?"

Brother Anselm forgot that this was the Abbot, a wise and holy man of whom he stood in awe. This was an elder monk, someone like St. Placidus to whom he could talk freely. He poured forth the story that Bart had told him, of a baby born while he was in Japan to a woman who would not marry him.

"I advised him," Anselm said in conclusion, "that he must see this girl and demand the truth."

The Abbot leaned back in his chair. "And now you have come to the conclusion that your advice was wrong. Why?"

"The girl is married. He must not hurt her marriage. Marriage is sacred."

"And the child?"

"He does not know if it lived. She said that it died. If it lived, it might have been adopted. Or it might be in an orphan home. I forgot my own experience when I advised him. He is a single man. He could not raise a child or care for it."

"And what would you advise him now, Anselm?"

"I would advise him to think of this girl's marriage and not to be the cause of trouble with her husband. I would advise him to stay away from the child unless he could be sure that he could do more for it than is being done. It is even better not to know than to know and to be helpless."

Some of an all but forgotten desperation thickened his voice. The Abbot looked down at the table top. "Is the girl a Catholic?" he said.

Anselm stared at him. In all of his thinking, that question had not suggested itself. "I do not know," he said.

"It may be the heart of the problem. If this boy has a child, its spiritual welfare is his concern, no matter how helpless he may be in temporal matters. He is responsible for the child and for the child's baptism."

"If she will not tell him?"

"He must use his ingenuity if his powers of persuasion fail him. I agree with you that he must use the utmost discretion as far as this girl's marriage is concerned. What did you have in mind, Anselm, apart from acknowledging your error of pride?"

Anselm lifted his head. "I would like to go to him, Father, to talk to him again as I have talked to you."

"Where is he?"

"I do not know. New York, I think."

"How would you find him?"

"His mother would know where he is. He may be with her."

The Abbot's eyes were no longer soft; they probed. "Anselm," he said, "is this a worldly desire?"

Anselm's eyes were steady. He was without doubt. "No, Father," he said.

The Abbot nodded. He leaned back in his chair and sat for a long two minutes, the tips of his fingers joined, his eyes raised to the crucifix on the wall.

"It may be, Anselm," he said slowly, "that this is a debt

that you owe in the world. The matter of the child's baptism is a grave concern to me. A soul may be seeking our aid. We cannot ignore so serious a matter when we have been made aware of it. I will see you again after the evening meal. Go now in peace."

Brother Anselm went back to his work at the guesthouse. He had not thought of the child as a soul and it was frightening to him that he had not. He had assured his own son's baptism but beyond that he had done nothing for him. Father Abbot had accepted him on probation, as an oblate, recognizing his past failure and the inability of such as he was to influence a son whom he did not even know. On that day, ten years ago, Father Abbot had said to him:

"You can touch your son's life with prayer, if in no other way. Live your responsibility to your family here, since that is your decision and since, manifestly, normal family life is no longer possible for you and the woman you married. Live it well, trusting in God."

At the Abbot's request, he had given him Dora's stage name and the name of a theatre, which was the only address he had. The Abbot said that he would write to her, so there was no doubt that he had done so. If he ever received a reply, he did not mention it. Anselm had never heard from Dora himself.

He had lived that life of prayer and he had been aware of his son as a soul, of Dora as a soul. It was strange that he had no awareness of a soul in this other, this child who would be his grandchild. The screen he was removing trembled in his hands. His son's problem was suddenly clear, not only to his mind but to the emotions that had been so long under control. That child, his son's child, his grandchild, could not be lost, abandoned, unknown. He raised his eyes to the blue and the white of the sky.

"Blessed Lady, help us," he prayed.

The day rolled over him. He came again to the Abbot's study in the evening. Father Abbot had a number of papers and memos under his hand.

"I have talked to one of our friends in New York who made inquiries for us," he said. "He informs me that Dorinda Daly is in Boston with a theatrical production.

She will return to New York next week. He was unable to tell me anything of your son. It might be prudent to wait until she returns to New York. Do you feel that you should go to Boston?"

"Yes, Father."

"Why?"

"Because of my advice, my son may not think about the importance of the girl's marriage."

"And if he is not with his mother?"

"I will tell her what I would tell him."

The Abbot studied him quietly and Brother Anselm met his eyes. Father Abbot picked up two envelopes. "The train leaves our station at seven twenty-six tomorrow morning, Anselm," he said. "It will arrive in Rochester at nine-eight and another train will leave there at 11 A.M. You will arrive in Boston at 8 P.M. Here are your tickets and sufficient money for your needs. I have instructed Brother Macarius to procure clothing for you. You will go to him in the morning."

Brother Anselm accepted the two envelopes. He had forgotten about money. It had not entered into his plans, nor had he considered for an instant that he would need it. He had been long away from such necessities. The full impact of his decision reached him then.

He was going back to the world, and he was afraid.

## CHAPTER 2

There was an envelope in Bart McBride's box when he came down to breakfast. It had been addressed to him in care of the ball club, forwarded to Dorinda's apartment, which was the only address he had, then reforwarded. He studied the feminine script in which "Algonquin Hotel" was written. Mary Norbert, undoubtedly, had written that. It was odd that he did not know her handwriting, had never had a letter from her.

He opened the envelope. There was a hundred-dollar check enclosed and a note that read: "Thanks, pal. Good luck. Lefty."

It was money out of the sky, found money. He had loaned money in the Army and in other places he had been, never expecting to see it again once he surrendered it, and usually correct in his negative expectations. He did not recall exactly when he had loaned this money to Lefty, or why, but he had a vague impression that it had been in Colorado Springs or Pueblo one night in August. Lefty was a tall, rangy pitcher named Hollen who came from a small town in Arkansas. He could throw a baseball through a brick wall but his control was only fair, and he usually tired after five or six innings. He probably wouldn't go any higher than the Western League, either. Bart, holding his check, had a warm feeling of kinship for Lefty Hollen. They had shared some tense moments together.

He walked out into the warm sunlight after breakfast with the vague idea of shopping for something that he could not afford, something in the luxury line that didn't cost more than a hundred dollars. The high temperatures were holding and the sky was clear. This October was one of Summer's children cast in a winter role and not up to it. There wasn't a topcoat in sight.

A man could buy records or books that he would not ordinarily buy, or a gun or fishing gear. Bart wandered in and out of record shops, bookstores, sporting goods houses. All of the luxuries that seemed desirable, and that were desirable, belonged to men who lived somewhere and who had some place to put them. He had disposed of all his Cornell possessions when he went into the Army, except for the contents of one trunk. His acquired possessions from the Army and Western League did not quite fill another trunk. The two trunks were in storage. He had three suitcases which held his wardrobe. There wasn't a whole lot of point to shopping.

He walked Fifth Avenue, and then Fifty-seventh Street, looking at window displays. He wanted to buy a present for Dore, and he had been capable of doing that once, but he was no longer tuned in to her needs, wants, or enthusiasms. She was somebody now who had so many personal possessions that the thrill of buying for her was gone. She did not need anything that he could buy for her.

He had bought her many presents in the course of the years, for birthdays and Christmas, and various occasions. For some reason one inconsequential present stood out in his memory. It was when he was eight or nine, in Minneapolis. He had run errands for a crusty old stage doorman all week and the man gave him fifty cents. He had felt important and wealthy and he had walked boldly into a department store while Dore was on stage for the matinee. A comb with bright stones in it attracted him. It was designed to be worn in a woman's hair and not merely to be used for combing it. He had never seen Dore wear such a comb, so he assumed that she must need one. He bought it.

When he gave it to Dore after the performance, she had stared at it for a long minute, then looked at him. There were tears in her eyes and she hugged him hard. That night in their room, she demonstrated his comb for him, sweeping her hair one way and then another before the mirror, wearing the comb a dozen different ways and changing her expression each time so that she looked like a number of different people. She never wore the comb on the stage or anywhere else, and he got the idea, eventually, that it wasn't a very good present; but that night it was wonderful and he never forgot it.

Dore hadn't changed as much as he had. She would be as happy today over a wrong present as over a right one, but he was no longer a daring buyer.

He was tempted several times by telephone pay stations that he passed. The simple, logical, desirable thing would be to phone Mary Norbert. With Dore in Boston, Mary might be free to take a few hours. It would be fun shopping with her and she would be a big help with the problem of what to buy for Dore. Pride checked the impulse with a firm hand. She hadn't left a single door open to him the last time he saw her.

He walked Madison Avenue, still shopping. There were a number of shops specializing in unusual gadgets, gimmicks, and folderols for women, but they were risky things for a man to buy alone unless he had clues to follow. He looked at the displays in several antique shops. There were things that a man would enjoy owning if he had a place where he could fit them in. He saw a pair of book ends, brass figures of Harlequin and Columbine. He stood before the window with his hands in his pockets and he wanted them. He had a few books that he particularly loved. They were in his trunks. He could imagine them between the book ends. There had been other books, many others, that he had given away. He would repurchase some of those if he had a permanent, or semipermanent, base somewhere. There were books, too, that he would like to own, that he had never owned.

He jingled change in his pocket, and he looked at the book ends, then he turned away. If he stayed in baseball, he might be out in the West again, or shipped to some league in the South or the East. He thought of Alex Waringly and the tentative offer of a job. If anything came of that, he might live in New York, or in any one of a dozen other cities in which there were Waringly plants and subsidiaries. He would at least live somewhere and not merely exist in motion.

The sun had followed its own routine through the hours while he was listening to records, looking at books, gazing into windows. Now the sun had completed its day in New York and it was heading west. It would linger in Wichita, Omaha, Des Moines, Sioux City, Lincoln, Pueblo, Colorado Springs, and Denver—all the cities of the Western League that he had known. He could close his eyes and see, vividly, any one of those ball parks, remembering scores of dramatic or humorous incidents that had occurred in them. He could see the downtown sections of the towns, and the hotels, and the hotel rooms. The sun would be shining for a couple of hours all over the West. If he could travel west with the sun, he would have as little to do in the lesser towns as he had in New York.

"To hell with it!" he said.

He put pride out of his life and strode out for Park Avenue. He was concerned suddenly lest he be too late, lest Mary Norbert be gone. He swung into the quiet lobby, past the doorman in the red-wine uniform, and rode up in the elevator. He paused outside the door of Dore's apartment and he could hear the clicking of typewriter keys. He rang the bell.

There was a long pause, and Carter Brill opened the door. Carter Brill looked startled, then he laughed. "If I may read expressions," he said, "you've just seen the devil."

"Not that bad!"

There was a moment when dislike of Carter Brill flared up in Bart McBride, resentment that the man was at home in this apartment. He faced it, swept it aside, and put it behind him.

"I'll admit," he said, "that I wasn't anticipating you."

"I don't look much like the little Norbert. Come in, won't you?"

"Not if you're busy."

"I need a break."

Bart walked into the autumn room. There were papers scattered across the top of Mary's desk, a sheet of paper in the typewriter. Carter Brill was in his shirt sleeves, without a necktie. "Mary had a date," he said. "I had work to do, so I did it here. I've been baby-sitting with her telephone. It cries and I answer."

"Can you work that way?"

"Practically uninterrupted. The only thing that disturbs me is silence, the country brand of silence where a cricket sounds like a Diesel truck."

Carter Brill was seated behind the typewriter again and Bart was seated under his own picture. It was the first time that Bart had been alone with Carter Brill. There was a strangeness, a lack of ease between them.

"I spent the weekend with some friends in Connecticut," he said. "They are great admirers of yours."

Carter Brill kissed his fingers. "Discerning people!" he said. "May their tribe increase!" He reached for a cigarette. "Connecticut, you say? Oh yes. Your telegram to Dorinda came from there."

Bart leaned forward. "You were in Boston? How was the opening?"

"Splendid. For Boston."

Carter Brill sat, relaxed, and talked about *The Seventh Wife*. Bart found it easy to relax with him. Once he was

met halfway, there was a friendliness in Carter that made
even a solo passage, such as his description of the opening,
seem like a conversation. He was a pale man in his middle
forties who normally created an impression of softness or
flabbiness, but there was vitality in him when he spoke,
and a rather compelling force in his gestures. His voice
softened when he mentioned Dore.

"She's carrying the show," he said, "but she isn't starring
in it—yet."

"What do you mean?"

"Nobody else in the world would do it. Rico Moreno
was afraid of a Broadway show. If he stayed frightened,
this one would be a bust, no matter what Dorinda did. So
she has let him run away with it. He isn't afraid any more.
He thinks he invented musical comedy."

"She can't afford to let him run away with it."

"She knows that. She has merely given him a head
start."

"Can she get back in command?"

Carter Brill looked worried. "Time will tell. It's hell's
own tough job. When a performance starts flowing strongly a certain way, it's like water flowing downhill."

He digressed into a discussion of performance, of the
rhythm of shows, the intangibles that establish, or change,
the balance of a production. Watching him, and listening
to him, Bart had the conviction that Carter was talking the
generalities of show business rather than the specifics of
Dore because he was concerned about her, and because
Dore was an emotional subject as far as he was concerned.
In the middle of a sentence Carter stopped suddenly, snap-
ping his fingers.

"I seem to have forgotten that you are not a typewriter," he said. "I shouldn't hammer you with words this
way."

"I've been enjoying it."

Carter smiled. His smile lifted one side of his mouth.
"It's folly to encourage me," he said. "I'm liable to take
out on you the frustration of my many conversations with
actors, in which I never opened my mouth." He looked
swiftly at his watch. "How about having dinner with me?"

The evening stretched emptily before Bart McBride. The

emptiness would be particularly stark if he had to think about Mary Norbert's date which took her away from the office early.

"I'd like that," he said, "but I've got to level with you first, so I won't have the feeling that I exploited an opportunity. I'm committed to asking you a favor."

Carter's eyes lighted with interest. "Name it."

"I am the only one committed. You're not. So I'll ask it. If you refuse, we'll go to dinner anyway and forget it."

"Fair enough."

"Somebody I know, Roger Vannin, has written a play. He'd like your opinion on it."

Carter Brill grimaced. "Now *I'll* level with *you*. Normally, I would rather drink ink. But I've only had a few words to write this afternoon and they've been tougher than writing a second act. Reading somebody's play might be a relief."

"It's something that I haven't any right to ask."

"You can ask anything. I could say no if I wanted to say it, and I would. The play might even be good. If it is, I'll feel like God's society editor. Where is it?"

"In my room at the Algonquin."

"Suppose you grab a cab and get it. I'll author two or three more words, then I'll break out some ice for us. We'll read this latter-day *Hamlet* and still get a reasonably early dinner. Okay?"

"Right. And thanks."

Bart went out and he was mildly astonished at how easy it had been to ask a favor of Carter Brill. It was even easier to like the man and to look forward to an evening of his company. That was something that he had not anticipated. It forced him to look at facts or run away from them. He preferred to look at them.

Carter Brill was Dore's kind of person. He spoke the language of her world. There was an inherent decency in him, and subtle intuitions, and understanding. He did not create awkward situations for other people. All of that was good, and Dore needed that. She could not live in a vacuum, nor thrive in loneliness, nor be what she was without someone to lean on, someone to trust. Whatever her relationship to Carter, it was necessary to the being she had become, and she could not go back. If she had married Carter Brill, the marriage would be no more acceptable to the Catholicism of her husband and her son than was the indefinable relationship that existed now. Bart shook his head.

There wasn't any answer that he could supply, and he did not feel called upon for an answer. It was beyond him and out of his experience. Feeling as he felt now, his earlier attitude of antagonism seemed childish—and yet he knew that there was an instinctive antagonism within him still, something that had to be controlled. There was no explaining it or reasoning with it; it just was. He was glad, however, that he had this opportunity to know Carter Brill. Liking a man for himself was always a net gain over not liking him. He had to leave it at that. He thought of Dore. She was the one he had to think about, not Carter Brill.

"There's nothing that I can do for her now," he thought. "Nothing at all. And God knows I want her to be happy. She shouldn't always have to swim upstream."

His own world closed in upon him again when he entered the hotel. He picked up his key at the desk and there was a telephone memo for him: "Please call Mr. Alexander Waringly."

He rode upstairs and picked up Roger's play. He stood for a moment, frowning at the telephone. The call from Alex might be the knuckles of Destiny knocking on his door. He shrugged his shoulders. He was not in a mood for Destiny.

The door to Dore's apartment was open when he returned and Carter was in the spring room. There were two decanters on a tray, a small silver bucket of ice, water in a pitcher, and two glasses. Carter poured two drinks, accepted the playscript, weighed it in his hand, then crossed the room to Dore's cabinet phonograph.

"I read to music," he said. "I hope you don't mind."

"I'm glad that you do."

"I've got Beethoven's C sharp minor quartet on here. To me, it's the greatest thing a mortal man ever wrote in any medium," Carter Brill said. "It will keep my critical faculties humble."

He sat in a big chair under a floor lamp. He wore glasses for reading and he looked older under the direct light. He turned the title page of the manuscript. The music of the strings made a gentle entrance into the room.

Bart McBride sat motionless. The music was sufficient in itself to fill this hour of his life. He did not know what it was saying, but all of his faculties listened. He thought, briefly, of Dore, whose room this was, of Mary Norbert, who was somewhere with someone, of his father and the quiet of the cloister garden. His thoughts of people would not crystallize. The music rode out into some realm beyond the world of flesh, so far beyond it that it renounced itself. He was aware of it as a presence in the room, but not of its parts. It was not melody or song, nor fugue, nor scherzo, nothing that, at any moment, could be named and thus imprisoned within a word or a definition; he experienced it.

The smooth-walled cylinder of his dreams imprisoned him momentarily in desperation, then the wall dissolved into a long stone corridor under arches. He walked soundlessly over the stones, and the distance did not diminish. Time did not exist. He had the feeling that he was on the verge of a great discovery, that the answer to life was almost within reach, then, suddenly, the music ceased its flow and the corridor vanished. He came back to the room slowly. Carter Brill gestured to him without looking up and Bart walked over to the phonograph. He turned the record on the turntable.

The music resumed, presto, and he was aware of two violins, a cello, and a viola. The spell was broken. Something was gone, something that had been his, and he could not find it again. He was in a room with Carter Brill, who was reading Roger's play. Carter read poker-faced, guarding his verdict. Bart wondered if the play was good, and if the lives of Roger and Aleta would be changed by it. He wondered if Aleta had written the letter to him, and if her letter might not change his own life more drastically than Roger's play could ever change hers.

He thought about Mary Norbert. It was a reflection of his own selfishness that he knew so little about her and about the people she liked. He had walked with her on the streets of his life, but he had not strolled, window-shopped, or explored on the streets of hers. It stood to reason that anyone so strikingly lovely, so magnetically attractive, would be a target for men, and that anyone so feminine would enjoy the role of target. Men would seek her and she would be flattered by the seeking. Why not?

The green flags of jealousy waved in the music that swept through the room. He recognized them for what they were, but he could not haul them down. He wanted Mary to be attractive yet not to attract, to be feminine yet not be the companion of men, to be challenging and not challenge anyone but himself. She was sharing something with someone tonight and he could not stand the thought. It was absurd and indefensible, like the latent hostility to Carter Brill, but it was there inside of him, and he had to struggle with it.

Like a disembodied spirit from another world, the music vanished. It was present, then it was gone. Life, suspended in its presence, asserted itself once more. Carter Brill laid down the manuscript and picked up his drink. Bart looked with surprise at his own glass. The ice had melted in the drink that he had not tasted.

"I never heard that music before," he said, "nor anything like it."

"You never will hear anything like it," Carter Brill said slowly. "The man who wrote that was dying when he wrote it. He was suffering greatly. His work was bigger to him than his own suffering or his own death, and he did not weep into his work. I wish that I had watched you listening to it instead of reading."

Bart stared at him. "I would like to do something in the world that I could feel about in that way," he said, "bigger than I am, more important than my life or death."

"So would I," Carter Brill said. "So would I. But that's the way of greatness." He laid his drink down and lighted a cigarette. All of his movements were deliberate, in slow time. "Is this chap a close friend of yours?"

"No. I don't know him very well. Why?"

"For one thing, his play is no good. For another, I know him very well, after reading his play. He wouldn't be worth a damn as a friend."

Bart looked at the playscript. A man's hopes had been wrapped up in that package. Illogically or not, he had the feeling that those hopes had been entrusted to him and that they were his to defend.

"I'm sorry that I didn't read the play myself," he said. "I don't know anything about it, but Roger is an admirer of yours. He would like to write like you."

"We are not amused," Carter quoted. He leaned forward. "When a young playwright writes a play, the leading character is usually himself. That's all right. It's expected. This young man is steeped in pity for himself, even as a character in a comedy of manners. That won't do. He doesn't think straight or write straight. Forget him."

Bart thought of Roger as he had been at their first meeting, and as he had been when he left him last night, sodden and unconscious. There wasn't much that he could say about him.

"He married the wrong woman," he said.

Carter Brill was watching him, smoking quietly. "Any woman would be the wrong woman," he said. "Believe me! The man is all there, in his play."

He rose abruptly. "You take responsibilities too seriously," he said. "Let someone else tote that bale. I'll write this Roger a charming letter in the morning and the little Norbert will mail his book back to him. Axes have fallen more rudely on better men."

He snapped out the light above his chair. Bart went out with him and Carter Brill suggested a Belgian restaurant in the East Fifties. Bart tried to forget Roger Vannin. As they walked across town, he told Carter about the hundred dollars and the fruitless shopping tour.

"I still have all of it," he said, "so I'm buying the dinner."

Carter laughed softly. "I never heard a better argument against my picking up a check," he said, "so I'll concede to you if you'll explain how getting your own money back is finding money."

"Do you know any ballplayers?"

"Sorry. No. I know a lot of actors. Will they do?"

"I don't know. My own specialty is ballplayers. The hundred dollars that came back is still miracle money to me and I've got to buy something with it."

"Okay. Take it away," Carter Brill said.

They dined in leisurely fashion, which was the only way that the restaurant permitted one to dine. For some reason of his own, Carter Brill seemed to be keeping a careful check of time. He glanced frequently at his watch. He reached a decision with the coffee.

"You hear a lot about the cutthroat jungle of show business," he said, "and anything you hear along that line is apt to be true. But there are a few human beings mixed in with the jackals, wart hogs, and boa constrictors. Did you ever hear of Maude Rariden?"

Bart concentrated. "The name rings a faint bell. I've heard of Brian Rariden, of course."

"Maude is his widow. Brian was the great romantic interest in the days of Viennese operettas, Victor Herbert cream puffs, and other stylish schmaltz. He made a lot of money and kept some of it. Maude still has the house in the East Eighties, with the top-floor stage. She is one of the human beings. She gives unemployed talent an opportunity to express itself. Every Tuesday there is a review of sorts on that stage. Almost anyone is likely to turn up in the audience. Kids have walked out of the Rariden house into jobs. The list of Maude's successful protégés is long. Many of them contribute to the fund that keeps her in operation."

Carter paused and Bart waited for the point to develop. "That is where the little Norbert is tonight," Carter said.

He timed and delivered the line with an actor's guile. Bart was caught off balance. "What?" he said.

Carter glanced again at his watch. "She has the star turn," he said, "so she will go on late. I promised that I would look in, but I think that it would be more interesting if you did."

"Why?"

"You came around to the apartment looking for her, didn't you? What's the matter with finding her in a more interesting spot?"

"I couldn't do anything for anybody with talent. You could."

"I wouldn't do anything for any of them. I'm not casting. I was only going to catch the one act, and I wouldn't be interested in doing anything about any talent that Mary Norbert might have."

"Why not?"

"I would hate to reach the point of liking her talent better than I liked her."

"It wouldn't necessarily follow."

"It necessarily does, unfortunately."

Bart studied him across the table. He wondered how Carter Brill reconciled that statement with his obvious feeling for Dore. The answer followed on the heels of the question. Carter Brill would not have liked Dore when she was merely a talent on the way to Broadway. He would have nothing at all in common with the Dorinda Daly that Bart knew best. Carter Brill met the mature artist in the years of his own maturity when they had much to offer each other. The solution of a mystery was there for a philosopher to unravel. Bart was not that philosopher and he knew it. He brushed thought away with one broad hand.

"I don't belong at this thing," he said. "They would throw me out."

Carter Brill was amused. "Actors! I don't believe that a whole team of them would be capable of throwing you out."

"Maybe not. So, perhaps, it wouldn't be fair to put them in a spot where they might feel that they had to try."

"Actors don't feel anything; they merely strive to please. They will not notice you; they will be absorbed in being noticed. Maude, who believes in everything unbelievable, will suspect you of being an angel in disguise. And the little Norbert will be surprised."

Bart considered that. "Why can't we both go?" he said.

Carter shook his head. "With me along, you would merely have an experience; without me you will have an adventure."

He rose and as they walked out between the tables Bart knew that he would go to Maude Rariden's to watch Mary Norbert perform, that Carter Brill was very right about it. He had enjoyed the older man's company, but Carter was still an older man. Bart had felt maneuvered and led, skillfully but surely. He had been less than himself. Among his own contemporaries, it would be different. His shoulders straightened.

They stood for a minute before the restaurant. Carter lighted another of his interminable, unending cigarettes. "This has been a great evening," he said. "I feel that I know you. I don't know what you are going to do with your life. I would be politely bored if you tried to tell me. But it must be something idealistic. By all means, idealistic." He laughed a little self-consciously and flipped the freshly lighted cigarette away.

"Like teaching French to the poor, starving Navajos," he said. "Something of that sort."

A cab pulled up to the curb and Carter waved his hand. "Yours," he said. "You race time. My best to Mary."

As he settled back into the cab, Bart wondered if Carter Brill had been making fun of him. The surface value of his words made it seem so, but Bart did not believe it. The man had given him liking, or more than that. Carter Brill, after that slow, groping start, had treated him as though he were his own son.

## CHAPTER 3

The Brian Rariden house belonged to the brownstone-stoop era when kitchens and dining rooms were on ground level, entry halls, parlors, libraries were one floor up, bedrooms on the floor above that. Extra floors provided servant quarters and whatever else an owner might feel that he needed. Brian Rariden had needed a stage and a private theatre.

Carter Brill said that no one answered doorbells on Tuesday night. "Walk in and climb stairs till you reach the racket," he said.

Bart McBride felt like a burglar climbing the stairs, but he did it. The light was dim until he climbed the last flight. He saw light ahead of him then and he heard laughter.

He stumbled two steps from the top and the sound made by his slipping foot echoed appallingly down the stair well.

One of the tiniest women he had ever seen stepped through the partly open sliding doors into the hall. She was no more than five feet tall and exquisitely slender. Her round Irish face was framed in a soft cloud of white hair. Bart straightened to his full height as he regained his balance. She stood with her hands on her hips, looking up at him.

"You seem to be sober," she said. "Who are you? St. Christopher?"

Bart grinned. This had to be Maude Rariden. "Yes," he said. "Want to see my medals?"

"Never mind. I've seen them. Last time I saw you, you were in a church in Venice and you were thirty-five feet tall."

"I know. This climate doesn't agree with me."

Shrewd blue eyes had been measuring him. Now they twinkled. "You're probably a traffic cop, you damned liar," she said, "but come in and keep quiet!"

She led the way through the sliding doors. The room was dark except for a lighted stage at the far end. There were mortuary-parlor chairs arranged in a rough semblance of order. Bart sat in one of them and concentrated on the stage. A whirling couple completed a dance turn; then a short man in tattered clothing walked out and announced solemnly that he was not a Korean, and never had been.

> *"We hear much of such* [he said],
> *Much ado about much*
> *Of people who are occupied.*
> *And the great dark horses*
> *Of occupation forces*
> *That are trampling over each hide.*
> *So, for something new, to do,*
> *We give to you*
> *Not horses, but discourses.*
> *Our trouble is, you see*
> *Ex-plicit-ly*
> *We are the unoccupied.*

*Nobody occupies us, nobody sympathizes,*
*With or without tea.*
These are our lives.
*We give you*—The Flea House and the Greasy
Spoon."

The curtain went up to laughter and the laughter continued as five people moved into a psuedo-dramatic scene
in which the dialogue was fast-paced patter. Bart, who had
not seen *The Teahouse of the August Moon,* which was
being parodied, missed much of the humor that brought
laughter from the audience. He spent the first few minutes of the sketch looking for Mary Norbert, or expecting
her momentary entrance. After he conceded the fact that
this was not her act, his interest was mild.

The curtain came down to enthusiastic applause and
the performers took bows; then a heavy-set man in a
rumpled suit shuffled out on the stage.

"We don't offer much," he said apologetically. "Merely
a preview of something that hasn't happened yet. Maybe
it won't happen like this. Then, where are we? If, should
be, it happens next week, you will remember that these
artists were good prophets. Better you should remember
that these artists were artists. I give to you—Norbert and
Turillo in *The Lady and the Tenor."*

The good-natured kidding from the audience indicated
that the stout man was well known and liked. He seated
himself at a concert grand that was angled to the stage. A
spot centered on him and he played the introduction to the
*Pagliacci* prologue. A dramatically dark young man in an
opera cape and a flop-brimmed black hat stepped out before the footlights and bowed, right, left, and center, in
exaggerated opera fashion. He swept his hat low.

*"Signore! Signori!"* he said.

He held the bow for a solemn moment, then turned and
bowed to the wings as a girl in a strapless blue evening
dress walked out. She had her hair swept back and it gave
golden reflections to the light. There was an expression of
mingled delight and surprise on her face. She wiggled her
fingers at the audience in acknowledgment of the applause

and looked at the young man, her head on one side, her hands clasping slowly, chest high.

She was Broadway meeting the Met. She was more than that. In timing, in expression, in gesture, she was Dorinda Daly.

Bart sat forward in his chair, unbelieving. She had warned him that she did impersonations, but this couldn't be! The man at the piano played. The music was different now. The young man sang.

> *"La donna è mobile*
> *Qual piuma al vento . . ."*

He did not sing it as the Duke's aria, he sang it as though it were a love song. Mary Norbert retreated and he pursued. He had a fine tenor voice and he sang with great intensity. He took her hand.

> *"Muta d'accento,*
> *E di pensiero . . ."*

He got the *dolce* into it, and when he let his voice out, it soared.

He sang *"Bella figlia dell' amore"* and then Mary came in under his voice, singing "la la la la." They sang together and it was a love duet even though she was not singing words. Her voice was clear and true, and there was an emotional quality in it, a quality like Dore's.

Frank Turillo came down from the top of his range and then she was singing to him. She was Dore, then, Dore in *Buffalo Nickel*.

> *"I want nothing that you won't bring,*
> *No hours, no flowers,*
> *No anything."*

He sang under her voice and she took the well-remembered refrain alone:

> *"This day, this hour, this moment,*
> *This mad delight,*

*This dizzy height,*
*This loving you."*

Her voice was sweet and wistful, as true as a tuning
fork. As the man sang with her again, she was interpreting
the lyrics for the audience, sending each word out to be
understood, emphasizing a word or a syllable as Dore did,
yielding no beauty in the bigger voice, complementing it,
fulfilling it. They reached the finale with the tenor singing
the *Rigoletto* music and Mary singing *Buffalo Nickel*. The
audience erupted in applause when they blended their
voices for the last time and bowed. Doc Epstein at the
piano shared the bow, beaming. Somebody called out
"More!" The man at the piano shook his head.

"Right now they are good," he said softly. "In five
minutes, who knows?"

Bart McBride sat dazed. He had just seen, and heard,
something extraordinarily good. The magic of make-up
and mime had enabled Mary Norbert, a pretty girl, to
look very like Dore, who had never been pretty, and to
project, as Dore did, with a rare type of beauty. Mary had
created the illusion of Dore. Her voice was lighter and
smaller, lacking Dore's flexibility, but she had every trick
of inflection and emphasis, and Dore's purity of tone. In
duet with the first-rate tenor of Frank Turillo, she had
served her own voice and her own music well; yet, sur-
prisingly, the big voice and the big music had seemed all
the finer because of the contrast.

It might be, as Doc Epstein had implied in the introduction, a preview of what would happen when two singers
from different worlds met in *The Seventh Wife*. "La donna
è mobile," which seemed an odd choice at first, had been
artfully chosen for this presentation; the only tenor aria in
the repertoire, probably, that could have been blended
with "This Loving You." The aria problem would not
arise next Tuesday night. There were no arias in *The
Seventh Wife*.

A young man whose appearance suggested Fred Astaire
was doing a dance routine. He was obviously a regular at
Maude Rariden's and accustomed to closing shows because
he performed brightly in the face of much audience con-

versation and movement. The evening had climaxed and he was the afterpiece, but someone had to hold the people where they were while the principals removed their make-up. He was not, Bart thought, an object of pity. He was like the eager young football players who come off the bench in the last five minutes of the last quarter with the score 62 to 6. His playing might not mean anything, but he was playing.

The music faded, the dancer bowed, and the lights came on. The audience, as Carter had promised, was decidedly mixed: young men and women, an old man, two old women, and representatives of both sexes in all the ages in between. The great majority were, obviously, actors and actresses, but some of the people present might be anything. There were at least forty people, some of whom might have appeared in specialties or sketches earlier in the evening.

Mary Norbert was in the center of a congratulatory group, so Bart helped some of the younger males who were folding the chairs and stacking them against the wall. The group around Mary had been reduced to four when he decided that he had waited long enough. Maude Rariden was one of the four and she saw him before Mary did.

"You'll not be wearing that eager look for me, Christopher," she said.

"Why not? You look like somebody I could lift."

"I've been lifted and I've been put in pockets, and, God forgive me, I've got a weakness for big men, but that's neither here nor there."

She turned to Mary. There was startled surprise in Mary's face. "Christopher?" she said.

"That's his story, the brobdingnagian creature," Maude said. "St. Christopher, no less, with all the medals!"

Mary shook her head. "He lied to you, Maude. He's Othello, the Moor."

Maude Rariden raised her eyebrows. "Ah, the voice of experience from one so young! Have little to do with him, my dear. I detest men who hold pillows over the faces of girls."

Mary Norbert's mouth opened and color flowed into her face. The two women and the man, who formed the group around her, laughed. "Come away from them," Maude said. "They know each other."

Bart was left alone with Mary. He stood, looking down at her.

"So you tried to show off!" she said.

Her eyes met his. She had removed her make-up and she had left the illusion of Dore in the dressing room. She made a small, helpless gesture that was more than a little exaggerated. " 'What wouldst thou write of me, if thou shouldst praise me?' " she quoted.

Bart turned pages swiftly in his mind. " 'She that was ever fair and never proud, Had tongue at will and yet was never loud.' "

"Right play, wrong line," Mary said. "But I was right. You are Othello."

"The line was Iago's. That makes no difference. You were pretty damned wonderful tonight."

Her eyes were wide and deep. A man could drown in them. "Thank you, Bart," she said. "I would rather hear that from you than from anyone else." She looked swiftly around. "Do you suppose we could go somewhere?"

"I hoped you would."

"Did you? Well, wait a minute."

She vanished through a door to the left on the stage. Frank Turillo was holding court for a half dozen of the younger people. Most of the older members of the audience were gone. Mary returned and she was wearing a cape of deep blue velveteen. They said good night to Maude Rariden and then they were standing on the steps outside. The street was strangely silent, the traffic sounds muted and far away.

"I could take you down to see the fish market," Bart said.

"I've been missing it. Nobody ever takes me."

"On the other hand, I've never been out with you before when you weren't wearing an old sweater or something."

"I never wear old sweaters. I'm always neat, even when not elegant. I pride myself."

"I'm sure you do. Well, tonight you are gorgeous, so that changes everything. We will have to find a place that has tablecloths."

"Tablecloths will be nice. And clean dishes?"

"Clean dishes. Absolutely."

They were walking toward Fifth Avenue, which offered their best hope of a cab. Bart was aware that the last time they walked together they had not been speaking to each other. He knew that she must be aware of it too. It was not a thing to remember. Memory should be like a place that one enjoys revisiting. It should be beautiful as a garden is beautiful, or one should dig it up and replant it.

"Tired?" he said.

"Not at all. I'm exhilarated. Floating. It's a very strange sensation. Like I'm two people—and the real one has wings."

"The one I'm talking to is the imitation?"

"I'm afraid so. Something like that. Do you mind dreadfully? I'll be all together in one dull package after a while."

"Fly while you can," he said. "If you feel yourself falling, scream and I'll catch you."

He knew what she was experiencing. He had felt detached and afloat, too, after some of the big games when he played football for Cornell. It was a feeling that a professional baseball player rarely had, if ever; perhaps it was an experience reserved for amateurs to compensate them for being amateurs. He whistled shrilly for a cab that was about to pass the intersection. The girl jumped like a startled rabbit and the cab stopped.

"You sound like a locomotive," she said.

"I had to make the man know we wanted him."

He gave the driver the name of a hotel on the West Side. "I'm sorry that I'm not wearing a dinner jacket," he said. "It limits us. But this place is all right."

"I'll love it. Do you mind if I float again?"

"Float."

Mary Norbert closed her eyes and rested her head against the back cushion. Bart had the idea that she was unhappy despite the surface exuberance. He did not know what could have gone wrong with her evening, but whatever it was, he could only stand by and take his cues until he was needed. When he helped her out of the cab, she pressed his hand. "Thank you, Bart," she said.

The Frat Room was as he remembered it: a long room,

dimly lighted, with the colors of a score of colleges worked into the decorations, fraternity plaques on the walls, tables decently spaced around the dance floor, and a small combo playing hot music. Mary made a beautiful entrance. The blue gown clung to her slender figure and her skin had a creamy glow.

"This place is a bit young," he said. "Pretty collegiate. But I've never danced with you. I wanted to."

They had a table on the raised tier, against the wall, under the insigne of Alpha Phi Delta. The combo was playing "That's Amore."

"First, I will have a drink," Mary said. "A tall one that I can take slowly. After that, I will have a turkey sandwich." She looked up and repeated her order to the waiter. She looked around at the other tables.

"Did you ever bring *her* here?" she said. "Or is it fair to ask?"

"It's fair. And I didn't. I didn't know any girls in New York. Somebody always had a sister or a cousin."

"With two heads."

"Some of them. I danced a whole evening once with a girl who claimed that she only spoke Hungarian. Her cousin interpreted for her. I discovered later that she was an English major from Barnard, but I never saw her again after I discovered that." Bart grinned. "You are my first date in this hallowed spot, the first I chose."

"I'm glad."

The waiter brought their drinks and Bart tilted to her. "To Mary Norbert!" he said. "I bow low. I had no idea that you were so very good."

"Did you really believe that I was?"

"I know that you were."

"That's sweet to hear. I'm so glad that you came tonight. I needed somebody." She touched her lower lip with her teeth. "It was the best opportunity I ever had, the best thing I ever did, the best audience. I wanted to remember that part for a little while, and feel it inside of me, and walk with somebody, feeling it, and scuff my slippers on the clouds."

The music stopped and the dancers were returning to their tables. She looked at them, then looked back at Bart.

There was a film over her eyes. "You helped a lot," she said, "because I had to face it finally. I just plain missed."

He shook his head. "You're crazy. It was a terrific performance. I ought to know. I'm an authority on Dorinda Daly. Or have you forgotten that?"

"No. I remember. But you noticed that we did not do an encore."

"I wanted you to give one."

"So did other people. It would have been good for Frank. He was very angry with me. We had another number, better than the one we did, a better showcase for his voice. He sang Canio's aria and I sang the "Did You Know" number from *All the Girls*. We got tears into it, but I couldn't handle it."

"Why not?"

"I wasn't 'pro' enough. I could only be Dorinda in one mood: the light, easy one. And Doc Epstein put that together for me, and held it together, and kept me from falling out of it. We worked all afternoon but even he couldn't carry me through the other one."

Bart looked away from the anguish in her face. He had to believe her that she was not as good as he thought she was. Experience had taught him that the person doing something has a more certain instinct about performance than the spectator has. There were flashy ballplayers who made a big impression on the crowd without deceiving other ballplayers for a minute. He had grown up in show business with a real professional, but he was an amateur. He had not done, nor tried to do, the thing that he had lived with Dore.

"If it was easy to be Dorinda Daly, Bianca," he said softly, "she would have more competition."

Mary smiled at the "Bianca." "I didn't shoot that high, Bart. Nobody expected that of me. But I learned something, a desperate something, working with someone as good as Frank, under a director like Doc. I learned what Dorinda tried to tell me—that I haven't got it, that a professional has to learn a lot, but that she's born with something that can't be learned."

The film over her eyes was wet now. Bart wanted to take her in his arms and comfort her. It wasn't the place, probably not the time. He felt closer to her because he had seen her wounded. "Does it mean so much to you, Bianca?" he said.

She laughed. It was a shaky little laugh, with a slight break in it. "No," she said. "It really doesn't. It doesn't at all. That's what makes all this so silly. If I hadn't gone back and tried again, it wouldn't mean anything at all."

It did matter to her, and he knew it, but there was nothing that he could do for her. The music started again. They were playing "Stranger in Paradise." He rose and held out his hand to her.

"You'll have to wait for your sandwich," he said.

They danced. She was slim and lithe and her body had no will of its own; she followed his lead. They found their own rhythm within the pattern of the music and nobody wrote the steps for them. They did not talk and they would never compliment each other on their dancing, because the way they danced together was right and inevitable, something that could not be any other way than the way it was. "Stranger in Paradise," Bart thought, was a song to remember, to remember always. He led her back to the table and sat looking at her, and she was the most beautiful girl in the world.

"I've been all sweetness and blight, haven't I?" she said.

"You fell and skinned your knees," he said. "The iodine stings."

The waiter brought her sandwich and Bart thought that he would like to tell her what Carter Brill said. "I am not interested in any talent that Mary Norbert might have because I would not like to reach the point of caring more for her talent than I care for her." He didn't tell her that because it expressed too well what he felt himself, and the words belonged to someone else. Mary finished her sandwich and touched the tip of one finger with the tip of her tongue.

"The iodine doesn't sting any more," she said.

"What, never?"

"Hardly ever."

They moved out on the floor again and most of the dancers were younger than they, from Columbia or City College or N.Y.U. or Manhattan, or from the college of

Let's Pretend, which confers no degrees. They were let's-pretenders themselves tonight and Bart was thinking, "This is the girl I should have known in college. This is the girl with whom I should have shared all the things that are fun." They danced to the crazy beat of "Hernando's Hideaway" and he did not think any more. The rhythm built and they were two bodies answering its challenge, moving together in answer to it.

They danced the other dancers out of the room and the music into silence. Somewhere, outside, it was morning, but as they passed through the shadowed lobby of the hotel Mary touched his arm.

"Let's not go yet," she said.

He led her to a chair in the corner and there was a single torchère alight. "I haven't asked you anything about your weekend," she said, "or about anything." She paused, then dropped the line casually. "Was she as beautiful as you remembered her, Bart?"

He drew a deep breath. "We'll either talk that subject through," he said, "or we'll let it drop. If we talk it, I'll have to crack down on you."

"Go ahead and crack!"

"I prefer not."

"I want to talk it."

"All right." He concentrated, thinking hard, reaching deep within himself for the words that he wanted. "When you make it difficult for someone to discuss something with you, Bianca," he said, "you close a door. Maybe it can't ever be opened again; by you or by anyone else."

Her eyes were level, partly shadowed. "If you mean that I acted badly the other night, I know it."

"That isn't what I meant. I don't want to watch my step, or avoid certain subjects, when I talk to you. If I want to discuss something, and I discuss it honestly, I won't feel guilty about it. Another person may make me regret discussing it, but I still won't feel guilty."

"Another person, if she is a woman, may feel just as strongly about listening as you do about speaking. There are subjects that she will refuse to abide meekly. She won't feel guilty, either, in refusing, vehemently if necessary, to be your listener."

Mary's voice was soft. Her eyes did not waver. Bart frowned into the palms of his hands. It seemed to him that an irrelevancy had crept into the discussion. He had been able to see the trees clearly when this started; now there was a whole forest in the way.

"Let's take an example," he said. "A man's past is over. He can't change it. If he shares it with you, it's unreasonable to act as though he could change it. All that he can change is his willingness to discuss the past with you. You lose something if he does that. You can't gain anything."

"What about my past?"

He stiffened. "What about it?"

"Suppose I told you that I had an affair with a man, an older actor, when I was in summer stock?"

"Did you?"

"We are supposing. Would you discuss the whole matter pleasantly, and be perfectly reasonable about something that was over, something that I couldn't change?"

"Yes," he said. "Did you?"

She laughed. "I am tempted to test the strength of that yes. I won't. I'll let you off the hook. I was only supposing."

"And there wasn't anybody?"

"I won't go that far. I had heroes. I've always had heroes. I've been a little bit in love with somebody most of the time."

"But . . ."

"Show business is a rough place," she said. "You played football, didn't you?"

"You know that I did. What does that have to do with it?"

"You got roughed up, didn't you? You knew that it would be rough. You knew that people would be trying to tackle you, to knock you out. So did I. You came through it. Nobody wrecked you. Well, that's how it was. I came through too."

He stared at her and she was smiling at him, looking very small in the big chair. "In answer to that last unspoken question," she said, "it is none of your business, but there have been no affairs, not even a little one, for you to be reasonable about."

"I wouldn't have been unreasonable."

Mary Norbert nodded. "You still haven't told me about your weekend," she said.

Bert hesitated a moment, then he laughed. "All right," he said. "Maybe you do it with mirrors."

"Do what with mirrors?"

"Never mind. Breaking mirrors means seven years of bad luck. I don't want to break any."

He relaxed into his own chair and he told her about the weekend, briefing a lot of it but giving her Aleta and Roger as they were, physically and otherwise. He climaxed with his ultimatum to Aleta and shrugged. "So that's it," he said. "That's the package."

Mary sat with her elbow on her knee, her chin in the palm of her hand. "This Aleta likes to pull the wings off creatures so she can watch them writhe," she said softly. "She won't send you that letter."

Bart's fists clenched instinctively. "Yes, she will," he said grimly. "She knows that I won't spare her, that this means too much to me. I have to know. I didn't leave her an out."

"It isn't like getting a taxicab on Park Avenue, Bart. She isn't helpless. I'll make you a bet."

"Name it."

She thought a minute, looking at him gravely, then she shook her head. "No. I don't want to bet. I want you to get that letter."

The lobby clock chimed three times and they both looked up startled. Bart rose and held out his hand. "I'm sorry," he said. "You must be dead after the day you've had."

Her hand clung to his after she had regained her feet. "No," she said, "and my knees are all better and the iodine doesn't sting any more, and I'm sorry that I was unreasonable."

"You gave me a new slant on that," he said.

It was the dark hour of the night. There was a blue haze over the Hudson River and a few yellow lights on the Jersey side. They had a taxi in three minutes.

Bart held her close to him in the curve of his arm as they rode across town. They did not speak. They rode close to each other, sharing the silence as they had shared the music. When he stood in the shadows with her in front of her apartment house, she rested her hand lightly against his chest, holding him away from her. Something within him seemed to be holding him away too.

"Look, Bianca," he said huskily, "I'm falling in love with you."

It was clumsy and awkward, and he knew it, but the words tumbled out and arranged themselves that way because he couldn't think of words. Mary's eyes met his and there was tenderness in them.

"Falling?" she said.

He shook his head. "Fell."

The admission seemed to chain him to inaction instead of releasing him. The girl thrust lightly with her hand and his arms closed around her. She seemed so small, so fragile, so infinitely precious in that moment that he feared to crush her.

"When you fall, your knees get skinned," she said shakily.

"And more than that, much more . . ."

He kissed her. He kissed her as he had kissed her on the deck of the ferryboat, but with a greater, more urgent need. He was in love with her. He needed all that she was, forever. She seemed to float in his arms, then she freed her lips from his and buried her face against his shoulder.

"Be sure!" she said. "And tell me in some special place. Tomorrow night."

"I am sure."

"No. Let's wait."

He continued to hold her there, lightly against him. It did not have to be tomorrow night. He had been absurdly, incredibly slow. He loved Mary Norbert as he had never loved anybody, wanted her as he had never wanted anybody. Her voice came up to him, muffled.

"Please, Bart."

He released her slowly. There had to be magic, of course. There had to be a place that they would remember always and not merely a shabby side street and a three-step stoop. He had all of his lifetime ahead of him, all of it that mattered, and she would be part of it. The knowledge lay between them, as close as their two hearts, and it was her knowledge no less than his.

"Tomorrow," he said.

She stepped out of the circle of his arms and ran up the three steps. She turned with her key in the lock and her hair was soft around her face. There was beauty in her, and grace, and all that a man might dream of. She touched her fingertips to her lips.

"God ye good den, St. Christopher," she said.

"God ye good den, Bianca."

He watched the door close and then he turned away. He walked westward and he felt her still, like a light-footed ghost, beside him, sharing this dark street and all the streets of his life to wherever the streets might lead.

## CHAPTER 4

Brother Macarius had a workroom with a skylight, a long table, a sewing machine, and two lines on which hangers supported clothing. He was a short, broad, stoop-shouldered man with hands and arms of surprising strength, a fleshy face dominated by a hawklike nose, and nearsighted eyes that blinked constantly. Of all the monks, he was the one least appreciative of the virtues of silence. He surveyed the tall, rangy figure of Brother Anselm with his head on one side, making a clucking sound with his tongue.

"So, you are going out in the world, Brother Carpenter," he said. "It is God's grace that you are an ugly man. You will be spared many temptations. I will have my trouble with you. The Holy Abbot says that you must be suitably attired. What would be suitable, do you think?"

"I had clothing when I came here," Anselm said gruffly. "I haven't outgrown it."

Brother Macarius chuckled. "Some beggar at the gate had it long ago if one showed up with your peculiar build, as one doubtless did." He moved along one of his lines, shaking his head. "It's for the best, Carpenter. Your clothing doubtless had profane associations."

He studied two black suits on the second line. "Suitable?" he muttered. *"Vanitas vanitatum."* His hand darted out. "Here! Nothing could be more suitable. Father Leo, him that died in '48, was a big man, too, and oddly made. This suit has waited for you, Carpenter. It will protect you. The odor of sanctity is on it."

Brother Anselm accepted the black suit without comment. He accepted the black shirt, the seminarian's collar, and the straight black tie, shutting out of his mind the flow of comment that came from the tailor monk. He thought of Brother Marcarius, in normal serenity, as Brother Thimble and had a warm feeling for him; but on this difficult morning the man was a trial to bear, a living testimonial to the ancient wisdom which silenced a monk's tongue.

It was many years since Brother Anselm last wore the clothing of the world. His fingers were clumsy with buttons. The trousers that had been worn by Father Leo were wide in the waist, a trifle full in the seat. The measuring eye of Brother Macarius noted that. He fingered a fold.

"If I had time . . ." he said. "But it is a minor matter. People will think that you are a Jesuit who has lost a little weight on a retreat."

"It makes no difference what people think," Anselm said.

"In the world they think about one another, Carpenter. They have nothing else to do, saying no prayers."

Macarius was rummaging through his supply of shoes. Anselm would have walked out with the first pair that he tried on, but on that point the small monk was uncompromisingly firm.

"Vocations have been lost because feet hurt," he said. "An ill-fitting shoe is a danger to the soul." He looked up apologetically. "I do not make a pun. I spelled 'soul' correctly in my mind."

He tried still another pair of shoes over Anselm's protest. "It is of great importance, Carpenter. If such a humble man as myself, in that German monastery where-ever it was, had taken such care with the feet of Martin Luther, doubtless we would have been spared his heresy."

He made Anselm walk around in the solid, black, broad-toed shoes. When he was satisfied, he produced an assortment of black felt hats. He brought out a small suitcase, too, and tossed two extra shirts into it and some socks and handkerchiefs. His eyes twinkled with amusement when he looked at the man he had clothed.

"It is too bad that you can't turn the collar around, Brother Carpenter," he said. "You're too old for what you look like."

Brother Anselm met the mocking eyes. "Thank you, Brother Tailor," he said. "I will carve you a good cross when they bury you."

He walked down the hill to the station. There was a bus which carried the retreatants and those who had business at the Abbey, but no monk would think of taking a conveyance for a journey of one mile. He walked with his eyes front, resisting the clamoring desire to look back. He was already lonely, with a loneliness that blotted out any sense of anticipation that he might normally feel. All of the security, peace, joy, well-being, and love of his life lay behind him on the hill, within the walls, under the towering spire and the gold cross.

He felt strange and uncertain when he boarded the train, clutching the ticket tightly in his hand, not trusting it to the unfamiliar pockets. He sat stiffly in his seat beside a stout man who was reading a newspaper. He did not look at the other passengers. Their very presence, the number of them, all strangers, in such a small space, smothered him, and the sound of their voices was a vast discord which lacerated his nerves. The conductor punched his ticket and the stout man left the train at the next station. Brother Anselm sat next to the window then, saying the rosary, as the bright colors of autumn flashed by.

The trip to Rochester was short and he had to change stations. He had no impression at all of the city, merely of traffic and confusion and noise. The big station was a marvel to him. He had forgotten the excitement of human activity in a railroad station. After the first few stunned minutes on a bench, staring straight ahead, he became aware of people as people, men and women engaged in incomprehensible enterprises, hurrying about with no interest in himself or malice toward one another. He watched them fascinated. The women, particularly, interested him. He had not seen a woman in ten years and here they were a commonplace, moving singly and in clusters and in the company of men, creatures of color, of bright attire, much given to gestures and shrill speech.

His interest in women was untainted by sensuality. He no longer thought sensually and his disciplined mind had long ago closed the gates to concupiscent imagining. He no longer fought because the thing with which he once fought had been rejected, and rejected utterly, even as an opponent. The storms of desire and the revolts of the flesh were with a man through his lifetime and he knew those, periodically, but they were an assault from without, and not weakness from within. When temptation came to him, it came in the garments of the past, tempting him to relive what he had been; seldom as something of his own age and time. Sitting in the Rochester station, he looked at the world and the people in it with the innocent wonder of a child, not feeling part of it, merely looking.

He had nearly two hours between trains, but after a half hour he obeyed the nervous impulse to check the train schedule, to make certain of what he already knew. He slowed his striding pace to look at the newsstand. He had forgotten that there were so many magazines and he did not remember the little, brightly covered books. He looked at the racked cigarettes and the cards advertising them. So many of the brands were new! He had smoked cigarettes for years, alternating from Camels to Lucky Strikes to Chesterfields, aware of other brands but rarely smoking them. There were brand names now that were completely foreign to him, names that were not even in the dimly remembered list of those he had not smoked. Coca-Cola was advertised as it had always been. Its very familiarity gave it a special allure. He fingered coins in his pocket. The Abbot had been generous. He could buy a Coca-Cola. He could have the coffee, which sent fragrance to his nostrils. His fingers tightened on the coins, then relaxed.

"For your needs," Father Abbot had said.

A monk did not need luxuries, nor anything more in these surroundings than the food that was ample for his sustenance in the monastery. The money was not his. He smiled, thinking of whose it was, whose clothing he wore. Everything in the Abbey was "ours" and no man said "mine." It was a joke at first with the young brothers and the postulants, before dignity and sobriety came to them. In the inevitable jostling and roughhousing when they hurried to finish ablutions before meals, someone would be stepped on and someone else would say: "Pardon me, Brother, for stepping on our foot."

Brother Anselm could not spend "our money" in the railroad station of Rochester for "our Coca-Cola" which he would drink alone.

He returned to his bench and a new temptation assailed him. People around him were smoking and the odor of burning tobacco was a tantalizing fragrance in his nostrils. He watched other people casually inhale and exhale the thin blue smoke. He remembered how it used to be: calming and quieting, a pleasant thing to do. There was no evil in it, no Church pronouncement against it; but the life of a monk was a firm setting aside of non-essentials, a renunciation of those things which did not contribute to the greater honor and glory of God. He had not needed the solace of tobacco where a greater solace abounded, but the craving came to him now disguised as a need.

In the scales against him was a priest who walked through the station smoking a cigar. It was the priest's right to smoke it, and it was a small indulgence that did not reflect upon him in any way; he did not live monastically, and could not, while he served the Church on the parish firing line. Anselm's eyes followed him. He wondered about those new brands of cigarettes. It seemed to him that there must have been a new development in tobacco, a new taste, to justify and popularize new brands. He wondered about that theoretical new tobacco taste and he fingered the coins in his pocket again.

Two young sailors seated themselves near him. They were disappointed, or annoyed, about something and they cursed fluently, dredging up the old, foul, familiar words of oil fields and barrooms long ago. Brother Anselm glanced at them and they became aware of him as a religious. Their profanity flickered out and they rose abruptly, walking away. Anselm was neither shocked nor startled, but the self-consciousness of the young men in his presence reminded him that he was a monk, one of a long, long line that stretched back over the centuries.

His fingers released the coins and sought the rosary. He prayed five decades for the two young sailors who had walked away from him. In the peace that followed prayer, he was once more indifferent to tobacco, and its odor, and the names with which men branded and packaged it.

The train for Boston left Rochester at 11 A.M. Brother Anselm rode in the day coach and he was more at ease now. It had all come back to him in the station, the way of things in the world and the acceptance of them. He had asked for and received one of "our breviaries" and he read the daily office. His simple vows did not require him to read the office, but the prayers, which were chanted at the canonical hours, and which he read now, were part of his life: he wanted them as these men around him wanted newspapers or magazines or conversation. He sat for an interval with the black book in his lap and thought about that, and of how difficult it would be to explain. He couldn't explain it to the man he had been, or to any man such as he had been; he could not even find a place where he might start an explanation.

He startled the waiters in the diner by the austere simplicity of his meal, and he startled them again at the dinner hour. The well-filled plates of the other diners interested him but did not tempt him. He knew, with the experience of ten years, how much food was enough; more than enough was gluttony.

A group of men passed down the aisle of the coach. They were laughing when they passed his seat and the fragrance of whisky hung in the air behind them. To Brother Anselm, at the moment, it was a rare fragrance, a rich, pungent aroma out of the past that brought memories flooding in upon him.

The pleasant memories came first. He could remember the hard days on a drilling platform in the old cable-tool days when a man worked a twelve-hour tour. He would come into town too weary to sleep. The oil towns were noisy and bright, waiting for him. He could remember gallon jugs of corn liquor and the harsh, hot bite of it that brought life and power back into a man's muscles, banishing the weariness. There was laughter, then, and jokes, and sometimes singing. There were dance halls and music. A man felt big with the labor he had performed that day and the liquor he had drunk that night.

Brother Anselm's body was wet with sweat under the clothing that Father Leo had once worn. He stared straight ahead, holding the breviary tightly in his hands. There were other memories and he faced them.

There was a time, a long time, when the joy of labor was absent because he performed no labor; when he still drank whisky, and drank without joy, because he was in slavery to it and had lost a man's right to say yes or no to it. There were rooms in which he lay helpless, and hospitals and cells in jails. He couldn't, in justice, blame whisky; the fault was his own. Still, whisky had not been a friend to him.

He remembered a sermon of Father Alberic's when he was a postulant, new to the Abbey and to the way of life that it represented. It had impressed him greatly because, although not yet a carpenter, he had worked with wood. He had never forgotten it.

Father Alberic stood before them with his cowl pushed back, his thin gray hair shining in the reflection of light, a man of bony features and intent earnestness and fiery speech.

"We are all makers of the cross," Father Alberic said. "We, each of us, through sin, fashion a cross for our Saviour to die upon. Some men, through contrition and penance, through grace and the sacraments, through faith, hope and charity, and the love of God, reduce the weight of their evil work. Other men build recklessly, remorselessly, selfishly, indulgently, viciously. They build the cross heavy and huge and rough-surfaced for another to bear."

Father Alberic paused and his eyes glowed. "Is it unjust, then, that when their work is done a Voice should say to them: 'This you have built. It is yours. Carry it'?"

The memory of Father Alberic faded. The other memories vanished as the fumes of whisky had vanished. The train was slowing and they were coming into a big station. This at last, at eight in the evening, nearly thirteen hours away from St. Urban's, was Boston.

"It may be, Anselm, that this is a debt that you owe in the world," the Abbot had said.

Brother Anselm left the train and he was afraid of that world, afraid of all that lay ahead of him, unsure of himself, a stranger in strange garments in a city he had never known.

He walked from the station to the hotel which was named on the paper that the Abbot had given him. He had to ask directions three times, and when he reached the hotel, it required an effort of his will to enter it. He had never in his life had experience with large hotels and he was in awe of them.

The clerk at the desk told him, with lifted eyebrows, that of course, at this hour, Miss Dorinda Daly was at the theatre. There was no Bart McBride registered.

He walked to the theatre, without knowing quite why, and stood looking at that name in lights above the marquee. There were pictures of Dora, a Dora that he would not have recognized, and pictures of other people. There was a ticket window and, although he was late and nobody seemed to be selling tickets, he imagined that he would be able to buy a ticket and go in. He was tired and curious and he fingered "our money" in the pocket of the black suit.

It was something that, he felt, the Abbot would approve, but he stood there hesitating, and then he turned away. He walked back to the hotel and sat in the lobby, waiting. His feet were very sore and he yearned for the comfort of "our sandals." It was the only craving that he had and the world could not satisfy it. "Our sandals" were home in "our cell."

## CHAPTER 5

*The Seventh Wife* glowed and glittered, shimmered and shone, on the stage in Boston. Mary Norbert watched it in a half-comprehending daze: enjoying it, marveling at it, but unable to separate the part from the whole. If anyone, even with the credentials of a major prophet, had predicted that she would be like this while watching Dorinda's new show for the first time, she would have rejected the prophecy with scorn. Yet here she was!

Dorinda was up there, singing to Rico Moreno. Her number was one that had given her trouble; "The New Leaf You Turn May Be Mine." There was certainly nothing the matter with it tonight, nothing that Mary could detect. It was one of those light, amusing numbers with punchy lyrics that Dorinda did so well. Every word came across the lights and the music was memorable, hummable. Dorinda, in character, looked young, innocent, confused. If Rico was dominating the show, as everyone seemed to believe, Mary could not see that either.

"I won't be able to give her one constructive comment," she thought. "I'll be just like anyone from the suburbs, gurgling about how wonderful she is, without telling her how or why."

Weariness pressed her down into the theatre seat. It had been an incredibly long day. She had left Bart just before dawn and she had not wanted sleep then; she had wanted only to move among her familiar things, touching them, assuring herself that they were the same even if she was changed. She had wanted to lie awake and relive an incredible evening, all that she had done and said, every word that Bart had said. Ultimately she sank into sleep and it seemed to her that the bells of awakening met her on the way. Dorinda called, and then Carter Brill.

She had to pick up the book of *The Seventh Wife*,

which Carter had, and catch a plane, and fly to Boston.
There had been barely time to call Bart before she left.
She awakened him, too, and he hadn't made much sense.

In Boston, she had found Dorinda's affairs in a complete
and terrible mess: letters and notes unanswered, some of
them unopened, telephone calls unreturned, telegrams un-
acknowledged. Dorinda had not even kept them together.
They were wherever she had read them, or intended to
read them: in her dressing room, her bedroom, anywhere
in her suite. There were invitations to one thing or another from people who could not be ignored, notes of
congratulations and good wishes, inquiries from editors of
important magazines, other letters difficult to classify from
people who knew her well. With the New York opening
just around the corner, it was no time to offend or antago-
nize people. Mary had gone to work on the stacks, after
she had first assembled the stacks. She had worked right
through the day. Dorinda had insisted that she see the
show.

"I don't feel quite right about it," Dorinda said. "Let
me know what you think, lamb."

Mary was trying to look at it, but her eyes weren't
focusing too well. The plot, inasmuch as any musical had a
plot, was being tied in a knot. The composer-hero was
stuck with his gay bachelor role, which he had assumed
to win the backing of the oft-married playboy. The playboy's seventh wife was critical of him and his supposed
way of life, using her influence against him. All that he
had to do to please her was permit her to reform him, so
that he would be a good example to the husband whom
she had reformed and whom she intimidated. Emmet Dane,
the TV personality, playing the role of the pupil who
first advised him to hire a mistress by the day for atmosphere, now reversed his stand. The composer-hero must
get rid of her. It was very easy. "Just tell the lady she's
fired," he sang.

The song sparkled with innuendo. It was the kind of
thing that could be sung with added lyrics in night clubs,
and probably would be.

Dorinda came back then. As the model hired to act as
the hero's mistress, and already in love with him, she was

suddenly aware of the situation and convinced that she must leave. Her song was "Now or Never," one of the most melodious, most poignant numbers she had ever had in any show. It brought the curtain down to a thunder of applause. Mary Norbert sat in her seat, blinking.

"It's fabulous," she said. "There isn't anything the matter with it. There can't be."

She needed only one glimpse of Dorinda back in her dressing room, however, to know that there was something wrong, very wrong, as far as Dorinda was concerned. Dorinda seemed to have forgotten that she had ever wanted Mary's opinion. When Mary volunteered a few faltering comments, Dorinda cut her off.

"I'm working on it," she said curtly.

She was tense, sharp with her maid during the costume change, nervously intent upon her make-up. It was a time to let her alone, and everyone did. Mary made a list of the telegrams which were pasted on the dressing-table mirror and on odd surfaces around the room. There were a great many telegrams.

"I wish that I could snap out of it," she thought. "I can't be half asleep now."

She saw part of the last act from the wings. Rico had another show-stopping song in "The Something I Had for a While," then he and Dorinda had a humorous number that they did together: "But That Ain't Opera." No one who saw the sparkling Dorinda of that number would suspect that she was ever any other way. After the final bow, she came back swiftly to her dressing room.

"Get me out of this, Janet," she said savagely. As the maid unzipped her, she ran her right hand through her hair. "God!" she said.

Mary rode back to the hotel in the limousine with her and Dorinda was quiet, sitting with her head back, her eyes half closed. She spoke only once.

"I wish to hell Carter had come back with you," she said.

Mary wished that he had too. He would have known what was wrong with the show and he might even know what to do about Dorinda. It would be good to talk to him about it, although Mary felt that even talking to Carter Brill would be too much tonight. All that she wanted from life was a quick shower and a bed to which she could surrender her consciousness.

Dorinda swept regally through the hotel lobby followed by Janet, her maid, who had the key to the suite. Mary stopped at the desk for mail or messages. The clerk dropped his voice to a confidential whisper.

"Miss Norbert," he said, "there is a man waiting here in the lobby for Miss Daly. He has been here for hours."

Mary shook her head. "Impossible! She cannot be disturbed after a performance."

"I was certain of that. He is a clergyman of some sort."

"Oh!"

Mary had a premonition before she turned and saw the man in the black suit who had risen from one of the lobby chairs. She walked toward him.

"I am Mary Norbert," she said. "I am Miss Daly's secretary."

He nodded his head jerkily. He was holding a black hat in his hands. There was a small, cheap bag on the floor beside him. "I have to see her," he said. "I am Brother Anselm."

"I'm afraid that it is quite impossible. She is very tired."

Brother Anselm looked as though he might be tired, too, but he did not say so. "I must see her," he said. "I have made a long trip and I cannot stay."

Mary knew him. She could not see much of Bart in the lean, angular face, but there was something of Bart there, an indefinable something. She had been prepared for the grotesque improbability of a monk in this hotel lobby from the moment that the clerk said "a clergyman of some sort." She thought of the distance between St. Urban's Abbey and Boston.

"I wish that I could do something for you," she said. "Perhaps in the morning?"

He shook his head. "I cannot wait. If her son is here, I do not have to talk to her."

"Bart? He is in New York."

She read momentary disappointment in the man's eyes. His lips tightened. "Then I must see her."

Mary wavered. She did not want to face Dorinda with

any request tonight, much less with a "must." There was, however, a rather frightening determination in this Brother Anselm. He had a compelling, invincible right, too, if he was strong enough to exercise it. He was Dorinda's husband.

"It is about her son. Tell her that," Brother Anselm said.

Mary's shoulders straightened. "Wait right here," she said. "I'll go up and talk to her."

"Thank you."

When she turned away, relaxing the necessity for concentration, her own weariness swept over her again. She did not want to do anything or face anything. She had to drive herself and it seemed to her that she was moving in a situation of stark unreality. She and Bart had not had their special date tonight, but they had had last night. That solemn man in the black suit would be her father-in-law someday; Dorinda Daly would be her mother-in-law. That did not seem real, either, but it was real and it involved her in all that concerned them. The thought strengthened her, banished some of the fatigue.

Her heart was hammering and she moistened her lips with the tip of her tongue as she walked through the silent suite. Dorinda was lying face down in her bedroom and Janet was giving her a massage. Mary did not hesitate.

"Dorinda," she said. "I have to talk to you."

She was accustomed to using the "Dorinda" when they were alone, never in the presence of strangers, seldom when Janet was present. The voice that had charmed a packed theatre tonight came muffled from the pillow. "Go to bed!"

"I've got to talk to you. Alone!"

Dorinda turned with a cat's speed, and with much of a cat's fury. "What do you mean?"

"I mean that I have to talk to you alone."

Their eyes dueled. Dorinda sat straight and pulled the big beach towel across her body. "Leave us, Janet," she said, "but be ready when I call you back."

Her eyes followed the maid, who left precipitately, then came coldly back to Mary. "This had better be good," she said.

Mary had her own instinct for timing. "Your husband is downstairs, Dorinda," she said quietly.

Dorinda's eyes widened with horror. She stared at Mary and she breathed in through her partly open mouth. She seemed to collapse from deep inside, her body falling in upon nothing. "My God, no!" she said. "I can't! It can't be. Not now. Send him away!"

"He has made a long trip to see you. He has to go right back."

"I didn't ask him to make a long trip. I didn't ask him for anything. I won't see him."

"He says that you must, that it is about Bart."

"Bart!" Dorinda's body lunged forward. The towel fell away from her small, firm breasts and she did not notice. "Bart hasn't come to the show. Not in New Haven. Not here. He isn't—he can't be! Mary, he isn't going to make a priest out of him?"

Mary smiled and shook her head. She was suddenly strong and sure, above weariness. Dorinda was afraid and vulnerable now as she, herself, had so often been. Her voice was gentle.

"No," she said. "It isn't that. But you must see him, Dorinda."

Dorinda closed her eyes. Her fists clenched. "I can't. I'm tired. I'm all shot. I've got nothing to give. Nobody knows what it's like out there. This damned show!"

Mary waited quietly. Dorinda ran her hands through her hair, then stopped suddenly. "How do you know that he's my husband?"

"His name is Brother Anselm."

Dorinda's long fingers gripped the towel, loosened, tightened again. "God!" she said. "Why must this happen? I thought that he had to stay in that place."

She fixed her wide eyes on Mary's face. "He isn't wearing some kind of Norman Bel Geddes outfit, is he? A hair shirt? Or that something over his head?"

"No. He looks like a priest except that he isn't wearing a Roman collar."

"God! That's bad enough. I can't see him. I won't. I couldn't talk to him."

Mary bent over her and took her hand. "He's tired too,

Dorinda," she said softly. "You can tell, just looking at him. And this is important to him. It may be important to you, too, and to Bart."

Dorinda returned the grip of her fingers, held her hand for a moment, then released it suddenly. "All right," she said. "Bring him up. I've been a coward. I still am. I'll be ready for him."

She rose swiftly, the towel dropping unnoticed to the floor. She had a straight, hard, conditioned body, such a body as few women have even in their twenties. Mary wanted to say: "This is a monk, not Carter Brill. Don't shock him." There was irony in the thought, and grim humor. After all, the man was Dorinda's husband, the only husband she had ever had.

"I'll be right back with him," Mary said.

Brother Anselm was waiting patiently and he rose when he saw her. She nodded to him and he picked up the suitcase. The elevator boy tried to take it from him but he shook his head. There was something grim and controlled and strong about him, but nothing confident or poised. He moved awkwardly and the black suit fitted him badly. He did not speak to her at all and Mary had the idea that he was pent up, as frightened as Dorinda, wanting this meeting no more than she. He stumbled getting out of the elevator and his inhalation of breath was audible when Mary opened the door of the suit. He walked in behind her, faltered a moment in his stride, then turned back and laid the bag on the floor inside the door.

Dorinda's reception parlor was a huge, high-ceilinged room with heavy green drapes on the tall windows, heavy furniture spaced around the room, two floor lamps glowing brightly but leaving most of the room shadowed. Mary had taken it for granted until this moment but now she saw it suddenly with the eyes of the monk.

"It must look like Grand Central Station to him," she thought. She turned with a smile. "If you will be seated for just a minute," she said.

He inclined his head with that queer, jerky movement, and remained standing. She crossed the room and passed through the door at the far end which opened on a short hallway. Dorinda was standing in the middle of the room smoking a cigarette. She seldom smoked, but she was puffing hard on the cigarette she held now. She was wearing her blue suit, a fine plaid weave with traceries of red in it. An inexperienced eye would be unaware of make-up, but it was there, a liquid film smoothing her skin, touching it gently with color. She looked small and young, gallant rather than glamorous, the deceptive simplicity of the suit underplaying her figure without betraying it, touching the soft curves but not flaunting them. Her eyes still looked haunted, but she was in command of herself, ready to play any role required of her.

"I want you right there, Mary," she said. "I won't be alone with him."

Mary shook her head. "I couldn't."

"Why not?"

"It wouldn't be fair to him, Dorinda. It wouldn't be decent."

Dorinda bit her lip. She frowned, then snapped her fingers. "Maybe you're right. But wait right there in the entry hall. Stay out of sight if you want to, but stay right there!"

"I'd rather not."

"You stay there! Don't argue! I'm playing this on my nerves. I won't go through with it if——"

"I'll stay there."

Mary walked out, smiled at the man who was looking past her, and continued on to the entry hall. Behind her she heard Dorinda's velvet voice say: "Hello, Bartholomew," and the hoarse voice of the man say: "Dora!"

## CHAPTER 6

The bedroom was her dressing room, the short hallway was the wings, the parlor was her stage. Dorinda Daly had it all in her mind and she knew her role. She did not have lines, and she was not good with lines unless someone wrote them for her, but that couldn't be helped. She refused to think about them, or think at all. That was the best way. She could handle the incidental business of any scene, even if there weren't any lines, and she could always do something to any cue; it was merely a matter of moving around, not letting herself feel anything, obeying her instincts. She wouldn't be frightened, and wouldn't make a fool of herself, if she did it like that. She let Mary Norbert take five steps into the room, then she made her entrance.

"Hello, Bartholomew," she said.

He looked like Boris Karloff in a straight role: black as a vulture, cadaverous, terrible, with that scarecrow suit flapping around him and that prison haircut. He croaked like a crow when he said "Dora." She hated the sound of that "Dora" and she had never let anyone else call her that. She moved front, center, with her back to the mantel and gestured with one hand.

"Sit down, Bartholomew," she said.

He was holding a black hat. He laid it on the small table beside the chair that she indicated but he did not sit down.

"Dora," he said. "I never thanked you for all that you did for me. It was——"

"You didn't suddenly come here in the middle of the night to do that, did you?"

"No."

"Then skip it. It was an idea. An urge. I owed you something. If it worked out, then that's fine."

She was brusque, sharp, not unfriendly but emotionally detached. He had conceded command of the situation to her with his first sentence, and that was fine; she didn't have to think about him. He was just somebody, anybody.

"It worked out." The man straightened his lean body and there was dignity in the way he timed his pause. "I owe you a lot. I can't measure it," he said. "Only God can."

"God doesn't know I'm on earth. I never bother Him."

Bartholomew looked right through her. She avoided his eyes, moved away, made him turn his body to face her. He looked awkward, out of position, standing now with the chair on his left, nothing behind him.

"Why did you come here, Bartholomew?" she said. "What about Bart?"

"He's in trouble."

"How in trouble?"

She moved three more steps to his left, bent over a small table, and took a cigarette from the box. When he did not answer her, she looked up. His face was grim, thinner, older, not the face she remembered but one that she would forever recognize. He gestured toward the divan which faced the chair that she had selected for him.

"Sit down, Dora," he said.

"I prefer not."

He stood there, looking at her. He made no gesture, issued no ultimatums, did not even change expression; but she felt suddenly silly and childish. The room wasn't a stage; it was a room. She tapped the cigarette against the back of her hand and strolled back across the room, taking her time.

"What kind of trouble does Bart have?" she said.

He stood, waiting, and she tried to tell herself that he was stubborn and that she could take it out of him, but he seemed less stubborn than patient, and she was very tired. She seated herself on the divan and drew her skirt down over her knees, holding it there, the cigarette between her fingers. Bartholomew seated himself in the chair. He was all legs and arms.

"Bart came to me," he said, "and I am grateful that you told him where I was. It was good of you not to poison his mind against me. Not many women would have been like that. You made a good Catholic out of him, too. I'm thinking of all those things, Dora."

She watched his face, not letting herself think anything or feel anything. "You gave Bart to me," she said flatly. "That's more than I gave you, or gave him. What's this trouble?"

"He had a child by a girl. He doesn't know where the child is."

Her eyes flickered. "That's a long time ago," she said. "The child isn't anywhere. It died."

"That's what the girl told him. He doesn't believe her."

"It probably wasn't his in the first place. The girl was a tramp, a gold-plated floozie. It's all over." She leaned forward, pointing the cigarette at him like a small gun. "What stirred it up again? You and all that religion and stuff up where you are?"

The man watched her gravely. "Bart talked to a girl who was an orphan. He was always worried about it. The girl told him about the orphan home. He didn't want his child in one."

Dorinda's thought moved on a straight line to Mary Norbert. She didn't want to think. She swore under her breath. "Look," she said. "You came here in the middle of the night when I'm half dead to tell me something I knew all about long ago. He was young and he didn't know half of what he should have known. This tramp knew it all. After he was in the Army, over in Japan, she sprang this baby business on him. He was crazy enough to want to marry her. By proxy, no less! He wanted me to arrange it. Me! I wouldn't have anything to do with it."

"You were wrong, Dora."

"Wrong? I should have delivered him to somebody like that? No, thanks." Her voice rose beyond her control. She struck a match savagely and lighted her cigarette. "If that baby lived or died, it makes no damned difference. Bart's out of it. It's over."

She jumped to her feet and paced again. "I shouldn't have sent him to you," she said. "And you shouldn't have come here."

The man sat quietly, watching her. "Bart asked for my advice," he said. "I told him that he had to see her, that he owed her a chance to tell the truth, and that he had a right to demand the truth."

Dorinda turned, horrified. "You damned fool!" she said. "You sent him back to that bitch?" She took three short steps and stood over him. "Is he mixed up with her again?" Her hand darted out. She shook the man's shoulder. "Is he?"

Bartholomew rose slowly, brushing her hand aside. "I made a mistake, Dora," he said. "My advice was wrong. That's why I'm here. I want to set it straight."

"Set what straight? If you sent him back to her——"

The man towered over her and a dimly remembered emotion came back to her, as remembered emotion always came back to help her in roles she played. This emotion did not help her. It was the memory of Bartholomew's hard, stubborn immovability, of his big body towering over her like this, and of hammering against it with voice and fists, futilely, to no purpose. She had pounded against him, screaming at him, getting nowhere. It was long ago, but it defeated her all over again. He was stronger now because he had no need of her. He looked down into her face and there was no warmth in him, neither anger nor caring.

"This girl is married," he said. "Bart must not do anything to set her husband against her. I did not think of that when I talked to him. Nobody has a right to do anything that will undo a marriage."

Dorinda took a backward step. She was fascinated by the intense earnestness in this man who had been her husband. He took a step after her, walking her down, taking the stage away from her.

"A man alone cannot provide for a child," he said hoarsely. "I forgot. I shouldn't have forgotten that. He hasn't a chance. A man alone can do more harm to a child than good. Bart is a better man because he was yours. I'd have done him no good. Harm maybe. He'd do that too. If the child has been baptized and is in good hands, he must stay away."

"Suppose Bart marries, then what?" Dorinda's voice was little more than a whisper. Bartholomew stood silent, looking down at her. She saw the bewilderment building up behind his eyes. He hadn't thought of that.

"A woman doesn't take kindly to a child like that, Dora," he said.

"Some women wouldn't."

"Most wouldn't."

The carefully thought-out words had carried him only so far. He was lapsing now into the old manner of speech, speaking as he once spoke.

"What do you want me to do?" she said.

"Tell him to let this woman and her marriage alone. No good can come of making trouble. There's ways and ways of finding out what he wants to know, maybe the ways you used in finding me."

Dorinda walked away from him. She took four steps and turned, the divan behind her. She felt stronger, more sure, when she faced him with space between them.

"Bart can't raise the child if he finds it," Bartholomew said. "Tell him that a man alone can't do it. If he doesn't raise it, it will never be his. It's better in the hands of God and whoever takes it."

There was sweat on the man's face. His skin glistened with it. He had said all that there was in him to say and he obviously felt that it wasn't enough, that he hadn't convinced her. The last word was hers, no matter how strong he was, or how stubborn. She could do as he wanted, or not do it. With the return of dominance, she felt pity. The emotions that she had sought to bar from this hour of her life had riddled her defenses.

"I did a good job with Bart, all things considered, Bartholomew," she said softly. "You couldn't ask more than he is. I couldn't. You let me do it. You didn't get much out of it."

"You had the doing."

"I had the fun of doing, too." She paced, turned half away, then faced him again. "If I didn't have Bart with me, I wouldn't have made it," she said. "I had to be something for him that I wouldn't have been for myself. You didn't have that."

"Is that why you took me out of the gutter?"

"If it was a gutter, I didn't know it. I wouldn't let them tell me anything. I wanted you found and I wanted you to have whatever you needed. That's all I wanted."

"It was a gutter. You gave me something you didn't have yourself. You gave it to Bart."

She bent over, found another cigarette, lighted it. "Don't start something that I won't let you finish," she said.

"I've got more than you have, Dora," the man said. He swept his arm in an awkward scarecrow gesture around the room. "You made it possible for me. I'd like to share it, somehow. I don't know how. I've prayed."

Dorinda broke the match in two and dropped it in the

ash tray. "It isn't for me," she said. "I've looked at it when Bart was seeing it. He was just a kid. He could see it. It wasn't there. Not for me. There wasn't anything."

"Looking wasn't enough."

"I've thought of that. God—if there is a God—won't be impressed with any show I ever did. He probably never paid any attention to them. What I've done with my life won't mean anything to Him. I know that. I've always known."

She moved back and forth, reaching for words, feeling them before she released them. "If I've got a chance with Him," she said, "it's got to be through other people. He may like that. I haven't hurt people. Really hurt them, I mean. Maybe I've given Him something in other people——"

Bartholomew was tense. She saw the drawn whiteness under the tan of his face. "It isn't enough," he said huskily.

"No? Probably not. It's what I had to give. There have to be people like I am. Don't ask me why. I just know."

The man did not understand and she knew that he did not understand. How could he? There was no need of such people as she in the place where he lived. There hadn't been any need of the kind of person that she thought she was in the life that they had had together. He wanted the person that she didn't want to be. Maybe that was what God wanted too: somebody to have a lot of children and clean places that would never be clean, and wash clothes that didn't look like anything when they were washed, and cook meals that she couldn't eat herself after they were cooked. It all built up inside of her and she saw the man standing there in that hangman's suit, looking like all the buzzards that ever hung around waiting for someone to die.

"You and God!" she said. "You and God!"

Her voice rose shrilly, out of her control, and when she pulled it down it broke like a wet aspirin tablet in her throat, choking her and filling her mouth with a foul taste. She swayed and then she was crying, crying with her whole body, bending double with the sobs, unable to hold them in.

Bartholomew reached her in two strides and his arm

was around her, holding her up. "Dora!" he said. "Dora! What can I do for you?"

Dorinda felt the fatigue maggots crawling in her nerves, and the sobbing that she couldn't check was like nausea. Bartholomew picked her up as though she weighed no more than a rag doll. He stood in the center of the room with her and Mary Norbert was in the room too. He spoke to Mary.

"Where will I take her?" he said.

"Into her room. I'll show you."

Mary ran on ahead and she called for Janet. Bartholomew walked easily, swiftly. Dorinda fought vainly for control. They had to ring down the curtain on her. She couldn't finish the scene. Bartholomew laid her gently on the bed. She looked at him through the slits of her eyes and he was not looking at her. There was a faraway look in his eyes and his lips were moving. He made a small sign of the Cross three times, over her forehead, her lips, and her heart; then he stepped back. Janet was beside the bed then and Mary Norbert was speaking to Bartholomew.

"Please wait for me in the lobby," she said. "I must talk to you."

Dorinda Daly wept and could not stop weeping. She had not even had the last word. That didn't make any difference. She knew that it didn't make any difference. She wasn't crying for that nor for anything that existed in the world. She was crying for the cow-eyed, conceited girl who loved a big, rough, proud boy a long time ago, and never got over loving him.

## CHAPTER 7

Mary Norbert knelt beside Dorinda's bed, listening helplessly to Dorinda's sobbing, stroking Dorinda's arm. "You mustn't, darling," she said. "You are shaking yourself to pieces."

She felt a gentle tap on her shoulder. Janet was standing behind her, broad, capable, her dark skin glowing. "Ill take care of her, Miss Norbert," she said.

Mary rose slowly. Janet had always been deferent to her, self-effacing, meek in any wild mood of Dorinda's; but Janet was decisive now, deferring to no one. There was assurance in her, and dignity. Mary nodded, paying that dignity the tribute of silence.

The big room looked shatteringly empty. Dorinda's partly smoked cigarette lay across another partly smoked cigarette in the ash tray. A feeble plume of smoke waved back and forth above it. Brother Anselm was gone and Mary feared for a few minutes that she would not find him in the lobby. When she stepped from the elevator, however, she saw him, seated in the chair that he had occupied before. He was staring straight ahead and he held his rosary in his hands. She walked softly and stopped about ten feet from him. He finished a decade and she moved forward again. He turned his head and saw her, then rose slowly, stiffly, wearily.

"If you will spend the night here, Brother Anselm," she said, "I will arrange for a room."

"Thank you," he said. "I will go to the train."

"It is very late and you must be tired."

He smiled, a faint smile, but he did not share the private joke that he enjoyed. "I stayed because you asked me to stay," he said.

"I want to talk to you. I am the girl who told Bart about the orphans."

"You heard all that we said up there? You listened?"

Mary flushed. "I did not want to do it. I wasn't eavesdropping. I work for Dorinda. She wanted me to stay."

The words spoke themselves. Until they were said, Mary did not realize that they were defensive words and that they might not be fair to Dorinda. She was too utterly weary to be wise, or to be discreet, or to regret too much.

"It is all right," she said. "I am going to marry Bart."

The man seemed to grow taller, to tower over her. He had a frightening quality. His voice should have been thunder. She awaited it, tense, half expecting that it would be thunder. He spoke softly.

"I am glad that you want to talk to me," he said.

He looked around for another place to sit where they could be together and something within the girl whispered, "Not here." This wasn't his setting. It wasn't fair to him. He wasn't at home here. He would not be at home anywhere probably except in his monastery, but this ornate hotel lobby robbed him of too much. The very chairs were supercilious, as the clerk had been supercilious: "a clergyman of some sort." Mary touched his arm.

"If you really must go back tonight," she said, "I will go to the station with you."

"You would have to come back alone," he said. "It is late."

"I will take a taxi."

She liked the protective thought, the concern for her. She was touched, too, by his hesitant gesture when he reached into his pocket. She was a woman. His instinct was telling him that he should stand any expense involved. She knew that a monk had no money of his own.

"Brother Anselm," she said softly, "I am the employee of a theatrical company. I have money for my expenses. I do not have to spend my own money."

That was not literally true, of course. She was not the employee of a company, she was employed by Dorinda Daly. He might, however, have some self-consciousness about that. It was best to keep the money impersonal, as something belonging to an institution. She read indecision in his eyes.

"Let's go," she said. "We can talk better in the station than here."

Brother Anselm sighed. It was a slight sound, but there was relief in it, and she knew that she had been right about the atmosphere of the lobby. He was feeling it too. He picked up the shabby bag and they walked out into the clear, cool night. There was a taxi waiting with the driver napping at the wheel. Mary awakened him.

"South Station," she said.

She knew by the way he looked at everything, the uncertainty in his manner, that Brother Anselm was not accustomed to cabs. She was appalled to think that he had walked to the hotel, carrying his bag, and that he had been prepared to walk back. He looked from side to side, out of the cab windows, and there was a slightly puzzled expression on his face. He was not an initiator of conversations.

"This is my first trip to Boston," Mary said, "and I have seen very little of it."

"I was in Rochester this morning. In the morning, I guess this one would look the same."

Brother Anselm was no longer interested in the streets over which they traveled. He rested the back of his head against the seat cushions. Mary could feel fatigue as a tangible thing in the cab, his and her own. When they alighted at the station, she had to brace her shoulders back with conscious effort.

"Will you have coffee with me?" she said.

Again, there was that momentary hesitation, that weighing of yes and no. Brother Anselm shook his head. "I had my supper on the train," he said.

On the train? His supper? How long ago? she wondered. She looked up at him. "You could take coffee."

"I do not need it."

"I do." She touched his arm. "Brother Anselm, if I had not been called to Boston, I would have had a date tonight with Bart. It would have been a very special date. We did not have it. I would like to have coffee with you."

"All right," he said.

Absurd though it seemed, he made that decision sound like something reckless. There was no table service at this hour. They sat side by side at the counter and he was ill at ease again, unsure.

"Will you have a sandwich?" she said.

"No, thank you."

He was swiftly decisive, so she did not press the point. "I'm going to have toast," she said, "because I feel suddenly hollow. Will you have toast with me?"

He shook his head and she leaned toward him. "Brother Anselm," she said. "Bart and I didn't know until last night. I haven't told anyone. Not Dorinda or anybody. You are the first. I am glad that you are the first. This is my engagement party."

He looked at her gravely. There was emotion, deep

emotion, behind his eyes. "God is very good to me," he said.

"He has been good to me too. He must have wanted us to know each other."

"Yes."

The waitress came for their order. Mary ordered her toast and coffee. When the man hesitated, she said softly, "It is a party."

Brother Anselm straightened. He spoke to Mary rather than to the hovering waitress. "There was a roll I used to like," he said. "It had white icing on it and jelly in the center."

Mary held her breath. She did not dare look at the waitress. Such rolls were commonplace at counters everywhere, but in the middle of the night? It would be catastrophe if they did not have it. She raised her eyes. The waitress had turned away. She had to move less than a dozen feet. She came back with the roll on a plate.

It was a discouraged-looking roll, dry-looking, with skimpy white icing and sticky red jelly in its center. Brother Anselm's face lighted up. "That's it," he said.

Mary had a momentary conviction that she was about to cry, that she would start crying right here at the counter and not be able to stop. "Drown the stage with tears," she thought, "and what would even be worse: drown the brother's bun!"

She knew then that she was all right. She wouldn't weep. She would eat her toast like a lady. She looked at Brother Anselm's face. He was savoring the fleshpots of his Egypt, eating that tired old station roll with the joy of a gourmet tasting a rare dish. She had to look away. She couldn't bear it. He could reject that craved delicacy as easily as he ate it. He had obviously rejected it for long years. Tonight he had accepted it because it was her engagement party. He had done that deliberately, too, making his decision with no compulsions of habit or desire driving him.

"He is the only free man I know," she thought. "He has absolute freedom. Bart hasn't, and I haven't. Nothing chains him. Nothing at all."

She looked at him again, at the strong lean profile. He was still enjoying the roll. After tonight he would probably never taste another. She wondered if he would long for one and regret. Probably not. It was of his own free choice that he lived as he lived, and it was magnificent. It was chilling, too, and frightening, but wreathed round with glory.

He looked at her suddenly and he was embarrassed. He had come to her party and he was neglecting her. The embarrassment was written in his face. A third of the roll remained on his plate.

"Are you a Catholic?" he said.

"Yes."

He nodded. "I knew that you would be."

"How?"

"I prayed for it."

It was that simple. She stared at him, wondering. "This is where it comes from," she thought, "that basic simplicity and honesty, and faith and trust. Scrape away the added things—Cornell, and glory, and Dorinda, and that woman, whatever her name is—and this would be Bart."

"I love your son very deeply, Brother Anselm," she said. "Ill try to make him happy."

"Let him make you happy," Brother Anselm said.

He took a sip of his coffee, and his eyes were far away from her. It seemed to her, suddenly, that there was wisdom in what he said. She was seeing Bart with a great white light beating on him, seeing him clearly from this seat of vantage beside his father. Bart would serve needs, but never a great ambition. With a woman who expected of him what was not in him to give, he would be a failure. His great gift was the gift of finding magic in simple things: a ferryboat in the rain, a bench in Washington Square, the sharing of tag lines and memories, the sharing of anything.

"What else is there?" she said.

She was not aware that she had spoken aloud until Brother Anselm turned to look at her. He had taken another bite of the roll.

"It's a strange thing," she said swiftly. "I had an idea that Dorinda took me under her wing because she wanted me to meet Bart, and she thought I'd be all right with him. She was afraid of some girls that he might meet. I resented being picked. I still do, a little. I didn't want to be the safe and sane one. I didn't want any mother to select me. I wanted a man to want me."

"He did, didn't he?"

Brother Anselm was chewing his roll, not looking at her. In the face of the simple question, her long speech seemed more than a little ridiculous; the ones she had made to herself, to Carter Brill, to the photos of Bart in the spring room.

"Yes," she said. "He did. He does."

"Would you be willing to take his child?"

She drew a deep breath. The question was like a sudden shower of ice water. "I never faced that," she said slowly. "It doesn't seem real to me. After all the thinking that I've done about it, it still isn't real. I don't know."

"It's a hard thing for a woman."

"Yes."

"How do you feel about children of your own?"

"I want them. I want a lot of them."

She felt on more certain ground here. She was afraid that she had made a bad impression in the matter of that unknown child which hovered like a phantom on the edge of Bart's life and hers. Her words tumbled out. Great fatigue was like liquor, she thought; it made a person talkative. She could not, however, stop.

She had always been interested in families, ever since she left the orphanage, she told Brother Anselm. Because she didn't have anyone of her own, she was interested in those who had. She had theories about large families. She would have many children if she could. But she would do something about the youngest. The youngest was usually spoiled by the older ones and led to expect more than they had.

"Because the youngest expects more, he probably needs more," she said, "but often he gets less because the family money and everything else runs out on him before he grows up."

Brother Anselm listened patiently and with flattering attention, nodding his head. "The eldest has to give up a lot to the younger ones," he said, "helping to raise them."

Mary stared at the sign that advertised something that

was very desirable and good for mankind. It was a splash of color, a focus for her tired eyes.

"Bart's child would have to make sacrifices for mine, and help them," she said thoughtfully. "I never considered that. I've been very selfish, haven't I?"

"The child is a baby," Brother Anselm said gravely. "It wouldn't know any woman but you. A woman can put a lot of herself into a baby."

Mary saw the sign through a wet mist. "Dorinda did," she said.

"Yes," the man said. "And without a husband to help her."

"I didn't mean that."

"It is true."

This was sacred ground. She could not walk on it. Whatever had happened between a man and a woman long ago was forever beyond her understanding. Bart was the result, and she loved Bart. She loved Dorinda. She knew, with certainty, too, that she loved this big awkward man who was Bart's father. It seemed a miracle that she had had this chance to know him.

"I want to tell you something," she said. "This isn't just a party. This is the very special date I was going to have with Bart. I'm having it with you, and I'm glad. I am very happy that it is like this." She paused and bit her lip. "Tonight, in some place touched with magic, he was going to ask me to marry him."

Brother Anselm turned to her, startled. "I thought that it was all settled."

"It is. I'm growing up, I think. I know tonight that a special place isn't important, or a man asking a woman. The important thing is needing each other, and knowing it. We knew last night."

Brother Anselm smiled. "I am very happy for my son."

The waitress came back. "More coffee?" she said.

Brother Anselm shook his head. Mary did not suggest that he have another roll because she knew that he would not. The party was over. They both rose and Mary took the check. Her engagement party had cost her forty cents. She left a quarter tip. She had spent twenty cents on Bart's father. She had bought him something that cost twenty cents. Never again in her lifetime, probably, would she be able to buy him anything, or give him anything.

They walked out into the big, echoing station, hushed with the emptiness of the predawn hours. She was tired still, but not as tired as she had been.

"We should have asked about your train," she said.

"I asked when I came in. A train leaves at 5:55 A.M."

She looked at the clock. It was nearly three. "You have had no sleep."

"God gives me sleep when I need it. He had other plans for me tonight and I am grateful."

They walked to the taxi stand and stood for a moment, facing each other. The tears were starting again and the girl fought them back.

"I am so glad that I know you," she said.

Brother Anselm's lips tightened. He swallowed and looked away. His eyes came back to hers. "Tell Bart," he said huskily, "that I will pray for both of you every day, and for your happiness."

"I will."

Mary wanted to kiss him as he stood there, tall and lean, ungainly, in his badly fitted black suit, with the kindness in his eyes and the long patience in his face, the patience which, like a garment, covered all his pain.

"When you are married," he said, "if you let me know, I will ask Father Abbot to say a Mass for you."

It was the gift that he had to offer, and he offered it, the something that was not his, yet, parodoxically, was his. Mary took his right hand, a rough and callused hand like Bart's, and raised it to her lips. Brother Anselm's left hand rested lightly on her head, and when he withdrew his right hand, he made the sign of the Cross over his own heart with it.

"God bless you forever, Mary," he said.

He helped her into the cab, then, and he was standing alone when the cab pulled away. Mary turned and waved to him before the tears swept her. She fought with them, chewing hard on a corner of her handkerchief.

"I don't know why I'm crying," she said. "I wouldn't change places with anyone in the world."

The taxi driver turned his head. "That's all right, lady,"

he said. "I ain't likely to change places with anybody neither."

## CHAPTER 8

The station at three in the morning had the vast, brooding calm of a cathedral. It absorbed such sound as there was into a near silence as it absorbed light into shadow. Brother Anselm sank onto one of the benches gratefully. He was aware of his feet and he tried to banish them from his awareness. He drew his rosary from his pocket and his fingers moved on the worn beads.

He prayed for the safety of the girl who was riding in a taxicab back to the hotel and he prayed in gratitude to the Blessed Mother who had so richly and generously forgiven his arrogance at her shrine. Not until he had completed the five decades did he permit himself thought.

It had been a fearful and a wonderful day. In a few hours he would board another train. He would ride through another day to Rochester and change stations. He would reach St. Urban's by 8:20 P.M., in time for Compline. It was all written with precision into timetables, a material and physical predestination governing the lives of men.

He was aware that he had spent very little of the money which the Abbot had entrusted to him, and that he might have passed the night in a hotel. He had not elected to do so. There did not seem to be any purpose in it.

He did not know whether Dora would correct his bad advice to Bart. She did not see it as he saw it, nor place the same importance on it. It made no difference now. God had foreseen what he did not, that Dora would be indifferent to the child because her feeling against the mother was stronger than her understanding. The girl, Mary, was miraculously present to do what Dora might not do, the one person in the world who could be depended upon to do it. To him there was significance in the fact that her name was "Mary." His fingers touched the beads again as he thought of it.

She was a fine girl and she had opened her heart to him. She had paid him respect, as Bart had done, and she had given him liking, affection. He blinked, remembering that she had kissed his hand. Her soul was fine, too, for all of the fact that she had a woman's prejudices. Bart was no longer alone with a problem that no solitary man could handle; he was a man with a woman to walk beside him.

Brother Anselm gloried in the great hush of the station. There had been too much noise, too many voices. He had spoken too many words himself, and more than a few of them were idle words. He had prayed diligently, however, for his tongue's guidance and he had not, within his knowledge, erred greatly in his speech.

He thought of Dora. She had not changed as it appeared that she had changed. Watching her, he had seen only illusion, a person who was different in a manner of dress and of speech, in an elegance of living. When he no longer watched her, nor cared that the room in which they talked was beyond anything that he had ever known in luxury, he heard the real person speaking, and reasoning, and feeling. That person was the Dora he had known and there was little change in her.

There had been panic in him when she wept, as there had always been panic in him at the sight of her weeping. He had remembered a thousand things, perhaps, in the few minutes during which he carried her in his arms. They were not evil things to remember. She was his wife and he had loved her. He had loved no other woman. For a few moments there, in that great room, she had needed him as she had often needed him in the time that they had together; but if he had not been there, she would have been taken care of by the people who cared for her when he laid her down.

She had found that life for herself, without him, long years before he found his own life without her. God had worked in him, and in his life, through her, and that was a great mystery.

He thought about her name in lights above the theatre marquee, and her pictures outside the theatre. Someone had put those lights in place, someone had taken those pictures and printed them. He had only a vague idea of what happened inside the theatre, but she was a very important person there and people would wait on her, taking care of what she needed or wanted. He had seen the place where she lived and he imagined that she lived in some such place in New York, with people treating her respectfully and working for her and doing whatever wanted doing. There was only one thing which she needed which those people did not, and could not, supply. She needed prayers. He looked up into the vast emptiness of the station, thinking of that.

"Live your marriage here, since that is your choice, and be faithful to it," Father Abbot had told him many years ago. He had tried. It had been difficult at first, but easier later, with the grace of God.

He said another rosary for Dora. The hands of the clock moved slowly and human weariness racked him. His eyes were heavy, but he was afraid that he would miss his train if he slept. He had not been aware of anyone else in the station, but a woman stood before him, and as her shadow fell on him, he looked up. She was a young woman, thin and poorly dressed.

"Excuse me, Father," she said. "Would you please watch my babies for a few minutes? I will be right back. I am afraid to leave them alone, or just with anyone."

He rose awkwardly, feeling a stiffness in all of his muscles. "I'll watch them," he said. "Take your time."

"Thank you, Father."

He did not correct her impression that he was a priest. She probably would not understand what an oblate was, nor the humble designation of "Brother." It did not make any difference. A man did not have to be ordained to watch babies. He would probably do as well, or as badly, as one of the anointed. He lumbered after the woman as she led the way to another bench fifteen or twenty feet away. His feet were sore and the heavy shoes made a stamping sound despite his effort to walk softly. There were a surprising number of people in the station. "I must sound like a horse," Brother Anselm thought.

The children were not literally babies. The boy seemed

to be about three, the girl probably a year younger. They were curled up together on the bench. The mother's coat was spread as a pillow and the little girl had her head resting on it; the boy slept with one arm under his head with only the hard bench under him.

"Thank you so much, Father," the woman said again.

She was gone then and Brother Anselm sat beside the children, hoping that they would not awaken. If they were afraid of him and started to cry, he would not know what to do. He said a prayer to St. Joseph, protector of the Holy Infant, and rested his faith in him.

He had never had much experience with children nor had he been around children when they were growing up. He had been the youngest of six himself and there hadn't been any younger children in the house during his growing years. His mother had died when he was twelve and his eldest sister had looked after him. His father was killed in an accident when he was fifteen but he was working by that time, so it hadn't made much of a change in his life. The family scattered and he did not know where they were, any of them. If his sisters and brothers had children, as they probably had, he had never known any of them.

He had one vivid memory of childhood and he knew that he must have been pretty young, although he was going to school at the time. It was a Catholic school and the teachers were nuns. He, and a number of other children, were taken to the church for some reason that he had forgotten, and the nun left them there. He, with several other boys, discovered that they could make an impressive and shocking noise in the quiet of the church by raising the kneelers a few inches and letting them drop. The girls were horrified and the boys were laughing when the nun returned.

He was very frightened then and because of the fright he probably remembered it all more vividly than he would have otherwise. The nun's face was very stern and she pointed her finger at him, ordering him out of the pew. He and three other boys were standing, badly scared, in the aisle when a priest came out of the shadows near the altar. He was a stout, elderly priest and he spoke to the nun when he came down the aisle.

"Do not be too hard on them, Sister," he said. "They are only children and they are in their Father's house."

Nothing happened to him except a scolding, but he never forgot the priest, nor what the priest said. Up till then, "God" had been little more than a word, in spite of the Catechism lessons that he learned and recited. After that, God, the Father, meant in a very special and personal way *his* father. The church, somehow, belonged to him and he took pride in it, discovering beauties in it, because it was his Father's house. He never lost that feeling, even when he was older and when he grew careless about his religious obligations. That feeling, which was deep in him, made it easier to find his way back when he was lost.

The children moved, or shifted position, several times, and Brother Anselm held his breath. Once the girl sighed deeply, half opened her eyes, and went back to sleep. The man studied both of them, strangely moved. They were so very small and dependent, yet they were complete human beings, needing only time to be as were those who cared for them.

Brother Anselm thought of Mary, the girl who loved his son. They had talked together tonight of babies unborn, hers and Bart's. Those children were over the horizon of time, as the railroad station at Rochester was to him, farther away, but out beyond Bart and Mary, waiting for them. They would be very much like these children on the bench beside him, the babies of Bart and Mary, very much like them: helpless little creatures with flushed faces, capable of sleeping like monks on hard, comfortless surfaces, as trustful as monks, certain that their needs would not be neglected or ignored.

Brother Anselm drew a deep breath. Those distant children, whom he would never see, were a part of his own life. Because he had lived, however unworthily, they would have life. It was a mystery as great as the Trinity of God that life should pass from such as he to, perhaps, countless human beings across the generations, sinners and saints.

He sat on the bench, looking at the sleeping children, and all of those other unborn children seemed very close to him. The woman came back. He heard her heels clicking sharply before she stood before him.

"Thank you, Father," she said.

He rose again, with all of his muscles protesting, and balanced precariously on his numbed feet. "They were very good," he said.

He went back to the bench that he had occupied before and raised his eyes to the clock. It was nearing five. There would be dawn color in the east. He braced his back against the unyielding wood of the bench. It was time for Matins. He opened the breviary to the prayer for Thursday.

*Bless the Lord, O my soul! O Lord, my God, thou art exceedingly great!*
*Thou hast put on praise and beauty and art clothed with light as with a garment.*

Brother Anselm read and his weariness dropped away from him. The station faded into its ultimate reality as a mere illusion in stone. The great words marched across paper and the mind of the man followed them.

*The young lions roaring after their prey, and seeking their meat from God.*
*The sun ariseth, and they are gathered together: and they shall lie down in their dens.*
*Man shall go forth to his work, and to his labor until the evening.*

The labor of Brother Anselm until the evening would be the riding of the train. There would be the many stations whose names he did not know, and Rochester where he must wait.

*All expect of thee that thou give them food in season.*
*What thou givest to them they shall gather up. . . .*

The hands of the clock moved slowly, but Brother Anselm did not notice it. His soul was at peace. He read on, hearing in his mind the chanting of the monks who praised God and greeted a new day in the choir stalls of St. Urban's.

*I will sing to the Lord as long as I live; I will sing praise to my God while I have my being.*

Those were the voices of his brothers, the music in his Father's house. Nothing around him had solid existence; he was already home.

On the thin edge of sleep, with the weight of the day pressing her into the mattress, Mary Norbert struggled upward, reaching for the phone. She shook her head and her hand dropped limply.

"It's too late," she said, "and he has had a full day. If only he waited, if only he didn't do anything about anything! I'll call him in the morning if only it isn't too late."

She was too sleepy to come to focus, but Time was a menacing ghost in the room. Bart's father had done all that he could and he was right about Bart. Marriage was sacred. Bart must not do anything to cause trouble in a marriage, even if the girl let him down again, as she would let him down. He must not do anything about his child until they could do it together. They could do so much together.

"He's had a whole day," she whispered. "If only he waited. I hope he did! It's my fault. I should have asked him to wait. I knew. I knew before I talked to his father. I just didn't let myself see it."

The day was gone, and most of the night, so she was helpless. The heavy weight pressed on her again and she slept, fretfully, uneasily.

## CHAPTER 9

Wednesday, October sixth, had a wide, gaping hole in it from the moment that Mary's phone call came through. Bart McBride stood under a cold shower and awakened slowly even with the icy water driving the breath out of him. His first impulse was to fly to Boston, either with Mary or after her, because there was no point to being in a city where she was not. Reason overruled impulse but he was reluctant to accept the verdict.

The blunt fact was that Mary had work to do in Boston, or she would not have been summoned there in a hurry. He did not have anything to do in Boston. He would be in the way, cluttering up time and space for those with responsibilities. To look at a fact that was even more blunt, he did not have anything to do anywhere. Call this a vacation after a season of damned hard work, and whatever one called it, he still did not have an oar to pull; he was a passenger in the boat. A vacation could not stretch out indefinitely. Even a vacation should have an object of some kind.

He toweled vigorously and his blood, awakening, awakened his entire body. He looked at the telephone as he was pulling on his shorts, then, through a natural association of ideas, his glance traveled to the dresser top. He had a message there to call Alex Waringly. On the reverse side of that telephone message there might be a job, an oar that he could pull, a useful thing that he could do, a regular pay-roll check that he could cash.

"If you are not worth ten thousand a year within twelve months, I'll fire you," Alex said.

He could do many things on ten thousand a year. He and Mary could have a lot of the things that were pictured in the magazines. They could live somewhere and put down roots, and own books and play music.

Alex Waringly, however, was Aleta's father and Bart was forever barred from honesty with Alex. He liked Alex as a person, although they were seldom on the same wave length. Alex, he knew, liked him. As far as Alex was concerned, the offer of a job to Bart had nothing to do with Aleta. For Bart, it was not such a simple matter. He knew Alex, and had the regard of Alex, solely because he had first known Aleta. A job with Alex meant the entering of her world, the world she had opened to him. He wanted to be done forever with Aleta and all that she represented, so he could not, short of blatant hypocrisy, accept anything from Aleta's father. He did, however, have to return the call and he might even have to permit Alex an opportunity to offer him a job if that was what Alex had in mind. There was such a thing as a debt in courtesy.

He stared at the telephone. It was too early to call a man who had to commute from Connecticut, a top man. The lower faces on the totem pole were already behind desks, whether they commuted or didn't. He would be one of the lower faces, himself, if he belonged to the Waringly empire and that part of it would be all right if the other angles were not all wrong. For the moment, he would go down and have breakfast, allowing Alex ample time to reach his office.

"There may be a letter from Aleta," he thought.

So many things hinged on that letter. Whether he received it or not, it represented something big in his life, bigger than ever now that he had Mary to consider. If Mary was going to share his life, there must be no shadow in it that he could clear away.

Mary! He thought about her, of the strong tide in which they had swum last night, the magic of her performance, the music to which they had danced, and the certainty that had grown between them. He saw her as she sang, so incredibly like Dore, yet so completely herself. He shared again her need for floating, for tasting her success before she faced her failure. She did not have to do what she had tried to do, and he was glad that she couldn't do it, but he had tasted anguish with her, knowing how it was. They had met head on where their viewpoints differed and they had not been hurt, either of them. She was lovely, she was the incredible realization of the lonely dreams men dream, she was *his*.

There was no letter in his box and his mood turned grim. He ordered and ate his breakfast without being aware of it save as something that he did out of habit, and of necessity. When he returned to his room he stood looking at the telephone and flipped a coin. He put the coin away without looking at it and called Alex Waringly. He ran the gamut of secretaries before Alex's booming, hearty voice came over the wire.

"Bart? You're harder to reach than the president of the Fifth Avenue Bank."

"Sorry. I didn't get your message till late last night."

"I'll bet it was late! I was young once myself. Well, listen! I want to talk to you. How about driving out with me tonight? We can talk on the parkway. Fine place to talk."

Bart hesitated only a split second. There would be no date with Mary tonight, magical or otherwise. Riding out with Alex should enable him to kill all the dark birds with one stone.

"Fine," he said. "I'll like that."

"Good. My office, four forty-five."

Alex Waringly hung up, and that was half of it. Bart placed the second call long distance, person to person. Aleta's voice came to him, cool, detached, curious, but not eager.

"I didn't get your letter, Al," he said.

"You didn't? Not yet?" she seemed amused.

"Did you write it?"

"As a matter of fact, no."

"Why not?"

"It's a bore. A stupid, juvenile, unfunny bore, that's why! It's over. Forget it."

"Did you think I was bluffing the other night?"

"I didn't think about you. You were tiresome."

"You gave me your word that you would write names, dates, and places, that you would mail me the letter."

"Did I?"

"You know that you did."

"I'd have given you arsenic, or carbolic, just to get rid of you."

"You didn't get rid of me. I warned you that you wouldn't. I'm riding out with your father tonight."

"Meaning what?"

"Meaning that, if I have to do it, I'll lay the whole story right on the table: for Alex, Florence, Roger, and any of the neighbors you care to invite."

"You wouldn't dare!"

"Five minutes after coffee, in the living room, no matter who is present or absent," he said. "If you stay away, it won't make any difference."

He hung up without waiting for her reply. Anger seethed

and boiled in him. He stalked out of the room and the Algonquin's one elevator took a long time in coming, as it invariably did. He cooled, waiting for it. There was nothing to hit, nothing to break, nothing to knock over. Cold anger was like the bearing of a grudge; he wanted none of it. Anger in him was a swift and violent storm; when it had no immediate action focus, it blew out to sea.

The next move was Aleta's and he would not compromise with her. It would be a relief to be done with secrecy, to be done with misrepresentation and dishonesty, to do just as he had told Aleta he would do: admit it all, accept his facts accomplished, and take whatever blame, reproaches, or condemnation came to him as a result. Alone, considering only himself, it would be a clean, deck-clearing thing. He couldn't, however, think only of himself. He had no right to hurt Alex, or Florence, or Roger, as he would have to hurt them, nor the right to betray the confidence that Aleta had once placed in him. He could not inflict pain on others to obtain relief for himself. If only relief were involved, he would have no course of action open to him; but the issue here was his child and he had given Aleta every chance to play fair with him. Because the child was more important than the lot of them, he wouldn't give a damn who got hurt if Aleta remained stubborn.

"She won't," he said grimly.

Bart strode through the lobby and out onto the sidewalk. The sunlight was spilling warmth into the streets of October. New York knew that summer was over but could not prove it. August was lingering into senility. He turned to his right at the corner and walked north on Sixth Avenue. The street signs said that this was the "Avenue of the Americas" but nobody believed that except strangers from out of town. People who lived on the avenue, or had stores there, wrote their addresses as Sixth Avenue and the post office delivered their mail. There were many stores. Only one block west of Fifth Avenue, Sixth was another planet. Stores sold secondhand magazines, secondhand phonograph records, secondhand anything, or new merchandise at secondhand prices. People in small shops fixed broken jewelry, repaired watches, pressed suits while the wearers waited, mended china and bric-a-brac, refinished furniture. One flight up, with a large sign in his grimy window, there was an old man who made violins. Bart strode past them all, past the Radio City Music Hall, too, home base for the famous Rockettes; and the Ziegfeld Theatre where Alfred Drake was playing in *Kismet*. He remembered Drake. Dore wanted to do a show with him once, but something happened. They would have been a good team.

He reached Fifty-ninth and he knew that there had been aim in his aimlessness. Before him lay Central Park, that great oasis of trees and lakes that extended from Fifty-ninth to 110th. Because he knew the Plaza entrance best, he walked east to Fifth Avenue. The horse-drawn hansom cabs waited there for passengers, as they waited day and night. He and Dore had ridden one of those cabs through the park when she was starring in *Buffalo Nickel*. Dore had been so excited that she had made him feel adult and superior. They had spent another day visiting the zoo. It was the greatest of all the zoos that they had visited, and the last. He wondered if Dore ever went to the zoo, or yearned to go, now that he was grown. He wondered, too, how Mary felt about them. A zoo couldn't just be visited; it had to be shared.

He walked into the glory of trees that were green and scarlet and gold. On either side of the wide park, the tall apartment buildings stretched like mountain ranges in long serrated lines. In the valley between these ranges, children rode ponies, sea lions sported in pools, tired adults rested and energetic adults hiked. He remembered the old theatre doorman downtown who was once a prominent welterweight fighter. "I used to do my road work in Central Park," the old man said, "running around the reservoir." Some young fighter might be doing that today. There were small boys sailing boats in a pond, competing with two solemn middle-aged men who had elaborate scale models. There was a huge impressive bust of Beethoven, and an obelisk that had weathered centuries under the sun of Egypt.

This, too, was New York. This was the New York of simple, honest, uncomplicated nonsense, where a man could come in his distress and his confusion to find perspective. Central Park was within walking distance of almost anywhere if one's legs were sound, and it was big enough to be lost in. There were authenticated stories of hermits who had lived in the park for long periods of time, foraging for their food amid the leavings of others, and supplied with every other need by nature and the City of New York.

Bart McBride walked in it and the odd pieces of his personal jigsaw puzzle fell into place. He was able to separate the idea of ten thousand dollars from the idea of Aleta, and the idea of work from the idea of wealth, the idea of fulfillment from the idea of gain, the idea of giving from the idea of taking. He knew where he stood in relation to Alex Waringly and his soul was tranquil. There was nothing that he could do about the decision that Aleta, not he, must make; but to that decision, which was out of his hands, he brought faith. She was not a person who would take the ultimate risk; she valued herself too highly.

He had his luncheon in the cafeteria near the pavilion. In mid-afternoon he walked back to the Algonquin and changed clothes. He reached the Waringly Building, a huge modern glass affair like a miniature United Nations, five minutes before his appointment time. Alex came out, bustling with energy after his day. There was nothing of the tired businessman in him.

"Glad to see you, boy," he said. "I should have had you come early enough for a tour. We've got a few impressive things around here. They'll keep. Let's go while the traffic is merely fierce, before it is terrible."

Alex Waringly's car was delivered to him. He took it over in front of the building and slid under the wheel with a grunt of satisfaction. "I like to drive my own car in all this insane mess," he said. "Ridiculous though that may seem, it relaxes me."

"It makes sense to me," Bart said.

He could understand the combative something in a man that New York traffic would challenge and satisfy. They drove across Forty-fifth Street and the one-way street was a slow-moving production line which picked up trucks, taxis, and private cars indiscriminately. For several blocks there was more boredom than challenge, but beyond Broadway the pace accelerated. They drove up the ramp to the elevated West Side Highway and then they were really into it. Traffic sizzled and hissed along and the pace was fast. Alex concentrated, his jaw thrust forward, eyes narrowed. He was a good driver and his enjoyment was obvious.

To the left, there were the great ocean liners of the Cunard and the French lines, and the deep blue of the Hudson River; then Riverside Park was under them. They rolled past the Soldiers' and Sailors' Monument, Grant's Tomb, and the great silver arc of the George Washington Bridge. Most of Manhattan was behind them and Alex, safely into the rhythm and with the traffic pattern resolved into an orderly flow, relaxed into conversation.

"Have you thought about that job I offered you?" he said.

"You didn't offer it to me. You talked about offering it to me. But I thought about it." Bart looked through the window at the kaleidoscope of traffic, two-tone cars in a bewildering variety of colors. He chose his words carefully. "I'm grateful to you, but I couldn't work for you. I wouldn't earn my check."

Alex chuckled. "I expected that reaction," he said. "Saw it coming. Hell, boy, I've got eyes and some savvy about people. You were quite a thing with Aleta once and now she snipes at you. She snipes at everyone, for that matter; but you'll just never get along with her again. You won't ever get along with Roger, either. So you don't want to step into something that looks like a family deal where you have to play on the same team. Right?"

Bart nodded. "That's part of it."

"I knew it." Alex chuckled again. "Well, you wouldn't be working for Aleta, you'd be working for me."

"I have no right to accept a job from you. I'm already in your debt."

"For what? A few drinks and sandwiches?"

"More than that."

"I can't see it. You were one of the young fellows Aleta brought around. The best of the lot for my money!" Alex cleared his throat. "I'll admit right now, with no women present, that I kind of wanted you in the family. You were one hell of a football player, boy, and it never gave you a swelled head. I got a bang out of you. How in hell could you owe me anything?"

"It meant something to me, knowing you, being welcome in a home like yours."

"Some of the damnedest people know me. It isn't much of a trick."

They were rolling through Westchester County now on the wide divided highway, with the fall colors dimmed by dusk. Bart was vaguely unhappy. Alex Waringly's direct, uncomplicated liking for him was an emotional involvement: Alex, obviously, was building slowly to the unveiling of an idea to which he had given much thought. The job, when he did offer it, would not be an opening on desk eighteen, nor a new desk with no work on it. Whatever it was, Alex had planned it, and Bart would not accept it. He knew that with certainty, but the refusal would not be easy. It was, he discovered with some surprise, more difficult to deny someone the joy of giving something than to refuse to give something to someone.

"Football has always been more than just a game to me," Alex said. "Kids grow into men fast playing hard football. They develop drive and initiative, the qualities we need in business. Football players, good ones, don't wobble around. They've learned how to concentrate on goals and on getting there. They see straight and they are hard to stop."

Bart looked at him, startled. "Do you believe that football develops all of that in a man?"

"Certainly. Don't you?"

Bart shook his head. "If it does, it uses those qualities up as fast as it develops them."

"Come now! You're kidding."

"I've known football players who, off the field, would look helplessly at their shoes, not able to make up their minds which one to lace first."

Alex laughed. Before he could reply, the car swerved sharply and the left front wheel started to bump. Alex swore under his breath and pulled into one of the trouble areas off the road. Bart got out when he did. The tire was completely flat.

"It can't be," Alex said. "Those are blowout-proof, puncture-proof tires."

"Something let the air out."

"I had them check my brakes today. Do you suppose. . . ?"

Bart nodded. "Some cluck in the garage let the air out. You've been running on the reserve. Let's get the spare on."

He took the key and opened the trunk. Alex cleared his throat. "Hell of a thing," he said. "Do you mind if I don't help you? I've had a few flurries with my heart. I'm scared to death of a thrombosis."

"It's a one-man job anyway," Bart said. "Think nothing of it."

He jacked up the wheel and he thought of what a slight exertion this was. He thought of those Western ball parks, of the bases he had run, the wild men he had caught. A man wasn't aware that he had a heart, never gave it a thought. As he lifted the big tire out of the trunk and bounced it, he was aware of Alex watching him wistfully; Alex who played golf, and ran a strenuous business, who looked fit, and who wasn't. He put the spare tire on and tightened the lugs. He put the flat back in the trunk.

"I'm glad you were along, boy," Alex said. "I got those tires so that nothing like this would happen to me."

"The tires are probably all right. It was a manpower failure, I imagine."

"Most failures are manpower failures. Products, good ones, are better than the men who buy them and abuse them." Alex was back at the wheel, frowning at the road. "A good man doesn't have to be grateful to someone who offers him a job," he said. "That somebody has one hell of a time finding good men. Remember that, boy. It's the eternal truth."

He drove for a mile, concentrated. "You wouldn't want something where you'd have to be mixed up with Aleta," he said, "and maybe Roger. I can see that. I've thought about it. We're moving in on Denver. It's a place where you have to buy land from the great-grandchildren of the original squatters if you want to do business, but it's a good town and it's on the boom. We're opening an office out there in one of their new buildings. You played baseball out there, didn't you?"

"Not for Denver. I played against them. Same league."

"Well, it's got publicity value. I'll send you out there as production manager."

Bart smiled. "I couldn't produce shavings from a pencil sharpener. I've never managed anything or anybody."

"That doesn't make any difference. We're not going to produce anything out there for at least two years. We're going to talk about production. You can lose your shirt trying to do business in the West before they are used to you. Your job will be to do that talking. You've got a title and you will give interviews to newspapers. You will talk to luncheon clubs. You will get around. You can make friends for us. It's a natural for you. After you've been operating for a while, those people out there will forget that we are Easterners and that they are against us. They'll start pressuring us to start production. That's when we can deal to advantage with them. Not until then."

"You make it seem important."

"Believe me, no. It is important. It's the way we have to operate. By the time we're ready to operate, we'll not only build a plant, we'll have subsidiary interests building homes for workers to buy, and we'll have the city extending services to those homes. It's a package: plant, worker homes, street paving, utilities, sewers, water. You'll put money into a lot of pockets and a little into your own."

The enthusiasm in Alex Waringly's voice was genuine. This was the life he lived and the game that he played. This was one of the visions he saw and he was a man whose visions were realized. He had had another, a different one, for Roger Vannin, who was a different type of man: the vision of a new product replacing the old, of inventive genius acting as a bulldozer in uprooting the deeply bedded habits of mankind.

Beside this Western vision, Bart saw one of his own. He and Mary could start fresh in a town they both knew. The girl who had been an orphan in Denver might have

children of her own there, children who would never have
to experience what she had. He and Mary could see that
plant come into being, and all those houses, feeling themselves part of a city's growth, citizens of a boom. He shook
his head. The vision of Alex was genuine and true because
it grew naturally out of all that Alex was. The parallel
vision of Bart was only a mirage because there was de-
lusion in it.

Some very fine people put their lives into the doing of
something that they were never built to do. They did it
because they let something irrelevant lure them on, something outside of, and apart from, the thing itself. They
never managed to do more than fairly well with the thing
they chose. They were forever confused, vaguely unhappy,
as futile and as desperate as the essentially decent characters in a Marquand novel. Bart had thought all of that
through during his day in the park. Mary had wanted
stage glamour and had tried desperately for a stage career because she wanted that glamour; but the glamour
was irrelevant and the essential qualities of mind and
spirit that were Mary's would not adapt to the demands of
a stage career.

Bart looked now at his mirage which was the pale sky
reflection of Alex Waringly's vision. It was a mirage and a
reflection because it existed on only one reality: the ten
thousand, or ten thousand plus, in dollars, and the things
that those dollars would buy. A week ago, he might have
jumped at Alex's offer because the rewards were great,
and great reward would have been an irresistible temptation. A man could grow a lot in a week if his personal
climate was right.

"It's a dream job, Alex," he said slowly; "a man who
could handle it would be a fool to hesitate over it. I
couldn't handle it."

"Nonsense. Why not?"

"I haven't got what it takes."

"You've got everything that it takes."

The car was taking the hills and curves of the Merritt
Parkway through the lovely Connecticut countryside.
There were no billboards, no signs. At intervals the road
widened and the extra lane curved off to the right, taking

cars off the parkway and leading them into the towns.
Alex had an hour behind the wheel in the morning, another hour in the evening. His home in Connecticut, with
its orchards and gardens, was as close to his office as
that. He lived well because he was doing the thing that he
was magnificently equipped to do. A man could perhaps
learn to love anything that provided him with comfort and
beauty, and, in the loving, serve it well. Bart shook his
head again. It was not all comfort and beauty. He remembered those unread books in the Waringly library, and
Alex frowning in bewilderment over the mystery of no
time. He remembered the daughters who were spoiled because the family couldn't put them out in the garage, and
of the men whom they married, who became spoiled sons-
in-law.

Something inside of him warned Bart that he was wandering into irrelevancy, but even the irrelevancy belonged
to a pattern into which he would never fit and never feel
at home.

"I'm more grateful than I'll ever be able to express,
Alex," he said. "I'll probably never be able to do as well
on my own, and never meet anyone else as generous as
you are. But I can't take what you're offering because I
can't give enough."

Alex caught the note of finality in his voice. He slumped
lower in his seat behind the wheel. "I wish I knew why,"
he said.

He drove a mile in silence, then shook his head. "I must
be growing old, boy," he said. "I don't understand your
generation. I can't get through to Roger. I can't get
through to you. If I had a son, it would probably be the
same thing. I'm damned if I know what you want that I
haven't got."

He drove onto the extra lane that suddenly opened up
ahead of him. He drove the long arc that took him onto
the state road. They were nearly home.

"I know what Roger wants," he said heavily. "He wants
all the soft things and nothing hard, all play and no work.
You aren't like that. What in hell do you want?"

Bart thought about the sermon in the Abbey. He had
stood before God's showcase tonight and the offer of Alex

had not been penny candy. Still, he had not wanted it. He had seen this afternoon, with terrible clarity, what he did want, but he had to talk to Mary. A man alone could choose for himself, but he was no longer alone.

"A year from now, I'll tell you, Alex," he said, "if you still want to know."

## CHAPTER 10

Aleta wore a scarlet blouse with a zigzag slash of gold. Her skirt was russet, flaring. She was dramatically autumn and she was in very good humor. She talked brightly of things that didn't matter and she treated Bart with impersonal friendliness. It was a mood that he had not expected, and evidently one that her mother had not expected, either. He saw Florence look at Aleta several times with a bewildered look in her eyes. Bewilderment and bafflement were normal to Florence, but this bewilderment was special. Alex carried his share of the conversation heavily. Roger was missing.

"I told him to stay in town and play," Aleta said lightly when Bart inquired about him. "He's still a college boy, you know. They've got some kind of a roar on at dear old Columbia tonight."

It was easy to carry on cocktail conversation with Florence at any time, and with Aleta in this mood. Florence told long anecdotes about people Bart didn't know and was content with an audience; Aleta settled for patter. Bart did not have a moment alone with Aleta until just before they went in to dinner.

"Well?" he said.

She looked up at him, her oddly narrow eyes drawn nearly shut. "I'm tempted to call you," she said.

"Don't! I would hate to hurt Alex or Florence, but I'd do it."

"I believe you," she said. "You'd do it. I should have reserved myself for gentlemen."

"What does all that mean—yes or no?"

"I mean that you win."

"When?"

"After dinner. I'll drive you to the station if you refuse to stay when they ask you."

"I'll refuse. But you can't trick me again, Al."

Her lip curled. "After tonight," she said, "I don't even want to hear anyone mention you."

She swept into the dining room ahead of him and she was as brightly cheerful about meaningless trivialities at dinner as she had been over cocktails. More than anything that she could have said or done, the bitterness of her exchange with him convinced Bart that this was the showdown between them, that she had conceded and that she was done with fencing and evasion. It was difficult to hold his place in the flow of conversation, feeling that sense of imminence, and Alex was no help. Alex was definitely glum. In the few minutes that they had together after dinner, the older man made an effort to recapture the mood of early evening.

"Sleep on what we talked about, boy," he said, "and ride in with me in the morning. Maybe we can clear up what's troubling you."

"We couldn't, Alex. I wish we could. I'll never work for anybody I like better."

"You're a damned fool, Bart. You could work for me."

Their eyes met and Bart felt very close to Alex Waringly. It would be a big thing to be Alex Waringly's son, someone who had grown up in Alex Waringly's world, absorbing his enthusiasm through the years, sharing his visions; but he wasn't the son that a lonely man wanted, and he couldn't be.

"I had better go back on the train, Alex," he said.

Aleta came back then and he tossed it to her casually. "Do you suppose you could run me to the station, Al?"

"Gladly," she said.

Florence protested his going and Alex shook hands with him warmly. Only Florence, of the four of them, failed to realize that this was the end of a chapter, the speeding of a guest who wouldn't return. Bart glanced around the living room. He had no good-bys to say to things, only to people. The Waringly possessions all wore mantles of impermanence, owing their presence in the house to their newness, to the fashion in interiors. No single piece of the furniture had ever impressed its personality upon him, nor established any association with the memories that he had of Waringly. That, perhaps, was significant; certainly it was sad.

He walked out under the stars with Aleta and his nerves were tight. She wore a short gold jacket and she strolled to the car with a slight swagger, humming under her breath. She started the engine and he slid into the seat beside her. The headlights slashed the darkness and gravel crunched under her tires as the car moved forward. She swung the wheel to the left as they cleared the pillars at the end of the driveway.

"Who's the girl, Bart?" she said.

"What girl?"

She laughed. "Who am I, Little Miss Muffet? Don't you think I can tell? All this sudden passion about paternity! Ugh! You're as obvious as television."

"Obvious or not, there is only one thing that I want to discuss with you."

"And she has coached you carefully in your lines! Just how you should go about it." Aleta laughed again. "I hope that she is a tough little peasant. She'll have to be. But don't tell me that she's subtle."

"I'm not telling you anything. I'm asking. You can't talk me away from the subject."

She was driving fast. Her tires screamed in protest on the curves. "Can't I?" she said.

"No! I took your word back there. The deadline was coffee."

"So it was. Only a skunk would set such a deadline."

"I made the mistake of trusting you last time." He was aware suddenly of the route, the familiar road. "You were supposed to take me to the station."

"I will. You wanted proof, didn't you?" Her lips curled. "Documents."

She swung the car off the road, into her own driveway.

Bart tensed in the seat beside her. "Listen, Al," he said. "If Roger is there, or Betsy, or whoever, it makes no difference to me, none in the world."

She braked to a stop and flipped off the ignition. Her narrow eyes, with their uplifted corners, were raised to his. "I never hated anyone so much in all my life," she said.

She slid out from under the wheel and walked stiff-legged toward the house. The house was dark and the cricket orchestra was playing in all the fields. The moon was trying to penetrate the low-lying clouds with light. Bart walked behind Aleta and the feeling in his nerves was the competitive feeling when a game was tight and the crucial action was swinging his way. Aleta's fingers touched a switch and the hall light came on. She walked into the living room and pulled the chain switch of the floor lamp beside the piano. There was a soft, low-intensity glow in the room. She turned slowly.

"I've hated you ever since you made me feel dirty with your damned proposal of marriage," she said tensely. "Your damned, arrogant, filthy offer to make an honest woman of me."

"It wasn't that."

"It was. You were taking a public bath, washing your sins away. You made me feel as though I'd done something disgusting and could only get clean again by marrying you. You!"

He stood there staring at her and he could feel the hot red color creeping up out of his collar. He had been young and confused, trying to do what he thought was right. He had been nerved up that day, facing a difficult task that he had had to force himself to face. There had been nothing in him, or in his experience, to prepare him for Aleta's reaction. He had had no idea that he would appear as he did to her. She walked up and down now.

"I can just see what marriage to you would be like. Sitting at home while you went on long, sweaty weekends with my father: hunting, fishing, golf. The he-men at sport! Long dull evenings while you sat around with him, and a lot of other go-getters, talking government contracts, plants, urban developments, and suds."

Bart's jaw tightened as he thought of Alex. "Those are the things that buy you what you want from life," he said.

"There's enough of it right now to buy me everything that I want for as long as I live."

"Your father knows more about that than you do. The stuff doesn't grow wild. It has to be cultivated, like a farm."

"A farm!" She looked at him and laughed, her head thrown back. Her hair was very black, her lips very red, her teeth very white; there was no softness in her. "A farm! You would think of that. You always were a stinking peasant. The man with the hoe! You don't know, and never knew, what fun is. You aren't even decently barbarian."

"I think that I know what fun is."

"Do you? Maybe you'll have it with that chunky Cinderella of yours. Maybe it will be what you call fun. My God! I can just see it!"

He took a step toward her. "Can you?" he said grimly. "Well, suppose you come back from Hysteria, charming though it be, and tell me the only thing that I want to hear from you!"

She faced him, her right hand opening and closing, her chin thrust forward. "Your child!" she said. "Your dear little child! You worried about that, didn't you? You sweated it out."

"You said it was a boy," he said.

"Did I? You wanted to marry me all over again, didn't you? You wrote me long, long letters. Do you know that I've still got those letters, Sir Launfal? What a humorist you were! On your knees, wallowing, you big clumsy ape! Drooling and slobbering!"

She lashed him and it was worse than the day she swung her hand against his face, slapping him. He had taken that and he took this.

"I burned your letters," he said, "so that no one would see them."

"The noble knight, *sans peur et sans reproche*. Always burn the letters of a pregnant woman! Chivalry demands it." She walked away, wheeled, and came back. Her voice was low, controlled, cold with hatred.

"You stupid bastard!" she said. "I wouldn't go through a pregnancy for any man on earth."

He stared at her, uncomprehending, and she laughed at him. "You liked feeling guilty," she said. "You liked making me feel guilty. I gave it to you. You were too far away to know better, so I gave it to you. I rubbed your nose in it!"

He knew then. He knew with a sick falling away of everything inside of him. There had never been a child of his, born or unborn. The little girl in the gray uniform didn't exist. The little boy who would play ball for the girl orphans didn't exist. All that existed was this sick, all-gone feeling in the pit of his stomach, the long months of anguish in Japan that were forever seared in his memory, the shadow over two years of his life, the desperate prayers, the frantic helplessness.

"You wanted it!" Aleta said. "And you got it." She looked up into his face, enjoying what she read there. "You conceited fool! While I was having that baby, I was out nearly every night with Roger."

His hands shot out then and gripped her. They had an independent, malevolent will of their own, needing no signal from his mind. He saw the stark terror in her eyes and knew only that it was a good thing to see. She had racked him on the most brutal rack in the world, and she had never relented. When he came back, and she had a second opportunity, she had put him on the rack again. She had kept him there until the last possible second, drawing it out.

The scream that she tried to release was a thin, dry, croaking sound in her throat. He spun her around and his powerful fingers moved toward that throat. There was a drawling, theatrical voice speaking then from the doorway.

"Very pretty. Just like a play. The husband's night out."

There was a break in the rhythm of destruction, a light flashing in darkness, the slow running out of a spin, the feeling of solid ground, a voice, words, a resumption of thought, the slackening of hands. Bart released Aleta and was aware that she reeled drunkenly away from him. He turned slowly to the door.

Roger was standing there. His face was sickly white and he had an ugly short-barreled revolver in his hand. "I always knew that this would happen sometime," he said. "I had a hunch lately that it would be the football hero."

Aleta had lost her fight for balance when she reeled out of Bart's grip. She had one knee on the floor, her left hand gripping the arm of a chair. "No, Roger, no!" she said. "It isn't that. You saved my life."

"Your life? Oh no!" Roger was very bitter, very dramatic. "Didn't you suppose that I'd know that this fellow was coming out with Alex? It was so damned sweet of you to suggest that I stay in town. Well, I warned you."

He held the gun steady and he was the length of the room away. Bart measured him, and measured the distance. It was too far. Aleta had told him that Roger was gun-happy. It was one time when she had told the truth. The man held the revolver the way a gun should be held. He was a slob, a crybaby who liked to indulge his self-pity in talk, but that didn't make him less dangerous when he had a gun in his hand.

"I told you that I'd shoot you and shoot the man if I ever caught you," Roger said.

Aleta was staring at him with terrified fascination. Bart had the idea that she did not quite believe in the reality of this, that some morbid thing in her was thrilled by it. She was somebody who liked to roast people over slow fires. She had probably done it to Roger often. Now he was doing it.

"It isn't that," she whispered. "Let me tell you."

What could she tell Roger? Not the truth. It would be as bad as what he thought. Bart shifted position and Roger's eyes flickered toward him.

"Don't be in a hurry!" he said.

Bart hadn't spoken a word to him. It wasn't the time or place for words. A word, the wrong word, could trigger that gun. The man was keyed up and he might not be all show-off. The self-dramatization might be only skin deep. Bart had a swift vision of what it would mean if he were shot here. He would have no chance to explain to Mary. She would always wonder. It would ruin Dore. There was his father in the monastery. Once a man was killed, he couldn't explain. How many men had died this way, with the world accepting the wrong explanation? He measured the distance again. It was a damned long room.

"Roger," Aleta said, "put that gun away. Please! It isn't what you think. I'll tell you. Please."

"You'll tell me." He looked at her bitterly. "You're always telling me." He leaned forward. "Do you know the worst thing that could happen to you—you and Dorinda Daly's little boy? I'll let you have each other."

He turned the gun toward his own mouth. Aleta screamed and Bart moved then. He took off from his toes and he moved as all of his life had trained him to move when a ball was hit or a signal called. He swept a heavy chair out of his way as though it had no existence. Roger had time for only one wide-eyed, incredulous stare, then Bart's left hand closed on the gun and Bart's right crossed to his chin, knocking him out into the hall.

Aleta shrieked and then she rushed at Bart. There was mad fury in her face and he stepped back away from her, holding the gun.

"You foul dirty brute!" she said. "You've hurt him. You filthy peasant!"

She struck and clawed at him, and he did not have to take that from her any more. He gripped her wrist and flung her away from him. She stared at him, afraid of him again, then threw herself across the prone Roger.

"Roger," she sobbed, "Roger darling. Did he hurt you?"

Bart did not look at her. He was looking down at the swinging cylinder of the gun he had opened, trying to absorb the last fantastic, incredible absurdity of the night. The revolver was empty.

He tossed it aside and walked past the two people on the floor of the entry hall. The night was dark and cool and he walked blindly. There wasn't any baby. There hadn't been any bullets in the gun. Roger and Aleta were two people who liked to tend the fires and tighten the thumbscrews, and turn the windlass of the rack, both of them. Maybe Roger hadn't been that way, maybe he had learned from Aleta. It made no difference. He was that way now. He had had some kind of an insane idea that Aleta would beg and plead him out of suicide tonight.

Maybe he would have enjoyed that in some perverse way. He had been careful, though, not to load the gun.

Aleta loved that kind of weakness, any kind of weakness, perhaps. She had to have a creature like Roger. Her nature demanded it. Roger carried coals for his own hell. A man couldn't feel sorry for him.

Bart McBride walked the dark road toward the station, then, suddenly, he stopped walking. He sat down on the grass beside the road and nausea swept him. He had learned tonight why men kill women, and how. The weapon of destruction which his two hands represented had not been empty.

## CHAPTER 11

Mary Norbert flew down to New York on Saturday evening before the show closed in Boston. She had talked to Bart several times over the phone, but the conversations had been unsatisfactory. He was cheerfully evasive, and the cheerfulness did not quite ring true. She knew that he had seen Aleta Waringly, and that her phone call asking him not to do so had been too late. Beyond that, she did not know anything.

"It can wait, Bianca," he said.

She had had to be content with that because he changed the subject when she pressed him. "A telephone is no good," he said. "I can't see the whites of your eyes."

Something had happened to him, and she could not imagine what, so she swung from curiosity to worry in the time that she had, which was little. The detail work in Dorinda's Boston life was staggering, and the detail belonged to Mary. Dorinda referred only once to her collapse on Wednesday night. Thursday afternoon, after her nap, she came into the parlor where Mary was working. She was wearing a peach negligee and she looked rested, fresh, as young as Bart.

"I made a fool of myself last night, didn't I?" she said.

Mary turned away from the typewriter and sat facing her. "No," she said. "It was a very human way to act. I loved you for it."

"Thank you, darling. It was still a balloon ascension, and no excuse for it. I even forgot that I had you out there listening to it."

"I didn't want to listen. I didn't hear anything that needed apology or explanation."

"I'm afraid that you did. I seem to remember shouting."

"No." Mary wanted very badly to tell Dorinda about Bart and herself. It was something that belonged to Bart as much as to her, or more so. They would have to tell Dorinda together. "I took Brother Anselm to the station in a cab," she said.

Dorinda's eyes widened. "Why?"

"He would have walked. He walked up here to the hotel after riding all day in a train. He was catching the train back at five something with another long day ahead of him."

Dorinda looked away. She bit her lip, shrugged. Her eyes came back to Mary. "Thank you, lamb," she said. "It was a sweet thought."

"I like him."

Dorinda rose. She walked the length of the room and walked back. "So do I," she said softly. "I always did. I still do. Those awful clothes! Why do you suppose he ever went into a place like that?"

Mary met her eyes. "What would you suggest?"

"A thousand things." Dorinda stood in the middle of the floor considering. She frowned slightly, then shook her head. "No, I guess not." She smiled at Mary, a bit rue-fully. "You know too much about me, darling, but if somebody has to know it, I'm glad that you're the one. This was a thing that always was too much for me. I was falling off merry-go-round horses before a real one threw me."

She left on the echoes of that enigmatic remark which obviously meant something clear and precise to her, no matter how vague it might seem to anyone else. She was back in a few minutes, standing framed in the doorway.

"Watch the whole show from out front tonight, Mary," she said. "It's not right yet, but it's getting better."

Mary watched it. She knew what was wrong with it from Dorinda's viewpoint before the first act was over. The backers were too far apart in their specialized interests. The men who had put up the money for this fabulously expensive production were, of course, eager for the show to succeed; but each of them wanted that success *plus* something else. The TV money was interested in Emmet Dane. The movie money was interested in Gilda Skara. Those people were valuable properties on loan to Broadway, so there were pressure groups working for each of them: a better song, a few more lines, some extra business. The minor elements of the show had been built up too much. There were people doing brilliant specialties who should be doing supporting roles, and only supporting roles. Dorinda was off the stage too often, with nothing to prepare for her return.

In the second act, Mary had a chance to see what Dorinda was doing about it. It was a subtle thing, and nothing that anyone actually could see, but Mary felt what Dorinda had done. She had changed the tempo, somehow. She had slowed everything that she did, not enough to disturb the fast pace of the show, just enough to draw the others in toward her, enough to establish herself as the focal point. There was no definition for what she did, and no one would ever write a manual on how to do it, but it was done. When Dorinda was on stage, she dominated it; when she was off, she was missed.

The curtain fell on the last act and Mary went backstage. "It was marvelous, Dorinda," she said.

Dorinda was looking into her mirror, her lips tight. "It will be," she said.

Carter Brill came up for the Friday performance and he was less enthused than Mary. "It's still an animal act and the animals aren't going through the hoops because nobody has a whip," he said. "Dick Cowlen isn't directing this show; he's running after it, wagging his tail."

So that was Boston, and Dorinda, and Carter. Mary flew down in the dusk and came in over New York when the lights were blazing from Coney Island to Westchester, when the tall buildings were standing small like castles seen from a cloud, and the lights were lying in lines over Brooklyn and Queens, and out into the harbor and the islands, and along the coast of Jersey. It was the biggest city in the world, and you knew it, flying into it. She felt a catch in her throat that was pure emotion and not related to anything save, perhaps, pride, pride that she was part of it all, that two small rooms down in that vast jewel box belonged to her.

She had told Bart to meet her at the airport terminal instead of at the airport and her feelings were mixed about that. She wanted to be with him on Manhattan and not out in the clutter of the airport. She wanted to have the trip behind her, all of it, when she saw him, and an airline trip to New York wasn't over until the airport bus set a person down on pavement.

"I want to be free when I see him," she said, and she did not try to define what she meant by "free," not even to herself.

He was waiting there, bigger than anyone, when she alighted from the bus and it made no difference that they had not had their date, nor the promised magic, that they had never said the things they had postponed saying. He stepped toward her with his arms out, and she melted into them, raising her lips to his. She did not consider what New York would think of it, and New York didn't think about it at all. New York flowed out of the bus and into the waiting room on two sides of them, accepting the fact that they were an island around which the stream must find its way.

"You walk in beauty, Bianca," he said huskily.

"I've been riding."

"Doubtless you rode in beauty, too. I wasn't there."

"There are practical matters. My bags."

"The place stays open. We will redeem them eventually."

He led her out into the noisy confusion of the streets. She had a feeling of lift, of rightness. There was something about him always that set a mood. He could make a play out of their most casual moment, very much as Dorinda did, but there was never anything of the actor in him. He had written her a letter to Boston, and in studiously avoiding any personal references to himself, he had revealed an amazing lot of himself. He had written several paragraphs about the importance of nonsense. "Even people who appreciate it," he wrote, "often fail to realize that nonsense has boundaries just as any other state has, that you leave it if you drive straight through, and that you get lost in it if you just drive around aimlessly. You are the only person I have ever met who knows where the boundaries are and who doesn't get lost."

Being what she was, and as she was, she would have to love a man who could write that in a love letter, in the first letter that he ever wrote to her. There was a language of nonsense, too, that was not silly, not exactly poetry, not anything that could be described in any other terms than its own. He spoke it fluently at the right times, and at other times he forgot it.

They had reached Forty-second Street. Grand Central Station was a massive pile of stone facing them, and the Commodore Hotel towered. Thompson's was a long window in the face of Grand Central; inside, it was a cafeteria with composition trays, well-worn silverware, and food without frills.

"I can offer coffee," Bart said.

"Accepted. *Gracias, señor.*"

"It isn't polite to speak Spanish after sundown."

They slid their trays along the rods before the display cases. Mary saw an icing roll with jelly in the center. She ordered it from the counterman.

"I'm going to eat this for somebody," she said. "Do you mind?"

He shook his head. "I wouldn't even mind if you ate it for yourself."

She sat across a table from him and she had the weird thought that this man could only be described in her life as "a familiar stranger" or, perhaps more accurately, as "a well-known stranger," which was very close to the language of nonsense. She knew those level eyes so well, and the smile, the strength and the ruggedness; but she did not know the white scar on his left cheekbone below his eye, nor the half-moon scar on his chin, nor was she quite ac-

customed to the fact that his nose was slightly out of line
and his eyebrows oddly flat. The story of physical punish-
ment was written in his face, but so much else was written there that she did not feel the horror that she normally
felt for the pain that people suffered.

"The diary, Bianca," he said. "The play-by-play. What
did you do?"

"Nothing. Please. You know what I'm dying to know
about."

He shook his head. "Not yet. Tell me about John Adams
and Paul Revere, and the Cabots and the Lodges."

"They were at a tea party all week," she said, "but
there was a show up there."

She told him about *The Seventh Wife*. At an adjoining
table two men were talking excitedly with many gestures
in a language that she did not recognize, a woman somewhere behind her was pouring out a long tale of mis-
fortune in a high-pitched whining voice; other voices rose
and fell, silverware clattered, people wandered aimlessly
around with trays, looking for tables. A person could talk
here in privacy, the privacy of hubbub. Bart listened to
her gravely.

"I talked to Dore on the phone," he said. "She sounded
all right."

"She is. But she has to be better than she has ever been
in her life. There is another thing——"

She hesitated and he pushed his chair back. "Let's go
outside," he said.

He led her through the door that opened on one of the
station waiting rooms. There were many people sitting on
the long benches, but he did not hesitate. He led her to a
balcony overlooking the vast concourse. They could see
the four-sided clock above the information booth, the people gathered around the booth, three deep, the thousands
of people hurrying to and from trains; where they sat, it
was quiet, isolated.

"I feel guilty taking up railroad sitting space after giving
my business to the airline," Mary said.

"You shouldn't. Look at all this space! If nobody sat
around, they'd have to close the place."

He grinned, then frowned at his hands. "I take you to the damnedest joints, Bianca."

"They're wonderful. They're New York. Nobody would ever fall in love here, or get married here, if they had to depend on places like the Stork Club. This place not only has privacy, it has splendor."

"And grandeur," he said. "It is the temple of the great god Transient. Now that we have that settled . . ."

"Yes."

She told him about his father's visit to Boston, softening the part where Dorinda cracked. She told him about that other station and her engagement party.

"All the McBrides are lavish and throw parties in glamorous places," he said.

"It was my party. I bought him a bun and coffee. And he is going to give us an Abbot's Mass for a wedding present. The Abbot will say it if Brother Anselm asks him to do it."

Bart looked away. His jaw line was taut. "Did he make that trip just to keep me out of trouble?"

"Yes. No hotel. No anything. Up and right back. All that way."

"It's something to know," he said. "Now I'll tell one." He drew a deep breath.

"There isn't, and never was, a baby, Bianca."

"Bart!"

"That's true."

He told her in curt, clipped phrases about a girl who wouldn't go through a pregnancy for any man alive, a girl who avenged affronts to herself with slow torture. She felt a little sick, hearing it. She gripped his hand.

"Bart, no! I can't grasp it. It was never real to me, then suddenly it was very real. I wanted to take that baby, Bart. I did. It was going to be our eldest."

He swept her into his arms wordlessly and held her there. She could hear the strong, steady beating of his heart. It was a long time before he spoke and it was enough for her just to rest there, close to him, feeling the hurt in him that was greater than any of those which scarred his face.

"She didn't hurt you, Bart," she said. "Not a crippling hurt. She couldn't. You're too strong."

She felt him draw air into his lungs. "No," he said. "She didn't hurt anybody. All the good and true and beautiful things came out of other people because of what she did, things I would never have known, never had. You! My father making that trip—you again, wanting to take the baby."

"I did, Bart."

"I know."

They were quiet, close to each other, snatching this moment in the place that they had. "Mary," he said at length, "we could live in Denver and have ten thousand a year."

"How?"

She listened while he told her of Alex Waringly, of the slow infiltration of big money into an entrenched town, and the function of a production manager who had nothing to do with production. "We could have a lot, Mary," he said. "We could grow big with the town."

He was being fair to this proposition, but she knew that he didn't want it, that he couldn't want it. She knew what he was, and if she had not known, it would have been clear to her after talking to Brother Anselm.

"Let's go back and catch in the Western League," she said.

"Do you mean that?"

"Absolutely."

"Why?"

"It would be a more honest expression of yourself."

"You're in this too. What about you?"

"I'm a girl who grew up cheering for boy ballplayers. Remember?"

"Yes," he said softly. "I do. There's something else, Bianca. I mentioned to you once that I had an offer from a small college. Athletic director. Coach. Instructor in English lit on the side."

She straightened inside the arc of his arms, freeing herself so that she could look at him. "You didn't want it," she said. "You told me that it was a personally conducted tour up your own dead-end street."

"My own blind alley. I don't have a dead-end street."

"I wouldn't know. I haven't seen the alley either."

There was a certain eagerness in him now. "The coach who took the job is quitting at the end of the football season," he said. "He likes to win games. A man can't win many down there. No alumni fund. No pros. There wouldn't be much glory and none of the kids would have a chance at All-American. A man would have to work with them for their own sakes because they wouldn't be good enough to make a reputation for him."

"Is that bad?"

"Not to me. I might be of some good in a place like that. If I couldn't teach anybody anything, I could help them to learn. I've thought about it, Bianca. People don't end up in blind alleys unless they're confused. I'm pretty nearly an expert on confusion. I know how to put up the detour signs and the warning signs, and where to put them. . . . But don't know——"

He faltered in his speech, stopped, and frowned at his hands. For a few minutes the dominance that was in him had powered his words, because the words expressed all that he was, a man who thought easily, naturally, instinctively, in terms of giving rather than in terms of taking. When his voice trailed off, Mary felt a little thrill of fright. "He could lose it," she thought, "that wonderful damn-the-torpedoes swagger that he has. He worried about me and he wasn't sure any more. I must never do that to him, or let him do it to himself."

"What is the town like, Bart?" she said.

"Small. About twelve thousand. There isn't much there, but it's a pretty town." His eyes lighted for a moment, then the light went out. "But, hell, it wouldn't do."

"Why not?"

His eyes came up to hers. "Because I can't kid myself when I talk it out loud, when it isn't just a daydream. There wouldn't be much for us, Bianca. Not at all what I want for you. It doesn't go anywhere. Not much chance for notice, or recognition or money."

"You know best. Maybe we're still catching in the Western League. Is it co-ed, Bart?"

"Yes."

She smiled into his worried eyes. "Maybe I can coach

too," she said. "I'm bright and willing, a good worker. I've learned a few things here and there."

They sat on a bench, looking at each other, and then she was in his arms again, feeling his lips on hers, floating in time between yesterday and tomorrow.

It was one of New York's railroad stations. More than a quarter of a million people arrived at, or departed from, Grand Central every day. Only two people noticed the man and the girl who kissed on a balcony bench. A ticket seller off duty turned and grinned at the ancient newsboy who limped along beside him. The newsboy shrugged.

"So maybe they're cousins," he said.

## CHAPTER 12

In the Abbey of St. Urban the twelfth of October was the Feast of Sts. Evagrius and Priscian, martyrs. There was a Requiem Mass in the chapel and a solemn procession to the cemetery. The bells of the Abbey tolled solemnly and the monks chanted the prayers for the dead that monks had chanted for other monks long centuries before the first European sailed up the river that was now called "Hudson."

Brother Basil, the keeper of the bees, had died in his sleep on Sunday night.

Father Abbot led the procession to the grave and said the final prayers as the body was returned to the earth. Brother Basil was wrapped in his habit with the hood of his cowl drawn over his face. They were no longer "our habit and cowl," they were forever his.

When the earth was shoveled into the grave, Brother Anselm fixed the cross in place, the cross that he had carved on Monday. It had been a shock to him when he was reminded by death that the brother's name was Basil. He had long thought of him as Brother Bumble. He lingered a moment at the grave, thinking about him. There was little to think about. Brother Basil had been old and stoop-shouldered. He loved the bees and understood them. He kept the monastery supplied with honey, which was a wholesome sweet.

Brother Anselm walked out of the cemetery alone. It had taken him only a few minutes to mark the grave with its cross, but the others, priests and brothers, had already dispersed to their labors. There had been no sorrow, no grieving, no regret. A good man had laid aside his labor and had answered the call of God. It was a natural thing, and as God willed it to be, so who could question it?

Brother Basil had had no relatives in the world who cared to come to his burial. Brother Anselm was glad for him, and for the Abbey, that this was so. Outsiders did not understand the ways of monks and their manners at funerals were unseemly. They lacked dignity and they disturbed the dignity that they found; which was, Brother Anselm decided suddenly, an uncharitable thought on his part and a sin of pride. A monk should not look for virtues in which to clothe himself; it was enough to walk in humility, leaving the distribution of virtues to God.

He said an act of contrition as he was climbing to the postulant dorm on the top floor. There was a need of a new sash-weight cord in one of the windows. Brother Anselm looked out into the clear morning and the sunlight was a golden haze close to the earth. The hives of Brother Bumble looked lonely and deserted. Sometime today, no doubt, Father Abbot would appoint another brother to the work and it would be forgotten in time that the old brother's name had been Basil.

Brother Anselm, looking down from his height upon the field of the old brother's work, was certain that he would remember him. He would pray for Brother Basil now and for a decent interval, giving him time to serve out his purgatory; then, if he had some difficulty in his work or some annoyance in his day, Brother Anselm would pray *to* him, trusting in the mercy of God.

In New York the day had been depressingly hot and the night was heavy, humid, impossible weather for October, a curse upon theatres with new plays that had opened early. The crowd of curious, the gawkers and the celebrity worshipers, had gathered on the sidewalk for the opening of *The Seventh Wife*. A mounted policeman was doing his best to keep a lane open for the arriving first-nighters. Tempers were short and there was much jostling among those who were waiting to see not the play but the spectators.

Backstage in her star dressing room, Dorinda Daly sat before her mirror doing nervous, unnecessary things to her make-up, her hair, her first-act costume. Carter Brill sat quietly smoking, watching her. She dropped her lipstick. It fell only as far as the shelf, a few inches from her hand, but she stared at it helplessly.

"Forget it, Dorinda," Carter said. "You don't need it."

"I know. I don't need anything and I need everything. This hellish heat! Why did it have to be like this, Carter? Why?"

"It just is. Let's leave weather to the weather men. We can't change it."

"But it will kill them. They'll hate the show. They'll hate everything."

"No, they won't."

There was a knock on the door and a voice calling: "Fifteen minutes, Miss Daly."

Dorinda stiffened. Carter rose, snuffing out the cigarette in an ash tray. This was it. The months of planning, working, memorizing, rehearsing, dressing, trying out, changing, rememorizing, working again—it all came down to this moment, fifteen minutes till curtain. He crossed the room and Dorinda rose, facing him. He laid his hands lightly on her shoulders, his fingers barely touching her flesh.

"You're the top, darling," he said, "the all-time top. Nothing can happen to you that isn't good. You'll hold them all evening in one small hand."

She lifted her face to him and he kissed her gently. "Thank you, Carter," she said.

Janet came in and the tick of the clock was loud, a steady, beating, relentless sound. "Nine minutes," it said, "eight, seven——"

Bart and Mary reached the theatre on a long zigzagging course that consumed an afternoon. They shopped for Dore's birthday present on Madison Avenue, and they had cocktails on the terrace at Rockefeller Center, watching chilled ice skaters on a warm afternoon. They prayed together in the cool dusk of St. Patrick's Cathedral and they dined in a French restaurant where Bart tried out his command of French and found it adequate, discovering at the same time that Mary spoke French more fluently than he did.

"They started me at the orphanage very early," she said, "when they thought that I could sing. Italian, too. There was a French nun there."

He shook his head. "There is so much about you that I don't know."

"Some things that you don't even suspect."

They laughed together and it was good to laugh about the unknown, to see a road through mist and to know that they would walk it together, not knowing where it led. It was good, too, to wonder about each other, to make discoveries about each other, to build their bridges to small intimacies across the sands of strangeness.

"I was always certain that I would never marry a man whom I hadn't known for years," Mary said.

He could understand that. As a cold, remote principle having nothing to do with fact, he could even approve it.

"I felt a little cheated sometimes," he told her, "because I didn't grow up in a neighborhood. It seemed to me that I never really knew anyone; that all the normal people grew up with their friends, and married the girl next door, and moved in down the block."

"I used to think that too. I was fascinated with families as well as with neighborhoods, because I never had either."

"I finally discovered that backstage is a neighborhood too," he said.

"Did you?" The idea excited her. "So did I."

They were coming out of Saks Fifth Avenue. She stopped on the sidewalk. "Let's go over to Walgreen's at Forty-fourth and Broadway for coffee."

"Why so far?"

"It's an idea."

They walked the long crosstown block and down Broadway. *Sabrina* was playing at the Criterion, *On the Waterfront* at the Astor. In Walgreen's drugstore Mary greeted several young people, introduced Bart to three of them. "Actors. Actresses. They hope." She looked around possessively. "My dates often took me here before I met you," she said. "It's the Sardi's of the bit players, the walk-ons, and all the people who live in casting office anterooms."

He felt a pang of doubt, looking at her. "You'll miss all this, Bianca."

Her eyes widened. "How will I? It's mine. I'll always have it."

"Even out in the sticks?"

"Anywhere. Everywhere. I've got everything that I ever had. As long as I remember, I have the things that I remember." She leaned toward him. "I had a weird thought about that last night, and about you."

"You mean that you remembered me after you left me last night?"

"I did. And I remembered how I used to go to motion pictures a lot. I figured back in time. I was going to pictures when you were at Cornell."

"Extraordinary! You astonish me."

"Don't be sarcastic. I was. I did. And every week they had a newsreel and highlights of the big football games." She paused and jabbed the table top with one eloquent finger. "Cornell was one of the big teams. I remembered because I always loved that word 'Cornell.' I was away out in the West and I didn't know anything about it, but I rooted for Cornell and wanted it to win because it was a lovely word."

There was intensity in her, a glow in her eyes. "Bart, I saw you play. I can't remember you as a player, of course, but you were up there on the screen, running with the ball, tackling people, and I was watching. I never knew, couldn't dream, that one of those men playing football would be——"

She ran out of words and stopped, breathless. He looked into her eyes, strangely shaken. Thousands of people who sat in stands and watched him play had forgotten him, and to other thousands who saw him on the screen he had been just a nameless football player going through a minute of motion; they did not know him any more than he knew them. Aleta was dead forever, in his memories and in her power to hurt him. There remained only himself and Mary, a football player off the screen and one small spectator, sitting in Walgreen's over coffee.

"We must go right away to a secondhand film shop," he said lightly, "and get one of those used newsreels. Then every Saturday night, promptly at eight, Peter Pan, who never grew up, will run through Yale in our living room. He always ran his best through Yale."

They laughed together again and they had another memory that no one could take away from them. She was forever a part now of all that he had been; she had seen him play when he was a hero.

They dressed for the theatre. He wore his dinner jacket and Mary wore the blue, off-the-shoulder gown. She wore his corsage, too, and Dorinda's blue fox which Dorinda had loaned her. She was, he thought, breath-taking in her loveliness. He went back into his mind for words and found nothing more eloquent than one of his earliest impressions of her. She was not merely face or feature, nor figure, nor carriage, nor grace: her quality was total effect.

"You are the most beautiful thing God ever made, Bianca," he said huskily.

Her eyes flashed upward to his face, then lowered. " 'It shall be inventoried, and every particle and utensil labelled to thy will,' " she quoted lightly. " 'As, item, two lips, indifferent red; item, two grey eyes, with lids to them; item, one neck, one chin, and so forth.' "

"That stops me. I don't even know the source."

"*Twelfth Night*, milord. I'll tell you sometime how I learned it." She lifted her eyes. "I'm glad that you consider me beautiful."

"You teach the torches to burn bright."

They had seats in the ninth row for *The Seventh Wife*. They settled into the cushions and made a pretext of reading their programs. "I feel guilty," Mary said. "I have not worried about Dorinda all day."

"Nor I."

There was a silence between them as concern crept into their preoccupation with each other. The big test for Dorinda was only minutes away. Bart stared at his program without seeing it. Tonight meant everything to her because her career meant everything to her. In the hour in which she failed, or was outshone, Dorinda would grow old. There was nothing beyond that hour that Dorinda would want, or that anyone could do for her.

The house lights dimmed in warning, then brightened again. Noisy people came down the aisle, talking loudly, wanting to be noticed. These people, and many like them, were the public, Dorinda's public, the people for whom so much effort had been expended. Beyond them, of course, were the others, in New York and out of New York, for whom the theatre filled a great need: the real people who borrowed daydreams and yearned for the glimpses of meaning which the theatre gave them, who rode the theatre's magic carpet above the cares and worries of their lives. These people mattered; but the first-nighters sat at the head table.

The orchestra was in the pit and tuned. The conductor came in. Bart felt again that smothering sensation that once he knew, digging in with his cleats, waiting for the whistle. The conductor raised his hands and the overture began. More people came down the aisle, talking loudly, wanting to be noticed.

The music was a medley of all the songs to come. It was the music of Dvořák, adapted to a popular medium. The obvious "New World" Symphony was not represented in the score, but the composers had borrowed from the Second Symphony, from the great cello concerto, the piano quintet, the quartets, the trios, the "Golden Spinning Wheel" and the "Midday Witch." The folk music of middle Europe which had filtered through the gentle soul of Anton Dvořák to emerge as enduring music was filtered back again to create the music of the people in another land. It flowed through the theatre, gay and hearty, with a touch of pathos in the gaiety, singing always, invoking the high gods of melody. Then it softened and the curtain was on the rise.

The highly original third wave of loud talkers came in,

looking like the first two waves, and acting like them. No one noticed them save with annoyance. Bart leaned forward slightly and he felt the pressure of Mary's hand in his.

Emmet Dane spoke the first line to Rico Moreno. Rico sang "The Little I Know about Women." His magnificent voice took a simple song and made something big out of it. His personality was warm, and when the chorus backed him up, he seemed to be having a good time, a friendly man out with friends. Then Dore came on.

Bart watched Dore's every movement. She knew how to portray timidity because she knew it and had suffered it. Bart, who had heard her berate herself for cowardice, had seen her cowardly. He had seen her brave. He had seen her gentle, compassionate, angry, unreasonable, strong and weak, hurt and happy. She mimed bewilderment on the stage and Bart remembered how often he had tried, and tried again, to explain something that was simple to him, baffling to her.

The nerves, the muscles, the delicate invisible antennae of an actress remembered all that he remembered but in a different way, recalling not the event but their own reaction to it, doing again what they had done before under similar stimuli. She could hold life in her mirror and reflect it back years later as a fresh, new, sparkling image.

Dorinda's voice made the music its own, and Dorinda moved through her scenes with a magic that concealed the authority of her many skills, making inevitable what she had contrived.

At the first-act curtain, Mary released her pent breath in a long sigh. "That's it," she said. "She has been working toward it all week, not quite doing it. Tonight she's done it."

"What?"

"Woven a thread through something that was a group of very good specialties done by very good people. She is in the middle now, and I don't know how she got there, but the show is revolving around her."

Bart frowned, concentrating. He had a sense that this was important, for some reason. "Let me get it straight," he said. "The show is actually a series of good songs and scenes, written for several good performers. That's the reality of it?"

Mary nodded. "Yes. And that was the trouble with it."

Bart groped for words, finding them one at a time.

"Then Dore took all of that illusion created by the other people and made out of it the illusion that she is the center of something that has no center?"

"That just about states it," Mary said.

Bart stared at the curtain and he understood Dore as he had never understood her before. Her whole life had been a series of victories over reality. She had done to the show what she had done to life.

The curtain went up again and he felt closer, if possible, to Mary than he had been before. They were living through an experience that meant more to them than to the people around them, but those people were moved. The audience was being swept, minute by minute, into the magnetic field of a great certainty. This was theatrical history in the making. This was a long, long run at its beginning.

Dore had a duet with Rico Moreno and she sang under his big voice, translating all that it said for her own people, not competing with him, but fulfilling him. Bart's hand was tight on the hand of the girl beside him. He was seeing again that stage in Maude Rariden's house.

"Those artists were major prophets," he said.

She sighed and her voice, when she spoke, was the voice of Doc Epstein. "Better you should remember," she said, "that those artists were artists."

*The Seventh Wife* picked up momentum, lifting the audience and carrying it along. When Dorinda Daly stood forlornly with the model's traditional hat box in her hand and sang "Good-by, Music," the theatre was like an Italian opera house on a good night. They didn't want to let her go.

Bart sat back in his seat as the final curtain came down. He looked at Mary and there were tears in her eyes. "Bart," she said, "she's magnificent. There's nobody like her in the world. Aren't you proud?"

"Yes," he said. "I'm damned proud."

He saw Dore come back for bow after bow, a radiant

Dore who had just scored her greatest triumph on this Columbus Day, 1954. It was her birthday and in the check room he had the birthday present that he and Mary had bought together in an antique shop on Madison Avenue: a little Dresden dancer like the dancer of long ago. He wondered if she would remember.

Carter Brill rose in the first box and started backstage. He was smiling and there was pride in his face too. Mary's fingers dug into Bart's forearm.

"I could cry for Carter," she said.

"Why?"

"He is desperately in love with Dorinda, Bart," she said slowly. "He gave her so much, and she needed him. Now she doesn't."

The audience was flooding out into the aisles. The play was over. It was a long drop from the high bright clouds of illusion to the solid ground of reality. Bart drew a deep and painful breath. "I guess that's right," he said reluctantly. "I'm sorry for him too. She doesn't need anyone now. Not for a long while."

They stayed in their seats, he and Mary, while the theatre emptied. There would be many, many people backstage. They would let the many thin out before they went to see Dore. He took Mary's hand in his again and he knew that he was no longer standing irresolute before the showcase of God. He had found what he wanted. He was without talent, but he had been very fortunate.

Mary looked up at him. "Don't go away," she said softly.

He came back to her startled. He made a half-apologetic gesture. "If I ever do, Bianca," he said, "I'll have a round-trip ticket."